REDEMPTION SONG

Melodie Murray

REDEMPTION SONG

FIRST EDITION trade paperback

September 2012

ISBN: 978-0-9851188-2-2

Part One

Stars Weren't His Only Creation

So the last will be first and the first last, for many be called, but few chosen.

Matthew 20:16

Chapter 1

Ethan

"Oh, Ethan, come on! Don't leave like this, baby. The party's just getting started!"

Ethan smirked and kept walking. Truth be known, it was three o'clock in the morning and the party had *started* over five hours ago. But that was Vanessa. She'd say anything to get what she wanted.

Ethan was finished answering to Vanessa Snow. He didn't even bother a backward glance as he jerked open the sliding glass door that led to the balcony of the upscale Hollywood loft. Of course, a normal person would escape through the front door, but with Ethan being the hottest new teen pop sensation since Justin Bieber, taking the risk of meeting anyone in the apartment building on the way downstairs was absolutely out of the question—especially considering he'd partaken in a few too many Tequila shots to seem convincingly sober. No, Ethan would be taking the fire escape.

Sometimes, fame could be so glamorous.

When Ethan had climbed down as far as the steel ladder would allow, he leaped to the dirty concrete sidewalk below, throwing his arms out to steady his wobbly balance. Shaking the dust off of his new designer jeans, he sighed and thought, *What a day.*

First, he'd tried to present some new songs to his agent, only to, once again, have them shot down with the slightest of glances. (Apparently, Ethan had enough talent to play everyone else's music, but not enough to perform his own.) Then, his mother flipped out when he refused to spend his entire night cooped up with her in their suite at the Roosevelt Hotel. Did she really think that he had nothing better to do? It'd been all he could do to get away without his bodyguard following him. And as if the aforesaid wasn't enough, Vanessa had decided to pick a fight with him in the middle of a crowd of her friends at the party, people that Ethan had never even met!

All Ethan had wanted was a little peace and some time to relax.

Ah, there it was. The means of escape that would grant him peace. Ethan felt a sigh of relief escape his lips as he laid eyes on the canary yellow Camaro that Vanessa had convinced him to purchase upon his arrival in California. It was parked in the shadows of the alleyway, simply waiting to offer Ethan the getaway he needed.

But there was a problem. He couldn't take the car. He'd been drinking.

Ethan allowed for a momentary pause, considering all of his options while he tried to keep his vision in focus. He could always call his mom to come pick him up. Ha! Yeah, right! She was furious enough with him already. There was no way he was going to admit to her that he was too drunk to drive. He knew precisely how well that would go over.

Ethan's eyes shifted across the street. Illuminated under a flickering street lamp was a bus stop. Okay, that was an option…if Ethan wanted to chance finding passengers on the bus that would recognize him and want to make a little cash by turning in photos of a celebrity taking public transportation because he was too inebriated to drive himself—yep, scratch that. Ethan reached his hand into his back jean pocket and felt for his phone. He'd have to take a cab. But wait. He'd given all of his cash to Vanessa earlier in the evening to buy party provisions.

Ethan let out a frustrated grunt and kicked the back tire of the car. What was he going to do? He couldn't just hang out in the alleyway all night. His eyes darted back and forth from the car to the bus stop, and a burning sensation rose in his gut, as though he was fighting some inward battle against himself.

He knew better than this. He had been raised differently. But what choice did he have?

I don't, he decided with an inward chuckle. *I don't have a choice in any other area of my life; why should this be any different?*

So against his better judgment, Ethan fell into the driver's seat. He twisted the key in the ignition, and the Camaro's engine revved to life. He blasted the radio in an attempt to silence the pestering voice in his mind telling him that he was an idiot. It was only a drive, he kept telling himself. A drive like any other. He'd driven tired before; wasn't that basically the same thing?

Ethan decided to allow some time to sober up a bit before heading downtown. He was fairly certain his mother was still waiting up for him at the hotel, and the last thing he needed to do was stumble into the suite and have her asking how he'd gotten there. So instead of endangering anyone on the crowded Hollywood streets, he would take a drive up the mountain where vehicles were scarce at that time of morning. What could possibly happen up there?

Ethan flashed a guarded glance down both ends of the surprisingly vacant street ahead, and determining that there were no visible cop cars, he pulled out slowly and headed for the edge of town. As he flipped through the dials of the newly installed stereo system, he finally settled on a station that fit his musical taste—102.6 Pop, Rock, and Hop. The latest Black Eyed Peas song rang out, and Ethan cranked up the volume to a deafening level.

Ethan struggled to keep his focus evenly split between the road and the glowing GPS as he followed its directions to Beachwood Drive. He wondered how long it would take the effects of the liquor to wear off to the point he could face his mom again. He understood why she worried about him; he was her only child, after all. But lately, she was bordering on overbearing. "You're only seventeen!" she'd say. "You're changing, Ethan." "You're out of control."

Ethan didn't agree. The only thing that felt out of control to him was his career. As much as he hated to admit it, what had started out as a passion for writing music that expressed his deepest thoughts, and an uncontrollable desire to sing those thoughts to the world, now felt like nothing more than an avenue to make some money. He was never allowed to sing his own songs. He had absolutely no say in how his concert tour was set up. Lately, it seemed that all of his decisions were being made for him.

Maybe that was the reason for his recent attitude change. Writing had always been a release—a means of de-stressing and screaming onto the paper every thought that he was unwilling or too afraid to say aloud. It was a way of telling the world who he really was. But now, Ethan Carter was just a name—a product to be marketed and sold. A puppet in the game they called the music industry.

Of course, Ethan's mom didn't share his viewpoint. She attributed his recent ill-thought judgment calls to the fact that underage drinking laws seemed to be nonexistent to a star of his caliber. Ethan fell easily into the after-party scene. A natural-born entertainer, it wasn't hard to fit in with crowds of unknown people, especially with a little liquid encouragement on his side.

It was in this scene where he met Vanessa Snow, the rich, unbelievably built daughter of Carl Snow, also known as the owner of Ethan's record company, Platinum Spins. Vanessa was one of *those* girls who looked air brushed even while sleeping. She was obviously a party girl, but Ethan felt as though he'd hit the big time with Vanessa. She had enough money that he didn't intimidate her, and although she wasn't famous in her own right, she was well-known enough through her father's name that she fit right in with his crowd. Granted, she was twenty years old, but that only fueled Ethan's ego. He liked the idea of dating older women.

But even Ethan had to admit that he didn't make the best decisions when it came to Vanessa. She rarely lured him into situations that ended to his benefit. And when she realized that she would be doing some modeling in Hollywood the same weekend of his concert, and insisted that they get together, he should have known that she was going to drag him to a party with a bunch of strangers.

Then there was the Camaro. Ethan wondered now what had possessed him into such an impulse purchase. Especially considering he had no idea how he was going to transport it back to New York. But then he remembered how Vanessa's legs had looked in the passenger seat as he'd test drove it down Sunset Strip—that might have been a small factor.

Ethan rolled down the windows of the Camaro, expecting it to keep him more alert, and started singing along with a dated Nickleback song. The cool night air served to be quite invigorating, further enabling Ethan's confidence in his intoxicated driving skills. He decided that maybe he wasn't as drunk as he'd originally expected and pressed his foot to the gas pedal, speeding up the mountain. If he was actually getting a little time to himself for once, he might as well enjoy it. And Ethan knew exactly where he wanted to go.

To the Hollywood sign.

Of all the places for a celebrity to go in Hollywood, right? Yeah, Ethan knew it was ridiculously touristy. But truthfully, he'd never been to the lookout spot on the mountain and he wanted to go—just like all of the normal tourists.

But the farther Ethan drove up the mountain, the heavier his eyelids became. He tried singing along with the blaring radio, but it was to no avail. He couldn't shake the grogginess that seemed to be oozing from his head to his toes like molasses being poured from a jar. He felt his consciousness slipping. A voice in the back of his mind screamed to wake up, to snap out of it! To pull over and sleep off the Tequila before he did something stupid! But the lingering haze blocked his body from responding to these subconscious warnings.

Slowly, Ethan's eyelids gave up the fight. A black world spun inside his mind, but he was still so comfortable, so tired, so...

Ethan wondered. Hadn't he been doing something? He'd been at a party. Something about a fight…He'd wanted to see the Hollywood sign…

Had he seen it yet?

No, he'd been on his way…

Ethan pressed past his comatose state, forcing his mind back to consciousness. He had no idea how long his eyes had been closed, but what he did know was that he was still behind the wheel of that car! Ethan popped his eyes open wide, and his stomach leapt to his throat. The road was no longer visible. A bright light was all that encompassed the entire front glass. No, make that two lights…

Headlights!

Ethan did all he knew to do, having little control over his extremities. He jerked the wheel to the left, swerving directly to the side of the oncoming vehicle, avoiding a head-on collision by mere inches. The Camaro jarred up the edge of the mountainside, banging and denting with every tree it ricocheted off of. Ethan held onto the steering wheel with a grip of unnatural force. He tucked his head between his arms and screamed in a tone he'd never before heard echo from his own mouth. Ethan's body flopped around the car's interior like a rag doll, his seatbelt lying comfortably in its original position, having never been used since he'd bought the car. Finally, with the steep incline becoming too great for the car's current angle, the Camaro flipped over on its side and skidded along the pavement until it eventually came to a screeching halt, lying perpendicular to the faded yellow lines of the dark road.

When the piercing sound of the crash eventually silenced, and the rolling motion halted, Ethan tried to clear his mind to assess the damage. Obviously, his car was banged up, but what about his body? He couldn't feel his legs. He couldn't feel his arms. He couldn't feel his head. He was numb all over.

The husky voice was barely audible over the jagged breaths exiting Ethan's throat. Or maybe it was because his radio was still going full blast. He hadn't even noticed the music while the wreck was happening, but there was the DJ's voice, ringing merrily throughout the broken car, going on about the weather as if everything were perfectly fine.

Ethan's shoulders cringed as the deafening sound of creaking metal shot through his ears and a bright light filled the car. Someone had yanked the dented driver's side door open and shone a flashlight into the interior.

"The driver is male. Conscious, but a little hurt. We're going to need a wrecker out here, for sure. The car is totaled." A pause. "Yeah, send an ambulance, and by the smell of this kid's breath, you better send me some backup, too. They're going to have to write this one up."

That was all Ethan needed to hear. He jerked his head toward his "rescuer."

"No no! That won't be nec...ess...essary!" Ethan slurred, squinting as pain shot through his head like lightning bolts. The bitter taste of blood slid down the back of his throat. It was coming from his nose. "I'm...f...fine. Everything is...everything is fine." He tried to smile but choked on a fresh gush of blood. "I...I just need to call my agent. He'll get this all straightened out."

"Your agent? Who are you, kid?" This time the man shone the light directly onto Ethan's face. "Well, well, who do we have here? The famous Ethan Carter! My daughter loves you."

Ethan grabbed the outer edge of the doorway and used it to pull his body out of the crumpled vehicle, flopping clumsily onto the pavement, forcing the man to dodge out of his way. His entire body was numb. He could have been badly hurt, but if he was he didn't feel it.

"Seriously, man, I'm fine! I'll sign as many autographs for your daughter as you want, but I need to call my agent before this becomes a bigger deal than it needs to be."

"Oh, I'm afraid that this is already a big deal, son." The man's eyebrows scrunched in a hard line of disapproval, his voice suddenly stern. "You see, that daughter who is such a big fan of yours is waiting for me to get home to her and that was my car that you almost hit back there. Now, I don't know what you're doing out here at this time of morning, driving like a drunken maniac, but I can guarantee you that this is a *very* big deal."

A sobering wave of guilt washed through Ethan, but was replaced by an equally nauseating wave as he gasped on another sharp pain shooting through his temples. "Look, I'm sorry I almost hit you! I've had kind of a bad day! I was just trying to kill some time before heading back to my hotel. I understand why you're mad, but if you haven't noticed, my car is the one that's busted up! If anybody's got something to be mad about, it's me! If you'll just help me get my phone, I'll fix everything and you can go home."

The man snorted with frustration. "Son, do you realize how lucky you are that time is the only thing you managed to kill tonight?"

Sirens sounded through the night as a caravan of flashing red and blue lights raced up the mountain to where the smashed remains of Ethan's hard-earned money rested on its side in the middle of the road.

Ethan's head jerked toward the noise and a nauseating feeling of panic rose up in his stomach. "Seriously, man! I've got to get out of here!" he pleaded once again with the man. "Do you have any idea what happens to people like me in situations like this? It'll be all over the internet by morning! You've got to help me!"

"I'm afraid I can't do that."

"What are you, a cop, or something?"

"Off duty, actually."

Ethan's head fell into his hands, and he let out a frustrated groan of defeat as the caravan came to a halt near where he stood, lighting the dark road with flashing lights so bright they seemed to illuminate the sky with a red and blue sun. If his mom was mad before, no word existed to describe what she would be now.

A paramedic raced forward, dropped his bag to the ground, and began a full head-to-toe assessment of Ethan's battered body. Swiftly following, a burly cop sauntered forward with a satisfied smirk. He shoved a breathalyzer in Ethan's mouth before he could even get a word out.

Ethan's world spun out of control all around him. The faces of his mother, his agent, his producers—everyone who worked so hard every day to help him live his dream—flashed into his mind, and a tidal wave of guilt washed through the pit of his stomach. And before he could swallow the vomit back down, Ethan spit out the breathalyzer, unsuccessfully attempted to miss the cop's shoes, and puked up the night's festivities all over the pavement.

As Ethan gasped to catch his breath between dry heaves, the DJ's voice echoed out through the craziness of the night.

"That's right ladies and gents out there in Hollywood land! We have it right here for you! The latest hit from the boy that all of your girlfriends want to date! Ethan Carter and 'Girl from My Dreams!'"

The cop let out a low chuckle. "Some irony, huh, kid?"

Chapter 2

Ethan

The clank of the jail cell door startled Ethan awake from his latest mini nap. Between the massive hangover headache (which the guards refused to give him any painkiller for) and his cell mate for the night (a fat, hairy tattooed man who snored to decibels above the capacity of the former Camaro's sound system), Ethan had not managed to get more than a few minutes of sleep at a time the entire night. He pried his eyes ajar in view of the cell door, but a ray of sun shone through the window on the opposite wall, forcing his arm to fold at his forehead to shield his eyes. Ethan glanced down, attempting to assess the bodily damage caused by his late-night adventure. Nothing appeared to be broken, but his muscles were sore to the point that he felt as though he'd spent a few too many hours lifting weights.

A grumbled laugh came from the other side of the barred door. An officer held a large key ring—the keys to Ethan's freedom. "Rise and shine, rock star. Somebody's busting you out."

Ethan jumped from the cot, grabbed his forehead once more in an attempt to suppress a shooting pain behind his eyes, and then realized that maybe he ought to rethink his anticipation. The thought of seeing his mom walk around the corner—having to deal with her livid expression—was almost enough to make him want to crawl onto the other cot and hide behind the snoring, hairy man. Jail had to be better than the prison he was about to enter at home.

But then he caught a break.

"Bruce!"

Ethan's agent, Bruce McCloud, pushed confidently past the cop to escort Ethan out of the cell. He wore a Dolce sports coat with a pair of designer khakis, and Burberry shoes from the new spring line. A pair of Ray-Ban's—the sunglasses that constantly remained attached to Bruce's face no matter how dark of a room he entered—rested comfortably at the tip of his nose.

"I'm so glad it's you, man. I thought you were my mom."

Bruce chuckled. "No way, kid. I take care of my clients."

Ethan and Bruce made their way toward the entrance of the police station while Bruce pulled out a huge pair of sunglasses and a hooded sweatshirt from the dark leather man bag that hung across his chest. "You better put these on. We've got places to go."

When they reached the front, Ethan stepped forward to peek out of the tinted glass of the double doors. He was amazed and a little confused. The parking lot was empty aside from the regular employee vehicles and the one that waited to take him away. Juicy gossip spread like wildfire in Hollywood. Paparazzi should be camped out in the parking lot, ready to pounce the second Ethan set as much as a toe outside of that door. Not that Ethan was complaining, but something didn't quite add up.

Ethan turned to Bruce. "What gives, man? Where are the reporters?"

Bruce smiled. "Not here."

"Yeah, I see that," Ethan said. "But why? How?"

"You'd be surprised what a little cash can accomplish when you want people to keep their mouths shut, kid."

"You paid off the medic guy," Ethan said, realization dawning. "And the cops? But that guy was really mad. Kept talking about going home to his daughter and how I almost killed him. There's no way he's going to keep quiet about this."

Bruce laughed. "He will, considering that his daughter needs braces. Look, kid, don't worry about it. Your pal, Bruce, has got things covered. Besides, if worse comes to worse and someone does squeal, then we'll use it to our advantage. Publicity is publicity. It doesn't matter if it's good or bad. This is your first offense. Sure, you'll have to put up with some hater columnists for a few weeks, but once the news dies down, this might be just what we need to jump-start the promotion of your next album!"

Ethan couldn't believe his ears. He was beginning to feel a pinch of relief, but then the sound of that low chuckle re-entered his mind.

"But, Bruce, I was drinking. I'm going to have to go to court over this."

"Nope, took care of that, too."

"But…they're cops…there are laws…"

An arrogant grin stretched across Bruce's lips. "Face it, dude. You're in Hollywood now. The cops here are more crooked than the road you wrecked on last night. I told you I had your back when I signed you on, and I meant it. As long as you stick with me, you've got nothing to worry about."

Ethan laughed, feeling a twinge of relief. Still yet, a different, weird, feeling kept creeping in. He knew he deserved every bit of what the law ordered in his situation, and he knew that it was unfair for him to get off just because he was famous. But that didn't mean he was going to turn around and march back into that jail cell and seal the door behind him. He worked hard every day to give his fans what they wanted. It would be downright cruel to allow himself to get into trouble when he had a solid way out. He owed it to them to get back out there and make more music.

Ethan took one more glance toward the cell that had been his home for the night. He pulled his arms and head into the sweatshirt and put on the sunglasses, just in case anyone was around outside who might recognize him. Bruce pushed the tinted police station door open, and he and Ethan jumped into the black Escalade that waited to rush him from his short-lived punishment.

"So, where are we going?" Ethan asked after a bit. He sat in the backseat of the Escalade, jammed in beside a suitcase and his bodyguard, Ted, whom he'd only heard say a handful of words since he'd hired him.

Bruce sped from the station, completely bypassing the turn toward the Roosevelt Hotel, where Ethan was certain his mom was presently sitting, brooding over all the ways to make his life hell-on-earth once he arrived. Instead, they exited onto US Route 101 toward Los Angeles.

Bruce's reply no longer held an amused tone. Instead, he sighed, seeming a bit irritated. "We are going to the airport. LAX." He ripped his iPhone from his pocket and began vigorously clicking away with his thumb as he glanced back and forth from the phone to the road.

Ethan didn't understand. "What are you talking about, man? I've got a show at the Staples Center in eight hours. We've got rehearsals, sound checks, makeup and wardrobe still to do....What is so important that we have to drive to the airport now?"

"Ethan, my man, you don't have a show tonight. Not anymore."

Ethan felt the heat rising in his cheeks, and he spoke through gritted teeth. "And why is that?"

"Because your mother said so."

There it was. Phase one of hell.

"What exactly do you mean, 'my mother said so'?"

"Look, kid, when your mom heard about the stunt you pulled last night, she called it quits on the show, packed you a bag, bought you a plane ticket, and sent me to pick you up."

"Are you kidding me? Bruce, she can't do that! Does she realize we're going to have to refund fifteen thousand tickets?"

Bruce grunted. "Fifteen thousand, six hundred, and twenty-one—to be exact."

"But...but..." Ethan stammered, trying to fight back his anger and clear his thoughts. "This is ridiculous! Just tell her that she can't do this! Too much is at stake...I can't disappoint my fans...the show must go on...whatever! I don't care, just tell her *something*!"

"No good," Bruce said, sounding bored with the entire conversation, as if he had already heard it several times that day. "Already tried all of that, and more."

"But, how is this possible? You can get me out of a DWI, but you can't override my mom on a decision to cancel one of the biggest concerts on my tour?"

"Sadly...no. Until you turn eighteen, technically, your career decisions are in her hands. I tried to talk her out of it, but she threatened to cancel the entire tour. I took the best we could get."

Bruce slowed the Escalade and made a wide right turn. Ethan looked out his window to see jets taking off from the runway. The Los Angeles International Airport stretched out in the distance.

"What exactly was the best we could get?"

Several things flashed through Ethan's mind at once. He imagined all of the worst possible places his mother could have dreamed up for his punishment.

"Know anyone in Alabama?" Bruce asked.

Ethan sunk down in his seat, and he let out a helpless groan. It was exactly as he'd feared. The worst possible place his mother could have sent him. The middle of deep south USA in the small town of Fairhope, Alabama—also known as his grandmother's house.

"Bruce, you've got to get me out of this, man. Do you have any idea what it's like down there? The woman doesn't even have cable!"

"Sorry, kid. Just look at it as a time of rest and relaxation. Ted's going with you. If you get bored, you can talk to him."

Standing over six feet tall, Ted was an African American man with a surly brow and muscles that threatened to break the seams of his jet black suit coat. To say that he was intimidating would be an understatement. Ethan glanced up toward Ted. The bodyguard's eyes never shifted. Ethan could barely even hear him breathing. Ted didn't budge an inch until the Escalade came to a stop at the entrance of the airport. Then, he grabbed Ethan's suitcase and stood outside the door, convincing Ethan that if a statue was ever made of a *Men in Black* character, it would look exactly like Ted.

Ethan let out one last exasperated sigh, popped two of the extra-strength Tylenol he had swiped from Bruce's man bag on the way there, and crawled reluctantly out onto the busy sidewalk.

On with phase two.

The plane ride to Birmingham was not quite what Ethan had expected. He realized his mom was mad when she insisted on banishing him to po-dunk USA for an indefinite time span, but he didn't realize just how mad she was until he got ready to board the plane at LAX. Ted had followed behind while Ethan made his way through the airport, being forced to slow down every two steps to sign an autograph or take a picture with a girl who was so obsessed with him that she couldn't even say hi without squealing and tearing up. Ethan hated that. The girls were cute, and they didn't seem like they would be such basket cases, but it was always the same story, no matter where he went. They all acted the same, dressed the same...flirted the same.

That's why Ethan preferred a private jet when he needed to travel long distances. It was much less invasive. But in this situation, just to keep from having to call his mom to argue, he would settle for the commercial jet. Ethan couldn't wait until he was seated in his big cushy first-class chair, a cold sparkling water in his hands and a hot towel behind his neck, and had the chance to lay back and relax the rest of his hangover away.

There was only one problem with this little scenario. Ethan's mother had planned for that, too. Relaxing was the last thing he was going to get to do. Instead, he reached the terminal to find out that his mom had booked him a seat in...COACH. Ethan got stuck between silent Ted and smelly Bob, a man who took up enough space that he technically should have bought two tickets.

It was a *long* flight.

Ethan spent the entire flight hidden inside the hood of his oversized sweatshirt, which was somewhat of an attention grabber in itself considering it was mid-June. His dark glasses never budged an inch. The last thing he wanted was to be forced to give a concert to the passengers midflight. After a couple of hours, Ethan was finally able to exit the plane into the Birmingham International Airport. Not surprisingly, his Tylenol had worn off and the stabbing pain in his forehead was swiftly returning.

"So...Ted..." Ethan began as his bodyguard pulled the last piece of their luggage off the conveyer belt. "Where to now? Do we have a car rented already, or do we need to find an Enterprise?"

Even though Ethan had asked him a question, he was still a little surprised when silent Ted voiced his reply.

"Mr. Carter, I believe our ride is already waiting for us." Ted gave a slight nod toward the doorway of baggage claim.

When Ethan caught sight of the man Ted was referring to, he almost laughed, realizing that this was not only the first time he'd ever heard Ted speak, but also the first time he'd ever heard Ted tell a joke. He was a funny guy.

But then Ethan took a closer look at the man in the doorway. He was tall and lanky and wore a plaid button-up shirt underneath a pair of partially unbuttoned denim overalls. What was that he was holding? A sign? The words were written in...crayon?

Welcome...(the penmanship was terrible)...Welcome Ethan...Carter.

"Oh, crap."

Ethan dropped his suitcase, leaving it behind for Ted, and ran to the man holding the sign, with his all too famous name on it, for the entire airport to see.

"What's the matter with you, man? Are you crazy!" Ethan was panting by the time he reached the man. He took a brief moment to clumsily readjust the hood of his sweatshirt again before reaching up and snatching the resemblance of a kindergarten craft project out of the man's hand and folding it in half, attempting to remove any evidence of his arrival. "You can't just go around announcing that I'm here. If the paparazzi receive word that I'm in Alabama, they'll invade the place."

"Ah, sorry bout that Mr. Carter, but...uh...your granny had that sign made speshlly for ya and she told me ta bring it. Kept sayin somethin bout how your mom wanted ya to have a proper welcome or somethin like that."

The man had one of the strongest Southern accents Ethan had ever heard.

"Yeah, that sounds like my mom, alright," Ethan muttered bitterly. Ted reached his side and sat his suitcase back down.

"I'm Ted, Ethan's bodyguard." Ted smiled kindly to the man and stretched out his hand. "Thank you very much for agreeing to meet us here on such short notice."

"Notta problem tal, sir. I'd do anything for Granny Mae. A famly member a hers, is a famly member a mine. We didn't even know Granny Mae hada famous famly! Name's Hank, by the way. Hank Hinkle."

Ethan snorted, trying hard not to let out a mocking laugh, but covered it up as though he was trying to suppress a cough. "So, uh,

Mr. Hinkle," Ethan began.

"No, no, boy! You call me Hank. Mr. Hinkle was my father!"

"Okay...Hank. Where is your car? I'm kind of exhausted, and I'm looking forward to catching some zzz's on the ride to Fairhope."

"Oh, we got somethin way better than a car, Mr. Ethan," An elated grin spread across Hank's cheeks, his eyes sparkling with excitement. "When your momma called, she said you liketa fly when you go places, and bi-gollies, she asked for me personally to come fetch ya! I was so honored. I never flown any famous people fore.

"She said that, did she?" Ethan gritted his teeth. This couldn't be good. There was no way that his mother was going to arrange a comfortable plane ride for him in the mood she was in. There had to be a catch. "I guess this is a lucky day for both of us."

Ethan tried to look on the bright side. How bad could Hank's plane possibly be? He imagined it had to be fairly small, but at this point, as long as he had room to lay his head back and catch a few minutes of sleep, it would be plenty big enough. Besides, it had to be better than the four hours it would have taken to travel by car.

But after about a two-mile hike to the small private runway that sat to the side of the huge airport, Ethan realized that he could not have been more wrong. When he caught sight of Hank's plane, Ethan became fully aware of just how ticked off his mother really was.

"Uh, Hank...what is that thing?"

The plane had two wings directly parallel, one on top of the other, on each side. Two little wheels extended out from beneath the body, and it had *no ceiling*! Two holes were visible in the top of the body that the passengers were expected to climb into. The plane looked like it had flown right off the pages of an American history book.

"She's a beaut, ain't she? This right here is called a biplane," Hank voiced proudly. "Been in the family for yers."

"So you were related to Amelia Earhart?"

Hank laughed, not catching the fact that Ethan's comment hadn't been a compliment.

"Yea, the girl's a lil' old, but she's still gotta lot left in her," Hank ran his fingers along the plane's body beside the propeller. I guess you aughta hop on in so we can get goin. Your granny's gonna be waitin on ya if we don't step on it quick."

Ethan glanced back up at Ted, hoping that by some miracle he felt as nervous as Ethan did about crawling into the 1920s hunk of metal, but it was to no avail. Ted had already picked up Ethan's suitcase, flung it into the front hole of the plane, and was beginning to climb in.

"Ted you can't be serious, man. This isn't a plane! It's a kayak with wings!"

Ted remained silent, but Ethan thought he caught the slightest hint of amusement in his expression. Ethan was nearing panic mode, but if he was anything, a wimp he was not. If silent Ted could do it, then so could he. Ethan reached a hand up to grab hold of the plane and hoist himself into the pit that would be his seat, but then he realized which hole he was about to crawl into.

"Uh...Ted...shouldn't we be sitting in the back?"

Hank answered for him. "Not less ya wanna drive cuz that's where the steerin wheel is."

"Never mind. I'm good."

Ethan paused to suck in one last deep breath before hoisting himself up into the plane to claim his seat beside silent Ted. He had never been afraid of flying, but he had also never ridden in a plane that didn't have a roof. So much for catching a few minutes of sleep. Granted, Ethan's eyes would be shut, but it definitely wouldn't be due to sleeping. Hank jumped into the plane with ease, passed a helmet to both Ted and Ethan (*a helmet??*), and flipped a few switches. The propeller puttered and spat in protest, but finally roared to life like a bumblebee on steroids.

"Here we go!" Hank cried with excitement from the back.

Yep, Ethan thought as the plane began its trek down the runway. He squeezed his eyes tight and gripped the edges of his seat to the point his knuckles turned white. *Here we go.*

Chapter 3

Ethan

By the time the biplane buzzed onto the Sunny Calahaun runway near Fairhope, Ethan had reached full-blown mental hysteria.

Number one: at that very moment, he should have been in his dressing room at the Staples Center gearing up for his show. Number two: he had just flown over one-hundred miles in a piece of tin piloted by the long-lost cousin of Elmer Fudd, with nothing to protect his head but something that slightly resembled a bicycle helmet. And lucky number three: the last five minutes of his death ride had restored in his mind all of the reasons why he'd hated visiting Fairhope past the age of twelve.

Fairhope, Alabama, was the hometown of Ethan's mom's mom, otherwise known as Granny Mae. The town was located on the edge of Mobile Bay, a small inlet off the Gulf of Mexico, and was a good four-hour drive from the airport. Fairhope was a small community of about eight hundred people, which resembled the population of a department store in Ethan's bustling hometown of New York City. Ethan had always thought Fairhope was pretty, but it was far too quiet for him...too country. Everyone moved at such a slow pace, and in Ethan's eyes, Fairhope was the black hole of the Alabama coastline. It was one of those rare places that seemed to suck in the people who visited, making it so that they never left. Other than maybe a few enchanting sunsets, Ethan didn't understand everyone's attraction to the town because there wasn't anything to do there. The thought of a night club was an absolute joke. There wasn't even a movie theater without having to drive to a completely different county.

Large farm land stretched out on the other three sides of the small town. The streets were quiet, a few vehicles passing slowly here and there. There were no tall buildings, no fluorescent lights, and no flashing marquees. It was simple. It was quaint.

It was boring.

"Looky there, Mr. Carter!" Hank bellowed from behind in the cockpit. "You granny jus pulled up. Perfect timin!"

Ethan sighed and slipped out an unenthusiastic, "Lucky me."

The landing was interesting to say the least. There's nothing like zooming nose first toward a concrete pad in a tin kayak. When Hank finally brought the plane to a complete stop, Ethan was tempted to jump out and kiss the ground beneath him.

Once Ted removed the bags from the plane, Ethan forced

himself to turn and face the grandmother he had refused to visit for the past five years. He assumed she would be short with him, probably mad that he hadn't found opportunities in his busy schedule to spend time with his family. She probably felt the same way his mother did. Probably thought he was full of himself and didn't care for things like family anymore. It was nothing like that. He was just busy, that's all.

When Ethan's gaze finally met Granny Mae's, he was shocked at the expression he found being returned. Granny Mae's lips stretched from ear to ear, and her entire face lit up like the Rockefeller Center Christmas Tree.

"Ethan! Welcome, honey! I have missed you so much!" Granny ran (if you could call that a run) to Ethan and pulled him into a squeeze surprisingly tight for a woman of her age. "Good grief, dear boy, you are skin and bones! Don't they feed you on that tour bus?"

Ethan pulled back quickly, ashamed of her eager forgiveness. He knew he should have visited his grandmother before now. She looked older than the last time he'd been in Fairhope. Obviously, she had aged five years, but it wasn't just that. She looked older. Not as healthy. The area around her eyes folded in wrinkles, and her skin was thin and looked easy to tear. He wondered for a brief moment if she was in good health.

"Nice to see you, Grandma," Ethan voiced quietly, a hint of shame in his tone.

"Grandma?"

"I mean Granny Mae."

"Hmm."

Ethan took off toward Ted, trying to ignore Granny Mae's confused glare that he could feel radiating through his back as he walked. He didn't get far before he was intercepted.

"OH MY GOSH! It really is you!" A little boy jumped out of Granny Mae's beat up old Plymouth and ran up to Ethan before he even knew what was happening. The kid looked to be about nine or ten. He was about a foot shorter than Ethan and had dark curly waves that hung from the edges of a beat up red ball cap that rested firmly on his head.

"Granny Mae told me you were coming, but I didn't believe her!" the boy voiced with excitement. "She likes to kid with me sometimes, but, wow, you really are here! My name's Ben, by the way. Benjamin, actually, but you can call me Ben. Can I call you Ethan? You know, you don't know this yet, but I bet we become best friends before long. I'm kinda awesome like that. I'm not being conceited or anything, I'm just being truthful. People love me. I don't know why. I guess just some people got it, and some people don't. Oh, and don't worry about anybody finding out you're in town. Granny told me you would want to keep it a secret, and you're in luck cause I'm great at keeping secrets!"

The boy gazed up at him with an expectant smile. Ethan wasn't quite sure how to respond.

"Um...thanks, Bob."

"It's Ben."

"That's what I meant."

Ethan's awkward forgetfulness didn't seem to faze young Ben in the slightest. Instead, his smile beamed even brighter and he skipped off toward Hank and his plane.

"Oh, man, Hinkle! That's the coolest thing I've ever seen!"

Ethan suppressed an amused snort. Obviously, Ben didn't get out much.

"So how has my Lil E been doing?" Granny Mae approached the car and motioned for Ethan to take shotgun before Ben returned and still had the chance.

"Wow, Granny Mae, I haven't been called that in..."

"Five years or so?"

"Yeah, something like that."

There it was. Ethan knew she was disappointed in him. He quickly tried to think of something to change the subject.

"So who's the kid?"

"Oh, Ben? I figured he already told you his name. I'm telling you, that kid has never met a stranger in his life. It's like he already knows everyone on Earth, they just haven't had the chance to know him yet." Granny Mae gazed toward the plane where Hank had hoisted Ben up into the cockpit. He was making loud engine sounds and pretending to steer. Her look was listless.

"I got that his name was Ben, but who is he? Are you babysitting or something?"

She laughed as though it was some sort of inside joke. "Something like that."

"What does that mean, Grandma?"

Granny Mae sighed, never veering her focus from Ben's direction.

"A few things have changed since the last time you were here,

Ethan. Ben was one of my Sunday school kids at church. One weekend his parents left him with his sister to take a drive up to Mobile to get some time away together. But they never made it home."

"What happened?"

"Drunk driver hit them before they ever reached Mobile. It's only a twenty-one-mile drive, but they only made it fifteen."

Ethan's stomach twisted into knots, and he recognized the familiar feeling of vomit rising in his throat. He wondered if this was a true story or a guilt trip.

"Granny Mae, did my mom tell you why I was coming to visit you?"

She gave him a sweet smile. "She sure did, honey, and believe me, I know what it feels like to be overworked. You deserve this break. I told your mom that you are free to stay as long as you like."

Ethan wanted to feel relieved that his grandmother didn't know the real reason for his sudden arrival, but her innocent kindness only helped to further his guilt. Ben's story was not some fictional story his grandmother had made up to cause him guilt. It was true. The kid had lost his parents in an accident similar to the one Ethan almost caused the night before. He wondered if his mom had known about Ben before arranging this little "vacation."

Ethan regained his focus. "So, I get that Ben's parents died, but why is he with you? Doesn't he have family who could've taken him?"

"Sure, sweetie," Granny Mae said. "He has me, as does his sister. We're not related by blood, of course, but I've loved those kids ever since the first day I met them. I couldn't just let them fend for themselves. Ben's sister is only seventeen. Technically, she could have handled things, I guess, but I figured that was an awfully young age to become a parent. So, I took them in."

"You mean they live with you? Ben *and his sister*?"

"Is that a problem, dear?"

Was that a problem? Obviously, Granny Mae had never seen how girls acted around Ethan. They wanted him to sign their arms, let them touch his guitar, dedicate a song to them. They squealed and screamed and even sometimes cried. Ethan loved his fans and he appreciated their support, but the obsessive crush act got a little old. Now he was going to have to live with it until his mom saw fit to let him return to his real life. But he couldn't expect Granny Mae to kick the girl out right after losing her parents just because he didn't want to put up with a crazed fan. He was stuck. Boy, his mom had really thought this one out thoroughly.

"No, Granny. Not a problem."

Ben bounded back up to the car, having a conversation with none other than silent Ted. Granny Mae was right. The kid definitely never met a stranger. Surprisingly, Ted didn't seem annoyed by the jabbering youngster. He actually seemed a bit amused.

"Granny Mae, can we go already?" Ben spouted as if they had all been waiting to leave on someone other than him. "I want to get home before Alaina leaves for work so I can introduce her to my new friend Ethan!"

"Who's Alaina?" Ethan asked, almost afraid to hear Ben's answer.

"That's my sister. I can't wait for you to meet her. She is going to llloooovvveee you."

Ethan let out an exasperated sigh and turned his head toward the side window, trying to figure out what on earth he could say to his mother to calm her down enough to let him come home from this nightmare.

"I can't wait, Bob."

"It's Ben."

"Right."

Chapter 4

Ethan

Stepping into Granny Mae's house was like stepping back in time to Ethan's childhood. Everything was exactly the same. The same old floral patterned couch and recliner set that had been there since before he could remember. The multicolored alphabet magnets on the refrigerator door. The pictures of Ethan from back long before the days of worldwide tours, guest appearances on talk shows, and confinement in the deep South due to episodes of drunkenness.

The carefree kid in the pictures smiled back at him innocently, and Ethan suddenly felt a little confused. In the stillness of his younger self, Ethan noticed something that he hadn't seen in a long time. The kid looked really happy—content. What had been so great back then? Even then Ethan had desired to be a big star. Why did the kid who had nothing look happier than the teen who had everything?

"C'mon, Ethan!" Ben's voice broke into his thoughts, bringing his focus back to the reality of his arrival. "I want to show you our room!"

Our room?

Ethan turned and found a guilty-faced Granny Mae standing in the entryway.

"Sorry about that, Lil E, but there are only so many rooms. Ben's got a bunk bed so it's not like you'll have to sleep on the same mattress. Not to mention, he's asleep by eight almost every night. You probably won't even notice he's there."

Granny Mae turned to silent Ted and offered an apologetic smile. "I'm so sorry, Ted, but I'm afraid that all I can offer you is the couch."

"That will be perfectly fine," Ted replied. "Thank you for your hospitality." Ted slipped the large vinyl duffel bag off of his shoulder and made his way over to the floral excuse for his new bed.

Ethan had no desire to share a room with Ben. He could take the couch and stick Ted in the room with the kid, but when he parted his lips to offer this suggestion, he closed them just as quickly. He was all out of fight. He just needed sleep, even if he had to get it in the same room as the ten-year-old. Now, if only he could get to the bed without being spotted by Ben's sister. He needed a nap before he would be ready to deal with living under the same roof with some squealing girl who would probably faint when she found out she was sharing a house with *Ethan Carter*.

When Ethan reached the doorway of his new bedroom, he found

Ben perched on the top bunk, smiling ear to ear like the king of his own little mountain.

"We missed my sister, but oh well. You can meet her later. Can you believe this?" Ben beamed. "We're going to be roommates!"

Ethan smirked. "It's definitely unbelievable."

Ben's smile grew even wider. Ethan had to admit; the kid was kind of cute in his own annoying little kid way. It was as if he glowed when he smiled that big.

"I've never had a brother before!" Ben continued. "Sure, I've got Alaina, but she's a girl and that's just different, you know? Do you have any brothers or sisters, Ethan?"

"Nope. Only child."

"Oh, that's too bad. Alaina gets on my nerves sometimes, but I guess she's pretty cool. She takes care of me and reads me stories at night and takes me to movies sometimes. It's too bad you didn't have a brother, but I guess you don't need one when you have a million friends on Facebook."

Ethan let go of his suitcase, not even attempting to remove it from the middle of the floor. He collapsed onto the bottom bunk bed. "How do you know how many followers I have on Facebook? Aren't you too young for Facebook?"

Ben snorted. "I'm young, not stupid. I just gave them a fake birthday. And you knew I was on Facebook already because you accepted my friend request last year. I figured you recognized me when you got off the plane."

Ethan almost laughed. Like there was any way he would remember some little kid who added him to one of the numerous social networks that his PR people had him involved with. Ethan didn't even check his Facebook page. He had people to do that for him. He hadn't even realized he'd made it to a million friends. That was actually kind of cool now that he thought about it."

"So do you remember?" Ben asked eagerly.

"Remember what?"

"Do you remember accepting my friend request?"

"Uh, not exactly. I don't check that. Other people check it for me."

Ben was quiet for a brief moment, processing Ethan's honesty. Finally, he spoke.

"That's stupid."

Ethan scoffed. "Why?"

"What's the point in having all those friends if you don't talk to any of them?"

"It's for publicity."

"Like advertisement?"

Ethan yawned. All he wanted was to take a nap and forget where he was. "Yeah, Ben. It's like advertisement."

"But don't you think it would work better if you did it yourself? I bet if people knew that it was really you posting all those status updates, they would check it a lot more often."

The kid had a point, but it only enhanced the level of his annoyance.

"Don't you have like a train set or a plastic tool table or something that you can go play with?"

Ben giggled. "I'm ten, not four. I'm gonna go play Xbox. I got the new SpeedNeed game the other day. It's totally cool. You wanna play with me?"

"Nope."

Ben jumped in one swift, graceful motion from the top bunk to the floor. "Okay, well, I'll see ya later, Ethan. I'm glad you're my roommate!"

Ethan didn't reply. Instead, he lay with heavy eyes, facing the light blue papered wall. He couldn't believe where the last day had taken him. How had it come to this? Exhaustion finally took over, and Ethan fell asleep; his unopened suitcase still in the middle of the floor, and his shoes still on his feet.

Ethan awoke to the rhythmic sounds of Ben's breathing drifting down from the top bunk. The room was pitch-black, and the only other sound came from the faint click of the ceiling fan motor. Ethan rolled over; trying to get comfortable enough to drift back to sleep, but something was bothering him. A pain. His stomach. When had he eaten last? Not on the plane...not in jail...not at the party...

Ethan hadn't even realized. It was going on two days since he'd last eaten. He was starving!

The poorly lit trip to the kitchen was nothing other than painful. Three toe stubs and one bump on the head later, Ethan found his way to the doorway of the living room. Silent Ted wasn't so silent from his resting spot on the couch. His snores filled the room. A faint glow emitted from the kitchen. Ethan glanced to the DVD player. It was three in the morning. Who would be up now?

Ethan edged his way closer to the kitchen, trying to remain as quiet as possible. When he reached the doorway, he stopped in his tracks. Curled up on the barstool beside the island, huddled over a half-drunken glass of milk, tapping her fingers indolently on the countertop, was a girl.

Ben's sister.

Ethan turned to run back to his room before she had the chance to notice, but a burning sensation shot through his stomach and made him change his mind. He would have to meet her eventually. At least if he got stuck now he would be close to food.

When Ethan turned back around to enter the room, something made him pause. He hadn't taken a good look at the girl before, but for some reason, she made him take notice. She didn't look anything like the girls who he hung around. First and foremost, she wasn't blonde. Her dark hair was long and straight as a board with wispy bangs that crossed over her forehead, almost completely covering one of her eyes. She looked to barely top five feet and couldn't weigh over a hundred and fifteen pounds. Her nails weren't long and, surprisingly, weren't fake. They were short and painted jet black. She wore a light blue tank top and a pair of striped cotton PJ pants that only went to her knees. On her feet was a pair of pink fuzzy house shoes. She didn't have on a stitch of makeup, but her skin was a smooth ivory with the slightest tint of red in her cheeks and lips.

Ethan wondered. Had he ever seen Vanessa without makeup? He knew he hadn't. He was pretty sure Vanessa touched up her makeup before she got into bed at night so that she could look painted when she woke up in the morning.

Ethan couldn't help but find something about this girl intriguing. Her dark hair and nails gave off signs of rebellion, but her bright pajamas and fuzzy shoes made her look like a helpless little girl.

Why helpless? It was something in her expression. She was staring at that glass of milk with so much intensity you'd think she was trying to make it boil with her mind. She sat only feet from him, but her focus seemed miles away. It almost made Ethan feel like he was intruding by entering, but a loud growl in the pit of his stomach snapped her out of her trance. He caught his breath when her gaze shot up, instantly meeting his, eye to eye.

"Oh...hi." Her voice held a soft, sweet tone, but there was something else there, too—a hint of melancholy.

"Hi," Ethan said cautiously.

He cringed, waiting for the girl to jump up from her seat and run to him with a shrill scream and beg him for a hug, but she just sat there keeping her gaze locked on his eyes. What was it about her doing that that made him uncomfortable?

"I'm Alaina, Ben's sister."

"I'm Ethan."

An awkward silence. Her eyes never veered—as if she expected something more from him.

For the first time in his life, Ethan didn't know what to say. Who was this girl? Why wasn't she acting like a psychopathic obsessed fan? Ethan couldn't even go to a gas station for a pack of gum without having to give hugs and sign autographs. This girl acted as though he was just another person, like every other person in the world—like she couldn't care less that she was sitting alone in a room with *Ethan Carter*.

Ethan had to admit—it was throwing him a little off guard. He was out of practice in the acting-like-a-normal-person department.

"What are you doing in here?" His question came out quickly and more harshly than he'd intended.

Great. That came out all wrong. His tone was more accusatory than inquisitive. It sounded like he expected her to have some reasonable motive for being in her own kitchen. Like he even knew her...like he even had a right to know why she was sitting in a kitchen...in the dark...staring at milk....

Chill out Ethan. It's just a girl like any other girl. You're freaking out!

Ethan gave his head a slight shake to clear it. "I just mean...it's really late to...be in a kitchen...."

She finally veered her eyes away from his—Ethan let out an involuntary sigh of relief—as she reached for her glass of milk. She took a slow sip and smiled. "I could say the same for you."

Her teeth were really white.

"Uh...yeah. I kind of forgot to eat yesterday. I woke up hungry."

"You forgot to eat?"

"I think so."

She looked amused, but there was something else. Pity?

Ethan shrugged. "I was just busy, you know?"

Ethan wondered how much Alaina really did know. He couldn't imagine she knew about his recent confinement for drunk driving or surely she wouldn't be this civil toward him. Not after what had happened to her parents...,

Alaina rose from her stool and strolled to the refrigerator in her little pink slippers. "I can't say that I've ever been too busy to remember to eat, but I guess we live very different lives." She opened the refrigerator door and bent over to view its contents. "Let's see here. How about leftover lasagna?"

"Sounds great," Ethan said.

Alaina removed the frosted Tupperware dish from the fridge and stuck it in the microwave. She took a step toward the stove and rose to the very tip of her toes to reach a plate in the cabinet above. She was so tiny. She grabbed a fork from the drawer and turned back to the island and paused.

"Are you...going to come in...or do you want me to bring it over there?"

"Oh, right." Despite his awareness, Ethan had not budged from the doorway since he'd realized there was another inhabitant in the kitchen aside himself. "I guess I'll come in."

Ethan pulled out the stool next to the one Alaina had sat in. A few minutes of silence passed. Not awkward silence. Just silence; eventually broken by the loud ding of the microwave.

Alaina removed the Tupperware dish and spooned the lasagna onto a plate. She placed the fork carefully on the edge of the plate and slid it across the island to Ethan.

"Wow, thanks," he said.

Alaina grinned. "Thank me after you've tasted it."

Ethan wasn't sure what that meant, but he was too hungry to care. He took a heaping bite, letting a little fall from his mouth because it was still piping hot, but delicious.

Alaina watched his every move. She made him very aware of his actions. Why had he let food fall from his mouth? That was stupid, right? He looked like he didn't even know how to feed himself. He should say something.

"This is really good. I had forgotten how much I missed Granny Mae's cooking."

Alaina smiled proudly. "Actually, I made that. Granny Mae hasn't done much cooking lately. She stays tired a lot."

"Well, I'm impressed. I don't think I know one girl who can cook her own food. They all have their maids do it for them."

"Really? Maids? Wow, that must be nice."

He'd done it again. Why did everything he said seem to come out wrong? He quickly tried to correct himself.

"Not that they all have maids...well some of them do...but I just meant that I think it's really cool that you know how to cook."

"Thanks, Ethan."

Ethan. Other than his parents, hardly anyone ever called him by his first name. From his agent, it was kid or superstar. From his fans, it was Ethan Carter. Never just his first name, but both the first and the last—like together they formed one word.

Alaina continued. "Cooking is something I used to do with my mom. She taught me everything I know."

"I bet she was great."

Alaina glanced up quickly. "Was? I guess it's safe to assume that Granny Mae told you about Ben and me."

"She mentioned a little."

"I don't blame her. She probably wanted to prep you in case Ben decided to unload the whole story out of nowhere. It would be a lot to handle if you hadn't been forewarned."

Ethan didn't know what to say. He had never dealt with death before. It was one of those awkward subjects that made him uncomfortable .

"Well, anyway," Alaina said, changing the subject as quickly as it had begun, "I think it's really nice that you took a break from your work to come visit your grandmother. She's so proud of you. She talks about you all the time. Well, to us at least. She keeps quiet about you in town. Said she wants you to be able to visit anytime you want without having to put up with obsessive fans."

Ethan suddenly felt very full. The lasagna stuck like a huge lump in his throat. "She told you I took a break so that I could visit her?" he said.

"Yep."

Ethan couldn't bring himself to tell Alaina the real reason for his sudden arrival in Alabama. Taking time out of his busy schedule to put his family above his career definitely sounded like a better story than what had really happened.

"She said you were on a tour or...something about a new CD...," Alaina said passively, rising from the island to wash her empty glass out in the sink.

A tour or something? It wasn't just a tour or something. It was the biggest and best thing that had ever happened in Ethan's life.

Ethan swallowed down another bite of the lasagna as he studied Alaina's expressions. He had trouble reading her. "I dropped a new album about a year ago, and I've got another one coming out around six months from now. The tour is named Love Jam. We were in Birmingham just a couple of months ago. I can't believe you didn't hear about it...."

The more Ethan rambled on about his career, the more clueless Alaina's expression became. He was starting to think that she had no idea what he was talking about. Who was this girl?! Most girls knew every detail about Ethan's life from which city his tour was at on different nights all the way down to what his favorite color M&M was.

Ethan let out an awkward laugh. "You have no idea what I'm talking about do you?"

A faint red hue flushed in Alaina's cheeks. Her eyes shifted downward with guilty embarrassment.

"Do you even know any of my songs?" Ethan pressed.

Alaina grazed her bottom lip with her teeth in nervous anticipation until finally, she said, "I'm sorry, but I really don't know anything about your music. Your grandmother plays your CD in her bedroom all the time in the mornings, but I've never really listened to it. Don't be offended, it's nothing personal."

Ethan laughed out loud. He couldn't believe his luck. He had come expecting some love crazed fan who would never leave him alone—wanting to know every single stupid detail about his life in Hollywood—but instead he'd found someone who only saw him as Ethan. It was overwhelmingly refreshing and instantly brightened his mood.

"You really don't listen to any of my music?"

"Not really."

"Is it because you don't like it?"

"Not exactly."

"Oh, you like Country music, huh. Figures, you being from Alabama and all."

Alaina laughed. "No, don't really care for Country."

"Well then, what do you listen to?" Ethan asked curiously. He knew for a fact that his songs were played on every alternative/rock station on the FM frequency. Other than Country, what was left?

She answered immediately—proudly. "Christian music, mostly: Toby Mac, Skillet, Newsboys, a little Flyleaf...it all just kind of depends on my mood."

Christian music. So that was the difference. Alaina wasn't like the other girls Ethan knew because she was a Christian. Ethan had never put a lot of value into the idea of a supreme power being the creator of all existence. The idea had always seemed so farfetched and, well, impossible. But Alaina seemed so confident in herself. She was alone in a tiny room, in the middle of the night, with one of the biggest teen idols of her day, and she acted as if it was just another night. Why was she not just a little excited to meet him? She didn't seem to be a snob. Ethan didn't think it was an issue of her thinking she was better than him or that he was unimportant. She just didn't seem to...care.

Ethan let his eyes find Alaina's, and this time he held her gaze willingly. Her eyes were big and brown and sparkled with the slight glow of the moon entering in through the kitchen window. This time he didn't allow himself to become squeamish in the intensity of her gaze. He held it and studied her expression, suddenly feeling an unexplainable urge to try to figure her out.

"Can I call you Ali?"

Ethan wasn't sure where the question came from, but the more he thought about it, the more her full name seemed too formal.

A slightly pained, reminiscent look flashed in her eyes. "That's what my dad used to call me."

"Oh, I'm sorry."

Way to go, Ethan—you idiot. Of all names to call her, you pick the one that her recently dead father chose. Real smooth.

"It's okay. Don't worry about it." Alaina shrugged. "I really liked that nickname, but I'm afraid the person who called me that was pretty special. The next person to call me Ali is going to have to earn the right."

Why did Ethan suddenly have the desire to be that person? What was happening to him? Just a few hours earlier, the thought of being stuck in Alabama made him want to scratch his way out of Ben's bedroom with his own fingernails, but now...now he was forgetting why he hadn't come to visit earlier. What would he be doing right now if he had stayed in LA? He would've had a packed out show at the Staples Center, which would've been fun, but what about when it was over? He probably would've been at some stupid party with Vanessa trying to keep up with everyone who was living the life. The thought now seemed almost exhausting.

Ethan wasn't sure what he expected, but he knew he couldn't ignore his desire to get to know this girl better. "Alaina, would you like to hang out with me tomorrow? There are a few things I'd like to do while I'm here in Alabama."

Their gaze held for several more seconds—what felt like an eternity. Finally, Ethan had all he could handle and turned his focus back to his lasagna, feeling the heat rise in his cheeks.

Alaina gave a soft giggle. "Sure, why not."

Chapter 5

Alaina

The alarm clock blared into the faint dream world that came from a restless night's sleep.

Alaina stretched and stifled a long yawn. The bright sunrise shone through her window and made her squint to keep from seeing spots. Her muscles ached with fatigue, and all she wanted to do was roll back over and pass out for the rest of the morning. She was going to have to find a way to get more sleep at night. Maybe she could find something today that would help.

Alaina rolled out of her bed and moved to the little table and chair that sat next to the bay window in her room, as was her morning ritual. The window overlooked the quaint garden area in the back of Granny Mae's house. Early in the morning was Alaina's time to reflect and regroup. The time she spent with her God. Sometimes she prayed. Sometimes she read her Bible. Sometimes she wrote in her journal. And sometimes, she just cried.

No matter what challenges the morning brought against her, Alaina felt she could face them after a little one-on-one time with her Savior.

Alaina had not always been so spiritual. Sure, she had always been a pretty well-behaved, responsible girl—and thank God she hadn't done anything too crazy before realizing the big picture—but she had definitely stepped up her Christian walk since the death of her parents. When Alaina had received the news of their passing, two choices flashed through her mind simultaneously. A part of her wanted to run screaming—destroying everything in her path, including herself—until she used enough energy to get rid of the rage that raced through her blood stream. But something else inside of her felt like a pull. Like someone was tugging on her very soul saying, "You don't have to destroy yourself just because they're gone. I'm here with you. I'll help you through this."

Alaina hit her knees that night and hadn't left them since. Without her relationship with God, and her love for Jesus, she knew she would not have made it. One day, she was a normal, carefree teenager. The next, she was on her own to be the only parent her younger brother had left. She'd had to quit every activity she was involved with in school so that she could get a job and support herself and her brother. She'd had to deal with bankers and lawyers to try to get her parents' finances straightened out. She was even the one to handle all of the arrangements for their funeral. It had taken everything Alaina had in her, but she'd made it through the storm. But she knew it was not without help.

If it hadn't been for Granny Mae, Alaina didn't know what would have happened to her and Ben after the accident. She knew of having no family members other than her parents, but what she wouldn't have done to have a grandmother like Granny Mae. Technically, she did have one now because they had become like family. Alaina felt eternally indebted to Granny Mae for her hospitality and generosity of taking in two kids off the streets.

Alaina grabbed her concordance off of the table. She needed help with her latest storm. She didn't know how she was going to have the strength to handle much more, but that's why she read her Bible. She wanted to find her strength, and she knew God could help her find it.

Scriptures on worry, anxiety, and fear.

Alaina thumbed back and forth through the passages listed until she found the one that spoke to her—Philippians 4:6—:

> Do not be anxious about anything, but in everything, by prayer and petition, with thanksgiving, present your requests to God. And the peace of God, which transcends all understanding, will guard your hearts and your minds in Christ Jesus.

The peace of God, Alaina thought. That's what she needed. A sense of peace and confidence. All it took was prayer and petition with thanksgiving. She could handle that.

Alaina looked up a few more scriptures, jotted a few notes down in her journal, and said a quick, heart-filled prayer before rising from the little table.

She looked around her room trying to figure out what to do first. This was the first day she'd been off work at the little restaurant on the pier in almost a month. Her summer days were filled with helping Granny Mae around the house, spending time with Ben, and then it was straight to work for a six- to eight-hour shift of hard waitressing. It wasn't a bad job—good tips, actually—but work was work, and eventually it all got a little old. But it provided her with income. Something her parents hadn't left her much of.

It wasn't that her parents had been poor or bad managers of their money. They just hadn't been given enough time to pay off their debts. When couples sign up for mortgages and vehicle loans and such, they don't expect to be gone before everything is paid off. Luckily, Alaina had been able to sell their house and the vehicle with the highest payment to make enough money to break even. Her dad's life insurance had covered the credit card debt and the remaining balance on the other vehicle, which she now used for her and Ben's transportation.

But with the recent onset of unexpected expenses, Alaina was pulling a lot of shifts at the restaurant, which didn't allow for a lot of playtime.

That was one of the reasons why when Ethan had asked her to hang out with him today, she had almost refused. Sometimes Alaina forgot that it was okay for her to have fun. She was so busy being the responsible one that she tended to forget that she was still a kid.

Alaina had quite a few friends before her parents' accident—been in the popular crowd, in fact—but when she was forced to turn her friends down every time they called for her to come hang out because she was too busy working or helping Ben with homework, eventually they just quit calling. She didn't blame them, and although at first she'd been mad, she realized now that it was unreasonable to expect anything different. All of those people had no idea what it was like to live in the real world. They didn't understand what she was going through.

Then there was Ethan Carter. Alaina wasn't quite sure what she thought of Ethan yet. Granny Mae had warned her yesterday morning about how her super-famous grandson would be coming to visit, which seemed a little strange considering he was mid-tour, but who was she to judge when a boy wanted to see his grandma?

What she hadn't expected was to meet him in the middle of one of those nights when she couldn't sleep. The tall guy on the couch just about scared her to death when she'd groggily strolled through the living room to get to the kitchen. And she knew Ethan had been asleep because she'd heard him snoring when she peeked in to check on Ben. He must have awoken when she shut the door. Despite the messy bed hair and ridiculous fuzzy house shoes, she figured that had been as good a time as any to meet him.

Alaina hadn't known what to expect from Ethan. She knew he was insanely famous, but that kind of life was so foreign to her. And she had no idea what people like him acted like, but she had to admit, she'd expected him to be annoyingly conceited. To Alaina's surprise, from their chance encounter, she hadn't gotten that from him, but then again, there's not a whole lot fifteen minutes with a person could tell about them.

Ethan had definitely taken her by surprise by asking her to hang out with him. What were they supposed to do? Where could she possibly go with him around this area that was anything compared to the places he'd been and seen? The boy had toured the world on a limitless tab. There wasn't much competing with that.

Oh well, Alaina thought. He had asked *her* to hang out with *him*, not the other way around. She wasn't going to worry about it. She'd leave all that up to him. It wasn't like they were going on a date. HA! That thought cracked her up. Her on a date with the most desired teen boy in the country. Yeah, right. Besides, Ethan had a girlfriend, or so she'd discovered with a little help from Google.

Okay, no, she wasn't a psychopathic, stalking, Ethan Carter lover. It was more a case of this guy being from a world totally separate from hers, yet he was going to be sharing a room with her little brother. Of course, she trusted Granny Mae's judgment of character, but it was still her responsibility to figure out who would be hanging around Ben. Her little brother had been through a lot in the past year. He didn't need anything else.

Alaina stripped from her bed clothes and put on her bathrobe. The disadvantage to living with Granny Mae was the fact that there was only one shower on the whole top floor, and it was attached to neither her nor Ben's room. She cracked her door open and peeked into the hallway. Ben's room was only two doors down, a closet behind the door in the middle. The bathroom was located at the very end of the hall.

Alaina stepped carefully into the hallway. She knew that if she didn't sneak quietly, Ben would hear her and want her to come into his room to play before she had a chance to shower—which on any normal day would be fine, but there was no way she was traipsing into that room in her bathrobe with some boy in there.

When Alaina reached the stairwell, she heard Ben downstairs talking to Granny Mae and some man—must be the tall man from the couch. She figured Ethan was still asleep so the coast was clear. Just to be safe, she covered the remaining distance to the bathroom door quickly and reached for the door handle, but it turned before she touched it.

The door swung open, and her plan to reach the bathroom unseen was clumsily shattered. Ethan stood before her with a towel wrapped around his waist. His sandy blonde hair swept across his forehead in dripping strands. His wide surprised eyes locked in on hers, and she immediately noticed how unbelievably blue they were.

"Uh...hi," he said a little awkwardly.

"Hi." Alaina was suddenly very aware that Ethan had no shirt on—finding it hard to shift her focus from the indentions of muscles in his waist just above the towel—and dropped her gaze, finding something extremely interesting to stare at beside her left foot. "I'm sorry. I'm...uh...not used to having to wait my turn for the shower. I'll give you a minute."

She turned to race back to her room, all too eager to get away from this situation as soon as possible, but Ethan spoke before she could move.

"No, it's fine. I'm all done in here. I wasn't sure what everybody's schedules were so I just took my chances. It's all yours. I'll get out of your way."

Still refusing to raise her gaze, Alaina let out a quick, "Thanks." Ethan stepped around her into the hallway. She was shutting the door behind her when she heard him speak again.

"Are we still on for today?"

Alaina concentrated on moving her gaze to Ethan's eyes only. "Sure, I've got the day off. I'm just going to clean up, and then I'll be down."

Ethan gave a slight grin and nodded as he turned for Ben's room.

Alaina closed the bathroom door and breathed in the steam that still filled the room from Ethan's shower. A nice aroma of floral and cologne filled her senses; she guessed a combination of her body wash and his shampoo.

One thing Alaina knew for sure. She was going to have to get used to sharing the top floor with someone other than her brother—which meant being much more careful with what she walked around wearing.

After a quick, reinvigorating shower, Alaina made certain that the hallway was clear before making her way back to her room to get ready to spend the day with Ethan.

Chapter 6

Ethan

Ethan's unexpected encounter with Alaina had taken him by surprise. Did her skin always look that fresh? She had to have just woken up, right?

Ethan descended the narrow staircase to the lower level of the house as an old familiar smell filled his senses. He hadn't smelled anything that good in a long time. Granny Mae's homemade biscuits and chocolate gravy. There wasn't a five-star restaurant anywhere that could beat that breakfast.

"Good morning, Lil E!" Granny's smile lit up when Ethan entered the kitchen. The darkness of the previous night had vanished. Bright rays of sunlight lit the room through the glass doors that opened to the small garden out back.

Ethan felt like a little kid again. He flashed back to days of storming down the staircase and jumping into one of the island bar stools. Granny always made his favorite breakfast when he came to visit. Even after five years, she hadn't changed a thing.

Had he really only been there for less than a day? The realization slapped him square across the cheek—it was happening.

The effects of the Fairhope black hole.

Ethan could almost feel the sick pull in his stomach from being sucked back into this place, this life...this lifestyle. He loved his Granny, but he had moved past this. He had worked his butt off to move past all of this.

He needed to get out of there, and quick.

"Are you hungry, sweetie?" Granny asked. Silent Ted sat as silent as ever in a stool next to Ben, who was greedily spooning chocolate gravy to his mouth like he was eating pudding. "Oh, of course you are. You're thin as a rail. I swear those big shot music people don't feed you enough. Get over here and eat. I made your favorite."

For a split second, Ethan wanted to run, jump on the bar stool, just like old times, but he held back. He wasn't the same innocent little kid Granny used to make breakfast for. He was an irresponsible teenager who had been sent to this house against his will because he'd been bad and then been too dumb to keep from getting caught. And now, here was his sweet grandmother—whom he had neglected to visit for a large portion of his lifespan—making him breakfast like he was still that sweet well-behaved little kid. She couldn't have known why he was there. There's no way she would be doing all of this for him if she did.

This thought only helped to fuel Ethan's anger toward his mom. Not only did she confine him to this southern prison, but she also did it so that he would be unknowingly guilt tripped every time his grandmother did something nice for him. If she wanted to punish him, why didn't she just yell, or take away his phone, or take away his driving privileges...something that normal parents did. No, instead she had taken away his entire life. Who does that?

"Ethan, honey, are you okay?" Granny asked when Ethan didn't answer.

"He wooks wike he might pook." Ben grumbled through a mouthful of gravy that dripped from his chin.

He might be right, Ethan thought.

Ted remained silent.

Ethan glanced up to three sets of inquisitive eyes. "I...uh...I think I need to make a call." He dashed from the kitchen into the little garden leaving his puzzled grandmother behind.

As the door slapped shut behind him, he heard Ted speak. "He'll be fine. He's just going to call his mom."

How did Ted know that?

It took five rings for her to pick up.

"Hello!" Her voice was calm and happy, as though she'd been looking forward to his call all morning. Not at all what he had expected.

"Mom?"

"Hey, honey! How's Alabama?"

"How do you *think* Alabama is, Mom?! Have you completely lost your mind, shipping me off here like some convict?! Do you have any idea what all goes into canceling a concert...and the Staples Center of all places?!"

Her tone remained the same, as if she hadn't heard a word he'd said. "Well I'm glad you're having a good time, honey. Tell your grandmother I send my love."

"Mom, are you hearing anything I'm saying? This is torture! Look, I understand I messed up and I'm sorry, but I've got a career to worry about here. I can't just take random vacations whenever I feel like it!"

His mom finally broke the act and got real.

"See, Ethan, that's where you're wrong. You are only seventeen years old, and for at least the next year, your life is in my hands. And until you prove that you're responsible enough to be a role model to those fans who pay big bucks to idolize you, you won't be around for them to praise."

Ethan's cheeks flushed crimson.

"You can't do that! All I have to do is call Bruce, and he'll fix all of this. I have my own money, you know. I can leave whenever I want."

"Oh, Ethan, don't be so naïve. Bruce knows his place, and he's been instructed to leave you alone or he'll be forced to find a new star to make his money for him. And as for your money, I've had all of your accounts frozen except for one. You'll find a debit card in the front pocket of your suitcase. That should hold you until you've learned what it's like to be a real kid again, depending on how quick a learner you are, of course."

Ethan clenched his fist and contemplated punching out a fern hanging from the patio next to his head. "Mom, please! This is ridiculous. I'm famous for crying out loud! What am I supposed to do here when people realize who I am? They'll flood the house! Paparazzi will be everywhere! I won't even be able to stick my head out of a window!"

"Then you'll get plenty of rest, but until that happens, you might want to keep a low profile. And might I suggest not drinking and driving. That usually helps one stay out of the public eye. You know, just a suggestion."

"Very funny, Mom. Hilarious, really." Ethan let out a frustrated sigh as he paced back and forth in the garden. He gave a swift kick to a ceramic flower pot sitting at the base of the porch swing, but it didn't make him feel any better; it only made his toe hurt. "I can't believe you're doing this to me."

His mom's tone abruptly changed from mocking sarcasm to blatant disappointment. "Ethan, there are a lot of things you've done lately that I can't believe."

To this, Ethan had no reply. Even he had to admit, there was no arguing that one.

"So how long am I stuck here?"

His mother's tone softened. She could sense that Ethan was giving up the fight. "I guess that all depends on you, honey. When you find the old Ethan—the one that sings and performs because it's what he loves to do and not because it's what makes him money— you call me back and we'll talk about it. Until then, get some rest and take advantage of the time off. Your Granny Mae is getting older, and there's no guarantee how much time you have left with her. Use this time wisely."

Ethan could already see there was no getting out of this. He knew his mother well, and when she got that tone there was no backing down. He'd seen it a thousand times with his producers. If she didn't want it, they couldn't talk her into it. There was nothing he could do.

His final plea came out more as a whimper. "Mom...please..."

"Honey, I love you and I want the best for you, and sometimes that means doing things you'll hate me for. I'll talk to you later."

The flat silence on the other end of the line let Ethan know that his mother had hung up.

That was that.

Ethan remained unmoving, taking on the appearance of a statue at the edge of the tiny garden. Given a pointy hat, he could've passed for a really tall gnome. He thought about his next move. Was it worth it to call Bruce? No, probably not. He knew his mother well enough to know that she had already taken care of any avenue Ethan could use to get out of this place. That only left one option.

Stay in Alabama.

Well, of one thing Ethan was entirely certain; if he was going to have any hope of leaving the house during his stay in Fairhope, he was going to have to do something drastic to keep from being recognized. He knew what he had to do...and the thought made him nauseous. His image consultant was going to kill him—it was his signature look and everybody knew him by it—but he had no other choice.

The hair had to go.

Her voice broke through Ethan's fog of panic, startling him with a tiny jump.

"Hey, you okay?"

Ethan looked up toward the patio doors. Alaina gazed back at him with an odd expression. He wondered how long she'd been there. Had she heard any of his conversation with his mother?

"Yeah...I'm fine. I was just talking to my mom."

"Oh."

What was that in her tone? Concern? Why did he already feel calmer? There was just something about this girl's confident presence that seemed to soothe Ethan's nerves.

Alaina had been the first and only person his age to treat him like a real human being and not a rock star since he'd quit high school and began his music career, and he was surprised by how much he was looking forward to spending the day with her. He just hoped she knew a little something about hair.

Chapter 7

Alaina

Alaina was a little surprised when Ethan's directions landed them in the parking lot of the Wal-Mart Supercenter.

It hadn't dawned on Alaina that Ethan was without personal transportation, but considering Granny Mae had picked him up from the little airport upstate, it only made sense. So Alaina's vehicle was providing the transportation for the day and Ethan was enjoying playing navigator from the passenger seat.

Although conversation between them had begun on the awkward side, it escalated smoothly. Sometimes, it was so hard for Alaina to believe that Ethan was a worldwide superstar. He acted so normal around her—well, except for when they reached a stop light and he put his hand on the side of his face and hunched down in his seat to keep from being seen by the vehicle next to them. That was a bit strange, but understandable, she guessed.

As they drove through the enchanting downtown area of Fairhope, Ethan regaled on memories from his childhood visits there. Shopping at the market with Granny Mae, learning to surf in the Bay, skating and riding his bike in the huge parking lot of the abandoned warehouse on the edge of town. Ethan's bright blue eyes glazed over in a sense of nostalgia as he pointed here and there as she drove. At times, Alaina picked up on slight alterations in his expression, hints of regret...or possibly sadness. She wasn't sure what that was all about, but she figured that everyone, no matter how famous, had their own personal memories that acted like triggers on their emotions. She knew she sure did.

Alaina chose the safe road and just let Ethan do most of the talking. She actually enjoyed hearing his stories. He had a kind of raw sarcasm that in one sense made her want to laugh, but in another, made her take every single one of his words seriously. He spoke from his heart, however vulnerable and exposed it made him seem. She wondered why she hadn't gotten that same vibe from his music. His songs were all about some impossible idea of love—a love that could never exist, no matter how perfect the couple.

Did he really believe in a love like that?

Alaina was more of a realist. When she experienced love for the first time, she wanted it to be a real, God-sent kind of love. The kind of love that wasn't always easy and wasn't always fun, but was never, ever boring. The kind of love that, in one moment, filled her stomach with butterflies, and in the next, made her want to throw something.

She knew it sounded crazy—or maybe just a little masochistic—but Alaina had witnessed this kind of love firsthand, and she knew that, although it wasn't always a bed of roses, it was effective when it came to longevity. Her parents had loved each other that way. At times they seemed to hate one another, but at other times, there was such an unbelievable, passionate companionship between them.

Memories flooded Alaina's mind with the intensity of a tropical storm. Why had she reminisced? It was always like this. She gave her head a quick shake, doing all she could to focus on Ethan and get rid of the huge burning lump in her throat. This was why she had agreed to come with him in the first place—to get out of her normal routine and get her mind off of her old mountains and the new mountain she was about to climb.

"So...Wal-Mart...," Alaina said unsurely. Per Ethan's instructions, they were parked in the very back corner, in the most possibly remote parking spot on the lot. This wasn't quite what she had expected when he'd asked her to hang out with him.

"Yeah...well...," Ethan spoke slowly, being extra careful to choose the correct words. Finally, he sighed and spit it out. "Okay, here's the deal, and please don't take this the wrong way because I don't want to come off sounding like a total jerk, but...I can't really hang out with you looking like this."

Alaina blinked, quickly hiding the offended scowl from her expression. She glanced down at her black and purple tank top with matching Converse shoes, paired with faded blue jeans with a frayed hole in the left knee. She didn't know how the girls Ethan was accustomed to being around dressed, but she hadn't realized there was a dress code stipulation involved in this outing. "I'm sorry...." She wasn't sure what to say.

Ethan's eyes widened in understanding, and he jumped to try to cover his tracks. "No! I didn't mean you! I meant me! There's nothing wrong with how you look. You're beautiful. I just meant I can't go out in public looking like *Ethan Carter*. I'm going to have to change my look up, or something. I thought maybe some hair color, a new cut..."

"You think I'm beautiful?"

Ethan slowed his rant and his cheeks flushed. He glanced down and started picking at a bit of nothing on his shorts. "Oh...well...yeah, sure I do." When she didn't reply, he went on. "So, I wondered if maybe you could do me a huge favor." His eyes met hers, and he gave a timid smile.

Alaina grinned. "You want me to go in alone and buy you hair color so you don't get mobbed by the masses of the Fairhope Supercenter?"

"Something like that."

"Is it really that hard, being you?

Ethan shrugged and gazed out the front glass. "Being famous definitely has it perks. It's the normal part that I have trouble with. People don't like to let me just be normal."

Alaina had never thought about it like that. When she saw celebrities on TV, she never gave a second thought to what their real life was like off screen, but then again, this was the first celebrity she'd ever known personally.

She resituated in her seat, regaining her confidence. "So, Ethan Carter, pop sensation of the twenty-first century," Ethan gave an amused laugh, "what identity would you like to try on today? Platinum blonde beach dude? Black-haired Emo kid? Fiery hot-tempered red head? Or maybe just plain old brunette all American boy? What's your look of choice?"

Ethan remained silent for a moment, contemplating his options. Finally, his eyes sparkled and a mischievous grin spread across his cheeks. His description online had nailed him perfectly, Alaina thought involuntarily. He was one of the cutest boy's she'd ever seen, but that grin looked like he was up to something.

"Uh...you're not going to do anything crazy like green or orange, are you?" she said. "Because I'm pretty sure that will draw more attention than your normal hair."

Ethan laughed. "No, not green. And definitely not orange."

"What then?"

"You pick."

Alaina snorted. "I'm sorry, I think I heard you say, 'You pick,' as in you being me in this particular situation."

"You heard correctly."

"Are you crazy?"

"Maybe a little. By the way, how are you with a pair of scissors?"

Alaina let out an exasperated sigh and reluctantly took the cash from Ethan's outstretched hand. As she made the hike toward the entrance of the store, she turned back once to view her car. Ethan's currently blonde hair was no longer visible in the passenger side window, undoubtedly because he was hunkered down in the floor board attempting to remain unseen.

By the time she reached the front door, Alaina had considered the situation and decided that she was definitely going to have to choose wisely or forever be known worldwide as the girl who messed up Ethan Carter's perfect hair. But it wasn't a hard decision. She already knew exactly what she wanted to get. A picture of Ethan's wide smile plastered in her memory, she easily found the perfect color to suit him. Ethan wanted to look like a normal guy. So Alaina chose a normal brown for a normal guy, just like he wanted, and just like she wanted for him.

Chapter 8

Ethan

Ethan suppressed the urge to mock Alaina as she grabbed small sections of his freshly colored hair and lifted them to the scissors that rested tightly between her fingers. She gave a frustrated sigh—her brow scrunching in a tight line of concentration that made cute little wrinkles form on her nose—and released the hair back to its original position without so much as a snip from the scissors.

Ethan sat in a straight back wooden chair next to the bay window in Alaina's bedroom. A bed sheet was draped around his shoulders. He'd tried to take his shirt off to keep the hair off of his clothes, but Alaina had insisted he keep his white tank top on—which he found a little amusing.

He looked around her room wondering if it would give him any clues to her personality. Her bedspread was a deep purple. A picture of his talkative young roommate, Ben, sat on a nightstand beside the bed in what appeared to be a frame made of cardboard and construction paper—a present, he guessed.

Posters hung here and there from her walls, mostly of different bands—several Ethan had never bothered listening to. They were mostly Christian rock bands. Ethan had never really bought into the whole Christianity thing. If he couldn't touch it or see it, he didn't see the point in believing it. Where was the proof? On the little table in front of him sat a soft leather-bound Bible that was clearly worn. Colorful bookmarks stuck out of random pages. A journal lay under the Bible and a cup with pencils and highlighters beside those.

Was that really what made Alaina different than the other girls Ethan had met? Her faith? Was that the source of her smooth confidence? Ethan only hoped she wasn't one of those religious fanatics. What did they call them? Jesus freaks? That would ruin everything. He liked Alaina because she seemed to accept him as a real person and not a superstar, but that didn't mean that he wanted to be judged for all his little vices. He knew he wasn't perfect; he didn't need to be reminded of it every day.

But that's what this little visit to the South was all about, wasn't it? To serve as a constant reminder of what he had done. The danger he'd put himself and others into when he drove that car after drinking all of that Tequila. What had he been thinking at the time? Why had he let Vanessa get to him like that? What's funny is that he hadn't even received so much as a text from her since arriving in Fairhope. Not only did Vanessa not know where he was, but she hadn't even bothered to call to find out. She was probably still mad at him. He couldn't believe she'd gotten so upset just because he had refused to dedicate his latest song "Girl from My Dreams" to her at his Staples Center concert. He was with her and everyone knew it—especially considering she never passed up the opportunity for a photo op with him when they were being swarmed by the stupid paparazzi. Why did he have to announce it to fifteen thousand fans during a concert meant for entertainment purposes only? It seemed like a little overkill.

"Ethan, I'm...I'm not sure I can do this."

Ethan turned to find the color swiftly draining from Alaina's cheeks. He held back a smirk. She looked hilarious, but cute as heck. He loved her style. Her little purple tank top, loose fitting faded jeans, and her signature Converse shoes. Her hair was long and dark, and he noticed that she did wear a little makeup during the day. Her style was very punk rock, but by her current expression, fierce was the last adjective he would use to describe her. She looked like a terrified kid standing there, holding those scissors.

"I thought you said you'd cut Ben's hair before?" Ethan said.

"Well, I have, but that was different. Ben's ten and if I messed up, we just combed it funny for a couple of days and hoped nobody noticed. You are not ten, and if I mess up, people will definitely notice."

Ethan smiled. "Calm down, Alaina. You're stressing out. It's just hair."

"No, it is *Ethan Carter*'s hair, and that little bang flip thing you've got going on there is known worldwide. They call it the 'Carter Cut.'"

Okay, this time he couldn't hold it back. He had to laugh. "The Carter Cut? Seriously? Where did you hear that?"

"I...might have...read it somewhere."

"You Googled me, didn't you?"

"No!" She sighed and her lips pursed.

He could tell by her guilty grin and the way her eyes darted from his that he was right.

"You did! You Googled me!"

"Well, what did you expect? You're sharing a room with my brother. I have to look out for him. I'm all he's got."

Her comment cut Ethan like a knife as flashbacks of his overturned Camaro on that dark mountain road came to mind. Once again, he hoped he would never have to tell Alaina the real reason he was in Alabama. Instead, he made a joke to mask his unease.

"Whatever. You're a stalker. Just admit it."

"Yeah, okay," she replied sarcastically. "That's why I had never heard even one of your songs until yesterday. If that's my best attempts at stalking, then I'm terrible at it."

Ethan paused, unsure if he had heard correctly. "You had never heard my music until yesterday? But you said you'd heard it from Granny Mae's room?"

She shrugged. "Yeah, but I never listened to an entire song or anything."

Ethan felt his mouth hanging open slightly. "Wow. I don't know whether to be insulted or insanely impressed."

She shrugged. "I told you I don't listen to that kind of music."

"So, how was it?"

"Your music? It was...cute."

"Cute?"

"Yeah, cute."

What did cute mean? Was that good? Ethan had never heard of his music being referred to as cute. Rockin, sure. Jammin, maybe. But cute? Never.

"What does that even mean?" he asked incredulously.

She grabbed his chin and rotated his face back toward the window. Running her fingers lightly through his hair, she grasped a strand and made her first cut, her courage returning.

"I don't know," she said. "The songs have good beats, and your voice is amazing, but I guess now that I've met you, I don't really see you singing those songs. The lyrics are so poppy and sappy. It just doesn't feel like you mean what you're singing. Like you're just singing for the sake of singing, not to get out a message. Does that sound weird?"

Ethan laughed to himself. "Nope, that doesn't sound weird at all."

How had she picked up on that? Alaina had known Ethan for less than a day. How could she—when even his own mother couldn't—figure out that he hated singing those stupid songs?

Ethan raised a brow. "So I should be singing messages?"

"Oh, you know what I mean," she said. "You are so famous, Ethan. You have the ability to make a difference in so many people's lives. I would love to have that kind of opportunity. I wouldn't waste it by singing corny little love songs about relationships that don't even exist in the real world."

Ethan grinned. "I wish you'd just tell me how you really feel."

Alaina laughed. "I'm sorry. I have this little problem of voicing my opinion even when people don't ask for it."

"No, it's okay. I think I might like that about you."

Alaina stopped mid-snip, and Ethan felt a twinge as the tension between them increased.

"What would you sing about?" Ethan asked, changing the subject.

Alaina paused. "I don't know. Thankfulness, maybe? Or loss. I would sing about things that could provide encouragement for people going through situations like mine. Something that would help them step back and take a look at the big picture, you know? And I think I might sing about Jesus."

There it was. The J word.

Their gazes met through mirrored reflections. When Ethan remained silent, Alaina asked, "What? Is that weird?"

Ethan considered this. "No. Not weird." He paused. "Just, I officially feel like a total jerk."

Alaina laughed and squeezed her eyes shut tight; her nose scrunched into a cute little line of embarrassment. "I'm sorry. Your music is great, really. I like it...."

"No, that's okay," he interrupted. "You were just being honest. And in a way, you're right. I don't sing about anything important like that. But if it's any consolation, I have no control over my song selection. Everything I've written is still a well-kept, treasured secret."

She looked surprised, continuing to run her fingers lightly through his hair, making the occasional snip here and there. The touch of her fingers in his hair sent chill bumps down his arm.

"Why is that?" she asked.

"I don't know. You'd have to ask the big-wigs at my label."

Alaina moved around to the front to work on his bangs. She studied him carefully while continuing to snip at his hair. Why did Ethan get so uncomfortable when she did that? Why did he feel like he owed her more of an explanation? Her huge brown eyes were wide with concentration as she twisted his head slightly from side to side; trying her hardest to make sure that the cut was even. When she was satisfied with her work, she reached for a bit of hair gel and ran it through a small chunk of his hair in the front. Finally, she grabbed a large hand mirror off the nightstand and handed it to him so that he could view the back of his head. The cut was short on the sides and in the back, but spiked just a little right around his bangs. The brown color made his eyes seem extra blue. And he had to admit, it was one of the best, and cheapest, haircuts he'd ever received.

"Well, I'm no big-wig, but personally," Alaina's eyes appeared just above his shoulder in the mirror, "I'd love to hear an Ethan Carter original sometime."

Ethan ran his fingers through his new hair. He couldn't believe the difference it made in his appearance. With a hat and some sunglasses, it was possible that he might actually be able to walk around like a normal person while he was there. Suddenly, Ethan felt a glimpse of something he hadn't felt for a long time. Freedom. And it was all thanks to Alaina.

And she wanted to hear his real music. It had been a long time since Ethan had played one of his own songs for anyone, but he was interested to see her reaction to his lyrics. He enjoyed and appreciated her honesty. In fact, he just enjoyed her company.

Ethan shifted his gaze and met her reflecting eyes in the mirror. "Alaina, for you, I think that can be arranged."

Chapter 9

Alaina

Alaina was thoroughly impressed with her skills as an amateur cosmetologist. She loved Ethan's new look, and he'd been right. The change in color and style seemed to alter his looks just enough that people might not realize who he was. Besides, nobody in Fairhope actually knew that Ethan Carter was the grandson of Granny Mae. Apparently, it was a well-kept family secret. No one would be expecting to see him roaming the streets of Alabama. Maybe if they weren't looking for him, it would be less obvious that it was him.

Alaina only hoped it would work because Ethan was itching to get out of the house. He had already asked her what people around there did for fun on a summer Monday night. Alaina informed him that, normally, she would be working, but everyone else usually hung out down by the pier. Which would have been a great outing for them aside from the fact that "hanging out at the pier" was code for getting wasted on the beach, and Alaina had way too much on her plate to be mixed up in the drama of high school parties. She mainly kept to herself, which made it difficult when Ethan asked if she wanted to go out that night and do something fun.

Alaina had sort of forgotten how to have fun.

The latest doctor's appointment had been almost more than she could handle. She had felt so helpless. Alaina knew chemotherapy couldn't be comfortable for anyone, but she always just sat there speechless, waiting for it to be over. That kind of stuff was so far out of her league it was ridiculous. And now, another appointment loomed ahead in only a couple of days. Would it get any better this time? Would she be inspired with amazing words of comfort at the perfect time; something that would turn the entire situation around? Probably not.

Alaina merely wished there was something she could do, but she wasn't a doctor. She was a teenager whom, only a year ago, thought she had lost everything, only to realize that she still had so much left to lose.

Alaina had lost a piece of herself after her parents' untimely death. A piece that she didn't think would ever fully fill in. How many pieces did she have left? She didn't think she could stand to lose any more chunks of her heart to the death of someone she loved. It was too much. So she did the only thing she knew to do.

She prayed.

Alaina found her strength in God. That was the cause of the

wear and tear on the ragged Bible that sat on her little table by the window. Countless nights, when she couldn't sleep, her Bible was the only thing that calmed her nerves to the point that she could keep her body tied to her bed. Her mood shifted constantly. On her helpless nights, she simply sat and stared, unable to move a muscle, trying to find some way of coming to terms with what was happening. On her angry nights, she wanted to run out into the streets and scream at the top of her lungs until someone pointlessly challenged her to shut up. On her hopeless nights, she stuffed her face in her pillow to keep Ben from hearing her uncontrollable sobs. She didn't want to scare Ben. He didn't need that. He was too young. She was all he had. She needed to be strong for him.

And then, out of nowhere, Ethan Carter walked into her life.

Ethan might have just been using her to help him stay undercover, but Alaina couldn't express to him how much of a comfort the distraction of his presence was. He obviously had no clue what was going on, which made her a little sad, but he would find out in due time. It was inevitable.

Alaina had almost reconsidered when Ethan asked her to go out with him. She was afraid to leave Granny Mae. Alaina held a huge responsibility to her. Granny Mae had taken her and Ben in when they needed her the most, and there was no repaying that. The last thing Alaina wanted was to inconvenience her in any way.

But when Granny Mae caught a glimpse of Ethan's new look and heard that he wanted to get out of the house and do something normal for a change, she had insisted that Alaina go.

"Sweetie, believe it or not, you are still a kid and you have the right to a little fun every now and then," Granny Mae had said. "Now you go spend some time with Ethan. He's surrounded by adults all the time. I bet he's glad to have found a friend like you."

So that was that. Now, Alaina sat alone in her bedroom wondering what on earth she and Ethan could possibly do in Fairhope that he would find the least bit entertaining. What should she wear? She didn't want to dress like a bum in case they went to a nice restaurant, but she also didn't want to get too dressed up. Obviously, Ethan Carter was not asking her out on a date (as if she even had time to date). This was strictly a platonic outing. She didn't want him to think that she had gotten the wrong impression.

After changing outfits about five times, she finally settled on some calf length leggings with a little sundress and a different pair of Converse's than she'd worn earlier in the day. Alaina had never been much for heels. She didn't see the point in forcing herself to walk around in something that made her want to cut her own feet off by the end of the night. Granted, she could have used the extra height, but heels still weren't worth it.

Alaina was grabbing her clutch purse and heading for the door when she was surprised to hear a tiny knock from the other side of it. No one ever knocked on her door.

She did one last mirror check and reached for the knob. She turned it slowly to reveal the source of the knocking.

Ethan stood before her with an excited grin plastered on his face. His dimples showed when he smiled that big. His eyes were the brightest blue she'd ever seen. He wore a pair of long khaki cargo shorts with a deep blue, polo-style, short-sleeved shirt. In his hand was a single yellow rose, just like the ones that grew out back in the garden.

"Hey," Ethan said a little sheepishly. "It's hard to pick someone up when you live in the same house. I'm sorry. This was the best I could do."

Alaina was speechless. She reached out for the rose as Ethan handed it to her. "Wow, thanks."

"I just wanted to do something to thank you for all of your help today. It's not every day you get some paranoid pop singer asking you to do his hair."

Alaina smiled and held the rose to her nose. She loved the smell. "No problem. It was fun...and I think the new cut makes you look...handsome."

There went her big mouth again. She could feel the heat rising in her cheeks.

"You do?"

No backing out now. "Uh...yeah."

Alaina's eyes darted up quickly from their spot on the floor and immediately locked with Ethan's. Their gazes held for a brief moment until they simultaneously shook loose and turned their focus.

"Are you ready?" Ethan asked, stepping aside so that Alaina could make her way into the hall.

"Yeah, I'm just going to take a quick sec to check on Ben."

Alaina walked down the hallway to Ben's room. When she reached the doorway she found Ben on the top bunk of his bed. He was already tucked in his pajamas (at the early hour of seven o'clock), reading a book she had given him for his birthday about all of the creatures God created. It was almost all she could do to keep from turning to Ethan and canceling.

Alaina rarely got nights off from work. She felt guilty leaving Ben alone when she had the whole night that she could be spending with him.

"Hey sis!" Ben said when he saw her enter the room. "Hi roomy!" he added as Ethan entered. Alaina was always amazed by Ben's smile. He could light up an entire stadium with that smile. "Are you and Ethan leaving for your date now?"

And that was the bad part of having a little brother. Sometimes they could be embarrassing. She refused to even shoot the slightest glance in Ethan's direction.

"Ben, sweetie, Ethan and I are not going on a date. We're just going to grab something to eat."

"Then why did Ethan change clothes like five times and redo his hair twice? And why are you holding a flower? Looks like a date to me!" Ben averted his attention back to the book as if he was just making normal conversation.

Ethan let out an awkward laugh from behind her. "Thanks, little guy."

Alaina couldn't help but laugh, and she was about to turn to leave when she noticed the flushed, pale look to Ben's skin. As his mother figure for the last year, she knew that look all too well.

"Ben, are you running fever?"

He replied almost before she had finished asking. "No."

"Ben, don't you make me climb up there because you know I will. Get over here."

Ben looked up from his book defeated, groaned, and crawled to the edge of the bed. Alaina placed the back of her hand on his cheek and reached up on her tip toes to kiss his skin. He was definitely warm.

"Ben, you are running fever! Why didn't you come get me and tell me you weren't feeling well?"

"Because I *do* feel well."

"Then why are you running fever?"

"Because that's what I do?"

"What does that mean?"

Ben flashed a stubborn little boy look. "It means that Granny Mae already gave me some medicine and I'm not sick. You are just a big ol' worry wart. And I didn't tell you because Granny Mae told me not to. She said you wouldn't go out tonight if I told you."

Alaina let out an exasperated sigh. "Well, she was right. I'm not leaving you here with Granny Mae when you're getting sick. She doesn't need to deal with that."

"Oh yes she does!" Granny Mae's voice startled Alaina from the doorway of the little bedroom. "Ethan, take Alaina out of this house at once before she gets to the point you have to drag her out and chain her to the seat of the car."

Ethan cast a look of confusion.

"Really, Granny Mae," Alaina pleaded. "Ben is my responsibility. I'll stay with him."

"You have way too many responsibilities, my dear," Granny countered. "And tonight, the only one you have to worry about is showing my grandson what it's like to be a normal teenager for once in his life. Now, I want you kids out of this house immediately and on the town having fun. Alaina, don't worry about Ben. I might be old, but I've had kids of my own. I know what to do with a fever."

"But...," Alaina started to argue.

"Nope! No buts. And Ethan, I want you to forget about agents, and producers, and screaming fans. Relax and have a good time tonight. You work hard, and you deserve a night to yourself."

Granny Mae looked at both of them dead in the eye. It was amazing how she could do that without shifting her eyes at all. She looked remarkably tough for such a frail woman. It must be a grandma thing, because it was working. "Are we clear, children?"

"Yes, ma'am," Alaina and Ethan chimed together.

"Very well," Granny Mae smiled. "Now, Ben, get down here. I made your favorite dinner.

Ben jumped down from the top bunk in one swift motion. Alaina cringed. "Grilled cheese sandwiches and chicken noodle soup?" he asked eagerly.

Granny smiled and brushed the top of his head. "You know it, kiddo."

Ben ran from the room, and the sounds of his steps could be heard as he bounded down the staircase.

"Oh, and Ethan," Granny continued before they could exit the bedroom. "There's a little surprise for you outside. Your friend Ted picked it up for you today." Alaina had almost forgotten about the tall man on the couch.

Granny Mae took them both by the shoulders and guided them

into the hallway to the stairs. Ethan gave Alaina an amused grin. She returned it.

"Okay, bye kids! Have fun!"

When Ethan and Alaina reached the front porch and peered out to the drive, they found the surprise. Beside the driver's side door of a beautiful jet black Dodge Charger, Ted stood holding a set of keys.

"I thought you might like the freedom of your own vehicle, Mr. Carter," Ted said as they made their way across the yard to him.

Please tell me he didn't just go out and buy a car, Alaina thought. But when she got closer, she noticed the tag on the key had the name of the rental place in town. She was surprised by Ethan's expression as he grasped the keys from Ted.

"Wow, thanks man," Ethan said slowly. "Are you sure this is okay?"

Why would it not be okay? Alaina knew Ethan was busy, but he surely had his license.

"I think it will be okay just this once," Ted smiled. "But try to bring this one back in one piece, Mr. Carter. I'm sure Alaina would appreciate it. And technically, per Bruce's orders, I am to accompany you on this outing in case you are discovered and mobbed by crazed female adolescents, but if it's all the same to you, I think I'd rather wait for a call or text to come to your rescue."

Ethan's eyes gleamed. He was like a little kid who had just been told he was free to run around unsupervised in a Toys 'R' Us. He reached out and shook Ted's hand as though some sort of silent agreement had been reached between them.

"You are welcome, Mr. Carter, but please do remember that my job is on the line here. I would appreciate it if you didn't make me regret this."

"No way, sir."

Alaina wasn't sure what was taking place between Ethan and Ted, but she didn't have time to ask. Ethan grasped her hand and led her to the passenger side of the car. He opened her door and waited for her to be seated before shutting it. Then he ran around the back of the car, gave Ted one last wave, and fell into the driver's seat.

Ethan turned to Alaina. His eyes sparkled with excitement. His wide smile stretched from ear to ear. Alaina felt a sensation in the pit of her stomach that she wasn't familiar with. For some reason, she decided in that moment that she could look at that smile all day and it wouldn't bother her a bit. She loved Ethan's smile. She loved that he was happy. She worried that she was beginning to care a little too much about whether Ethan Carter was happy or not. It shouldn't matter to her in the slightest...but it did.

Ethan turned the key and the Charger's engine purred to life.

"So where should we go?" he asked.

Alaina thought for a moment and decided she could care less. She actually had a night to be a kid again. The first in a long, long time. And she didn't care where Ethan took her. All she cared about was that wherever the night took her, Ethan would be there with her.

Chapter 10

Ethan

Ethan could hardly believe what was happening. He had never expected Ted to talk, much less to go rent him a vehicle so that he didn't have to rely on Alaina to drive him around. He had felt a little pathetic asking Alaina to go out with him that night and then having to take her vehicle. But Ted had solved the problem. Ethan understood what Ted was laying on the line for him, and there was no way that he was going to mess that up.

The night had begun as a desperate desire to get out of Granny Mae's house. To break free from his prison of punishment. But Ethan didn't feel that now. When Alaina opened her bedroom door, and he'd seen her beautiful dark hair and cute little outfit with her signature shoes, he decided that maybe this night was a little more about her. Ethan had been curious about Alaina since their chance encounter the night before in the kitchen, and the more time he spent with her, the more he wanted to know her.

Alaina was beautiful, and down to earth, and natural. She had an inner beauty that he didn't quite understand. A calm peacefulness that he'd never felt in his own self. And even though she'd gotten a little frantic about leaving Ben, that only fueled Ethan's desire even more. It was a sign of passion and loyalty mixed with a bit of anxiety. Alaina was going through something Ethan didn't understand, but he wanted to do something to help her. She had helped him when there was no one else around to do it, and he wanted to return the favor.

Surprisingly, he wanted her to...smile. Ethan loved her smile. He wanted to make her happy tonight so that he could see her smile. The entire situation made Ethan realize how long it had been since he'd cared about someone's happiness other than his own.

"So I was thinking we might go grab some food at that restaurant on the pier," Ethan said after a moment. "I've always liked the looks of that place. It's pretty, sitting out there on top of the water."

Alaina giggled.

"What?"

"That's where I work. I'm a waitress."

"Never mind, scratch that. You're probably sick of the food by now. We can go somewhere else."

"No, it's okay," she said. "I actually never get to eat the food. I'm always too busy working. It'd be nice to experience that place as a normal customer for once."

It was a night of new experiences for both of them. As Ethan drove through the sparkling downtown area of Fairhope, the sun was beginning to set over the ocean's horizon and the town was coming alive. The light poles that lined the streets of the town were wrapped in beautiful greenery and white lights. The streets were clean. People walked here and there on the sidewalks. Mostly couples, but a few families with children also. Ethan had forgotten how slowly life could move when he wasn't on a tour bus bouncing from city to city.

Ethan remembered the way to the restaurant easily and arrived there within ten minutes of leaving the house. He and Alaina chatted back and forth about areas of the town that they liked the most. They laughed when Ethan's latest hit came on the radio. He cranked it up and sang along in a pretend voice so that he sounded terrible. Alaina laughed and seemed to make the entire vehicle sparkle.

When they arrived at the restaurant, Ethan parked the car and walked to Alaina's side. He reached out his hand to help her from her seat. She took it slowly and stepped out. The fruity scent of her hair lofted up to his nose. Her smooth, soft hand lay gently in his. When she was standing, Ethan was about to release her and move to shut her door, but something stopped him. He didn't want to release her.

So he took a chance.

Ethan held loosely to Alaina's hand and began to move away from the car, cautious to see how she would react.

It was apparent that she was about to pull away, but in that instant, their eyes met, and to his astonishment, after a brief moment of hesitation, Alaina moved with him away from the car, allowing her hand to remain comfortably rested in his.

When they reached the entrance, a smartly dressed hostess greeted them at the door.

"Hey girl!" the young girl voiced with surprise. "What are you doing here on your day off...and who is this?" The girl ran her eyes up and down Ethan as if he were a statue for her very own viewing pleasure.

"I'm E...," he began.

"This is my friend from out of state," Alaina cut him off with an odd look. "This is...uh...Brandon...Matthews. I'm showing him around Fairhope tonight. We're just going to grab something to eat and then head out."

Ethan almost laughed aloud at Alaina's quick thinking. He'd been so wrapped up in the moment; he'd almost blown his cover before the night even began.

"Alaina! So nice to see you, dear!" A blonde lady, dressed in a tweed power suit, exited the kitchen area and hurried over to give Alaina a quick hug.

"Uh...Brandon...," Alaina said, trying not to smile. "This is my boss, Tina. Tina, this is my friend, Brandon."

"It's so nice to meet you, Brandon!" Tina exclaimed, grasping his hand with surprising force. "We don't see Alaina out of her uniform very often. I'm so glad you chose our establishment for your dining this evening."

"Oh, don't worry about us, Ms. Tina," Alaina said. "We'll just sit over in the corner out of everybody's way. I know what the dinner rush is like. We don't want to get in the way."

"My dear, you will do no such thing." Tina turned and flashed a businesslike smile at Ethan. "Brandon, any friend of Alaina's is an honored guest at my restaurant. You will be eating outside on the pier tonight."

"But that table is only reserved for really important customers," Alaina objected.

"Which is precisely why you will be seated there." Tina snapped her fingers toward the hostess. "Gabby, take care of everything, will you? You know how things work on the pier."

"Yes, ma'am," the girl said. "Wait here just a second, you guys. I'll be right back."

Ethan continued to grasp Alaina's hand as they waited. He couldn't judge the look on her face. Was it embarrassment or appreciation? He wasn't sure, but he could tell that she wasn't fond of all the attention.

"Hey, are you sure you're okay with this place?" he asked softly. "We can go somewhere else if you want."

She cast a slight smile and peered up to him. "No, it's fine. They're just not used to seeing me out without Ben or Granny Mae. The shock will wear off soon enough. And I've waited the table at the pier a few times, and it is beautiful. That was really generous of Tina to let us sit there." A sly grin spread across her cheeks. "Besides, if my friend, Brandon, wants to experience Fairhope, this is the way to do it."

"Brandon," Ethan laughed. "That was a good one."

The hostess returned then and led them through the main dining area and out a discrete door in the back of the building. They walked onto a sparkling white dock that extended far out into the water. In the distance, Ethan saw a glow of light coming from a small gazebo at the very end of the dock.

While they walked, Ethan listened to the hostess attempt to whisper to Alaina.

"Are you sure Brandon has never visited here before?" the girl murmured. "He looks kind of familiar."

"Nope, never been here in his life," Alaina said quickly.

"Well, you need to bring him around more often. He is *hot*."

Alaina giggled and Ethan looked away, pretending he hadn't heard.

When they reached the end of the dock, Ethan found that the gazebo contained a single table set for two. The ceiling was lit with twinkling white lights and greenery, just like the light poles in the town. The lights reflected and danced on the ocean water below. A tall white candle lit the table. Crystal place settings lay placed at each of the two seats.

Ethan unwillingly released Alaina's hand and reached for her chair. He pulled it out, allowing her to be seated. Then he took the remaining seat, directly across from her.

"Tina told me to go ahead and get your drink and food orders while I'm out here," Gabby said, pulling a small notepad and pen from her apron pocket. "What can I get for you guys?"

Ethan and Alaina placed their orders, and Gabby retreated back down the dock to the main dining room.

It could not have been a more pleasant evening. The sky was completely clear, every single star visible. Ethan couldn't remember the last time he had seen stars. The wind blew slightly over the calm ocean waves, and the fresh smell of salty sea air surrounded them.

Once Gabby was safely indoors, and out of earshot, Alaina gave Ethan an apologetic look. "Okay, so I'm totally embarrassed."

Ethan gulped down a big bite of the complimentary loaf of bread Gabby had brought out with the menus. "Why?"

"Because I told Ben this was not a date, but thanks to Tina, this is looking remarkably like a date." Her cheeks flushed a little, and she averted her eyes from his. "I'm sorry if you're uncomfortable. I didn't plan any of this and I'm sure Vanessa would have a thing or two to say if she saw you out here like this with some other girl."

Ethan almost spit out the sip of water he'd just taken. "Vanessa? How did you...oh you found that on the internet too, huh?"

Alaina gave a guilty grin.

Ethan thought for a brief moment, choosing his words carefully. He hadn't even considered the fact that Alaina thought he had a girlfriend. "Alaina, if the past couple of days have taught me anything, it's that Vanessa has a thing or two to say about everything, and I couldn't care less about any of it. We got in a fight before I left, and I haven't heard from her since. All she cares about is the publicity being part of a celebrity couple can bring her. I've known it for a while. I just haven't done anything about it. As far as I'm concerned, there is no 'me and Vanessa.' There is only Vanessa, doing who knows what, and me sitting here with you about to have an awesome dinner. Date or not, I'm having a blast and I'm just glad that you came."

Alaina's eyes gleamed. Was she excited? Ethan couldn't tell. He wished he knew what she was thinking. Was she as happy to be with him as he was with her? He knew that he was probably jumping the gun—honestly, who in their right mind falls for a person in only a day—but he couldn't help it. He was mesmerized by Alaina. If his mom called that very second and told him it was okay to go back to his tour, he wasn't sure what he would say. Fairhope was starting to grow on him. The black hole was swirling right in front of him, and he was running toward it at full speed. He didn't want to leave yet. He wanted to stay right in that moment with Alaina. He wanted more time to get to know her and show her that he was more than just a famous kid with a guitar. He was a person with his own thoughts and feelings, and right now, his feelings were all centered around her. Alaina wasn't worried about his fame or his money. She looked at him and talked to him like he was a regular person. Like she held expectations for him that other people let fall in hopes to gain his approval. He wanted to meet all of those expectations.

"So what was that between you and Ted earlier?" Alaina asked once their food had arrived. "What did he mean by 'bring the car back in one piece?'"

Ethan's stomach churned. He'd hoped Alaina hadn't caught on to that particular comment. What should he say? He couldn't tell her what really happened with his last vehicle. Her parents were killed by a drunk driver. If Alaina knew he wrecked his car because he'd been drinking, there's no way she would ever look at him the same again. The last thing he wanted to see in those huge brown eyes of hers was disappointment.

No, somehow, Bruce had kept the accident out of the tabloids because Ethan had Googled himself that morning and there was no news except for some speculation as to why he had postponed his tour dates. Rumors would begin to fly soon—of that he was certain—but so far, nothing about the accident. Alaina couldn't find out. That's just all there was to it.

"I...uh...," Ethan began slowly. "I had a wreck recently. Went around a curve too fast, hit some water, and hydroplaned. Totaled my car. Ted's been giving me grief about it ever since. That's one of the reasons I'm here. Mom got worried about me and wanted me to slow down for a while. Take a breather. Plus, I haven't seen Granny Mae in almost five years so I was overdue for a visit."

There, that was mostly the truth.

"That's terrible," she said softly. "You're really lucky you weren't hurt."

Ethan knew that. In fact, if it hadn't been for all of the alcohol in his system, he probably would have been injured. The paramedic even told him that if he had tensed his muscles, it could have broken his legs, but since he had been so numb, he just kind of flopped around. The more Ethan thought about that night, the stupider he felt. At the time, he'd felt on top of the world—like he owned it. What was it about alcohol that gave a person a false sense of confidence? Ethan was certain Alaina would have found his performance that night to be utterly pathetic.

"Yeah," he said finally. He couldn't bring himself to tell her the truth.

"God must have big plans for you."

Ethan paused. "What?"

"God protected you during your wreck. Think about it. If you totaled your car, it must have been a pretty bad wreck, but here you sit without a scratch. There's a reason He saved you. He has a purpose for you. You just don't know what it is yet."

That thought had never once entered Ethan's mind. Why would God, the guy who wanted everybody to act right all the time, protect a stupid teenage boy who had intoxicated himself half to death? Although he hated to admit it, Ethan knew that wreck was entirely his fault. Why would God save *him*?

"I don't know about all that," Ethan said cautiously, "but I do know that I was very lucky."

Alaina gazed directly into his eyes, digging down deep into his very soul. What was she searching for in there? He couldn't hold her gaze. He had to look away.

After a moment, she spoke. "You don't believe, do you?"

"Believe? Like, in God?" Ethan stuttered. "I honestly haven't ever put much thought into it."

"But don't you ever wonder where we came from? How we got here?" Alaina pressed. Ethan wanted to stop her, to tell her to please not start rambling about religious nonsense before she ruined their evening, but something in her expression sealed his lips. Something in her tone. A deep passion that Ethan had never noticed in, well, anybody. He was intrigued; all he wanted was to hear more.

"Look around you," she continued. "Look at the moon and the stars. This massive ocean. He created all of this for us. Can you not feel it? In the wind? In the air around you? His presence is everywhere."

Alaina closed her eyes for a moment and inhaled deeply. Ethan didn't know what she was talking about. He'd never been taught about God and the things He had created. Ethan had always just lived without asking questions. He couldn't feel what Alaina felt, but the way she sat there across from him, her arms wrapped around her chest, a glowing light in the scene around her, Ethan knew that he wanted to feel what she felt. He had traveled the world and done things most people had only dreamed of doing, but never once, in all his experiences, had Ethan ever felt as alive as Alaina looked at that very moment.

Ethan reached out and, once again, took Alaina's hand in his. This time without the slightest bit of hesitation. He didn't know the God Alaina spoke of, but if He was willing to grant him this one wish, it was worth asking. So Ethan opened a little piece of his heart, and for the first time, he spoke to his Creator. He knew he didn't deserve it, but he hoped Alaina's God would grant him this one request.

Please don't let her let go.

Chapter 11

Alaina

Dinner with Ethan was going much differently than Alaina had originally expected. She was curious as to what was happening between her and Ethan. They had only met the previous night, but she was beginning to feel as though she had known him forever. Was it possible to lose her heart in such a quick period of time? Amazingly, the thought didn't have the effect normally expected in these situations. It didn't cause cute little butterflies to swarm in her stomach. It didn't leave a cheesy grin plastered on her face. It didn't make her feel like dancing around her room when no one was watching.

It made her feel sick.

Alaina had lost the majority of her working heart to the death of her parents, and she was currently in the process of trying to hang on to what was left. She was afraid she would never have enough love left to share with anyone other than Ben. But there was Ethan with his smooth voice, his beautiful bright blue eyes that burned holes into her when he stared, and his old-fashioned gentleman tendencies. What was she supposed to do with that? She didn't want goose bumps to form on her arms every time Ethan flashed that goofy dimpled grin. They just did. She didn't want to feel the fire that ignited between them every time he took her hand in his. But there was nothing she could do about it.

Alaina couldn't figure out which emotion was holding dominance at that point. She was terrified that she was going to be hurt. Seriously, Ethan was a worldwide rock star! That alone should've been enough to make her run for the door! But to top that off, she was currently going through a crisis that she wasn't quite sure Ethan would be comfortable with. Alaina wasn't a normal teenage girl. She couldn't offer Ethan a stress-free relationship. The loss of her parents had left her with baggage, and there weren't many boys that were willing to deal with baggage, especially not the ones who bounced from one state to the next every other day.

Alaina could tell that Ethan was interested in her, but to what extent, she wasn't certain. How interested could he possibly be? What did she possibly have to offer him that he couldn't find in any other girl? He was *Ethan Carter* for crying out loud. He could have any girl he wanted.

And then there was that sobering fact that hung over their heads like a rain cloud waiting for the perfect time to let loose.

He would be leaving soon.

The entire situation made absolutely no sense. It was irrational. It was irresponsible. It was an impossible scenario.

Then why could Alaina not bring herself to walk away?

Tina had given them their privacy throughout the entire dinner, only interrupting long enough to deliver their food and a ticket marked with a zero balance and a little note saying that their meal was on the house.

Alaina and Ethan had talked throughout the entire meal. There were no uncomfortable moments. No awkward silences. Conversation flowed smoothly as if they were old friends. They countered each other's remarks, finished each other's sentences, and told stories of their pasts; each realizing they had more in common than either could have expected.

Alaina easily forgot the standard that the rest of the world held Ethan to. As they walked hand in hand along the breezy Alabama coastline, she saw him as nothing more than the vibrant boy who had a passion for music and who could take her mind off of everything but him with only the slightest grin.

The drive home was surreal. Alaina wondered how, after such a perfect evening together, they were to end it by entering the same house and walking the same staircase to their separate rooms.

When Ethan pulled the car slowly into the driveway, he cut the lights and flicked off the engine, but neither of them budged. Alaina wasn't sure about Ethan, but she was not ready for the night to end. She hadn't felt that carefree in so long; it almost felt like the first time. All of her cares and worries had been washed away with the slightest touches of Ethan's hand in hers. His arm wrapped around her shoulder as they had walked along the beach. He hadn't been pushy. He hadn't been disrespectful. He'd been cautious and sweet. Alaina didn't feel like Ethan expected anything out of her. She just felt like he wanted to spend time with her and get to know her, which made for an amazing night.

But all good things must come to an end, and there Ethan and Alaina sat, at the end, neither knowing what to say or do next.

Finally, after a few seconds of irresolute silence, Ethan finally spoke. His words were slow and deliberate as if he wanted them to come out perfectly.

"I had a really good time tonight."

"Me too," Alaina replied.

He laughed to himself. "No, you don't understand. I started

singing when I was so young. I don't think I've actually been on a normal date that didn't involve reporters and paparazzi...well...ever."

Alaina glanced down at their intertwined fingers. Ethan ran his thumb slowly over her knuckles. She looked back up, meeting his gaze instantly. "Was this a date?"

Ethan only hesitated for a split second, but he looked a bit nervous, which she thought was kind of cute. When he spoke, he had a slight grin. "Could it be?"

Alaina didn't even think. "Yeah. I think it could be."

Ethan's eyes never veered from hers. He bore deeper and deeper as though he was trying to find something within her that he didn't quite understand. Usually, she could break his gaze after this long, but not this time. He was holding strong.

He leaned closer, reached out a hand, pulled a piece of stray hair from in front of her eyes, and ran it down behind her ear. His fingers stopped at her chin where he felt her skin. His face was so close now.

Alaina's heart beat like a bass drum inside her chest. He was going to kiss her! How had this happened so quickly? Was she ready for this?

He shifted and drew even closer. She could smell the faint aroma of his cologne. His hot breaths bounced off her cheek as his lips parted. Her eyes closed. So close now. She could imagine the feel of his lips on hers....

What was she thinking! She couldn't do this. She wasn't even being honest with Ethan. He knew what she had been through...but not what she was going through. He didn't know what he was getting himself into. She wasn't being fair to him.

The soft feel of his lips grazed across hers....

She pulled away and sighed.

"I can't."

Ethan didn't protest. He didn't push. He pulled away, gave her an understanding shrug, and said, "I'm sorry."

That stupid lump rose in Alaina's throat, but she swallowed it back down. She was getting good at that lately. "No, I'm sorry. I'm...I'm just not ready."

"It's okay, Alaina. I understand."

"Why don't you call me Ali?"

Ethan's eyes widened, and he understood perfectly what she meant. He held the back of her hand to his lips and gave it a soft, tender kiss.

"We better get inside."

"Okay."

Ethan reluctantly released her hand and climbed out of the vehicle. He walked to her side of the car, opened her door, and reached to help her out. They walked in silence up the little walk lined in perennials, then up the three white painted stairs to the front porch. They reached the doorway.

Alaina paused.

In a split-second decision, she turned quickly, rose to her tip toes, and planted the swiftest of kisses on Ethan's smooth cheek. She turned the door knob and entered the living room before Ethan had the chance to say a single word.

Alaina bolted for her room ignoring the sleeping tall man on the couch and the light he must have left on in the kitchen. When she didn't hear the door open behind her, she thought it safe and took a second to check in on Ben.

Her little brother lay comfortably on the top bunk, sleeping peacefully as if all was wonderful in his world. Alaina climbed high enough to kiss his forehead, analyzing that his fever had diminished throughout the night. She readjusted his hat so that it rested properly on his head, and ran from the room before Ethan had the chance to make it up the stairs.

When Alaina was in her room, safely alone behind her closed door, she collapsed onto her bed, attempting to slow the dizzying spin in her mind. She was a mixed-up mess of emotions. She ran over and over the events of the night, as if watching a black-and-white picture show in her mind. Ethan's broad smile was etched in her memory. The safe feeling she felt every time he held her hand in his. Then, that moment when their lips had almost touched....

There it was, when Alaina had thought it would never be possible for her again.

Little butterflies and a cheesy grin.

Chapter 12

Ethan

Ethan stood frozen on the porch.

Alaina liked him. She was obviously a little freaked out, but she'd kissed him; that had to mean something.

Ethan had never felt for a girl what he felt for Alaina. Things with Vanessa were always so complicated. No matter what they were doing, it was an inevitable fact that it would contain some sort of pointless drama. He'd just assumed all girls were that way.

But Alaina was different.

Her lips still burned on his cheek as he finally opened the door and entered the house. Ted's snoring gave away his position on the couch, but Ethan noticed a light still on in the kitchen. He made his way across the room to turn it off, but when he reached the switch, he was startled by the voice coming from a stool by the island.

"Fun night?"

Granny Mae looked at him knowingly and cast a sly smile.

"Uh...yeah. Really fun, actually."

"I figured you would like Alaina once you got to know her. Not quite the obsessive fan you were expecting, huh?"

Ethan scoffed, remembering that conversation. He couldn't have been more wrong.

"She is something, all right," Ethan said. He grinned to himself and moved to the sink to grab a glass of water.

Granny Mae's smile faded a little. "Ethan, honey, can I ask you something without you getting offended?"

"Sure, Granny. Shoot."

"Well, I see that you and Alaina are getting to know one another, and I know how these things go sometimes with kids your age..."

Ethan wasn't sure where she was going with this.

"...but I think that you need to know that Alaina has been through more in the last year than most people go through in their entire lives. She can't afford to be hurt again. Are you following me?"

Ethan took the seat next to his grandmother.

"You think I'm going to end up hurting Alaina?"

"No, dear, I would never expect you to do anything on purpose, but it's just that you are not going to be around here forever. You and I both know why you're in Fairhope in the first place, and we both know that you'll be hitting the road again as soon as your mother gives you the permission to do so."

Ethan remained unmoving, refusing to meet his grandmother's gaze.

"You know the real reason I'm here?"

Granny Mae reached out and rubbed the top of his hand. "Of course I do, Lil E. I know you love me, but even I know you would never postpone a tour just to come visit your old grandmother. Your mother explained everything before you arrived."

Ethan let out a heavy sigh.

"Granny, I know what you think…"

"Do you?"

"Yeah. You think I'm just like all the other stars my age. I get a little success, make a little money, and all of a sudden I think I'm invincible and can do whatever I want. But it's not like that. It's…," Ethan sighed. "It's just not like that."

Granny Mae reached out and grazed her hand down Ethan's cheek, making him feel like the same twelve-year-old boy he'd been the last time he talked to her like this.

"I don't think that, Ethan."

"You don't?"

"No. I think you're a very special, talented boy who happened to lose his way for a while. Honey, just because you mess up once doesn't mean you can't fix it. I already see a difference in the Ethan sitting here and the one who climbed out of Mr. Hinkle's plane."

Ethan laughed remembering that terrifying, ancient plane and its extremely southern pilot.

He sighed and continued. "I don't know, Granny Mae. I messed up pretty bad this time. I…I don't even know what I was thinking. I knew not to get in that car. I was just so fed up with it all. I felt like everything was snowballing on me and…I freaked. I guess you're pretty mad at me, huh?"

"No, baby. I was a little disappointed when I heard, but I know that you'll fix everything in the end. I have faith in you."

"Now you sound like Alaina."

Granny Mae smiled. "I'll take that as a compliment. She's pretty special, don't you think?"

You have no idea, Ethan thought. But he highly doubted that Alaina would be so quick to forgive like his grandmother was.

"She doesn't know the real reason I'm here, does she?" Ethan asked quietly, already knowing the answer.

"No."

Ethan sighed. "She can't find out, Granny Mae. Her parents were killed by someone doing the same stupid thing I did. That guy I almost hit could have died, and his daughter would have been left behind just like Alaina and Ben. She will never understand."

"I wouldn't be so quick to assume that, Lil E. Alaina is a mature young lady. Don't you think she deserves the truth from you?"

"Alaina makes me want to be a better person, Granny Mae."

"She tends to have that effect on people."

"It doesn't matter what excuse I give her; she won't understand why I did that."

"Ethan, do you care for Alaina?

Ethan looked up at his grandmother with a sheepish expression. "Is it that obvious?"

Granny Mae gave him an understanding smile. "Something you will learn as you get older, sweetie, is that sometimes the hardest things we have to say are the hardest because they must be said to the people we care about the most. Regardless of whether Alaina finds forgiveness for you or not, it doesn't change the fact that she still deserves the truth. She might even appreciate you more for it in the end."

"I hope you're right," Ethan said lightly.

Granny patted his hand. "I usually am." She rose slowly from her stool. "Well, I'm pooped. I'm going to head for bed."

Ethan watched as his grandmother made her way slowly across the room. She looked so much older than he remembered. Weaker. His mind flashed back to the scene between her, Ben, and Alaina earlier that evening. Alaina had not wanted to leave Ben with Granny Mae. She seemed so worried. Why? Granny had dealt with children before. Why would it matter if she watched Ben for a while...unless there was more going on with Granny than had he realized.

"Granny, are you sick?"

Granny stopped short in the doorway of the kitchen and turned back to him. "Why would you think that, Lil E?"

"I was just thinking about earlier. How reluctant Alaina was to leave Ben with you."

Granny considered this carefully, taking her time to find the correct response. "Ethan, you may soon find that you're not the only one with things you find hard to say."

"What does that mean?"

"It means you don't have to worry about me, dear. I might be old, but I'm tough. And no, I'm not sick."

That was a relief, but still didn't explain Alaina's strange behavior. Maybe he would ask her about it tomorrow.

Once Ethan's grandmother left the kitchen, he dumped the remains of his water in the sink and moved past sleeping Ted to the staircase. When Ethan reached the top of the flight, he paused before opening his bedroom door, shooting one last glance down the hall toward Alaina's room.

He didn't understand everything that was going on, but he knew for certain that he was crazy about the girl that lay on the other side of that door. And he didn't know how much time they had left together, but he knew without a doubt that he was going to make the most of every single second of it.

Ethan turned the knob of his bedroom door, and before entering the room, under his breath, he whispered.

"Sweet dreams, Ali."

Chapter 13

Alaina

Alaina hit the snooze button several times as the sun stubbornly rose outside her window. It was a dreary, rainy Tuesday morning, and she had to get up and get to work. Alaina had been marked off the schedule at the restaurant for the previous day, but to make up for lost time, she had agreed to work a shift for one of the girls who wanted the day off. That put Alaina working a double shift. Needless to say, it was going to be a long day, but Alaina's desperate need for money highly outweighed her reluctance to roll out of bed.

She was already tired from her lack of sleep the previous night. Her outing with Ethan had left her on a natural high, incapable of allowing her to become the slightest bit sleepy until it was already too late.

Alaina began with her normal morning devotional. Today she chose to read about hope—an attribute she had been highly lacking in the past few weeks. She was beginning to realize that the concept of hope and faith in times of crisis was much easier talked about than actually carried out. Alaina was doing her best, but after weeks of the endless cycle of work, taking care of Ben, and bouncing from one doctor to the next, she was approaching complete burn-out mode. There were only so many grown-up responsibilities her teenage mind could process at a time before she felt like exploding. Her night with Ethan could not have come at a better time, and although she still wasn't completely comfortable with allowing herself to become close to anyone in her fragile state of mind, she was still more grateful for the distraction than he would ever realize. She knew it was only a matter of time, though, before she would have to explain all of the details. Clue him into what actually went into spending a day in her world. Would he leave? Probably. But what other choice did she have?

Alaina didn't have any chance encounters in the hallway that morning. She was successfully unseen throughout both trips to and from the bathroom. When she was completely dressed, her little black two-pocket apron already tied around her waist, she left her room to start her daily routine.

First stop: Ben's room. She gave a light two-tap knock and placed her ear against the door. She wasn't positive, but she thought she could hear two sets of heavy breathing coming from the occupants inside the room. Being much more careful than she normally was, Alaina turned the knob and tiptoed into the room.

Ethan lay on the bottom bunk, the covers lying loosely around his waist. Alaina tried to suppress a giggle to keep from waking him and Ben. Ethan looked hilarious snuggled into his big pillow, which was cased in pictures of little basketballs, footballs, and baseballs. He was slightly out of his Hollywood element. His expression was peaceful, and his skin was smooth and appeared soft to the touch. His full lips were parted slightly, allowing the air to flow easily to his lungs. Alaina imagined what it would have been like if she would've just let Ethan kiss her when he had tried. Did she have regrets? Maybe a little...but she knew it was for the best. As fed up as she was with doing the responsible thing, she knew it would eventually come to that anyway. There was a time to listen to her heart and a time to listen to her head, and right now, the best thing she could do would be to keep a level head.

Alaina placed her right foot lightly on the edge of the metal bed frame in front of Ethan. She grabbed the bars at the top and slowly lifted her body so she could peer at Ben on the top bunk. The metal gave a slight creak. She hoped neither had heard.

It was almost ten o'clock. Ben was starting to sleep later and later every day. When the summer had begun a few short weeks earlier, he had been up at six on the dot every day. Now, whether asleep or awake, he never left the bed before eleven.

Alaina lifted Ben's cap just long enough to give a quick check to his forehead. The fever was trying to return. Oh, how she longed to just be able to stay home with him when he wasn't feeling good. Most normal kids got that privilege when they were sick. One of their parents would stay home and give them constant care and supervision. Alaina was forced to leave him with Granny Mae, who had enough to worry about without having to deal with a sick little kid.

"Hey you."

Ethan's voice was a little raspy, and it was obvious he was trying to not wake Ben. His fingers wrapped around her bare ankle, and he gave it a slight squeeze, leaving a burning ring in its place.

Alaina lowered back down to the floor. "Good morning. Did you sleep well?"

He shrugged and cast a sly grin, "A little. How 'bout you?"

"A little."

Ethan's hand found hers, and he pulled her down to where she was sitting on the edge of the mattress beside him.

"You really worry about him, don't you? I've noticed how

protective you are of him."

Alaina looked into Ethan's eyes and saw nothing but true concern. She wanted so badly to tell him the truth right then, but she just couldn't bring herself to do it. There had to be a better time.

Instead, she settled for a different version of the truth. "Ben has been through a lot in a really short time. If something happened to him...I...I don't know what I'd do."

Alaina didn't realize that she had become silent. Ethan studied her carefully. He reached up and rubbed his finger along her cheek, snapping her out of her trance. "Hey, you okay?"

She replied quickly. "I'm fine."

He didn't look completely convinced, but his next comment surprised her.

"Why don't I hang out with Ben a little today, you know, since you have to work? That way, he won't be stuck here alone."

"You really don't have to do that," Alaina replied. Although her heart melted at the idea of Ethan offering to give up his free time in order to keep her little brother company, she knew that he had to have better things to do with his time. "He'll be fine. He's pretty used to it by now."

"No, it's okay. I don't mind." Ethan grinned. "He's actually starting to grow on me a little. Yesterday, while I was in here getting ready for our dinner, he gave me...the talk."

Alaina looked at him skeptically. "The talk?"

"Yeah," Ethan said. "You know, the talk. He asked me what I planned to do with 'all that money I'm raking in.' He asked about my intentions, except he called it detentions." Ethan laughed. "He even gave me a curfew."

Alaina laughed, but a part of her broke on the inside. Ben was the most special little boy on the face of the planet.

"You mean to tell me that my ten-year-old little brother managed to intimidate the famous Ethan Carter?"

Ethan laughed. "Maybe a little, yeah."

"Well, whatever you guys do," Alaina said, "just don't let him overexert himself. He hasn't been feeling well the past couple of days. He needs to take it easy."

"Yes, ma'am."

Alaina smiled and took one last look at Ethan, taking in all she could of his sleepy morning appearance, bed hair and all. Why did he get better looking every time she saw him?

"Well, I'm off to work. Unlike some people, we can't all take off when we get a whim to come visit our grandparents."

Alaina was joking, but a strange look flashed across Ethan's expression. However, it was gone so quickly she dismissed it as nothing.

Alaina rose from her spot beside Ethan and made her way for the door. Ethan hung on behind her, reluctant to let go of her hand. But finally, he did. When Alaina reached the door, she paused at the sound of his smooth voice.

"Have a good day, Ali."

Goose bumps rose on Alaina's arm, and the goofy grin returned. She didn't turn around. She just kept walking.

Chapter 14

Ethan

"So, Ben, what should we do today?"

The mid-morning sun beat down in warm, soothing rays on their heads as Ethan and Ben sat at the white wrought iron patio table in the little garden, surrounded by the rose bushes and all their glory. They had just finished off a plate of pancakes. Well, truthfully, Ethan had finished off a plate of pancakes. Ben had fiddled with a few bites, but none of them ever reached his mouth. Ethan figured Ben must not be much of an eater, but it still surprised him considering it was almost lunch time by the time Ben awakened. The kid could really sleep. Ben was in bed the night before when Ethan returned from his date with Alaina. He knew for a fact that Ben had not woke up once since then.

Now, Ben sat directly across from Ethan, wearing an eager grin along with his signature baseball cap. Messy brown curls hung out the bottom. Ethan wondered if Ben even took the hat off long enough to bathe. It wouldn't surprise him a bit to find Ben in a bubble bath with the hat remaining firmly attached to his head.

"How should I know?" Ben answered after a moment. "I'm just a kid."

Ethan smirked. Ben had been a bit skeptical when Ethan offered to spend the day with him. "Is my sister putting you up to this?" he'd asked. Ethan assured Ben that it was his own idea to hang out with him. Granny Mae had even given Ethan a strange look, but when he shrugged and gave a guilty grin, she understood his reasoning perfectly.

He was doing it for Alaina. Sure, Ben was a cute kid—and sometimes the things he said were hilarious—but would he be hanging out with Ben if it wasn't for Alaina? Probably not.

"I could teach you to play guitar," Ethan suggested nonchalantly.

"No way! For real?" Ben slammed his hands down on the table causing his fork to fly from his plate into a pot of tulips on the opposite side of the walkway.

Ethan noticed that Ben had Alaina's eyes. They caused the same igniting glow when they lit up.

"Sure, if you want."

"Could you teach me 'Fallen' or how about 'Reckless' or maybe…"

"Whoa, slow down big guy," Ethan laughed. Ben was naming

off all of Ethan's hit songs from the past year. "It took me a long time to learn to play those songs. Maybe we should start with a something a little easier...like 'Twinkle Twinkle Little Star.'"

Ben scrunched his nose up in a cute little line of disapproval, a trait that Ethan had also noticed in Alaina.

"Maybe if you get good at it, we can do a duet tonight for Granny Mae?"

This perked Ben right up. "Awesome!" he said.

Ben jumped up from his chair and darted into the house before Ethan even had time to rise to a standing position. Walking in from the garden, Ethan found his grandmother in the kitchen washing up some dishes from breakfast. Ted was nowhere to be found. Ethan guessed he was going into town for a while because the car was absent from the front drive.

"Ben and I will be in our room if you need us," Ethan said as he walked to the staircase.

"To learn guitar, I hear," Granny said with an amused grin.

"Yep."

Ethan reached the staircase as Granny Mae spoke again.

"I'm really proud of you, Lil E."

He paused and turned back toward her. "Why's that."

"What you're doing for Ben."

"Oh, it's nothing. What else am I going to do? I'm stuck here, remember." Ethan smiled realizing the difference in the tone of that statement from his conversation yesterday with his mother to now with his grandma.

Granny responded. "Well, it may be nothing to you, but I promise you that it is something to that little boy up there. Alaina might not have known much about you before you arrived, but Ben did. He really looks up to you."

Looks up to me? Ethan thought. Why on earth would anybody look up to him?

"Granny, I'm just a singer, not superman."

"Baby, you're much more than a singer to those young fans of yours. Think about someone you looked up to and wanted to be like when you were little. Now imagine them willingly offering to spend time with you. That's what you have done for Ben today. In his eyes, a singer is the least of what you are."

Granny Mae's words stuck in Ethan's mind with heavy dissonance. He had never thought about it like that. What would Ben think of him if he knew the real reason Ethan was in Alabama?

Would Ben still admire him?

Ethan didn't know, but Granny's Mae's words changed something in him. The entire day had begun as an attempt to do something nice for Alaina, but now, he felt somewhat of a responsibility to Ben, too.

Ethan nodded, showing her that he understood, and headed up the staircase. When Ethan reached the doorway to his bedroom, he found Ben sitting Indian style on the carpet; Ethan's guitar case was laid out carefully in front of him. Ben's knees tapped up and down with excitement.

"So, I thought about it," Ben started with a matter-of-fact tone, "and I guess 'Twinkle Twinkle' will be okay. I mean, everyone has got to start somewhere, right? Besides, you can't put the horse before the car." Ben paused. "Or is it cart?"

Ethan tried to suppress a laugh. That expression sounded comical coming from a ten-year-old. "Where did you hear that, Ben?"

"My dad used to say it."

Whoops. That was not a subject Ethan wanted to bring up. He hurried to pull his guitar out of its jet black case, trying to change the subject quickly.

Ethan started by showing Ben a few of the most common chords on the instrument and how to hold his hand properly so that he could place his fingers for each one. After Ben got the hang of those chords, Ethan showed him how to pick out a few notes with his other hand. Ethan was amazed by how quickly Ben caught on. When a little over an hour had passed, Ben was playing "Twinkle Twinkle Little Star" as if he had written the song himself.

Ethan was also a little surprised by how their lesson made him feel. He had never taught anyone how to play before. He'd always been the student, never the teacher. But Ethan got a happy little adrenaline rush every time Ben played a few chords correctly and lit up the room with his proud smile.

A while later, Ben seemed to be getting bored so Ethan suggested breaking for a while to do something else. When asked, Ben decided that he wanted to go hang out at the pier.

Ethan had initially objected, Alaina's words from that morning—"Don't let him overdo it. He hasn't been feeling well."— echoing through his memory as Ben suggested the idea. But when Ethan ran it by Granny Mae, she had agreed that it was a good idea.

Granny said Ben needed to get out of the house and get some fresh air. Said it might be good for him. At one point, she even said it could help. Ethan didn't know what that meant, but he didn't bother to ask. Ted had returned from town with groceries, which meant that the car was free for use.

Ethan and Ben hopped into the Charger and headed for the pier. It had been years since Ethan spent time on the beaches of Fairhope. He'd always loved going there as a kid.

The car ride with Ben was amusing to say the least. He had, of course, insisted on bringing his *Ethan Carter* CD. Ben sang every single lyric to each song at the top of his ten-year-old lungs while Ethan drove. They parked at a spot on the outskirts of Municipal Park, and after throwing a few pennies into the huge fountain that sat in the center of the park, Ethan and Ben made their way down to the beach.

Considering the great weather, there weren't nearly as many people out in the water as Ethan had predicted. It was a perfect 80° and holding; the waves were calm on the sea, and there wasn't a cloud in the sky. The brightest, clearest blue sheet hung above their heads like a mirror reflection of the sea below.

Ben started with sandcastles. Ethan helped a little, but he was fairly terrible at it. Ben, somehow, could make the perfect tower with no cracks to be seen. Ethan's towers, however, crumbled with the slightest bit of wind. Eventually, Ethan gave up and took to lying in the sand, watching Ben play at the water's edge. He couldn't help it, but his focus constantly shifted to the little restaurant on the pier, which was only a couple hundred yards away.

That's where Alaina was at that very moment, probably waiting on some vacationing couple, smiling and being polite in her own little Alaina way. His mind averted back to their almost kiss in the car.

Ethan had run through the events of the past night over and over again in his mind. Had he moved too quickly? He didn't feel like it. Ali seemed genuinely interested in him, too, but when he'd tried to kiss her, she'd pulled away. Said she wasn't ready.

What did that mean? Was she talking about her parents' accident? Was it too soon after their death for her to show interest in guys? Surely not. That happened over a year ago. Had someone broken her heart recently? Maybe she wasn't ready because she'd been burned in a past relationship? Ethan wasn't sure, but for some reason, he didn't feel like any of those hypotheses would ring true.

Alaina talked as if there was something going on right now that she was dealing with and that kept her from becoming close to anyone.

Ethan wanted to know what it was. He wanted to help her. Not because he wanted her physically, but because he wanted her emotionally. He loved talking to Ali. She excited and calmed him all in the same breath. Their personalities meshed. But he knew that as long as she was dealing with whatever was bothering her, she would never fully open up to him.

Ethan continued to focus on the pier as a shadow fell in the midst of his gaze. It was the shadow of a little boy. A dripping, sopping wet little boy. Ethan looked up to find Ben peering down at him as though studying him with a microscope.

"She's probably not that busy right now if you want to go say hi," Ben said, plopping down in the sand to begin work on another masterpiece castle.

"Who?" Ethan asked ignorantly, already knowing precisely who Ben was referring to.

"My sister, duh. I know you like her."

Ethan choked with a little cough, surprised by young Ben's candor.

"And how do you know that?" Ethan asked.

"Because you stare at her with googly eyes."

"Googly eyes?" Ethan wondered if googly was a real term or just a Ben term.

"Yeah, like this." Ben tilted his head to the side and put on a goofy smile. He widened his eyes and batted them, doing an impression that Ethan hoped he never truly resembled.

"I don't do that."

"Well, maybe not that bad," Ben giggled. His focus shifted back to his sand castle. "You do like her though, don't you?"

As strange as it felt to be having this conversation with a child, Ethan felt the need to be honest. "Yeah, I do. Is that okay with you?"

Ben thought for a moment. "I guess so. Just as long as ya'll don't go around doing that gross kissy stuff."

Ethan laughed. "Gotcha, dude. No kissy stuff."

Ethan couldn't help but feel a little bad for the way he had treated Ben when he first arrived in Fairhope. He'd been so ridiculously full of himself and his own self-inflicted circumstances that he hadn't even bothered to take notice of what kind of kid Ben really was. After spending time with him today, Ethan was beginning to realize that Ben was not like most little kids. Ben had this way of taking any situation, no matter how good or bad, and twisting it around until it fit happily inside his own beautiful world.

There was no bad inside of him. Only pure, innocent truth, love, and loyalty.

"You wanna go swimming with me, Ethan?" Ben asked a few minutes later.

"Sure, kiddo. Let's hit the waves."

Ben jumped up and dashed to the water's edge.

"I beat you!" he screamed as Ethan ran to catch up with him.

Ethan joined Ben out in the water, and they jumped and splashed and swam around in the briny sea. Ben giggled and jumped up and down as if it was the most fun outing he'd ever participated in. By the way he acted, Ethan thought, it seemed Ben hadn't left the house in months. But after thirty minutes or so, Ethan was beginning to notice a subtle change in Ben.

Ben was still playing as hard as he could go, but he was looking tired. Pale even. Ethan was several feet away when Ben suddenly stopped playing. Ben turned to Ethan, went to say something, but nothing came out. Ethan paused for only a second.

Something was wrong. Ethan didn't know what it was, but he could see it by the terrified expression suddenly washing across Ben's face.

Seconds before Ethan reached Ben to ask if he was okay, Ben's eyes rolled back in his head and his little body went limp. He collapsed into the waves with hardly a splash. Ethan panicked.

"Ben!"

Ethan dove to where Ben's lifeless body had been picked up by the rolling tide. He caught Ben only seconds after he submerged beneath the salty water.

"Ben! Ben!"

That's when Ethan first noticed. Ben's hat had lifted from his head in the rush of the waves and now floated next to them in the water. The cute messy brown curls that normally hung out of the bottom of the hat...continued to hang out of the bottom of the hat.

Ben's head was nothing but perfectly smooth skin. Too smooth to have been buzzed or shaved. The little curls Ethan had grown so accustomed to seeing on Ben had been fake all along. Ben had no hair of his own.

Ethan swatted to grab the hat before the tide could pull it out to sea. His other arm was wrapped around Ben's tiny little chest; Ben's head was limp against Ethan's shoulder. Ethan dug his toes deep into the sand and pushed against the current toward the water's edge, all the while trying to keep from having a panic attack. When Ethan reached the shore, he laid Ben down gently in the sand. Ethan racked his brain trying to remember anything he had ever heard or seen that would give him the slightest idea of how to handle this situation. Ben lay unconscious, but still breathing, at his knees. Finally, Ethan resorted to smacking Ben's cheeks, trying to be forceful enough to bring him to without hurting him.

"Ben! C'mon Ben!"

Ethan's heart did somersaults in his chest when Ben's eyelids gave a slight flutter. Ben opened his eyes slowly. A guilty expression washed over his features as he realized what had happened. Ben sat up and his hands slowly reached up and felt of his bald head. His eyes darted around, and Ethan knew instantly that he was looking for his hat. He handed it over, and Ben rushed to put the hat back in its rightful position on his head.

"Ben, what the heck was that? What happened to you out there?"

Ben's guilty expression only intensified, but he tried to hide it by flashing a fake grin, only it was too weak to fool Ethan. "Uh...I dunno..."

Ethan tried again. "Are you okay?"

Ben replied almost before Ethan got the words out. "Yep."

Yep? The kid almost drowns in Ethan's arms and all he gets is a yep?

"Tell me what happened, Ben."

"I got...tired...."

"You got tired."

"Yep."

Ethan had never heard of anyone being fine one minute and tired enough the next to cause them to lose consciousness.

"Ben, what happened to your hair?"

Ben thought for a moment and looked up, burning Ethan with his big brown innocent eyes.

"Bad haircut?" Ben suggested.

Ethan didn't believe it for a second, but decided not to press the issue. Ben had never before held back on anything when talking to Ethan. If Ben wanted him to know, he would have told him.

Ethan sighed and accepted his defeat. "We better get back," he said, trying to calm his racing heart. Ben's...whatever it was...had scared him to death.

"Do we have to?" Ben pleaded. His voice was frail.

Ethan didn't hesitate. "Yeah, we have to."

Ben's skin was pale, and he looked exhausted. Ethan wondered if this was what Alaina had meant by not letting him overdo things. Well, so much for that.

Ethan helped Ben to the car and drove directly for Granny's house. All he wanted to do was get Ben home before something else happened. By the time they reached the house, Ben still looked drained, but at least he wasn't passing out. Ethan helped Ben into the house and found Granny Mae in the living room reading from the Bible that she kept on the coffee table.

Granny took one look at Ben, and it was as though she immediately understood something that Ethan didn't. "Come on, sweetie," She took Ben's little hand in hers. "Let's get you to bed. Did you have fun today with Ethan?"

"It was awesome, Granny Mae," Ben said with weak excitement. "Ethan taught me to play guitar, and then we went to the pier and made sand castles, and then we went swimming and then..." Ben shot Ethan a pleading expression from behind Granny's back. Ethan realized that Ben didn't want him to mention what actually happened in the water. "...and then we came home because I was getting tired."

"Well, I'm glad you had a good time, baby," Granny Mae said gently as she led Ben up the staircase.

When they reached the boy's bedroom, Granny helped Ben change into a pair of PJ's before he climbed into his bunk. She asked Ben if he was okay and if he needed anything. Ben curled up into his pillow—his soaked hat was reattached to his head and left wet stains on the fabric. He insisted that he was fine.

Ethan watched the entire ordeal in bewilderment. It was obvious that Ben wasn't feeling well, but Granny Mae acted as though she dealt with it every single day. As if it was no big deal.

When Ben was tucked in and comfortable, Granny Mae turned to leave the room. She squeezed Ethan's shoulder on her way out, and he caught a glimpse of something in her eyes.

When Granny Mae was out of earshot, Ethan spun back toward Ben. He decided to try one more time.

"Ben, what happened to you out there today?"

"I told you I got tired."

Ethan wanted to press the issue further, but Ben did look so tired and so comfortable snuggled into a little ball with his bedding. Instead, Ethan let it go with a confused sigh.

He turned toward the door when he heard...

"Hey, Ethan?"

"Yeah, Ben?"

"Thanks for hanging out with me today. I know you only did it for my sister, but I really had fun."

Ethan paused. "It may have started out that way, little guy, but it didn't end that way."

He turned to leave and Ben spoke again.

"Hey Ethan...about what happened today...can you do me a huge favor?"

"What's that, Ben?"

"Don't tell my sister, okay?"

Chapter 15

Alaina

Alaina was down to the last hour of the longest work day she had ever experienced. Not only had the double shift been exactly double the amount of hours she wanted to be there, but the hours had drug by as if she was watching paint dry. It was such a beautiful day outside, and Alaina could think of about a million things she could have been doing besides serving food to tourists.

No matter how busy they got, or how distracted she attempted to be, Alaina was never able to yank her thoughts away from Ethan. Ethan spending the day with Ben was one of the sweetest things any guy had ever done for her.

But then again, there weren't many guys in Alaina's past, and the worst part was that she wasn't the only one who was aware of her previous lack of involvement with boys. The girls Alaina worked with were always trying to get her to go out with them to meet boys or to go on a double date with them. She always said no.

So after showing up out of nowhere last night with some guy they had never seen, Alaina naturally expected a few questions from her co-workers. What she expected, however, was nothing compared to what she'd been forced to endure the entire day. Alaina had been asked everything from "Who was that guy you were with last night?" to "Are you guys serious? to "How long have you been dating?" to "Is he the one?"

Alaina didn't understand what the big deal was. Could two people not have a nice dinner with one another without the whole world thinking they were making wedding plans? Her co-workers acted as if this was the first guy they had ever seen her spend time with, for goodness sakes.

Actually, now that she thought about it, she hadn't been seen with a guy since her parents' accident....

But still, Alaina didn't understand what all the fuss was about. It's not like she and Ethan were *dating*. Okay, sure, they had agreed to call their outing a date...but that was only a one-time deal. One date did not connote dating. Their relationship was merely...

Alaina didn't know how to finish that sentence. She did a quick mental re-evaluation of the entire situation. Ethan was an extremely famous superstar who had, for some crazy reason, chosen her as the person to help him conceal his true identity from the world; which had led into dinner; which had led into his trying to kiss her and her freaking out; which had led into his hanging out with her brother for no apparent reason while she worked.

It all sounded very nice and fairytale-ish, but no matter how Alaina looked at it from there, all roads led back to the exact same destination point.

Ethan leaving.

She sighed.

Nope, definitely not dating.

Alaina pulled her cell phone out of her apron pocket to get a quick time check. Only fifteen minutes to go. She and Gabby, the hostess from last night, were putting the finishing touches on the dining room so that the restaurant would be good and ready to go in the morning. Gabby had been one of the main interrogators thus far, and Alaina thought surely she was questioned out at that point. But that assumption proved too good to be true when Gabby's voice rang out, yet again, through the dining room.

"So are you and Brandon going to go out again before he goes back home?"

At the beginning of her shift, Alaina had wondered who the heck Brandon was. It had taken several conversations before she became accustomed to Ethan's new alias.

"I already told you, Gab," Alaina said, trying hard to not sound annoyed. "We were just having dinner last night. That was all there was to it. If we go out again before he goes home, I'm sure it will just be dinner then, too."

"Then why is he here?" Gabby persisted. "Why did Brandon come all the way down here from New York if he just wanted to have dinner with you? How did you two meet anyway?"

Alaina groaned under her breath. She hated having to lie to her friend, but she had no choice. It's not like Gabby would believe her if she told her the truth, anyway.

"Our parents were friends. We've known each other since we were kids but haven't gotten to see each other. He just came down to visit and get a little vacation time."

"Then why was he holding your hand last night?"

Shoot. Alaina had forgotten about Ethan holding her hand in the middle of the restaurant.

"Um, I don't know. I guess he's just affectionate."

Gabby shook her head and cocked an amused smile. "Oh, Alaina, give it up already! You were on a date! You were on a date with a hot guy, and you loved every minute of it!" Gabby paused,

studying Alaina's reddening cheeks. "Girl, you know I'm just giving
you a hard time because I want you to be happy, right?"

Alaina laughed. "That statement kind of contradicts itself, don't
you think?"

"Maybe a little, but whatever," Gabby said. "Alaina, I have
watched you in this restaurant for the past year, and I gotta tell ya,
girl, you have less of a life than my grandmother."

"You're right, Gab. That's very inspiring. Thank you."

"You know what I mean," Gabby continued. "You need to get
out and go on dates with hot guys. I'm giving you a hard time so that
maybe you'll realize that it's okay to have a little fun every now and
then. Brandon seemed like a nice guy. What's the harm in taking
advantage of the time you guys have left together? I know he has to
leave eventually, but he hasn't left yet."

Alaina remained silent. She continued to keep her focus
centered on the pile of silverware that remained to be rolled before
she could leave.

After a moment of silence, Gabby smirked and said, "I wonder
what Cam would think about you hanging out with Brandon."

This pulled Alaina from her trance, and she laughed.

Cam, short for Camaron Crawford, was a boy from Alaina's
school who she had gone on a couple of dates with before her
parents' accident. Needless to say, things had not ended well. Cam,
unlike Ethan, had been extremely pushy. He had wanted Alaina to
get much more physical with him than she felt comfortable with, and
then had not been very understanding when she objected. Then, to
top things off, when her parents had been killed in the wreck, Cam
had not so much as sent her a text message until months later. It had
been very easy for him to be with her when everything was going
fine, but the second things got a little complicated in her life, he had
bolted. Hence, the reason Alaina knew boys were not fans of girls
with baggage.

But recently, Cam had come back into the picture. Not by
Alaina's choosing, but by his own. He came by the restaurant about
once a week to apologize, which in the beginning Alaina found a
little sweet. That was, until she heard that Cam was still up to his old
routines. Saturday nights at the pier drinking and acting stupid with
his buddies. Sunday mornings in church with his family. He was as
wishy-washy in his spiritual life as he was in his relationships.
Alaina didn't have time for that mess—which was exactly why she
politely turned Cam down every time he asked her to go out with

him.

"Oh, c'mon, Alaina!" Cam would plead, taking her hands in his and sending goose bumps up her arms—and not the good kind, but the icky, creeped-out kind.

She always told him it was because she wasn't ready to date yet—that with everything going on in her life right now, she just didn't have time for a relationship (especially not the kind of relationship Cam would expect her to be a participant of).

Gabby was right. Cam probably wouldn't be too happy to hear that Alaina had been turning him down for dates for months, but that she had agreed to accompany some other guy to dinner.

Silverware almost rolled now, Alaina was itching to get out the door. She couldn't wait to flee the band of questioning and return to her normal routine of grabbing late-night dinner in Granny's kitchen, checking on Ben, and crashing into her bed. Alaina loved Gabby, but she'd had about all she could handle for one day.

Alaina heard a little jingle come from the tiny bell that hung from the door handle of the restaurant's front door. She ignored it, figuring it was just Tina returning from making the night's deposit at the local bank. That's when Gabby decided to start in again.

"So, speaking of Brandon..."

Alaina shot up, resisting the urge to slam her fist down on the table. "Gab, seriously, I really don't want to talk about this all night!"

"Talk about what?"

The voice was not Gabby's.

A tingle rushed through Alaina, and she felt her cheeks turn beat red. She turned slowly.

"What are you doing here?" she asked when she was facing him. She took a quick look and tried to memorize every little detail of Ethan's appearance that she could take in at once. He wore a loose-fitting pair of faded jeans with brown flip flops and a printed T-shirt. His skin appeared to be a little tanner, which made his bright blue eyes sparkle even brighter than they had before.

Oh, I was in the neighborhood," he replied with a sly grin.

"You were in the neighborhood?" Alaina asked skeptically.

"Uh...yeah...sort of..." Ethan laughed. "Okay, technically, I drove into the neighborhood on purpose, but I figure it's all the same in the end.

"How convenient for you," Alaina teased. Ethan came closer, only a foot or so separated them.

"Actually, I have something I want to do and I kind of hoped you'd go with me," Ethan said quietly.

Alaina searched his eyes and found a glow of excitement in them. She didn't know what Ethan wanted to do, but she wasn't going to miss it for the world.

"I...I'm almost done here," she said, spinning back around to the few remaining pieces of silverware that lay before her. "Just give me a minute, okay?"

"Oh no you don't!" Gabby voiced. Alaina had forgotten Gab was even in the room. "You have been here twice as long as I have. You go. I'll finish this up."

"Gab, you don't have to do that..." Alaina started.

"Yes, I do and I'm gonna, so get out of here." Gabby walked over to where Ethan stood beside Alaina and looked up to him. "Better take her while you can, babe. Free time for Alaina is a rare commodity. Take advantage of it before it's too late."

Ethan gave a half-hearted salute. "Yes ma'am." He reached down and took Alaina's hand in his and started pulling her toward the door. "Come on, we're busting you out of here."

Alaina giggled and followed behind. Before going through the door, she turned to shoot a thank-you look at Gabby. Gabby grinned, winked, and turned to finish the silverware that Alaina had left behind.

When Alaina stepped outside, she was met with a cool sea breeze and one of the clearest nights of the entire summer. Ethan continued to lead her down the pier toward the shore. When she reached her vehicle, she pulled her apron off, locked her tips up inside the glove compartment, and turned back to Ethan.

"Where are we going?"

"It's a surprise," he said.

"Can you give me a hint?"

Ethan laughed and put his arm around her waist, pulling her in tightly—a perfect fit—as they walked side by side back toward the edge of town, on the sidewalk running parallel to the beach.

"Um, let's just say I hope you like bright lights."

Chapter 16

Ethan

Alaina's dark hair wisped across her cheeks in the cool ocean breeze as she strolled with Ethan along the enchanting Mobile Bay coastline. Her arm rested gently around his waist, and he held onto her, just thankful that she didn't pull away. Her head rested perfectly inside his arm. Ethan was surprised by how much he had missed spending time with her that day. How was it possible that he had only known Alaina for a couple of days? What had occupied his thoughts before her?

"You still haven't told me where we're going," Alaina said after they had walked almost a mile.

"We're almost there now," Ethan said.

"Why didn't we just drive?"

Ethan considered her question and decided that an honest answer was probably best.

"Because I wouldn't have been able to hold you for the past fifteen minutes if I'd driven."

"Oh I get it!" She gasped, pretending to be insulted. "You think you're pretty slick, don't ya, superstar?"

"I have my moments," Ethan grinned.

"Well, I can fix that."

In a quick motion, Alaina spun out of Ethan's arm, playfully putting space between them, but Ethan caught her hand by the fingertips before she could get away.

"Oh, no you don't." Ethan pulled her back in. Alaina squealed, trying not to lose her balance, and landed against his chest. She looked up and met his eyes. His arms wrapped around to the small of her back, their noses only inches apart. Alaina relaxed her muscles and fell into his grasp, allowing him to hold her.

Ethan inhaled deeply, allowing her scent to flow through him, and then let out a slow breath. He could have stayed in that moment forever. Ethan searched her eyes. She looked...nervous. The chemistry between them was palpable, and all he wanted was to feel her lips against his. Ethan inched closer and closer to Alaina. His hand raised, and he ran his thumb carefully along her cheek. The tips of their noses met. His heart raced in time with hers. Ethan's eyes closed.

She pulled away.

Ethan didn't know what was keeping Alaina from becoming close to him. She acted like she wanted to kiss him, but then she backed out at the last second. But Ethan didn't push. He liked Alaina—a lot—and the last thing he wanted to do was make her feel uncomfortable. He peered down at her. She refused to meet his gaze. Ethan ran his fingers through her hair and pulled her close again. He planted a soft kiss on her forehead and pulled her back to her original position at his side.

"C'mon, we're almost there."

They continued on for another quarter mile. The walkway curved around a small hotel up ahead. The sounds of music and laughter drifted through the air as they walked. When they reached the other side of the hotel, a narrow beach—a different beach than the one Ethan had taken Ben to earlier that day—stretched out before them. A festival was being held right there on the sand, and there were people everywhere. Carnival rides were clustered in one area of the beach, and food and game stands lined their perimeter. A tall Ferris wheel circled above their heads, and boats lit the waters out on the sea.

"It's the Festival of Lights," Ethan said when Alaina paused to take it all in. "I saw a poster advertising it today when I was with Ben. I figured you already knew about it."

"I don't get out much," Alaina said blankly. "They have this festival every year, but I completely forgot about it this year." She turned to face Ethan and lowered her voice. "Are you sure you're okay with being around all of these people? What if someone recognizes you?"

Ethan shrugged. "My disguise has worked so far. Besides, I haven't been to anything like this in years. Well, not unless I was signed to perform at it. I really just want to experience this like everyone else does." Ethan's eyes sparkled, excitement rising in his voice. "I want to ride rides, and play games, and eat funnel cakes till I feel like puking!"

Alaina laughed. "I'm not sure everyone does that." She paused. "Actually, I'm not sure anyone does that."

"Whatever, smarty pants. I'm going to the festival, and considering I just walked you a mile from your source of transportation, it appears that you will be going with me—funnel cakes and all."

"And what if I refuse?" Alaina teased.

"Then I guess I'll have to beg."

"You wouldn't," she dared.

Ethan paused for only a moment before a wide, devious smile

spread across his cheeks. He fell to his knees at Alaina's feet, people walking by on all sides. "Ali, please go to the festival with me! Please! Please! Please!" Ethan folded his hands at his chest, stuck his bottom lip out, and gave her his best possible puppy dog face. People were starting to stare.

Alaina's head dropped into her hands and she giggled. "Okay, okay! Just as long as you get up...Brandon...before people think my new friend is a psycho!"

Ethan rose to his feet, laughing the whole way. He found his little stunt quite funny. He draped his arm around Alaina's shoulder and led her toward the carnival.

"You know, you could've had me with a bag of cotton candy and a grape snow cone," Alaina said. "But I guess that was fun, too."

Ethan received his night of normalcy at the Fairhope Festival of Lights. He and Alaina played games and messed with carnies. They rode the Ferris wheel four times. Alaina got her snow cone, and Ethan ate his funnel cake. In fact, he ate two.

Eventually, they were getting bored with the crowded carnival and decided to take a walk along the water's edge. Ethan walked hand in hand with Alaina. He had never had so much fun with any girl...well...ever. Alaina didn't spend the night worrying about how her clothes looked or making sure that not even a smidge of make-up wiped from her face. She didn't show off and talk loudly just so the people around her would take notice of her every move. She was there with Ethan, and that's all she seemed to care about. There might as well not have been another soul at the entire festival.

The only person Ethan had seen all night was Ali.

The world of flashing lights, and screaming fans, and the politics of fame seemed light years away as Ethan held Alaina firm against his chest; the water cascaded gently over their bare feet. The stars lit the night sky above the black water. Ethan had forgotten how much he loved stars.

Ethan's world as he previously knew it was gone. His world was Alaina now. He knew eventually he would have to leave Fairhope, but he would find a way to work that out. There had to be a way. Nothing could feel this right and not be able to work.

Alaina stood in front of Ethan with her back to him, facing the ocean. Her head rested tenderly on his chest. His arms wrapped around her waist. Ethan leaned down and brushed her cheek with his lips, pulling her into a tight embrace. He didn't kiss her to try to get her to kiss him back. He just did it because he needed to. It wasn't an embrace of expectation, but one of affection and admiration.

Alaina turned slowly in his arms and buried her head in his neck, returning his embrace.

A soft melody floated over the water from a dance being held at the festival. Ethan ran his fingers down Ali's arm from her shoulder to her fingertips. He intertwined his fingers with hers and began to slowly rock back and forth in time with the music. She peered up to him, a timid smile forming, but soon she fell into step with him. They swayed in the sand as the wind circled around, enveloping them in a tunnel of their own existence.

It was a moment that Ethan would remember for the rest of his life. It was perfect. It was magical.

"Well, isn't that ador...adorable." A slurred voice rudely broke through the flawless moment.

Alaina stopped in her tracks. Her muscles froze in a tense stance.

Ethan's head bolted up and found a group of people coming their way from a campfire lit area underneath a small pier down the beach. Ethan hadn't even noticed it before. The source of the comment was a tall bleach blond guy who appeared to have jumped straight off the cover of a summer edition of a Hollister catalog.

"Who the heck is that?" Ethan murmured.

Alaina sighed, obviously embarrassed.

"That is Cam. He's a...old friend."

"Old boyfriend, to be exact." Cam cocked an arrogant grin as he walked closer, correcting Alaina's description of him.

Ethan wasn't sure how to react. What was with this guy's attitude? He sauntered through the sand like he owned each individual grain. A part of Ethan wanted to deck the guy until he tasted sand, but another part of him knew that Alaina would find that childish and unnecessary.

That's when Ethan's gaze darted to a gleam coming from something in Cam's hand which hung down by his waist—a bottle. The source of Cam's overconfidence. Not only was he arrogant, but he was also drunk. Ethan knew the signs from a mile away. He had become all too familiar with them in the past few months of his life. Standing there watching Cam stumble to stay standing upright gave Ethan new found insight. He had never witnessed this kind of behavior without being a partaker in it himself. Had he looked that ridiculous?

Ethan observed Alaina's reaction. She had also noticed the bottle. Her eyes darted from Cam to each of his drunken buddies. Her expression was one of disgust. It was obvious that she, in no way, approved of his actions.

"I don't believe I've met your new friend, Alaina," Cam slurred.

"Uh...Brandon..." Alaina began awkwardly, "this is Cam. He's an old friend of mine. Cam, this is Brandon."

Cam lifted the bottle and took a big swig of its contents. "Now see, that's weird because I've never seen Brandon around here before."

"He's a friend of the family," Alaina said quickly. "He's not from here."

Cam's eyes shifted up and down Ethan. "Hmm, obviously."

"What can we do for you, Cam?" Alaina asked, trying to hurry the conversation along.

"Oh, Alaina...I can think of several things you could do for me." Cam gave a furtive laugh. "But I doubt your friend here would approve of any of them."

Ethan's temper flared, and he involuntarily took a step toward Cam. Alaina placed her hand, ever so lightly across his stomach, and he stopped. She was calm. She was in perfect control. How was it that he was getting so worked up about this guy and she seemed perfectly fine? The problem wasn't that Ethan hated the idea of Alaina having ever been involved with this idiot—although he definitely was bothered by that mental picture. Ethan was more disturbed by the fact that one of the things he loved the most about Ali was her innocence. It didn't seem right for some loser to be talking to her like that. It just felt wrong.

"C'mon, Brandon," Alaina said, attempting to keep her voice calm. "Let's get out of here."

Alaina grabbed Ethan's hand and began to turn away from Cam. Ethan's eyes met Cam's, and they locked in an intense glare. Ethan was about to turn when Cam decided to speak directly to him.

"So I guess Alaina has found some extra time in her busy schedule to fit you in, huh? I gotta say, I admire you, man. She's hot and all, but that's a lot of baggage to deal with just for a little one-on-one time, if you know what I mean."

That was it. Ethan spun back around and took that step toward Cam. "No, actually, I don't know what you mean."

This time even Alaina jumped in. "Cam, why don't you shut

your big fat mouth!"

"And why would I do that, Alaina?" Cam said bitterly. "You've been turning me down for months because you were too busy dealing with..."

"Shut up, Cam!"

"What, Alaina? You don't want me talking about your drama in front of your new boyfriend?"

"I said SHUT UP, Cam!" Alaina was beginning to lose control in her voice.

Cam paused, a wave of understanding washing through his eyes, and then started to laugh. "Oh, I get it! He doesn't know, does he?"

"Know what?" Ethan asked.

"Cam, please," Alaina pleaded, her voice a mere whimper now.

"Wow, I don't feel so bad after all!" Cam sneered at her. "I mean, at least you cared about me enough to not ask me to put up with it! Why are you with this guy anyway, Alaina? You know he's not going to stick around once he finds out."

"Finds out what?" Ethan asked again, clearly annoyed.

"Why not just get it over with now," Cam continued, speaking directly to Alaina. His voice lowered a bit. "Whenever you're feeling a little lonely, baby, you can come find me. No attachments. It's the perfect arrangement."

Ethan looked at Alaina. Her eyes welled in tears. She turned away from both of them and knelt down at the water's edge. Ethan had seen all he needed. He turned back to Cam, steadied his feet, and squared his shoulders.

"I think it's time for you to leave, man." Ethan said. His voice remained calm and steady, but by his body language, it was perfectly clear that he meant business.

Cam ignored Ethan's warning and lunged forward, dropping his bottle to the sand. His friends stayed behind, laughing.

"You better watch who you're talking to," Cam sneered through gritted teeth. His fists were already clenched.

To Ethan's utter amazement, he still remained calm. "Dude, you're drunk. I think it'd be best if you just go back to your party and sleep it off. Forget you ever ran into us."

Alaina remained knelt down by the water with her head in her hands, holding back sobs. She wasn't able to see the look on Ethan's face as he glared at Cam. The two boys stood, bowed up chest to chest, but Ethan never faltered. He remained strong, sending Cam a message that he was not backing down. Cam had a solid muscle structure, but Ethan was a performer. He underwent vigorous training on a daily basis to stay in the shape he was in. The dynamic dance routines demanded by his choreographer were not easy. When it came to whom was the more built of the two, Ethan won by a landslide. Not to mention, he'd taken Bruce's suggestion a few months back and attended self-defense classes. Cam talked a big talk, but Ethan didn't consider him to be much of a threat.

Ethan and Cam remained in their stare down. Ethan waited with intense focus to see what Cam would do next. Would he try to sneak in a punch? If he did, Ethan was ready for him. Would one of his buddies jump into the fight? If they did, Ethan would deal with it. He'd had training for that, too.

Finally, when Cam seemed unsure of his next move, Ethan spoke.

"So, what's it going to be, man?"

Cam's eyes broke first. They shifted from side to side, and he noticed that no one had jumped in to back him up. A moment of awkward silence passed, and Cam's lips formed back into their haughty grin.

"Forget it. It's not even worth it."

"You mean she's not worth it," Ethan countered.

Cam just shrugged, retrieved his drink from the sand, and returned to his group of friends. They laughed and stumbled back off toward the distant camp fire.

Ethan allowed his muscles to release and took a few deep breaths to calm his anger. Alaina remained silent with her back still to his. Ethan sighed. He didn't want to, but he had to say it.

"Alaina, what was all that about?"

When she didn't respond, he turned to where she knelt with her back to him.

"Ali, you have to tell me what's going on."

Alaina stood up slowly and let out a long sigh. "Cam's right."

"What?" Ethan said. This was not the response he was expecting.

Alaina spun to face him, tears staining her cheeks. When Ethan caught sight of her eyes, his heart sank a little. She was shutting down on him, just like she had done in the car after their dinner date, and just like she had done earlier tonight on their way to the festival. He moved toward her, but she held her arm up to stop him.

"Cam's right, Ethan. I don't know what I was thinking...I have been so stupid...so irresponsible...."

"Okay, Ali, cut the coded dialogue and please just spit it out. What do you mean, Cam's right? Right about what? He was wasted! I'd be surprised if the guy could tell his right foot from his left right now, much less be in the condition to give you relationship advice."

"That's just it, Ethan!" Alaina's expression was filled with confusion and pain. "There shouldn't be a relationship."

"What are you talking about?" Ethan could feel his stomach tightening. He tried to hide the panic in his tone. "You just decided that in the last two minutes because of some drunken idiot who's mad because you won't date him? Come on, Alaina! What's really going on here? Be honest with me."

"That's the problem," she said meekly. "I haven't been honest with you. I haven't lied to you, but I haven't told you everything," Alaina paused, sucking in a deep breath as if trying to sum up her courage. "I'm not like normal girls, Ethan."

"I know that! That's why I like you, Ali. The last thing I want is to hang around another clone of the exact same person I've dated before."

"You're not getting it, Ethan. My life is...complicated."

"Everyone's life if complicated."

"Not like mine."

"Are you talking about your parents' accident?" Ethan asked. "I get it. That was terrible, and it should have never happened, but you guys are making it. I know it's hard but..."

"It's not just that, Ethan! I can't...I can't give you what normal girls can give you. I work all the time because I have to. And when I'm not working I'm dealing with..." Alaina caught her breath and stopped. She turned her back to Ethan again, trying to hold control of her emotions.

Ethan racked his brain trying to figure out what she was holding in. That's when his memory flashed back to his time with Ben earlier that day. First, the strange look of sadness that his grandmother got every time she looked at Ben. Then the incident in the water. Ben's lack of hair. His sudden exhaustion. None of it added up for a normal ten-year-old.

Ethan spoke carefully. "It's Ben, isn't it?"Alaina sniffed, and her head dropped into her hands. "Alaina, what's wrong with Ben?"

She paused and took a second to wipe under her eyes with the back of her hand. She never turned, refusing Ethan sight of her face.

When her reply finally came, it was hushed and consumed with desperation.

"I'm losing him."

Ethan's eyes shut tight, and he tried to shake the feeling of dread that had been pulsing in the back of his mind all day in his own little form of denial. "Losing him how?"

"He's...dying, Ethan. Ben is dying."

He said the only thing he knew to say—the only acceptable option that he could wrap his mind around. "That's not possible. Ben can't be...dying. He's just a kid!"

Alaina turned slowly. Her voice had regained its control; her words were deliberate.

"It's possible, Ethan. Ben has a rare form of Acute Myelocytic Leukemia. A couple of years ago, he started having problems, getting sick a lot, and then a few weeks after my parents died, we finally got a diagnosis. He's gone downhill ever since. He has quit responding to the chemo. The doctors are saying that we're running out of options...."

Ethan didn't know what to say. All he knew was that he would do anything to remove the desperate look from Ali's face. He grabbed her arm and pulled her in to his chest. He wanted to hold her. He wanted to comfort her in the only way he knew how. She stayed for only a moment, but as he feared, she pushed away in the end.

"I can't do this, Ethan." She turned and started up the beach, putting space between them.

"Why not, Alaina?" Ethan followed swiftly behind. "Because of what Cam said? Cam's a moron. Just because he's a selfish jerk doesn't mean that I am. I'm not going to pretend to understand what you're going through right now, but I'm not going to run from it either."

Alaina spun on him. "Do you even hear what you're saying? What are you going to do? Stick around in little Fairhope and go to doctor's appointments with me? Try to maintain your sanity while you watch Ben wither to nothing? Because that is what my year has been like, Ethan! You've been here less than a week. This is not your nightmare! You have the perfect life. Why would you do anything to mess that up?"

"The perfect life?" Ethan scoffed. "Are you kidding me, Alaina? I get excited about a stupid little festival because I never have time to do things like that, and even if I did have time, I couldn't because I can't get any privacy. Sure, I have money, but I can guarantee you that there is nothing perfect about my life."

Alaina remained silent. Ethan thought for a moment that she was about to reconsider, but he was wrong.

"Please don't do this, Ethan," Alaina pleaded.

"Do what?" Ethan asked, moving close to her again. "Tell you I care about you? Well, too bad. It's too late for that. I care about you! And I'm sorry, but I can't help that! You are the best thing that has happened to me in a long time. You...inspire me, Ali. You make me want to be a better person...."

"Oh, Ethan, give me a break! You're a worldwide superstar! You could have any girl you ever wanted!"

"But I don't want any other girl, Alaina! I want you!"

"You don't understand," Alaina said desperately. "I can't do this."

"You keep saying that, but you still aren't telling me what that means."

Alaina gave a frustrated sigh. "I have lost everything, Ethan! I lost my parents. I lost my house. Ben was the only piece of my normal life that I had left and now I'm losing him too! I...I can't lose anything else!"

"Like what? What are you going to lose?"

"YOU!" She finally screamed. "You, Ethan! Do you have any idea how much I have tried to keep from developing feelings for you? I was doing perfectly fine before you showed up with your big bright blue eyes and your stupid adorable smile...."

"Alaina." Ethan moved toward her cautiously.

"You're leaving, Ethan! Maybe not tonight, and maybe not tomorrow, but eventually, you will leave me!"

A little closer now.

"Alaina..."

"I can't believe I was stupid enough to let this go on for so long. I should have known better." Alaina was talking to herself now. "I'm a masochist. That's got to be it...."

"Ali." He was directly in front of her now.

"What?" she snapped.

"Shut up."

Ethan lifted his hand to her cheek, ran his fingers through her hair, and grasped her head in his hand. Alaina sighed, all the fight finally leaving her. She didn't back away this time.

"Yes, I will have to leave eventually," he said gently, "but that doesn't mean anything has to change between us."

"You say that now...."

Ethan shushed her and continued.

"Just because I have a complicated schedule doesn't mean that we can't work through it. And I know that what you're going through is a lot for a guy to deal with, but I deal with tough decisions every day." Ethan paused, trying to make every word come out perfectly. "I don't want to lose you, Ali. And I don't want you dealing with this alone. We're going to get through this together, okay? Me and you."

Alaina peered up at Ethan. He gently wiped away an escaping tear from her cheek.

There was nothing else to say. Ethan and Alaina shared a gaze of understanding. They were both taking huge risks by agreeing to care for one another—but it was a risk they were both willing to take. They understood that sometimes love requires sacrifices, but that it's always worth it for the right person. Would it be an easy road? No. That concept was a fairy tale. But it would not be a road they would travel alone.

Alaina thought that God had rescued Ethan from his accident because he had big plans for him. Unfinished business for him to take care of. Ethan couldn't help but feel like this might be it. God's plan for him. Alaina needed someone to help her get through this storm, and Ethan wanted—possibly more than he had ever wanted anything before—to be that person for her.

It was a normal Tuesday night to the rest of the residents of enchanting Fairhope, but to Ethan and Alaina, it was a night of awakening, awareness, and honesty. And under the brilliantly clear Alabama night sky, lit by the glow from the huge moon overhead, Alaina finally gave into her heart. She didn't push Ethan away. She didn't hold back.

She reached up onto her tip-toes and allowed her lips to meet his. It was no more than a kiss, but Ethan remained respectable in every way. If this was all Alaina could ever offer him, it would be enough. He kissed her back with all he had, and in that moment Ethan Carter began to realize what it felt like to actually care about someone else more than he did for himself.

His heart was no longer his. It belonged to Alaina.

And he didn't miss it a bit.

Chapter 17

Alaina

It was Wednesday. The day of the week that Alaina immediately began dreading at precisely 12 a.m. each Thursday morning of the previous week. Wednesday was the day that Alaina drove Ben up to Birmingham for his weekly chemotherapy treatment. It was approximately a 4½-hour drive, which she had somehow, after repeated trips, managed to cut down to about four. Needless to say, the day was draining both emotionally and physically. Alaina would roll out of bed at four thirty, dragging her partially asleep brother to the car in his pajamas—with a clean change of clothes packed in a bag—and set out to make it to their ten o'clock appointment at the University of Alabama Cancer Treatment Center. They would pull back into the drive at Granny Mae's around eleven or so that night. It was dark when they left and dark when they returned.

The trip originally felt as if it took forever, but now that she and Ben had made it so many times, it almost felt like a brief drive down the road. They had landmarks memorized on all sides of the road and noticed instantly when a billboard had been changed. In the beginning, she and Ben passed the time playing car games and singing along with the radio. Recently, however, as Ben was becoming weaker and weaker, he tended to sleep the majority of the drive. Granny Mae had accompanied her several times to help break the monotony, but Alaina hated to ask her because it seemed to wear Granny out almost as much as it did Ben.

But Alaina didn't have to worry about that this time because Granny Mae would not be accompanying her today. Alaina had explained her mid-week routine to Ethan as he had driven them home the night before, and much to her surprise, he requested to tag along. She'd desperately tried to talk him out of going, not quite ready to let him feel the weight of her lifestyle. Things were going so well between them. They'd hit it off from the moment they'd met, and Alaina was still shocked at the wave of comfort she received every time Ethan wrapped his arms around her or flashed his dimpled grin. It was this simple fact that finally broke her resistance and led to her approval of his accompaniment. Each and every visit to the treatment center became harder for Ben to endure and harder for Alaina to watch.

The center resembled any normal hospital until time to step off the elevator into the children's ward. Alaina was still amazed with the change in atmosphere on that floor. There wasn't a bare wall anywhere; murals of oceans, skies, carnivals, space, sports, and countless other things covered every square inch. She and Ben had never met a nurse that wasn't smiling, and Ben was greeted each time like a long lost friend of the staff. In the beginning, it had thrown Alaina a little off guard. How could all of these kids who were going through these terrible diseases, fighting every second just to stay alive, be so content in a place like this?

In the chemo and radiation room, hospital beds shaped as race cars lined the wall. Several kids shared the same appointment time and kept each other company while receiving their treatment. Alaina watched every appointment, always amazed at the attitudes expended by such young people. Treatments always started with the IVs. The nurses came in and stuck a needle in one of each of their little arms. Alaina still cringed every time because she knew the dark purple bruise that would pop up the next morning from Ben's repeated sticks. They tried to place the catheter in a different spot each time, but it didn't matter. There were only so many places, and after a while, it was inevitable that the same spot would be stuck twice. After the IV tubing was in place, the treatment began. As the magic liquid flowed through their veins, destroying not only the cancerous cells but also a majority of other healthy cells, the kids laughed, watched movies, ate Popsicles, and drank smoothies. The bright lights and smiling faces were a great decoy, but Alaina wasn't fooled for a second. She had seen the deep sores that sometimes formed in Ben's mouth after a therapy session, causing him to go without food for up to a couple of days at a time. She had gotten up in the middle of the night with him as he violently threw up over and over until his stomach heaved but nothing came out. Every Wednesday, she passed time in the eerily quiet waiting room while Ben slept and recouped from the day's treatment. Still, despite it all, the kids, Ben in particular, never lost faith. They weren't angry. They lived each and every day as if it was their last and appreciated every single little thing that was done for them. Their strong spirits never ceased to amaze Alaina, and she thanked God daily for knowing them.

Ben had, thankfully, made a couple of friends who were going through the same obstacles as he. Playing with them at the treatment center was the only time she ever saw her brother remove his signature ball cap without shame and just be the carefree little boy she remembered from before he was diagnosed. Alaina knew one thing; she would not have been able to deal with Ben's treatments with as much strength as she had if not for the awesome nurses and doctors who worked with him. They provided her about as much comfort as they did Ben.

The medical team was definitely a source of comfort for Alaina, but her faith was her rock. Her heart was heavy that morning because Ben was scheduled to receive test results. She was hopeful for, but not expectant of, good news. So she focused her study on having faith in the hard times, expending most of her time Psalms.

When Alaina was finished with her devotional, she groggily finished up the touches on her appearance, feeling the effects of her lack of sleep during the night, and stumbled into the hallway. She wondered if Ethan had remembered to set his alarm, and if so, if he had managed to not hit the sleep button until it quit going off. She hoped so because it was almost five and they needed to hit the road immediately. When she reached Ben's bedroom and tapped lightly on the door, she was surprised upon opening it to find that the room was empty.

She backtracked and descended the staircase to find Ethan standing at the front door talking to Granny Mae and Ted. Alaina's stomach did a summersault upon sight of Ethan, and her feelings for him instantly magnified. Fully dressed and ready for the day, Ethan stood with his guitar case hanging from his back, and Ben lying peacefully asleep in his arms. She paused for a moment at the base of the stairs to take it all in.

"Good morning, hon," Granny Mae said sweetly when Alaina entered the living room. Ted gave a slight wave, and Ethan's head shot up, their eyes meeting instantly. He gave a slight grin and shrugged.

"When I saw the time, I figured you would want to leave soon so I went ahead and brought Ben down for you. I hope that's okay," Ethan said.

Alaina's heart melted. "Thanks," was all she replied. Their eyes never veered, and a silence fell in the room. The memory of Ethan's lips against hers flashed in her mind, and her cheeks grew hot. She sucked in a deep breath trying to calm her nerves as Ethan studied her from across the room. Neither realized that Granny and Ted were watching with intrigued expressions.

Finally, Granny cleared her throat. "Ethan, dear, why don't you take Ben out to the car before he wakes up?"

He simply nodded and turned for the door as Ted pulled it open for him. He carried Ben out to the Charger that still sat parked in the same place it had been when they'd arrived home from the festival.

Alaina reached for a couple of pillows and a blanket that Granny had laid out on the couch for her. On her way out the door, Alaina stopped to give Granny a swift kiss on the cheek and was handed a bag of goodies for the road. "Thanks, Granny Mae," Alaina said gratefully. Granny always had everything together for her early morning departures.

She ran to meet Ethan at the car. She opened the backseat door, placed the pillows on one side, and pushed the seats forward as Ethan carefully laid Ben down. Alaina took the blanket and spread it across him. He never budged.

Ethan insisted on driving, and as they reached the outskirts of the Fairhope city limits, he turned onto Highway 10 to Mobile, which would eventually lead to I-65 all the way to Birmingham.

"I can't believe you got around so fast this morning," Alaina said once they had been driving awhile.

He seemed a bit surprised. "What did you expect?"

"Oh, I don't know. I guess I just wasn't expecting you to be so...efficient."

Ethan scoffed. "Are you kidding? I'm totally efficient! Five a.m. is a normal morning for me."

"A big rock star like you?" Alaina jeered. "No way, I'm not buying."

"Okay, maybe it's not five every day," he smiled, "but it is sometimes. Like when I'm performing on a talk show or doing a radio show. I have to get there really early for wardrobe and sound checks. *Good Morning America* was the worst. That day started around 3 a.m. *The Ellen Show* wasn't too bad, being in the middle of the day, but I think *Letterman* and *Leno* were my favorites. They made for really late nights, but at least I didn't have to wake up at the crack of dawn and..."

Ethan paused when he noticed Alaina staring at him.

"What?" he asked.

"Nothing," she said quickly, trying to hide her smirk.

"Then what's with the face?"

Alaina gave a quick laugh. "You...amaze me sometimes."

"Oh yeah?" Ethan cast a proud grin. "And why's that?"

"I don't know. It's just, when we're together you seem so normal—helping my brother and going with me to the hospital—and then you talk about appearing on talk shows. I mean, who does that? It's a little...strange...that's all. Sometimes I forget what your real life is like."

"My real life?"

"Yeah, the life that doesn't involve lengthy hospital visits and sick kids and emotionally stressed-out girl...acquaintances...."

Alaina abruptly shut her mouth realizing she was about to call herself Ethan's girlfriend! What was she thinking? It was one kiss for goodness sakes. Only one kiss! Alaina didn't know what it took to be considered the girlfriend of the world-renown teen pop sensation, but she was fairly certain that their last two days together probably didn't qualify her.

After a short silence, Ethan spoke with a curious tone, his eyes never veering from the road ahead. "Acquaintances? Is that what we are?"

Alaina froze. "I...uh..." Her stomach twisted in knots, and she gave a slight grunt to clear her throat. "What...what would you like us to be?"

Ethan smirked, as if he found something in his own thoughts quite amusing. He reached down, took hold of her hand, and lifted it. His lips pressed gently to the back of her hand, and he held it tightly against his chest. "Whatever you want, Ali. I'll take whatever you'll give me."

Chapter 18

Alaina

The ride to Birmingham felt to Alaina as if it took only a fraction of the time it normally did thanks to Ethan's company. She could be so carefree with him. She didn't have to be anyone but herself. She didn't worry about not looking the right way for him, or whether she was saying all the right things, and even though she knew Ethan wasn't a believer, Alaina didn't have to hide the fact that she was. She made constant references to her faith, and Ethan just listened intently as if he actually might be a little interested to hear more. She sat in the passenger side of the rental with her bare feet resting comfortably on the dash in front of her. Her hair hung in a loose side braid, and her eyes rarely shifted anywhere but to the boy who sat beside her.

Ethan held her hand and pretended to tickle her until she screamed and smacked him on the arm for not watching the road. He told her she looked beautiful even though she knew she'd gotten way too little sleep to hide the bags that hung under her eyes. He sang her songs, usually making up his own lyrics to every song that came on the radio—either completely butchering the song or putting the original singer to shame. Alaina was nothing short of enchanted, and with each passing second of their time together, she fell deeper and deeper for the boy she knew hardly anything about. And it was almost...just almost...enough to distract her from the fact that Ben had not woken the entire trip there—which was a first.

It wasn't until Ethan pulled into the parking garage of the University of Alabama Treatment Center that Ben finally began to stir.

"Hey Ben," Alaina said lightly as her brother rolled over and grudgingly rubbed sleep from his eyes. He sat up slowly, eyes not quite open.

"Are we there yet?" Ben replied in his usual singsong voice he used when he knew exactly how far they were from the center.

"Yeah, bub, we're here."

"Really?" He seemed a little surprised. He usually just asked that question to be a pest. "Wow, I slept the whole way this time!"

Alaina's heart broke a little. Ben talked as though this was some kind of small accomplishment when she knew it was only because he was getting worse. She wondered how long it would be before this trip was no longer an option for him.

Ben shifted his focus, noticing that Alaina was not driving.

"Ethan! I didn't know you were coming!"

Ethan glanced at Alaina and grinned with a slight wink. "Sure thing, little buddy, and your sister told me you've got to do this treatment thing and it takes awhile but that you get to hang out with your friends while you're doing it so...I brought you a little something to pass the time."

Ben's weak eyes sparkled, and Alaina thought she saw a little life returning to them. "What is it?" he asked.

"It's in the trunk. C'mon I'll show you."

Ben scrambled out of the back seat and met Ethan at the back of the car. Ethan used the key to pop the latch of the trunk. The door swung open to reveal his black leather guitar case lying flat inside.

"Wow! You brought your guitar!" Ben smiled ear to ear. "Are you going to play for me and my friends while we get our treatment?"

Alaina had noticed Ethan's guitar strapped to his back that morning, but she'd been so tired, she hadn't thought a lot about it. He surely wasn't going to play for the kids. It would give away his identity to everyone there. She wondered what he had up his sleeve.

"Actually, rock star, I was thinking that maybe you could show off your new skills." Ethan gave Ben a little wink.

Ben's eyes widened. "Really? Do you really think I'm ready to go public?"

Ethan unsuccessfully tried to suppress his amusement. "Yeah I think you're ready. Besides, the girls will love it."

Ben smiled. "Cool."

Alaina watched, not having the slightest clue what either of them was talking about.

"Someone want to clue me in on this conversation?" Alaina asked.

Ethan spoke before Ben. "Don't you worry about it, big sis. This is a guy thing."

Alaina cast Ethan a skeptical look.

"Let's get you to that appointment, Ben." Ethan pulled the guitar from the trunk, wrapped the strap around his back, and his arm around Alaina, leading them toward the entrance. Ben reached up and grabbed Ethan's hand. Ethan glanced down at Ben's smiling face and his ball cap with the messy curls. Ethan looked a little surprised, and Alaina waited to see if he'd let go...but he didn't. He grinned at Ben and gave him a pretend punch across the cheek with their intertwined fingers. Ben dramatically acted as if it hurt. They both laughed as if it was a joke that only they understood.

Alaina knew that Ethan had chosen to hang out with Ben the day before, which by now she was pretty sure was just a way for him to try to impress her, but what she hadn't realized was how well they'd hit things off. Ben had been sound asleep when she and Ethan arrived home, and she hadn't been able to ask him how his day had gone. She hoped he'd had fun. She had to admit that the idea of Ben hanging out with someone who didn't know his condition scared her a little, but she really wanted Ben to have a chance to hang out with his idol without the worry of Ethan being nice to him strictly out of pity. Obviously, it had worked out fine because Ethan hadn't reported any problems to her. She was sure he would've told her if anything had gone wrong. As far as she could tell, he'd been honest with her about everything.

Alaina and Ethan managed to get Ben to his appointment a mere five minutes early. On the elevator ride, Ethan leaned over and murmured in her ear, "So what's it going to be like up here?"

She could detect the angst in his tone, and she knew it well because it was the same way she had felt the first time she'd taken that same elevator ride. She'd expected to walk into a stark white hallway filled with the echoes of children screaming in pain and parents crying in agony for them. That thought was comical now that she knew what it was really like.

"Let's just say it's not what you're expecting," she whispered back.

When the little light above the elevator doors reached the number five, a ding sounded and the double doors slid their separate ways. Ben immediately let go of Ethan's hand and ran to meet the nurses who looked forward to seeing him every week. Alaina paid close attention to Ethan's reaction as he stepped off the elevator.

It was just as she expected. Ethan's eyes widened, and he released her hand walking a little ways ahead into the large mural painted waiting area. "Wow," he breathed, not realizing she could hear.

"Told you," she grinned. "You haven't seen anything yet. C'mon, I'll introduce you to the nurses."

Alaina took Ethan's hand back in hers and led him around the corner to the nurses' station. There they found Ben, already seated in the middle of three of the nurses, laughing and licking a sucker. How that kid managed to find candy in the first five seconds, every time they arrived, Alaina would never know.

"Hey Ali!" One of the nurses, Katrina, waved with a huge, greeting smile from beside Ben in the station.

"What's up, Kat?"

Ethan leaned near her ear. "I thought only special people got to call you Ali."

"Yep, and you have no idea how special these people are."

The nurses were laughing and joking with Ben when they suddenly became very much aware of the fact that Alaina was not alone this time. They all became silent about the same time, eyeing Ethan, unsure of what to say. Knowing her and Ben's situation, they too were not accustomed to Alaina even talking about boys, much less bringing one to the hospital.

A tall African American nurse, named Raché, who Alaina had grown to love from the first time she'd met her, was, not surprisingly, the first to speak.

"Well, well, who do we have here?" she asked Alaina in an overly dramatic voice.

Alaina's head dropped, and she felt her cheeks grow hot. She knew these nurses pretty well by now, and she felt sorry for Ethan for what he was about to go through.

"This is my friend...Brandon," Alaina said, smiling at the use of Ethan's alias.

Ben's head popped up, and he let out his most disbelieving, argumentative ten-year-old voice. "No it's not."

Alaina's mouth popped open a little, and she turned to Ethan, unsure of what to do. She had completely forgotten to explain Ethan's situation to Ben and hadn't even considered the fact that Ben would never go along with the story unless prompted first. But then, once again, Ethan took her by surprise.

"It's cool, lil man," he said to Ben. "Sometimes I go by Brandon, too. I think we'll use that today. Is that okay with you?"

Ben cocked his head with a confused expression that was so cute that if Alaina hadn't been so worried about messing up Ethan's cover would've made her want to run and hug him. She thought for a second he would argue in typical Ben fashion, but Ethan had a way of talking to Ben that Alaina didn't think she'd ever master.

"Sure. Whatever, dude," Bed said, sounding much older than he really was. "If you wanna be Brandon today, it's fine with me. What should I be? How bout Will? Or maybe Chuck?"

Ethan laughed. "I like Ben. Just Ben."

Ben grinned. "Cool...Brandon."

The nurses remained silent throughout this entire exchange, but Alaina knew Ethan wasn't off the hook yet.

"So, Brandon," Raché continued, putting on a protective expression, "how did you meet our sweet Ali?"

To Alaina's surprise, Ethan didn't so much as flinch beneath her harsh gaze. "I came to visit my grandma. I think you've probably met her? Her name is Mae."

"Oh, Mae's your grandmother?" Raché went on, not lightening up a bit on her accusatory tone. "So I guess that means you are sharing a house with Miss Ali, and I see that you are holding her hand, so that leaves me with only one question." The nurses behind her giggled and so did Alaina. Technically, Alaina could have jumped in to rescue Ethan at any time, but sadly, she was kind of enjoying this. "I take it you are behaving yourself," Raché cleared her throat, "if you know what I mean...."

Ethan slipped Ali the quickest of glances, causing her to bite her upper lip to keep from laughing. "Yes, of course, ma'am."

Raché eyed him up and down one last time before turning back to her file that sat on the front counter.

"Mmm-hmm, you've got a long day ahead of you, child. We will see."

Once the nurses recovered from trying to hold back their laughter, all the while Ben was completely unaware of anything but his sucker, Katrina got up and grabbed hold of Ben's hand.

"C'mon Benny Boy, let's go get you hooked up. A few of your buddies are already here, and they've been asking about you."

Ben jumped up and walked with Katrina down the colorful hall, entering his usual room at the third door on the right. Alaina and Ethan followed quickly behind.

"That lady was a little...intimidating," Ethan said once they were past earshot of the nurse's station.

"Who, Raché?" Alaina pretended to be clueless. "Nah, she's just protective that's all. They kind of like me here."

Truth be known, these women had become a bit of a second family for Alaina. They had seen her through about everything in the past year. They'd made her laugh on days she never thought she'd be able to again. They'd cried with her on days she knew she couldn't laugh no matter what. They'd bought her and Ben birthday presents and Christmas presents. They'd even taken up a private collection a few months back when the transmission broke down on the car and Alaina was afraid she wouldn't be able to get Ben to his treatments. Their donation, along with the one from her church family, had been just enough to fix the car like new.

Albeit their job or not, these women were her family, and like she'd told Ethan earlier, they were very special.

They'd reached the doorway to Ben's treatment room, and Alaina paused before turning the steel handle.

"Ethan, I think there's something I should tell you before you go in there." She wasn't sure how to tell him this, and she wished she'd been more honest about it from the beginning. "Ben's hat...that he wears all the time...isn't just a hat. It's actually a wig. The chemo that Ben is on has made all of his hair fall out. He insists on wearing the hat at home, but he doesn't wear it here. None of the kids do. I just wanted you to be prepared before you see him like that."

Ethan opened his mouth as if he was going to say something, but shut it again quickly. Alaina didn't quite know what to make of it, but before she could ask, he spoke. "I'm not worried about whether or not Ben has hair, Ali. I just want him to get better."

Alaina let out a breath she hadn't even realized she'd been holding. She still couldn't believe she'd found a guy who was as understanding of her situation as Ethan was. She didn't say anything in reply. She did the only thing she knew to do to thank him for his consideration, the only thing she wanted to do. She reached up on her tip toes and laid the lightest of kisses on his lips and then turned the doorknob to the treatment room and walked in. Ethan gave her hand a slight squeeze and followed in behind her.

"Sissy, can I have another one please?"

Alaina sighed with an amused grin. "Ben, you've already had three!"

"Yeah, I know, but I think that four might make me feel a lot better!" Ben flashed his cutest grin, showing as many teeth as possible.

Alaina and Ethan were seated in straight-back chairs next to Ben's race car bed in the treatment room. The walls were covered in murals of a crowd-filled stadium with the brightest blue, cloud-covered sky. Around the base of the walls, a race track curved in a large circle around the room. There wasn't a dull color anywhere. Even Alaina's and Ethan's chairs were multicolored. The same few kids who received treatments the same time as Ben every week occupied the other beds that lined the wall. Their parents, or whoever accompanied them to the appointment that day, sat beside them. They colored and listened to music and put puzzles together on a little sliding tray. Anything to keep the kids' minds off of what was really happening to them.

"Aww, c'mon, sis!" Kat said as she stopped by to check Ben's IV line. "What possible harm can a fourth Popsicle do to anyone?"

"Oh, why not," Alaina caved, knowing she hadn't cared in the slightest to begin with. She just liked to play with Ben when he was getting his treatment. Anything to make him smile. "If fact, Kat, I think we could all use another one." She gave Ethan a slight wink, and he nodded in agreement.

"Comin' right up," Kat smiled, disappearing into a side room. A moment later, she emerged with an entire tub of Popsicles. She started at the bed at the end of the room, distributing one to the little girl who occupied it—she was three years younger than Ben—and one to each of her family members. Kat continued this process, allowing everyone to pick their favorite color until she'd covered everyone in the room. Ben, not fully understanding the concept of savoring his food, managed to scarf his down quicker than anyone—except Ethan. Those two boys had way more in common than Alaina would have ever guessed. And she couldn't believe the difference in Ben's attitude with Ethan present. Ben was always fairly good natured during his treatment, and he tended to have a pretty good outlook on the chemo despite the consequences he knew would soon follow when he got home. But today had been even better than most. Ethan made jokes about Ben's treatments, referencing the IV tubing to tentacles extending from Ben's alien body, which cracked Ben up and led him to holding his arms up and trying his best to act like a scary alien. He insisted on rubbing Ben's bald head for good luck, which in turn, led to Ben making each and every nurse stop and listen to his new business venture in which he charged ten cents per person to rub his head for good luck. Surprisingly, a couple of the nurses even took him up on it.

Ethan seemed more than comfortable with Ben in this environment and provided him with more comfort than Alaina could have ever offered. Alaina had trouble finding it in her heart to make light of what was happening to Ben, but after watching how Ethan approached Ben's disease, she realized that the humor actually seemed to relax Ben a little. He didn't have to concentrate on how sick he felt, or how different he looked, or how much better or worse he was getting. He got to hang out and have a good time. Alaina didn't know how she would ever thank Ethan for moments like these, when she got to see her little brother laughing and playing and...happy. She knew it was only a matter of minutes before he became too tired to play anymore, but if it was up to Ethan, Ben was going to make the most of every one of those minutes.

When everyone had finished their Popsicles and the kids were waiting for their IV's to finish, Ben looked up at Ethan, a bit of nervousness in his eyes.

"Is it time now?" Ben asked.

It took Alaina a minute to realize what he meant, but when Ethan reached behind his chair and pulled his guitar case around, she remembered their plans.

Ethan gave Ben an encouraging grin. "Ready when you are, big guy."

Ethan pulled the guitar from its case and placed it gently on his knees. Since Ethan had arrived, Alaina had yet to see him with his guitar, but as he sat in the straight-back chair next to her, looking intently to the head of the guitar and making delicate adjustments to the turning keys, she decided that Ethan and the guitar complemented one another. They were a perfect fit, as if God had created Ethan with that specific talent in mind. Alaina couldn't help but feel as though Ethan was wasting his gift. Sure, he was successful and had a career people only dreamed of, but in the end, what was the point? He wasn't promoting anything for God in thanks for the gift he'd been given. If only Ethan would believe, Alaina knew that he would understand why she felt that way. But now wasn't the time for that. Right now, as Ethan carefully passed the guitar to Ben and helped him maneuver the strap around his IV tubing, Ethan was using his gift for God whether he realized it or not. Ben was a child of God, and what Ethan was doing for him right now was something that Alaina would eternally be grateful for. She said a silent prayer, thanking God that he'd sent Ethan to Ben. She only hoped He would give Ethan a blessing in return—possibly something that would lead him closer to believing.

"Whatcha got there, Benny Boy?" Kat asked as she shifted from the bed to his right. She had been making another round between the patients.

"Eth..." Ben paused and giggled. "I mean, Brandon has been teaching me how to play guitar, Miss Kat. Can I play something for my friends, please?"

"Why of course you can, sweetie! Just let me go get the girls because they will want to hear you, too!"

Kat turned and ran through the door. Seconds later, she re-entered, joined by Raché and the rest of the nurses.

"Okay everybody!" Kat called, signaling for everyone to direct their attention toward Ben. "Ben has been learning to play guitar, and he wants to show you guys his new skills. Do ya'll want Ben to play you a song?"

The rest of the kids in the room called out, "Yea!" Ben beamed. Alaina couldn't believe the kid's nerve. If she was ever given that much attention, she'd freeze like an ice sculpture. She knew Ben couldn't have practiced very much, but that was the difference in her and Ben. Ben was fearless, and he lived every moment as if it was his last. All of the kids in that room were like Ben. With everything they'd been through, and the long road they knew was ahead, fear had a completely different meaning to them.

As Ben carefully placed his hands in their proper positions on the guitar, he looked to Ethan for his approval. Ethan gave a slight nod to let Ben know that he was doing fine. Ben held the pick up to the guitar, and Alaina thought he was about to play, but then he held it back down and, to her surprise, addressed the entire room.

"Since this is my first gig and all," Ben started. Alaina, along with several of the adults in the room suppressed amused chuckles. "I will be playing a simple song I'm sure you all know called 'Twinkle Twinkle Little Star.'"

Alaina leaned over to Ethan and whispered, "Did you teach him that announcement, too?"

Ethan grinned. "Nah, that was all him."

Ben once again held the pick to the strings and concentrated hard on the finger board, making sure his fingers were in the just right spots. Alaina wasn't sure what to expect considering the kid had never held a guitar in his life as far as she knew. She assumed the song would be choppy and consumed with sour notes. But it wasn't.

Ben's hands moved smoothly between chords, and the pick never once slipped. The tune was not the sound of one chord unevenly played after another, but a continuous melody of individual notes in which he progressed through smoothly and without interruption. Alaina would never think of "Twinkle Twinkle" the same way again. What Ben played was absolutely beautiful and more like a lullaby than a children's nursery rhyme.

He went through the entire melody of the song three times before finally ending with a combination of chords at the end. When Ben finished, a grin spread across his face that Alaina expected could have lit up the gates of heaven. The room broke into applause.

"Benny Boy, that was awesome!" Kat ran up and wrapped Ben in a big bear hug.

Raché approached next and looked Ethan straight in the eye, her stern expression returning immediately. "You taught him to play?"

Ethan flashed a quick glance at Alaina. "Uh...yes, ma'am...I did."

"Hmm...very good, Brady."

"It's Brandon."

"Uh-huh." With that, Raché gave herself leave to move on. Alaina giggled.

"I don't think that lady likes me very much," Ethan murmured.

"She's still feeling you out," Alaina replied. "Trust me, she's coming around."

"Well, I think that's a beautiful thing you did for Ben, teaching him how to play so well!" Kat said, finally releasing Ben. "You must be a wonderful teacher."

Ethan shrugged. "Nah, the kid's a natural."

"Now it's your turn!" Ben exclaimed, thrusting the guitar back to Ethan.

Alaina jumped in. "No, no, Ben. He doesn't have to do that. Not today." She cast an uneasy eye to Ethan. She knew the second he began to play a hit that everyone in the room heard ten times a day on the radio they would be able to tell exactly who he was. Then the questions would start. Then the pictures. Then the...who knows what else.

"Aww, c'mon please!" Ben pressed.

"Yes, Brandon, you have to play for us!" Kat insisted. "If you can teach Ben to play like that, you must be very good!"

"He's awesome!" Ben started. "Don't you recognize him? He's Eth..."

Alaina gasped. "Okay Ben! How about another Popsicle? I bet five would be even better than four!"

"Nah, I don't want another one. I want to hear E..."

Alaina put her hand over Ben's mouth, not knowing what else to do. "Uh..." She turned to the confused nurse and gave a guilty smile. Kids. Sometimes, they just don't know how to take a hint.

Alaina shifted her focus as she noticed Ethan wrapping the

guitar strap around his shoulder and readjusting it to fit his body instead of Ben's. "It's cool, Ali. I'll play."

Alaina gave him a questioning look. Inside she was screaming, *What are you thinking?!* He just shrugged, smiled, and said, "It's okay. I want to."

Alaina gave up and took a seat next to Ben on the bed.

Kat turned and got the room's attention again. "Okay kids, Alaina's guest has agreed to play for ya'll, too!" She looked back to Ethan. "They're all yours, man."

Ethan situated the guitar comfortably across his knees and looked up to the kids. "So you guys want to hear some music?"

"Yeah!" the kids rang out.

"How about some singing, too?"

"Yeah!"

"Well, let's see, have any of you ever heard the one that goes like..." Ethan's hands slid across the strings and the instrument erupted into a lively version of the first verse of "Old McDonald Had a Farm." The kids laughed and sang along. When he finished that, he said, "Okay, okay that was pretty good! How about this one?" This time he played "B-I-N-G-O," and even some of the adults joined in. Alaina and Ben sang at the top of their lungs along with Ethan, and she noticed that Ethan seemed to be having just as much fun as the kids. After a couple of rounds of "Farmer in the Dell" and "Three Blind Mice," Ethan was the hit of the entire room.

"That was awesome!" Ethan said. "You guys are really good singers!" The kids laughed, and there wasn't a mouth in the room that wasn't smiling. "Well, I think that's about all the kid songs I know."

The kids erupted in protest. Ethan laughed. "Can I play you one of my own songs instead?" The kids seemed to be okay with this so Ethan continued. "Nursery rhymes are a great place to start when you're first learning to play like my buddy, Ben, here, but eventually you can start writing your own stuff. I'm going to play you guys a song that I wrote all by myself, and you guys are so special because I've never played it for anyone else before."

The kids cheered like that was the coolest thing anybody had ever told them. They acted as though Ethan was the most famous singer on the planet, which was fairly close to the truth, but none of them realized it. He had them held captivated all on his own. No label or band or backup dancers. Just Ethan and his guitar, and Alaina could tell he was exactly where he wanted to be.

Ethan cast a quick glance at Alaina and with a sly grin he strummed the first note. "Here goes."

Alaina watched in awe as Ethan performed. It was a slow song with a pop flare. This was the first time she'd ever watched him play, and somehow he was different. When Ethan played, he and the guitar were no longer two separate objects, but one mechanism working together in beautiful harmony. His expression changed. He was passionate, and it appeared that nothing else in his world existed except him and his instrument. His voice was smooth, and he never missed a note. He was truly a professional, and Alaina was impressed. But once Alaina moved past how talented Ethan was, she started listening to the actual lyrics of his song.

He was singing about love. And not a mushy, fairy-tale, utterly impossible kind of love, but a messy, complicated, completely infuriating kind of love filled with passion and sorrow and heart-wrenching honesty. It was the exact same type of love that Alaina believed in. The only kind she thought was truly real, and Ethan had written a song summing up her very thoughts.

As Ethan continued to play, Alaina felt her heart softening even more for the famous pop star who sat before her. She dreaded coming to the hospital every week and racking her brain to find some way to help Ben get through his treatment with a positive outlook, but Ethan had taken care of all of that. He had come right in and brightened the entire room with his energy and his smile.

Alaina knew that she and Ethan had a lot of things in their relationship that needed to be worked out before they would be able to progress any further—for instance, the fact that Ethan held no belief in the God that pulled Alaina through each day of the hell she'd been consumed in for the past year—but after listening to Ethan's belief on love that rang out in the song he sang for those sick kids, Alaina realized that they had finally found one belief that they held in common. And in her eyes, that was a good place to start.

Chapter 19

Alaina

The last falling quarter clinked into position in the chamber of the buzzing, bright red soda machine that stood solidly in the corner of the hospital break room. Ben had finished his treatment almost an hour earlier and was lying down to rest. Alaina and Ethan, neither one being needed at the moment, had opted to go grab a soda and a bag of chips to tide them over for the afternoon. Ben normally needed a couple of hours to sleep and rest from his treatment before they were released to make the long trip back home.

"That was beautiful, what you did in there for those kids," Alaina said as they turned to retrace their steps through the maze of hallways leading back to the cancer ward.

Ethan grinned and grasped Alaina's hand in his. "It wasn't that big of a deal. It was fun."

Maybe to Ethan, what he'd done hadn't been a big deal, but to those kids, Alaina knew, he had made their entire day.

"So I've been wondering about something," Ethan said slowly, a moment later.

"Oh, yeah?"

Ethan paused as if carefully considering what he wanted to say. "Granny Mae told me about what happened to your parents and why you guys are staying with her..."

Alaina wondered where he was going with this.

"...and don't get me wrong, I'm glad I was able to meet you," he continued. "But I guess I'm just wondering why you had to stay with her in the first place. Do you not have any other family?" Ethan stopped them in the middle of the hallway, next to a long line of windows that overlooked downtown Birmingham. "I'm sorry. You don't have to answer that if you don't want to."

Alaina took a seat on a wooden bench that rested against the window. Ethan sat down next to her. "There's really not a lot to tell," she said. "My mom and dad were both only children. My grandparents on my dad's side both passed away when I was little. My mom's mom was put in the nursing home with Alzheimer's a few years ago and died shortly after that. My mom's dad ran off when my mom was a baby. I've never met him."

"Wow," Ethan breathed. "So you have been dealing with..." he looked down both sides of the hall "...all of *this* all on your own?"

"Not all on my own," Alaina said. "I've had your grandmother, which has been an absolute Godsend, and I've had the people from my church. And then, of course, there are Ben's nurses."

"But how did you get to keep Ben?" Ethan said. "I thought that they usually split kids up when stuff like this happens. Foster homes and stuff. How'd you get out of that?"

Alaina sucked in a breath through her teeth, making a hissing noise. "Now that is not such a simple story. Turns out, my parents had named me sole guardian of Ben in the event of an accidental death—who knew that would ever actually happen—but that was only valid after my eighteenth birthday. So I went to court and filed for a petition of guardianship that would hold until my birthday. I had to prove that I had a stable home for Ben—thanks to your grandmother, I did—and that I had financial means to support both of us. Granny Mae explained that she would be funding all of our utilities and food. Ben and I would go back to school like normal, and I would work to save up some money so that when I turned eighteen, we'd find our own place. It was a miracle, and we had to fight really hard for it, but it worked. They granted the petition."

"Then you found out Ben was sick?" Ethan asked.

"Yep. We got the news just a couple of weeks after our court date," Alaina replied, "which actually turned out for the best, because if we'd known beforehand, they probably would not have granted the petition."

"So where does all of this fit into the plan?" Ethan asked. "I know cancer treatment can't be cheap. How are you guys affording all of this?"

"I work at the restaurant to make enough for the minimum insurance payments. Ben qualifies for all kinds of free health care because of our situation, but it still doesn't pay for everything. So we carry extra insurance to help make up for some of the slack." Alaina rose from the bench and held her hand out for Ethan. "That's my story."

Ethan took her hand and rose to her side. He draped his arm around her shoulder and continued their walk down the hall. "That's some story."

"It sure is," she said. "And also one that I don't tell many people. I'm not even sure why I told you, but I guess there's no taking it back now."

"No. I'm glad you did," Ethan said. "It's not just a story, it's your life...and that's something I'm very interested in." He glanced down at her and cast a shy grin.

Alaina actually felt a little better after talking to Ethan about her life. People all over town knew bits and pieces of what she had been through, but she didn't dare talk to any of them about it. It wasn't their burden to bear. It was hers. But recently, it had begun to feel as if a heavy backpack was permanently stitched into the skin of her back so that she was meant to carry the weight of it around forever. Explaining everything to Ethan, actually saying it aloud, seemed to help lighten the load a little, as if maybe just a little something had been removed from the backpack.

"So tell me about your life," Alaina said, realizing how very little she knew about Ethan outside the shelter of his grandmother's house. "Everyone has a story with their parents. What's yours?"

They rounded the corner and walked through the cafeteria area of the hospital. Up ahead was another long corridor with winding hallways splitting off on both sides. At the end was an elevator that would take them back up to Ben's floor.

"Oh man," Ethan said. He looked thoughtful. "Well, my dad also ran off when I was little. It's just me and my mom now."

"Oh, I'm sorry," she said.

"No, it's cool. I don't even remember him. My mom was raised in Fairhope, but on a college trip with friends to New York City she met my dad, got pregnant with me, and moved up there hoping to find a way to make him stay with her. When it didn't work, she just stayed there."

"So where is your dad now?" Alaina asked.

Ethan gave a charismatic shrug. "Still in the city, I guess. Last I heard, he's some big advertisement executive." He paused. "As far as I'm concerned, he doesn't exist."

An empathetic look crossed her expression. "So your mom never married?"

"Nope. She'd just started dating a little when my video got discovered on YouTube. After that, things got crazy and we started traveling all over the country. There's not a lot of time for a social life when your kid's on tour."

"Imagine what it's like for the kid...." Alaina said under her breath.

"Hey now, don't start that again." Ethan stopped at the end of the hall, near the elevator. He pulled his fingers up to Alaina's chin and forced her to look him in the eye. "Ali, we've already talked about this. We'll make it work, okay?"

Alaina nodded, not wanting to expend the energy it would take

to argue with him. Instead, she turned away and pushed the button
for the elevator.

When they reached the treatment ward, Alaina led Ethan back
toward the visitor's waiting room. But on their way, they had to pass
by the nurse's station. Kat approached as they got to the counter.

"Alaina, Dr. Rouse informed me that we got the results back on
Ben's blood work."

Dr. Rouse was Ben's oncologist. During their last visit, Ben had
given more blood, and tests were being run to see if the
chemotherapy was making enough difference in the reduction of
cancer cells. Ben's cancer attacked the blood-forming cells in his
bone marrow. The disease had invaded her little brother's body fast
and with merciless aggression, and Alaina knew he was losing the
battle. Today was the last session in his third round of chemo, and
blood tests from the previous week would tell them if enough
difference was being made to give them reason to hope for a chance
of remission.

"He wants to meet with you, hon," Kat continued. Alaina could
tell that she was trying to keep a straight, nonrevealing face, but
Alaina knew these nurses too well by now. They cared for Ben as if
he was their own kid brother, and she could tell that Kat wasn't
happy with the news.

Alaina steadied her feet, trying her best to calm the dizziness in
her mind. She'd known the test results were coming, but she'd
expected to receive a phone call or a letter or something. She didn't
realize she was going to have to face them that day.

"Um...when does he want to see me? Is Ben awake yet?"

"Dr. Rouse is in his office now," Kat replied. "And Ben just
woke up a few minutes ago. He's watching cartoons right now, and I
think Raché is taking his vitals."

"Okay." Alaina cast a quick glance at Ethan, not sure what to
say. "I guess I'll..."

Ethan interrupted. "I'll go hang with Ben. You do what you need
to do, and we'll be here whenever you're ready, okay?"

The look in his caring blue eyes made Alaina think that maybe
Ethan meant "whenever you're ready" to not necessarily mean when
Dr. Rouse finished talking to her, but when she was actually ready to
face Ben.

"Thanks, Ethan," she said. He pulled her in and gave her a quick
peck on the forehead before turning toward the hall to Ben's room.

"Okay, Kat," Alaina sighed. "Let's get this over with."

Kat led Alaina to the far end of the treatment ward to an office that Alaina had been in way too many times before. When she reached the door, Kat knocked lightly, cracked the door, and said, "I've got Alaina here, Dr. Rouse."

Dr. Rouse rose from his desk chair, opened the door for her, and held his hand out toward the chair opposite his desk. "Good afternoon, Alaina," he smiled.

Dr. Rouse had been wonderful to Alaina, and she really liked him. It was hard, on occasions like these when she expected to hear bad news, to not hate the man just because he was the messenger, but she honestly didn't think she would have ever picked a different doctor to deal with Ben's illness. Dr. Rouse didn't treat Alaina as a child, as most doctors they'd previously seen tended to do. He understood her situation. That she was the person taking care of Ben at home. Dr. Rouse talked to her like an adult. He didn't sugar coat information and hobble in circles around what she needed to hear. He gave her the facts, followed by their options, and then he gave her the ability to make decisions on Ben's behalf. She respected him for that.

"Have a seat, Alaina," Dr. Rouse said kindly.

Alaina reluctantly took a seat and waited for the doctor to do the same. She cleared her throat hoping some of the nervousness would subside. "So, Kat told me we got the results back on Ben's blood work."

"We did," Dr. Rouse replied, rustling through a file on his desk and pulling out some papers. "Here is a copy of his lab report." He passed a paper across the desk to Alaina.

She had become accustomed to reading these over the past several months, understanding the meaning of the number counts of white blood cells, hematocrit, and platelets. And she knew instantly what the numbers on this current lab report meant for Ben.

"The chemo isn't working, is it?" The question came out as a half whisper, while Alaina prayed with all her heart for him to say she was wrong.

Dr. Rouse replied slowly. "No...it's not working."

Alaina opened her mouth to reply, but nothing came out.

"I'm afraid it's just the opposite," the doctor continued carefully, but still using the same matter-of-fact tone that Alaina normally appreciated from him. "The number of cancer cells seems to be increasing. All the chemo seems to be doing is helping to destroy what healthy cells Ben has left."

Alaina fought back tears as she tried to muster the strength to ask her next question. It came out frail and staggered. "Wha...what do we...do next?"

The doctor answered with a steady tone, but it was obvious to Alaina that he wished he didn't have to answer her. "I would suggest the next step we take needs to be looking into long-term pain management routines. We also have counselors available to help with making your home a comfortable place for this transitional phase. If you would like to speak with one of our emotional outreach counselors, we can arrange..."

"How long?" Alaina interrupted. She had heard all of his words, but they were all spinning around in her mind in a jumbled up mess of denial. "How long does he have?"

"I really can't tell you with any kind of certainty," Dr. Rouse replied. "It varies with each patient."

Alaina continued to remain silent, willing away the tears that wanted nothing more than to pour out of her eyes like tiny waterfalls. She'd known this news was coming. She even thought Ben had been expecting it—something in his eyes told her so. But none of that made hearing the reality of it out loud any easier for her.

The remainder of her visit with Dr. Rouse consisted of discussions over their plan for Ben's pain management. She signed all the necessary paperwork and asked all the appropriate questions. She was given pamphlets on things they could do at home to help keep him comfortable and pamphlets from every church in the region that had people willing to talk to her. Alaina took it all in stride, with a strength that she knew in her heart was not her own.

When Dr. Rouse finally excused her from his office, Alaina insisted that he let her walk back to the nurse's station alone. When she was on the opposite side of his closed office door, she felt her composure dwindling. She looked in both directions, not seeing anyone down either side of the hall, and took off in a sprint toward an unmarked doorway at the end of the hall.

To a normal visitor, this door would look like the entrance to a patient's room or another office, but after having countless hours to kill in this hospital, Alaina had managed to roam every nook and cranny to discover that this door was actually an unmarked stairwell. The door at the top of the stairs led to an office floor that was restricted to visitors. Luckily for Alaina, not one of the hospital staff ever used it. And she knew this because this was not the first time she'd needed to take advantage of the privacy it offered. The cancer ward offered rooms for families to use for grieving, but Alaina just found something odd about asking a nurse to let her in a room so she could bawl her eyes out for a few minutes. Alaina was much fonder of finding her own little hiding place to temporarily lose her mind.

And as she burst through the stairwell door and collapsed in a ball in the corner beneath the stairs, that's exactly what she did. She finally gave way to the tears, and the hurt, and the anger, and the unfairness of it all, and let it out. Having a lot of practice crying so that no one could hear her, in a silent moment of despair, Alaina buried her head between her knees and allowed her body to quake in remorse for her brother and what she was going to have to tell him. She prayed to God for His strength and guidance, because she knew without Him, she would not make it through this.

And there, desperately out of hope, crouched underneath an abandoned staircase in the middle of her nightmare, Alaina felt God fill her up with exactly what she'd asked for—the strength to be still and know that, through Him, she could do anything.

Chapter 20

Ethan

"So you really think I did awesome?" Ben exclaimed with excited eyes.

Ethan nodded. "Yep, I really do. Way better than my first performance."

When Ethan had left Alaina to go hang out with Ben, he'd entered his room to find him engrossed in an enthralling episode of *Ben 10 Alien Force* on Cartoon Network. Raché had detached his IV, taken his vitals, and gotten him another three Popsicles since he'd awakened. "What can I say?" Raché said. "The kid loves Popsicles, and I love the kid."

Now, with Ben back in his signature ball cap, looking more and more like the kid Ethan knew (aside from the dark circles under his eyes and the paleness of his skin), they sat together watching cartoons and waiting for Alaina to come back and give them the okay to head back to Fairhope.

Ethan wondered what the doctor had told her. By the look on her face as he'd left her, he didn't imagine that she expected good news. His heart went out to her, and he wished he could help her in some way. He had money. It wouldn't be the slightest inconvenience for him to simply pay off every debt Alaina owed, but Ethan knew she'd never accept it. Alaina was independent and headstrong. She'd consider it pity money. What could he do? There had to be something.

Suddenly, Ben jumped up and shot into the bathroom like a lightning flash, leaving Ethan dumbfounded in the seat beside his bed. He was about to ask Ben if he was okay, but then he heard it. The sound of Ben heaving up every single Popsicle he had eaten that day. Ethan had heard that puking was a side effect of chemo. Poor Ben.

Ethan heard the toilet flush and the sink run a few seconds before Ben sheepishly opened the door and crawled back into his spot in the bed beside Ethan's chair.

"You okay, Ben? Ethan asked once Ben didn't offer up an explanation on his own.

"Yep."

The kid was just as headstrong as his sister. He'd acted the same way when he'd almost drowned at the beach—pretending like nothing was wrong.

"Does that happen every time you have to get a treatment?"

Ethan asked slowly.

Ben shrugged. "Not every time. Just sometimes."

Ethan sighed, wanting to find a way to talk to Ben and let him know that he was there for him. Granny had said that Ben looked up to Ethan as a role model, and Ethan took that much more seriously now than he had a few days ago.

"Does it hurt?" Ethan said hesitantly.

"Does what hurt?" Ben turned to him with curiosity swimming in his big brown eyes.

"Cancer."

Ben sat thoughtfully for a moment. "It does sometimes. But then God puts me to sleep so that I can't feel it."

"God puts you to sleep?" Ethan didn't mean to be skeptical, but...

"Yeah. When it does hurt, it hurts all over. So I just close my eyes and ask God to make me go to sleep so that I can't feel it. Then I wake up later and the pain is gone." Ben smiled as if every word he said made perfect sense.

"Ben, are you sure that's not just the pain medicine they give you?"

"Nope, I can tell the difference," he said matter-of-factly. "It's definitely God."

"But how do you *know*?" Ethan realized in that moment that he was not asking this question to sway Ben from his belief, but to help his own mind come to understand something that had awakened inside of him since he had met Alaina.

"I don't know," Ben said. "I just feel it, you know?"

"Yeah," Ethan said quietly. "I think that maybe I do."

"Know what?" Alaina reached the doorway at that moment. Ethan noticed instantly that'd she'd been crying and had unsuccessfully tried to wash her face and hide it. On the outside, she was smiling at her little brother, but Ethan saw in her eyes that it was all for show.

"Uh...we know that Ben has officially set the hospital record today for the most Popsicles eaten in a single visit," Ethan joked.

Ben laughed. Alaina gave Ethan a questioning look, but let it go quickly. He could tell that all of the fight was out of her for the day.

"Well, Ben-ben, you think you're ready to make the trip?" Alaina asked.

"I don't know..." he replied slyly." You think Granny would

make me some of that strawberry ice cream cheesecake stuff if we call and tell her I feel really bad?"

Ethan couldn't help but laugh. This kid was amazing. Even after all he'd been through that day, he still had a sense of humor.

"It will be too late for cheesecake by the time we get home," Alaina said, trying to fake a genuine smile, "but I'm sure we can work on getting you some for tomorrow. How's that sound?"

"Sounds like I'm ready to go home!" Ben jumped off the bed and bolted toward the door. "C'mon, what's taking you guys so long?" With that, he was out the door and headed for the elevator.

Alaina turned for the door, but Ethan grasped her fingers before she could leave. "Hey, you okay?"

She didn't answer. She just gave him a pained grin and released his hand so that she could follow her brother.

The car ride home didn't hold many changes from this. Ben fell asleep, once again, in the back seat, and Alaina spent the majority of the time staring out the passenger-side window. Ethan didn't press things. He could tell that Alaina had received bad news from the doctor, and honestly, he wasn't any more certain of a topic of conversation than she was. The idea of hope running out for Ben's recovery was affecting Ethan in a way he never would have expected that first afternoon when he'd met the lively, overly talkative little boy at the airstrip. Between spending the day teaching him guitar and playing in the sand, and sharing a room with him at night, Ethan had developed a bond with Ben, and the thought of losing him was something he could hardly stand.

It was well past nightfall when Ethan finally pulled into his grandmother's driveway. He shoved the gear shifter into the park position and stretched his arms out in front of him, stifling a long yawn.

"Finally," Alaina said groggily. She opened her door, grabbed her bag, and climbed out of the car. Ethan followed and opened the backseat door as Alaina gathered up the pillows and blankets that Granny had sent with her that morning. Ethan reached in, got a good grasp on Ben's hips and shoulders and heaved him into his arms. As he moved away from the car, Alaina kicked the car door shut behind them.

"How on earth do you do this every week?" Ethan whispered as she pulled her key out to unlock the front door. "I know you don't carry him in like this."

"Nope," she whispered back. "I usually have to wake him up

and make him walk. This is a much better system though." She flashed him a slight grin—the first one Ethan had glimpsed from her since they'd left the hospital.

Ethan and Alaina crept into the house as quietly as possible. The light in Granny's room was off, signifying that she'd already turned in for the night. Ted lay on the couch snoring just as loudly as he had since he'd started sleeping there. It suddenly hit Ethan what an imposition it was for Ted to have to be here with him. Sure, it was Ted's job, which was the exact thought that Ethan held when he'd arrived, but now that he stood back and actually saw things for what they were, he realized what a little brat he'd been. Ted was stuck on a narrow little couch that was a good foot and a half too short for him, with the coffee table pulled all the way up to the edge to block him from rolling off onto the floor during the night. Ethan resituated Ben in his arms and took his first step up the carpeted staircase, making a mental note to go out the next morning and purchase Ted a cot, or at the very least an air mattress.

When Ethan reached his and Ben's doorway, Alaina turned the knob and opened the door for him. Ethan was then hit with the fact that Ben—the little boy who was fighting for his life from an illness that was zapping every ounce of energy he had—was stuck climbing up and down a ladder just to sleep at night because Ethan didn't want to be inconvenienced with sleeping in the same room as a kid, much less being stuck with the top bunk.

Not tonight, not ever again, Ethan decided. He was healthy. He was capable. Who was he to want everything to be perfect just for him? Suddenly, his actions from the previous few days flooded back to his memory. The reason he and his mom had gotten in a fight in the first place...she'd just wanted to spend some time with her son, but that was too much to ask. *Ethan Carter* didn't have time for his own family. He was too busy going to pointless social events and getting himself drunk. Oh and let's not forget about the driving and almost killing someone's father part. Then there was his grandmother, whom he'd been less than friendly to when she'd picked him up at the airstrip. What, five years wasn't enough time away from her? He needed a little more in order to really appreciate how loving and forgiving of a woman she was? And then there was Alaina, who he'd fully expected to fall all over him and annoy him to the point of insanity because, oh wait, that's what he'd expected every girl to do. And Ben...Ethan was nothing but hateful and rude and sarcastic for the entire first day of his and Ben's time together, yet Ben still idolized him. What had he possibly done to deserve that? Ethan felt as though his knees were going weak. It was as though a lightbulb—no, make that a spotlight—had gone off in his head and awakened him to reality. It was humbling and, honestly, made him a little nauseous....

"You okay?"

Ethan's thoughts were jerked back to focus by Alaina's whisper.

"Do you need me to help you get him up to the top?"

Ethan hadn't realized how long he'd been standing there, in the middle of the bedroom, with Ben still sleeping in his arms. "Uh...no," he replied. "I'm just going to lay him on the bottom."

"But that's where you sleep," Alaina said.

"Not anymore." He bent over and carefully rolled Ben out of his arms and onto the bed. Ben instinctively curled up into a ball. Ethan adjusted the pillow under his head and pulled the blanket up to his shoulders. Alaina watched his every move with a strange fascination.

"Wow, you do that really well for a guy with no brothers and sisters," she pointed out as they walked back toward the doorway.

"Oh yeah, you think so, huh?" When they'd made it to the hallway, he slowly pulled the door closed and gave her a mischievous grin. "Well, I guess it's your turn, then."

Alaina's eyes widened, not quite sure whether to believe him, but Ethan laughed to himself thinking that she didn't know him well enough if she thought he wouldn't. He leaned down, swept an arm behind her knees and braced her back with his other arm. In one quick motion, he swept her into his arms and carried her toward her bedroom just as he had Ben.

"C'mon, big sis, you've had a long day and it's time for you to get some rest, too," he grinned.

Alaina's cheeks turned a dark crimson, and she playfully kicked as though she wanted him to let go, but Ethan could tell she wasn't putting up a real fight. "I can't believe you're carrying me like some little kid!" she laughed as he reached her door. The sound of her laughter made him feel triumphant, a task he hadn't been sure he'd be able to accomplish that night.

Ethan carefully stretched out the fingers of his right hand just enough to shimmy the handle and open her door. He made the distance from Alaina's door to her bed quickly. He held onto her tightly with one arm and pulled her blankets back with the other. Vigilantly, he rolled her out of his arms, just as he had done Ben, and pulled her covers up to her shoulders. Her dark hair cascaded across the top of her pillow except for one section, which lay sprawled loosely across her forehead. Ethan took the slightest moment to take her all in. In the darkness of her bedroom, lit only by the moonlight shining through the window, her soft skin and big brown eyes seemed to almost glow a shade equal to that of the light reflecting off her pillow. He reached his hand to her forehead and gently swiped the section of hair back to its proper position behind her ear.

Alaina's eyes found his and held them for what felt like an eternity. Then, to Ethan's surprise, she pushed herself up to a sitting position, reached her arms out from the blankets, wrapped them around his neck, and pulled his body to hers. When their lips met, Ethan felt as if an explosion had gone off inside his heart. He melted in her arms and wanted nothing more than to stay in that moment. Forget the tour, and the producers, and his arrogant agent. He would give them all up in a heartbeat to stay in that moment with Alaina. Her kiss was soft and sweet and genuine. It wasn't needy or forced. It was long and deep and...perfect. When they finally parted, Alaina buried her head in his neck. Ethan sought to catch his breath and his heart.

"Wow, what was that for?" he whispered, refusing to let her go.

"Just cause," she said.

Ethan wanted so badly to ask Alaina what she'd been told in the doctor's office, but once again, a strong feeling in his gut made him stop before he said a word. Instead he decided to ask her a question that he'd been thinking about the entire drive home from Birmingham.

"Ali, can I ask you something?" he said hesitantly.

"Sure." Her head never left his neck. He continued to hold her.

"When you pray...to God," Ethan felt weird announcing His name out loud. "What do you ask for? And I don't mean when you pray for other people. I mean, what's the one thing that you want for yourself?"

"Hmm," she said. "Well, sometimes I pray for guidance, sometimes wisdom. But I guess I'd have to say that most often I just pray for strength, you know? Just the strength to get through each day as well as I did the one before." She turned to look at him and once again found his eyes. "Why do you ask?"

Ethan ignored her question. "And do you find it? Does God give you strength when you ask for it?"

She cast a small smile and replied without hesitation. "Yeah, He does."

"But how do you *know*?" Ethan persisted.

Alaina leaned forward and again allowed her lips to connect with his. When she pulled away, she said, "That's easy. I know because He sent me you."

~~**~~

Ethan took another glance at the miniature grandfather clock that hung on the wall above his grandmother's ancient television. She didn't have cable, but he'd managed to rustle up some of his grandfather's old Western VHS tapes. The picture was a bit bouncy, and every now and then the sound would fade in and out, but it was better than nothing.

Alaina had left early for work that morning. Ethan hadn't even caught a glimpse of her in the hallway. Ben was still upstairs sleeping. Ted had gone into town to run some errands for Granny Mae, and Ethan had sent his debit card along with instructions to pick out the nicest air mattress money could buy. The little house was quiet, and making the understatement of the century, Ethan was *bored*. It also didn't help that every time he looked at the clock, a span of only a few minutes had passed. Ethan didn't know why he was so antsy. It wasn't like he had bigger and better things he could be doing—although everyone involved with his tour was probably losing their minds at the moment wondering when he would be returning....

In fact, that exact question had been plaguing Ethan's mind as well. He knew he couldn't stay at his grandmother's forever. Obviously, he had a career he had to get back to. He had fans who paid good money to get tickets to his shows, and he'd already had to postpone two venues since he'd been there. It was more of an issue of making the call. Number one: he was going to have to face his mom when he called, and he knew he owed her a huge apology. Would he have felt that way a few days ago? Not a chance. But a few things had changed since then. Number two: he was going to have to leave Alaina. She had finally opened up to him. He just wasn't quite ready to go back yet.

He'd checked his calendar, and he only had one more concert scheduled in the next couple of weeks. He knew that one would be an easy reschedule because it was a fairly small venue somewhere up in Washington. He figured that if he could only hold out till then, it would give him and Alaina more time to figure out how they were going to make this complicated mess work. And to top all of that off, Ethan wasn't quite ready to leave Ben yet either. It seemed that Ben had gotten worse in the few short days Ethan had been there. What was going to happen when he had to leave for a couple of months at a time? Ethan shook those thoughts from his mind. They were too much to think about.

He needed something to occupy his time today—something to take his mind off of Ben and something to calm his racing heart from the memory of Alaina's kiss. He couldn't believe he wasn't exhausted because trying to go to sleep after she'd bid him goodnight had been next to impossible. He wanted to do something special for Alaina. And not something generic like flowers or chocolate. He wanted to do something that showed her how much he cared about her. A gift that showed her that there had been effort put into it. He wanted to do something that would mesh both of their personalities and show her how easy it would be for them to be together once they got Ethan's scheduling straightened out.

That's when he was hit with the perfect idea, as though he was being inspired by some little voice in his head telling him all of the right paths he should take.

Ethan jumped up from the couch, suddenly much more eager about the day ahead. He had a plan. He had a purpose. He needed help.

Ethan darted to the kitchen and hopped up into one of the stools at the island. Granny Mae stood on the opposite side holding a rolling pin, the entire front of her apron caked in flour. She was putting the finishing touches on the strawberry ice cream cheesecake for Ben and was starting on a homemade chocolate pie that Ted had placed an order for the day before.

"Hey there, Lil E," she smiled. "What are you so happy about this morning?"

"Granny, I want to do something for Alaina," he said a bit sheepishly. "And I think I'm going to need your help."

Granny looked up to him, and her smile widened. "I'd love to help you, baby! What did you have in mind?"

Ethan paused only for a moment, already knowing exactly what he needed to say.

"I need you to teach me everything you know about Fairhope..."

Ethan paused, not believing the words that were about come out of his mouth. "...and I need a Bible."

Chapter 21

Alaina

It was evening. A dark pink sun was starting its slow decent over the wide Mobile Bay coastline when Alaina finally pulled into the drive from a long day of hard waitressing. Tips had been great, which was definitely a plus, but that hadn't made the thought of coming home any easier for her. That morning, as per her normal routine of spending a few minutes with Ben before she left for the day, Alaina had been presented with what she knew without a doubt would be the most difficult question that she would ever have to answer.

Ben wanted to know what the doctor had said.

Alaina had thought of little other than the answer to that question ever since Dr. Rouse spoke with her, but that didn't leave her any more prepared to deliver the news to her little brother. She'd told him that they would talk about it when she got home from work. Alaina couldn't even deal with the possibility of it in her own mind. How was she to tell him? That would be like confirming that it really was happening. Alaina wasn't ready to lose her brother yet. Sure, he had driven her crazy growing up: getting into all her stuff, constantly wanting to be in her room when her friends were over, tattling on her for every little thing. But that didn't mean that she didn't love him or that she didn't want him around anymore.

It all seemed so unfair. There she was, seventeen years old, and she was living the life of a forty-year-old. This was not her job! She should have been the one breaking down and crying and getting consolation from her parents that everything would be okay, that they would take care of everything, and that they would all get through this hard time together. But no, she was all on her own, playing the role of mother, father, and sister all at one time. She had to be Ben's rock, but who was going to be her rock?

Her mind instantly flashed to Ethan, but she pushed that back just as quickly. She loved what they were becoming, but she would not use him as her crutch. This was not his battle. Granted, she couldn't imagine what that visit to the treatment center would have been like without him there—with his playful banter with the kids, his deep respect for the nurses, and his never-ending support that kept her from losing her grip.

The truth was, she'd already involved Ethan too deeply, but she just couldn't seem to keep him away. She knew it would be better for him to stay as far away from this mess as possible, to go on living his life as he always had before he'd met them, but every time he offered to spend time with her, Alaina just couldn't quite bring herself to tell him no. And time with her meant time with her complicated life. She wondered how long he would stay involved. When would it become too much for him? When would it be simpler for him to just pick up and go back to where he'd left off?

Alaina knew it would come eventually. What was developing between her and Ethan seemed too good to be true. They'd spent such a short amount of time together, but their connection was so much deeper than she'd ever experienced with anyone else.

Alaina realized then that she'd been sitting in the driveway for a good five minutes with the car still on, still in drive, with her foot pressed tightly to the brake. There was no more stalling now. She was home. There was only getting out of the car, walking in to face Ben, telling him the news of his fate in the most honest and delicate way she possibly could, and being as strong as she could be for him. There was no magic formula or secret trick. There was only doing what she knew she had to do. So, very reluctantly, Alaina shoved the gear shift into park, took a deep breath, straightened her shoulders, and forced her hand to the door handle.

The trek up the flower-lined walkway to the whitewashed front porch seemed ten miles long, and that was perfectly fine with her. She would have gladly walked many more just to keep from having to enter that house. As she climbed the small flight of white wooden steps and approached the front door, she could hear Looney Tunes echoing throughout the living room. When she opened the door and took a look around the room, her eyes instantly zoned in on the couch, and to her utter amazement, a small smile formed in the corner of her lips.

Ben was sitting on the couch curled up under Ethan's arm, a huge bowl of spaghetti in his lap and red sauce outlining the entire circle of his mouth. They were laughing together about the latest way Wile E. Coyote was using an anvil to cause himself bodily harm.

"Hey Ali!" Ben jumped off the couch and came over to his sister, wrapping her in a big bear hug. "How was work?"

Alaina instantly noticed the redness and strain in his eyes. He'd been throwing up today. She'd expected it—it was always this way the day after chemo—but it never got any easier to see. He looked pale and didn't show signs of having much energy, but he was still smiling, so she let out a little laugh and bent down to return his hug. "Not too bad. Mr. Carn came in to eat with his wife today."

Ben scrunched up his nose in a cute little grimace. "Is he the stinky one?"

Alaina grinned. "Yep, that's him."

"Eeeww! What'd you do?"

"I saw him coming through the window and took my break," Alaina replied with a sly grin. "Gabby ended up waiting on him."

Ben laughed. "Good one!"

Alaina reached behind her waist and untied her apron by pulling one string at a time. She pulled it off and flopped it down on the arm of the couch. Her eyes veered to Ethan, who was pretending to be engrossed in Looney Tunes. She appreciated that he was trying to respect her time with Ben. "So what have you two boys been doing today?"

Ethan glanced up. "Oh, a little of this...a little of that. We men don't share our secrets, do we Ben?"

Ben's shoulders straightened a bit, and he crossed his arms, the cutest scrunch forming in his nose. "That's right! We're men. We keep our secrets."

Alaina couldn't help but laugh. "Is that right? Okay, I guess I can accept that."

When Ben and Ethan both looked up with cheesy, not to mention guilty, grins, Alaina new that something was up. "Okay, I retract my previous statement. What's going on?"

Granny Mae entered the sitting room from the kitchen, pulling off her own tomato-splattered apron and hanging it on a hook in the interior door frame. "We're going out," she said with a smile of excitement.

"Out?"

"Yes, out. This family needs a break from this house, and we are about to get one." She grinned even bigger.

"Family?" Alaina had always thought of Granny Mae as family, but never put together the idea of her being Ethan's grandmother, too. What did that make the two of them? Weird. She noticed Ethan was thinking the same thing because an amused grin was playing across his features. He glanced up at her from the couch and flashed a quick wink. She tried to hide the blush in her cheeks and focused back on Granny Mae.

"So we're going out?" Alaina said a bit hesitantly. "Ben, are you sure you're up for that tonight? I can tell you've had a rough day. Are you sure you wouldn't rather us stay here and catch up on Looney

Tunes' reruns?" *And let me tell you that there is basically no chance that you will survive this cancer and you probably won't live long enough to become a teenager and experience all that life has to offer; like love and friendship and family and...Maybe this going out thing isn't such a bad idea after all.*

"Sis, I'm fine. Now let's go! We've been waiting all afternoon for you to get home, and we're burning some serious sunlight time. C'mon!" With that, Ben was out the door and headed for Ethan's rental. He could be heard inside the house from the front lawn. "No offense, Granny Mae, but we're taking the cool car tonight! Give the clunker a night off!"

No one could hide their laughter. Granny Mae called out to Ben, "That clunker is still in great shape I'll have you know!"

Ethan rose from the couch and reached down to a bag on the other side of the couch arm. When he stood up, he caught her eye and the accusatory expression on her face. "What?" he asked innocently.

"What's in the bag?"

He shrugged.

"You planned this didn't you?"

His guilty grin gave him away. "Maybe."

"Sometimes I don't know about you rock stars," Alaina said, "always sneaking around and planning stuff behind people's backs."

"Trying to do something nice for people we care about," he added, closing the distance between them and causing a slight chill to roll up her spine. "Your right, we're a despicable breed."

His breath was hot against her face, his lips only inches from hers. She wanted to retort with some equally playful comment, but all she managed to squeak out was, "You care about me?" He'd told her before, but each time it just got harder and harder to believe.

His grin immediately erased, and his expression became serious. He didn't reply. Instead, he let the bag fall to the floor and reached his hand to the nape of her neck, entangling his fingers in her recently ponytail-released mess of hair, and pulled her lips to his. He was gentle and his lips matched perfectly with hers. Alaina let out a low involuntary sigh and fell into his kiss even deeper. Sensing her approval, his arms moved to the small of her back and he pulled in her body so that it fit perfectly against his. Alaina's heart was racing...no it was about to reach light speed. In fact, it was a little much. Fighting every fleshly desire in her all too human body, she tried to force her muscles to pull away, but then she didn't have to.

Ethan released her with the gentlest of nudges, kissing the tip of her nose before completely letting go of everything but her hand. He gave her a guilty grin. "Sorry I got a little carried away." With that, he reached back down to pick up the mysterious bag and led her out to the car to meet the others; all the while, Alaina tried to catch her breath.

~~**~~

Ethan

The night was going better than Ethan could have ever hoped for. Ted had left early to map out the spot and couldn't have done a better job. According to Granny Mae's directions, there was a privately owned piece of land on the tip of a bluff at the outskirts of town. There was a single log cabin with a porch that extended out over the side of the cliff. It offered an idealistic, no competition view of the Bay and the most spectacular sunset.

Problem was, it was extremely pricey to rent. But to Ethan, it sounded perfect. He hadn't even made a dent in the allowance money his mother banned him there with. He wanted this night to be all about Alaina and Ben. Ben went on and on during their alone time together about how much he loved the ocean and the stars and how he never got to see them anymore because he was always sick. Alaina had once explained to him the beauty she saw behind God's creation. In Ethan's eyes, this was money well spent.

Ethan still wasn't sure about his personal feelings toward the whole God thing, but he was sure about his feelings for Alaina. And if being in the midst of His creation caused the same twinkle that formed in her eyes the night she'd first talked to him about her beliefs, well, he could stand to hear a little more about it. Anything to see her look that alive.

Now, they were all seated on the porch, warning Ben over and over again to not lean too far out over the railing and taking in the spectacular view of the setting sun out on the twinkling ocean horizon. Alaina was next to Ethan and reached her hand forward, taking his fingers in hers.

"This is amazing," she whispered, her gaze never veering from the view ahead. "This must have cost a fortune. I can't believe you did this."

Before Ethan could reply, Granny Mae jumped in. "Oh that's not all he did, darlin'." She cast a questionable glance at her grandson, and Ethan nodded, approving that she continue. "I told Lil E all about how you and Ben hate missing Wednesday night church on the days you go to the hospital, so he suggested that while we're here, we have our own little service."

The utter look of shock that flashed across Alaina's expression was impossible to not distinguish. She shifted her gaze and eyed him curiously. "You suggested that?"

"He even handpicked the passage to be covered," Granny Mae added proudly.

Alaina's confused gaze never faltered. "But, you..."

"Wanted to do something nice for you," Ethan finished for her. "But trust me, it wasn't without a whole lot of help from Ben and Granny Mae," he added quickly before Alaina presumed he'd been lying all along about knowing absolutely nothing about the Bible. The truth was that he *still* knew absolutely nothing about the Bible. Granted, as he and Granny Mae and Ben navigated their way through the overwhelmingly huge book that afternoon, he'd managed to learn a little. Granny Mae showed him the difference between the Old and New Testaments. She showed him how to use the index and the concordance. She even told him a little about the men who wrote some of the books. The more Ethan listened to his grandmother, the more he saw that same sparkle fill her eye that he always noticed in Alaina. It was the same with Ben. He was beginning to wonder if maybe they had more things figured out than he'd previously given them credit for.

Deciding to ignore the vulnerable feeling rising in him as Alaina continued to gaze into his eyes with a combination of confusion and astonishment, he turned away and reached for the bag he'd brought along from the house. In it were several Bibles that Granny Mae had managed to scrounge up from around the house: her own enormous wide print, black leather Bible; a thin, colorful paperback for Ben; Alaina's was a combination of soft pink and brown leather with what must have been a hundred multicolored shards of paper bookmarking various places; and finally, for Ethan, a dusty gray hardback, bound in a smooth leather carrying case that had once belonged to his grandfather. That was all Granny Mae had found. Ted would have to share.

But, to Ethan's own amazement, when Granny Mae spoke up and asked, "Who would like to start us off with prayer?" Ted pulled his own travel-sized Bible out of his back jean pocket and said, "I'll do it."

What? Silent Ted reads the Bible? Silent Ted prays?

Everyone bowed their head and closed their eyes. Ethan, quickly catching on, mimicked their actions and did the same.

"Father," Ted began, his voice suddenly strong and confident. "We come to you today with thankful hearts. We wish to thank you for friends and family and the opportunity to sit in the midst of your creation and offer words up to you."

Wow, Ted's pretty good at this praying stuff.

"Lord, there are many seasons in our lives and we pray that you will be the central focus of each of them. Whether we're taking on new members of our family (*Was that meant for Granny?*) or taking on new responsibilities we fear we can't handle (*Alaina?*) or dealing with changes that are scary and not always explainable (*Poor Ben.*) or trying to figure out what kind of people we will choose to become (*Uh-oh, that one was for me.*); God we pray that you will guide our decisions and that we will step back and be still enough to hear your guidance and allow you to lead as only you know how. Please bless these people, Father, and bless this study. It is in Jesus's name that we pray. Amen."

A light chorus of "amens" echoed around Ethan.

"That was absolutely beautiful, Ted," Granny Mae said. "Thank you."

Ted nodded and gave Ethan a slight wink. How had he not known before that Ted was a Christian? Because silent Ted hardly ever talked, that's why. But now Ethan understood why. There's no way Ted would ever approve of the types of decisions Bruce asked of Ethan every day.

"Okay, honey," Granny Mae continued, shifting her gaze back to Ethan. His stomach suddenly tightened, knowing exactly what was next to come. "Would you like to read the passage you picked out?"

He took a hesitant breath. "Uh, yeah sure." It amazed Ethan at his unexpected feeling of awkwardness. He could perform in front of thousands at a time, but when it came to reading a few lines from a book, he froze. It was just a book wasn't it? Ethan was beginning to wonder.

He placed his fingers on the bookmarked spot he'd made earlier that day and spoke; trying to locate at least a portion of the confidence he'd heard in Ted's tone as he prayed. "Well, I did have a lot of help, so this wasn't all my decision, but we picked Psalms 23."

Truth be known, Granny Mae had recommended that scripture. Said it would be very fitting for everyone's current situations. Maybe part of Ethan's nervousness was due to the fact that he hadn't actually sat down and read the passage the way he needed to. He'd skimmed over it, finally settling on it because he'd read so many random passages that day and hadn't had a clue what any of them meant. This one seemed the most direct, but he hadn't paid a whole lot of attention to the detail. He only hoped he would read it the way it was supposed to be read. Ethan took one last deep breath and a slight glance across the horizon. *Oh well, here goes nothing.* As he read, he concentrated on the meaning of each verse, determined to figure out why these people loved this book so much.

"Psalms 23," Ethan began. "The Lord is my shepherd. I shall not want. He makes me to lie down in green pastures. He leads me beside the still waters. He restores my soul. He leads me in the paths of righteousness for His name's sake." Ethan paused, realizing he hadn't taken a breath yet. He took one deep inhalation and continued, never allowing his eyes to lift from the page. "Yea, though I walk through the valley of the shadow of death, I will fear no evil; for You are with me. Your rod and Your staff, they comfort me. You prepare a table before me in the presence of my enemies. You anoint my head with oil. My cup runs over. Surely goodness and mercy shall follow me all the days of my life. And I will dwell in the house of the Lord forever."

When Ethan finished reading, he skimmed back over the passage again to make sure he hadn't messed anything up. It wasn't until a few seconds later that he realized everyone was silent. He raised his gaze and found all eyes on him. His stomach immediately tightened again.

Granny Mae flashed a loving smile. "Beautifully done, Lil E."

Ethan managed a self-conscious grin. "Thanks."

Now that Ethan actually paid attention to the words of the psalm, he understood why Granny Mae would want him to choose it. Alaina and Ben had faced that...what was it called...valley of death. They had faced that after their parents' accident. Now, Ben wasn't just facing the valley, he was walking right through the middle of it. Was it possible that there actually was a God that could provide enough comfort to Ben and Alaina that they didn't have to fear? Was He really with them? Would He really comfort them and make it feel as though they were lying in the middle of beautiful pastures without a care in the world? That was a beautiful thought, and just as Ethan was about to dismiss it, the strangest feeling seemed to flow through his veins as if he'd just injected some kind of happy drug. What was that feeling?

For the rest of the night, Ethan listened to everyone talk about the guy, David, who had written the psalm. Turns out, David was a song writer, just like Ethan. They each compared their favorite scriptures and read them out loud. He listened until the sun set entirely and the twinkling pink ocean surface was replaced with a jet black sheet of sparkling stars.

Yes, Ethan listened as he had never listened before, and with each word spoken—without his even realizing it was happening—Ethan's heart slowly softened and he finally began to believe.

Chapter 22

Ethan

The following week with Alaina was nothing short of magical. They'd spent each possible moment together. She'd even convinced him to attend church with the family on Sunday under his Brandon alias. That had been interesting, but not entirely bad either.

Alone time with Alaina was brief and usually only happened after Ben was tucked comfortably into bed. Since Ben's last appointment, the one in which Ethan accompanied, he had been put on an entirely new medication regimen. And it was extensive to say the least. Ben stayed so drugged up on pain meds that he was beginning to be asleep more often than he was awake. Alaina continued to work the majority of her days away, doing her seventeen-year-old best to provide enough money to at least make minimum payments on Ben's hospital bills. It made Ethan practically nauseous to wonder what the total was up to by now. He'd love to contribute—he had money to spare—but he knew Alaina would never accept it.

Ethan continued to hide away in the house most of the time, but even to his own surprise, he wasn't bored in the least. In fact, he had taken to writing again. The psalm of David had inspired him a little. He'd even peeked at a few of the other psalms when no one was watching. Ethan was always amazed at the feeling behind the words he read. Some were consumed with power, some with courage, and some with love. But in each was the same message over and over. They called upon a God who could offer them exactly what they needed in their present situation. They didn't fear. They didn't anger. They didn't back down. And in Ethan's eyes, that made for some pretty good lyrics.

When Ethan wasn't writing, he was thinking. His mother's plan, much to the sake of his pride, had been a complete success. Ethan had never felt like a bigger jerk in his entire life. What was he thinking getting into that stupid Camaro? Why was he even drinking in the first place? He was successful, with a lifestyle that ninety-nine percent of the world only dreamed of, and there he was, wasting it away on alcohol and a self-centered girlfriend. Mistreating his mom, who he knew was one of the few people who actually had his best interest at heart. And being too wrapped up in his own circumstances to even realize the types of tragedies that were happening all around him. There were people out there, kids in fact, who were suffering, and he was spending his time singing pointless little pop songs about love stories that weren't even realistic, much less possible. He hadn't understood it when Alaina first said it, but now he did. He was wasting his God-given talent.

Yes, God-given.

That was something else that Ethan had been considering this past week. Once he'd allowed his heart to open a little to the possibility of a Creator, everything just seemed to make a little more sense. He didn't just wonder aimlessly about where he'd come from, or why he was alive to begin with, or what the whole purpose of his time on this Earth was all about. To be honest, it was a little exhilarating to not claim to have all the answers.

But all of these new mindsets didn't change Ethan's current situation. Truth be known, he had still messed up (messed up big-time), and he was still in trouble with his mom. He was still mid-tour, with at least fifty more stops to go in the United States before its completion. And to top all of that off, he was still falling more and more every day for a girl who he potentially had no future with.

Whoever said that just because you believe in God your life becomes easier was totally delusional.

Ethan had already ignored five persistent phone calls from Bruce that week and wondered what his mother would say if she knew Bruce had been calling. He imagined Bruce would probably be in some trouble of his own.

Bruce's voicemails started out with humor. "Hey there, lil buddy. How's hillbilly hell treating you?" Then they'd turned to desperation. "All right superstar, you've got to pull it together. I've got upcoming venue owners emailing me angry letters to find out if you're going to be able to make it to your next concert. So far, we've only missed three shows. Right now, the press thinks you have laryngitis. Come back soon and maybe we can salvage this whole deal." The final message portrayed a tone of hostility that Ethan had never heard from his fun-loving agent. "Mr. Carter, I would like you to remember that you have signed a contract to complete this tour. It would be in your best financial interest to return to it as soon as possible before more drastic measures must be taken to assure your arrival."

Ethan raked his hands through his hair as he leaned backward in the patio chair at the little table in the garden. When had life become so complicated? Were these the consequences to bad decisions? He didn't want to think about his future, or his agent, or his tour right now. All he wanted was for Alaina to get home from work. Granny Mae and Ted had taken Ben to an arts and crafts show downtown, and Ethan was looking forward to some quality time with Alaina.

Ethan would be perfectly satisfied with a lifetime of moments just like the one's he'd shared with Alaina this week. Secret kisses in the hallway. Long talks in the garden until all hours of the night. Ethan sharing thoughts and feelings that he'd never told anyone else. He told Alaina about his dad leaving. About how he felt deserted and was still angry and bitter about it. He talked about how he felt like he needed to support his mom to make up for his dad's absence...one of the reasons why he worked so hard to be successful in his performing career. And Alaina always listened to it all with nonjudgmental ears. She always knew exactly what he needed to hear, whether it be just a word of advice, or something she'd read in a recent morning devotional.

And usually, at least once a day, there was a time that Alaina would allow Ethan to make her forget all the complications of her life. Those he always looked forward to. She'd sink into his arms, frail and tired in body, but alive and vibrant in spirit as her kisses filled him with an excitement unlike any other he'd ever felt. But Ethan was respectful and never pushy. He'd be angry with himself for being any different with Alaina. She deserved the best guy, and he could only attempt to be a fragment of that for her.

Ethan certainly couldn't deny his feelings for Alaina even though, at times, he'd tried to fight them. He understood her hesitation in their relationship. It was complicated, and most likely, it would only get worse as time progressed. But he was past the point of trying to fight the masses of obstacles. What he felt for Alaina was bigger than all of that, which was exactly what he planned on sharing with her tonight.

He glanced down at his watch. Quarter to eight. Alaina was working a double today so he had at least another hour before she would get home. He rose from the patio chair and made his way toward the sitting room, deciding that he might take a look at a few more of those psalms while everyone was out of the house. He'd just flipped the Bible open when a solid knock at the door resounded throughout the room.

Wondering who on earth could possibly be coming to visit at eight o'clock—surely not a salesman—Ethan rose from the couch, leaving the Bible open on the coffee table, and went to answer the knock. When he swung the door open, the bright mascara-doused eyes that stared back surprised him more than any salesman ever could. The girl wore a dress that belonged only in a city night club, with large platform heels and some of the longest legs Ethan had tried so hard to forget.

"Vanessa?"

The blonde beauty smiled slyly. "Hi love. Nice hair."

"Wh...what are you doing here?" Ethan's heart pounded, and surprisingly not because of how his ex-girlfriend looked. It was as if Ethan's two worlds—the crazy rock star world versus the calm figure-his-life-out world—had just collided together causing a massive whirlwind that raced through his mind like a southern state twister. "How did you know where to find me?"

"Bruce called me. He sounded a little desperate. Said something about your mom threatening to cancel the tour if he visited you, but that she had never mentioned a problem with my visiting you." She smiled. Her teeth were so white they could blind a person in pure sunlight. "So here I am. Now are you going to invite me in or not, silly?"

"I..." Before Ethan could reply that he didn't really think that was the best idea, Vanessa pushed passed him and entered the small sitting room. Her heels clanked loudly against the hardwood floors. Once in the room, her hands went directly to her hips and an amused grin surfaced on her features.

"Wow, no wonder Bruce said he had to tie you to the plane to get you here. This place is a dump! How have you managed to keep your sanity this long?"

Ethan instantly wondered what he'd seen in Vanessa...aside from the legs. She was a vain attention hog.

"That must have been a pretty bad wreck for your mom to banish you to this place," she continued, running a judgmental eye over every square inch of the room. "Exactly how drunk were you, anyway?"

Ethan paused. "Wait, how do you know why I'm here? Bruce told me the press thinks its laryngitis."

Vanessa let out a short laugh. "Do I look like the press, doll? I don't know one reporter who has legs like mine, and trust me, I know a lot of them." She shot him a wink and moved to the couch. When she sat, her dress rode up to her upper thigh, and as she crossed her legs in front of her, the high heels forced the muscles to protrude slightly in her calves.

Ethan shook his head and turned toward the grandfather clock that rested against the wall, trying to figure out what to do. Vanessa could not be there. Not now. Not ever. He had to make her leave, but how?

"Oh, double wow." With a disgusted look, Vanessa pushed the book on the coffee table around with the tip of her heel. "Don't tell me these people are Bible-thumpers too, E? How have you stood this for so long?

You must be losing your mind. I've got some stuff in my bag if you need a little..." She let out a mischievous laugh under her breath. "...coping juice."

Ethan couldn't believe his ears. Was that "coping juice" not what landed him here in the first place? And now she was offering it to him as if it was the perfect solution to his every problem in life. How could he have ever been so ridiculously stupid to believe that people like Vanessa really cared about him?

Ethan took a deep breath, silently cooling his temper. "Why are you here, Vanessa? Don't you have a party to be crashing or something?"

Vanessa rose gracefully from her place on the couch and turned to Ethan with a playful grin. "Bruce sent me to hurry this little rehab session along. He figured once you saw what you'd left behind, you'd be ready to come back. I've been worried about you, E. We all have."

"Well, Bruce was wrong." Ethan said. "And what's up with the timely concern? I've been here almost a month and haven't received so much as a phone call from you."

"Baby, I've been busy. I was signed to that ad campaign for Victoria's Secret the day after you left. I'm going to be an Angel! Can you believe it?" Vanessa's eyes glazed over as the imaginary camera flashes filled them. "Our dreams are coming true, E. You're on this great tour. My modeling is taking off full force. Soon, we'll be the most talked about couple in Hollywood."

Ethan smirked. A few weeks ago, Vanessa's daydreams would have sent his ego into overdrive. Now, the idea of that life seemed like a distant reality...one that he could definitely stand to do without. None of what Vanessa said included him living his dream because he loved to write and loved to sing and play. That life was about getting the most attention, no matter what the costs.

"Like I was saying," Vanessa continued. A sultry smile spread across her perfectly blushed cheeks, and she started to slowly step toward where Ethan stood between her and the kitchen entryway.

"I've missed you, E." Her voice lowered seductively, and she ran her fingertip down the length of his chest. "We have a lot to catch up on."

Ethan took a step back, realizing that just because he'd made the decision to leave Vanessa after their drunken fight, didn't mean that he'd actually voiced that to her. He'd just assumed she knew by the fact that he hadn't made an attempt to call her in so long. Obviously, she didn't catch on too quickly.

"About that," he said, working to maintain his focus as she sauntered closer and closer to where he was now backed completely against the wall beside the door facing. "I think that maybe I should have explained things a little more clearly...."

As if sensing her upcoming rejection, Vanessa took another step forward, but caught her heel on the edge of the center rug and flung forward. Instinctively, Ethan reached out to catch her, but Vanessa was quick and landed directly in his arms, their faces only centimeters apart.

"That's much better," she whispered. And before Ethan could move a muscle, her lips were pressed to his, hard and eager, pushing his head back against the solid wall. At first he tried to sway his head side to side to release the grip that her lips had on his, but when that wasn't working, he placed his hands on her shoulders and pushed her off.

But it was too late.

A soft gasp echoed in his ears, burning a hole in his memory that would last until the day he died. *No. Please no.*

Vanessa, also hearing the gasp, spun around, finally releasing Ethan from her strong hold. "Oh, who do we have here?" She ran her eyes up and down Alaina with the same expression she'd used on the furniture.

"Ali," Ethan voiced desperately. "Wh...what are you doing home so soon?"

Don't ask that, you idiot! That only makes it look worse!

Alaina's expression was flat, but Ethan could see the hurt welling in her eyes. He'd memorized those eyes.

"Slow night. Gabby let me come home early." Her voice held a brisk tone. "Who's your friend?" But then he saw her take a closer look, and a flash of understanding washed through the hurt. "Oh...Vanessa."

Vanessa eyed Alaina's waitressing attire and sloppy ponytail with a visible look of disdain. "Of course," Vanessa said, as if the entire world should know who she was without having to ask. "And...you are?"

Alaina gave her a look that under different circumstances would have made Ethan laugh, but he had absolutely nothing to laugh about in this moment. Instead, her eyes flashed to his and he felt as if she'd burned through him with her gaze.

An awkward silence filled the room, but Alaina finally spoke, trying to keep hold of a shake in her voice. "What's going on, Ethan? Why is Vanessa here?"

Before Ethan could even open his mouth, Vanessa rounded on Alaina, taking on her sassy stance. "Why shouldn't I be here? I am his girlfriend after all."

Oh, no.

Alaina looked like someone had punched her in the stomach. "His...his what?" She spun on Ethan. "Your what?"

"You thought one little alcohol-induced fight would be enough to break up the hottest couple in Hollywood?" Vanessa scoffed and turned to Ethan. "Seriously, E, who is this girl?"

Alaina's eyes grew wider, and Ethan knew that she was putting all of the pieces together. "I guess I wasn't aware that Ethan was a drinker."

It was obvious that Alaina was just humoring Vanessa now. Ethan knew it was time to step in.

"I...was..." he stammered. There was no way this was going to end well for him.

Vanessa butted in again. "E, don't be modest." She turned to Alaina. "This guy holds the A-list record for longest keg stand. He's a legend."

Alaina smirked. "Is that so?"

"Yeah, and he's usually better at not getting caught, but I guess fighting with me really did a number on him." Vanessa put her hand on Ethan's shoulder. He instantly jerked it away. "That wreck totaled out his brand new Camaro! But you can just get a new one, can't you, baby?" She smiled playfully, fully enjoying rubbing their money into Alaina's face.

At this point, if Ethan's mother had not taught him to never hit a girl, he could have knocked the paint right off of Vanessa's face. His head hung with his eyes cemented to his feet. He didn't dare look up. He could already feel Alaina's expression boring into the top of his head.

"The wreck," she said slowly, finally visualizing the whole picture. "The one that made your mom send you here. You were drunk? You drank and got in a vehicle and drove and got in a wreck?"

Ethan finally looked up with a grief-stricken expression. All he could do was whisper, "yes."

"And was anyone else involved in this accident?" Tears were visible at the corners of Alaina's eyes, and Ethan knew exactly why. She was remembering her parents' accident, just like he knew she would if he ever told her the real reason he was there.

"There was a man." Ethan voiced quietly. "I almost hit his car, but I veered at the last second and missed him."

Granny Mae was right all along. He should have just told her on day one. Any response from Alaina would have to have been better than the disgusted look of disappointment she held now.

Alaina didn't say a word. She just kept staring at him in disbelief.

Finally, Vanessa turned to Ethan and said, "What's her problem?"

That's all it took. Alaina spun and bolted for the door.

"Ali wait!"

Ethan took off after her, not even caring that a dumbfounded Vanessa was still standing in the sitting room wondering why he was chasing after this other girl. As he hit the lawn, a crack of lightning lit up the night sky, followed shortly by a blast of thunder. Alaina was already in her car and backing out of the driveway. Ethan bolted across the lawn, but she was gone.

He raced back into the house and into the kitchen where Granny Mae had left the keys to her car on top of the island. He hoped she wouldn't mind his borrowing her car, but he didn't have time to call and ask for permission. He'd just have to ask for forgiveness later.

"Ethan, stop chasing that girl like some love sick puppy," Vanessa called through his frantic state of panic. It's beneath you, doll. She'll never be like us, and you know it."

Ethan snatched up the keys and paused at the front door to voice his retort.

"Oh, I'm counting on it."

With that, he raced from the house, jumped in the car, and peeled out into the street. He knew his chances of changing Alaina's mind were slim, but if only for the sake of never having to ask "what if," he knew he had to try.

Chapter 23

Ethan

It was a long shot, but Ethan managed to find Alaina at the first location he tried. She was at the pier where they'd shared their first date, standing apron free, uniform shirt untucked, with her long, dark hair blowing wildly in the stormy wind. Her arms hung lifelessly to her sides, and she stared out across the black, choppy water. A faint light came from one lonely lamp at the end of the white boarded walkway, and it cast dancing shadows across the water. As he approached silently from behind, another flash of lightning rippled across the sky.

"Ethan, don't."

How did she even know he was there?

"Ali, please. Just hear me out for a second."

"My name is Alaina."

Okay, this was bad. The wall was back up, layered even thicker than it'd been the first time he'd met her. Alaina spun around, and her expression shattered Ethan's heart. It wasn't the wild eyes or the tear-soaked cheeks that did it. It was the disappointment. Of all the things Ethan had wanted to be for Alaina, this is what it had came down to. Her viewing him in the exact way he viewed himself. It wasn't supposed to end this way.

"How could you not have told me?" Alaina spouted. "You lied to me, Ethan."

"I know," he said. "And I'm sorry, but after I found out what happened to your parents, I just couldn't do it."

"Why?" she persisted. "What could possibly have kept you from telling a secret like that?"

"I...don't..."

She advanced on him. "Yeah? Spit it out."

Ethan sought to catch his breath. "It...it's just complicated, okay?"

Her mouth tightened in a thin line. "Complicated? What's complicated about telling the truth, Ethan?" Ethan turned around, unable to look at her expression any longer. Alaina continued.

"Look at who you are! Look at what all you have! What all you've accomplished! What could you possibly have to lose by just being honest?"

Ethan spun back around, mad that she even had to ask that question. He was losing control. His life was spinning out of control and so were his emotions. "I didn't want you to look at me with the look you're giving me right now, Alaina!"

"So instead you chose to lie to me?! How could you, Ethan? How could you drink and then drive like that? I have no parents right now because of someone who made that exact same decision! Ben is fighting cancer with no other support system than a teenager and your grandmother because of that decision! You could have been the cause of a similar situation for someone else!"

Ethan raked his hands through his hair. "Don't you think I know that, Alaina? I have done nothing but kick myself for the past three weeks for that stupid night. I know it was reckless. I know it was wrong. But I can't take it back! I'm sorry I wasn't honest with you, but I was..." He sighed and tried to calm his voice. "I was just scared, okay."

"Scared of what?" Alaina asked, exasperation filling her tone.

Ethan sighed as if the answer should be obvious. "I was scared of losing you." His shoulders slumped, knowing that this was the absolute worst time to say this, yet he felt like it might be his only chance. His voice softened, all the fight replaced by a sad desperation.

"I love you, Alaina."

Her face shifted, but only for a second. Then it hardened with that stubborn crease that she and Ben shared forming at the top of her nose. "You...you *love* me?" Her voice did not reflect the slightest hint of excitement. It was harsh and accusing.

Another crack of thunder sounded, and the sky lit up again.

Ethan's vulnerable emotions flared once more. "Yes! I love you! Is that so hard to believe?"

Alaina scoffed. "Well, considering I just walked in on you kissing your girlfriend, then yeah, it is!"

"I was not kissing her. She was kissing me."

"Oh really?"

"Yes, really," Ethan insisted. "My agent sent her down here as some ploy to try to get me to come back to the tour sooner than later. I had no idea she was coming. In my mind, we were broke up, but in hers, she only sees what she wants to see. Trust me, Alaina, you are the only girl I want to be with. Vanessa means nothing to me."

Alaina laughed out loud.

"What's so funny?"

Alaina crossed her arms and advanced on Ethan causing him to back up as if she were pushing him backward with her mind. "You love me, yet you can't even be honest with me? After everything we've been through together in the past few weeks, all the things you've opened up about and shared with me, you didn't think you could trust me with the real reason why you're here in the first place? Let's just call this for what it is, Ethan. You didn't not tell me because you were afraid of losing me. You didn't tell me because it was easier to play the sweet grandson role and make yourself look good rather than owning up to what you'd done and admitting you'd made a mistake! You're not someone worthy of pity, Ethan. You're a coward. If you really loved me, you would have thought I was worth your honesty, no matter what my reaction."

"You know what," Ethan bit his bottom lip, fighting back his anger. "You have absolutely no right to call me a liar. Look at you!"

Alaina gasped. "Me!"

"Yes, you! How long was I here, how close had we become before you let me in on Ben's little secret? You let me take him out for the day, knowing he was sick, and never even gave me a head's up about it or anything. When he passed out in that tide, I thought my heart was going to stop, and I had no idea he was even sick! A little honesty on your part would've been appreciated that day!"

Alaina paused for a moment, and Ethan thought he'd got her, but he was wrong. "Ben passed out that day and you never told me? Did you even tell your grandmother?"

Uh-oh. Ethan opened his mouth to reply, but after several tries, all he came up with was, "No."

"What. Were. You. Thinking!" Alaina looked incensed. "What if he needed to go to the hospital? What did you do, just take him home and put him in bed like it never happened?"

Ethan sighed. "Sort of."

Alaina threw her hands up in frustration. "I understand you didn't know he was sick, but losing consciousness tends to hint toward some kind of problem, Ethan! Why didn't you tell me?"

Ethan shrugged. "Ben asked me not to."

"Oh, so you listened to the ten-year-old? Are you sure it wasn't more like we told you not to let him overdo it, yet you did and were afraid to own up to it? Once again you've shown that you were too much of a coward to just be honest."

Ethan's temper flared. "So you think that just because you've led this righteous lifestyle that you have the right to tell me that I'm a coward!" He took a few steps in her direction, causing her to back up a few paces.

Ethan continued, his harsh tone never ceasing. "You hide behind your God and your religion as a means to not have to get close to anyone. You don't hang out with anyone you work with. You don't date. You talk to the people from your church, but that's as far as it goes. Just admit it, Alaina. You're scared to open your heart up to anybody for fear of getting hurt. So don't you dare call me a coward!"

Alaina's expression turned hostile. "If it wasn't for 'my God' I wouldn't have made it through everything I have in the past couple of years. So don't you dare accuse me of hiding behind Him! I don't hide in Him, I trust in Him. Maybe if you put a little trust in Him, you'd realize that you don't have to rely on lying to win your battles for you!"

Ethan let out a frustrated grunt and spun to face Alaina again. "Can't you see that loser who got in the vehicle and drove drunk is not who I want to be anymore, Alaina! Have you not paid attention to me at all since I got here? I'm different now; I don't want to be that guy, Alaina, and it's because of you! You are infuriatingly decent, and you prick my conscience with only the slightest bit of eye contact. I want to be better for you! I didn't want to lie to you, Alaina. I just didn't want you to be disappointed in me like you are now!" He closed the space between them, looking her dead in the eye. He wasn't finished yet. Somehow, he had to make her see. At that moment, another crack of thunder sounded, and the sky let loose, rain pelting the water all around them in heavy drops.

"I love you, Alaina, and I have been wracking my brain all week trying to figure out how we can make this thing work long distance. It's not supposed to end this way."

She took a moment to reply, but her voice still contained the same bitterly sarcastic tone. "So you're done. You're different. No more lies?"

"No more lies." His eyes were locked with hers. Their faces were so close. All he wanted to do was to pull her in and kiss her with a passion that would make her forgive him instantly. But he'd memorized those eyes, and there was no forgiveness in them anywhere. In fact, her next question took him so off guard that he backed up a little.

"So where does the press think you're at right now? I'm pretty sure if they knew the truth, your story would be all over the internet."

Ethan opened his mouth then closed it again. Finally, he spoke. "Bruce gave them a story...but that's not me, Alaina. That's my agent.

I didn't tell them anything."

Her voice was calm and controlled, the anger replaced with a pain that matched that of Ethan's. Rain rolled down her cheeks, and he couldn't distinguish it from the tears. "That's the point, Ethan. You may not be lying, but you're paying people to do it for you. As long as you're in this type of lifestyle, it will never work with us. There will always be too much distance, too many secrets."

"So you want me to give up my dream for you?" Ethan asked, not even attempting to hide the defensiveness in his tone.

"No," Alaina sighed, all the fight leaving her expression entirely. "I want you to ask yourself what level you're willing to sink to in order to reach your dream. Because the Ethan I know...the Ethan I *love*...is way too talented and way too special to ever have to succumb to lying and showing off in order to achieve his dreams."

Her words cut him like a knife. She was right and he had no reply. Instead, he stood in the pouring rain and listened to the next words that came out of her mouth, knowing that he would never blame anyone but himself for causing her to say them.

"I have to work early in the morning. When I get home, I expect you to be gone."

With that, Alaina turned and walked away out of his messed-up mesh of two worlds and out of his life.

Chapter 24

Ethan

Ethan awoke the next morning with a headache outmatching the hangover-induced one he'd arrived there with. The previous night felt like a bad dream, and he'd give anything to fall back asleep and change it all. How had everything reversed so abruptly? One moment, he was content in little Fairhope, Alabama, with Alaina in his arms, and the next he was being shipped back to live the celebrity life without her. It was all he could do to roll out of bed and jump the little ladder from the top bunk. Ben snored soundly beneath him.

Ethan trudged to the shower, then back to his room to get dressed and pack his things, then downstairs to the kitchen. All the while, he kept an eye out for Alaina, knowing with all his heart that she wouldn't be there. He'd messed up again. He should never have allowed Vanessa in the house to begin with, but he wasn't going to blame what happened on her. If Ethan had just manned up in the first place and been honest with Alaina, this could have all turned out differently. She'd been correct in her part of the accusations battle. He was a coward. But she was dead wrong about the other part. He did love her despite the fact that he'd lied to her, and he could already tell that it was going to be a long and painful road to get over her.

Ethan passed by Ted, who sat on the couch sipping a cup of coffee and watching the morning news. When he entered the kitchen, his grandmother immediately made the distance from the opposite side of the room and pulled him in for a loving embrace.

"Oh, Lil E."

"I gather Alaina talked to you already?" He didn't even attempt to hide the sadness in his tone.

She shrugged. "Not exactly. But I've lived with that girl a long time and I know when something is bothering her. She didn't have to say much. I take it she discovered your true reason for visiting Fairhope?"

Ethan repressed a sigh. "Yep. You were right Granny Mae. I should have told her from the beginning. Plus Vanessa showing up just in time for Alaina to come home certainly didn't help matters."

"How did Vanessa know to find you here?" Granny asked.

"Bruce told her." Ethan tried to ignore the anger burning in his gut. "Thought it'd get me back on tour sooner. Man, that guy is unbelievable. Guess it worked, huh?"

"What about your mother?" Granny asked. "How did you convince her to bring you home?"

Ethan shrugged. "It took awhile, but I think she could tell something was bothering me."

Granny pulled off her apron and hung it on its peg. "Now, baby, you know you don't have to go running off just because you and Alaina are having a conflict."

Ethan nodded and took a seat at the island. His own body weight suddenly felt much too heavy for his legs to hold up. "I know that Granny, but I have to go. Alaina doesn't want me here. I don't even know why I've hung around this long. I have a career to get back to. It was stupid to ever have left it in the first place."

"Now don't you start that, Ethan Carter." Granny stood opposite from him, leaned her elbows onto the island, and looked him directly in the eye. "The good Lord put you here for a reason and a purpose, and you have changed into the most remarkable young man since you've been here. I've never been more proud of you, Lil E. I think you've learned a lot during your stay here, and I hope you'll take it all back with you to that tour bus. Things don't have to change, you know. You can still be this guy, even out there on the road."

Ethan stared at his fingers. He had a billion questions, but only one surfaced. "Really, Granny?"

She flashed a loving smile. "Yes, baby. God sees us everywhere, not just where we see him. You keep up with reading that Bible...don't think we've haven't noticed you with it...and He'll keep up with you. He won't let you fall back to where you were if you'll just stay focused on Him."

Ethan struggled against a strange burn in the back of his throat. Was that really possible? The same God that all the men in Psalms wrote songs about could really be with him day in and day out as he toured the country, as he sang, as he spent time with his mom? Could it be possible that he really could find the strength to withstand the temptations of the rock star life if he just put a little trust in God like Alaina said?

What an overwhelming thought.

"Thanks, Granny," Ethan said quietly. He sat for a moment more, his thoughts swarming in his mind. Finally, he willed his legs to lift him upright. "I'm going to run upstairs and grab my things."

When Ethan reached the tiny bedroom that he'd shared for almost a month with Ben, he stood in the doorway and looked around, taking it all in. The thought seemed to smack him directly in the face. Not only was he leaving Alaina, but he was leaving Ben, too. He looked at the little ball of strength and courage that was wrapped up in the race car comforter on the bottom bunk and felt another chunk of his heart shatter. He'd learned more from this talkative little ten-year-old than any teacher in school had ever managed to teach him. What would happen to Ben? No, Ethan knew the answer to that and he couldn't even think it. Would he get to see him again before it was too late?

Ethan had to do something to thank Ben for all that he'd done for him. Ben was Ethan's fan through and through, but Ben's star-struck admiration didn't even hold a candle to what Ethan felt for him. He had to repay Ben somehow. But what could Ethan give him that would mean something? That would show Ben how much he cared for him. Ethan glanced down at his small pile of belongings and the answer came instantly. He took a seat at the computer desk with the rocket ship nightlight, grabbed a piece of paper and a marker, and began to write the words he'd been working on all week. When he was finished, he tri-folded the paper, and attached a separate note to the front.

To Ben,
Thanks for sharing your room with me, little buddy. I hope this gift will make you happy. Let it be a reminder that you can do anything you set your mind to.
Your biggest fan,
Ethan

When he was finished, he laid his gift on the edge of Ben's bed, placed the note on top of it, and left the room, unable to bear even one more look.

Ted awaited him at the bottom of the stairs, fully packed duffel bag in tow. When Ethan reached the landing, Ted gave him a slight nod, gathered Ethan's things, and took off toward the car. Granny Mae stood in the doorway with something in her hands. As Ethan approached, she swept him up in the most heartfelt hug he'd ever received, and he returned it with everything he had in him. When she finally pulled away, moisture pooled in her eyes.

"I love you, Lil E," she said with a sniff.

"I love you, too, Granny Mae."

She pulled it together quickly and offered a slight smile. "Don't you dare wait five years before your next visit."

"I won't, Granny Mae."

She reached out and took hold of Ethan's hand and turned it

over, palm up, and placed the object she'd been holding onto it. "I want you to have this."

Ethan's ran a finger over the smooth leather cover. "But...this was Grandpa's."

She nodded. "Yes, and it's yours now. I know you have a lot of questions right now, Lil E, and this book has every answer you'll ever need. In fact, when you get ready to start looking, I suggest you start with the spot I've bookmarked for you. You might find it...refreshing."

Ethan tightened his grip on the book and embraced his grandmother in one last hug before turning to join Ted in the car.

As Ted pulled away from the quaint two-story house from Ethan's childhood, Ethan couldn't help but feel as though his life was about to change. He was a new person, and he was going to be different. Even if Alaina never allowed him the chance to show her he was different, he was going to show himself.

The trip back to New York was long and allowed Ethan way too much time to think. It seemed as though Ted had suddenly become silent once more, having said hardly anything since they'd left the house—which left Ethan to do nothing but be still and listen to the voices inside his head.

Some told him he was the biggest idiot jerk-face who ever walked the planet. Some reassured him that everything would turn out fine. Some hummed lyrics that he'd been working on all week. And some schemed up ways that Ethan could somehow make things up to Alaina despite the fact that he was thousands of miles away and she technically didn't want to see him. In the end, the combination of all the voices just aided in the further increase of his headache.

The flight home from Birmingham to LaGuardia Airport turned out to be just as entertaining as the flight that brought him to Alabama. This time, not even bothering to suggest first-class seats to Ted, Ethan willingly purchased his coach seats. His hair color disguise held up until a fanatic fan recognized him about halfway through the flight. So he hugged every wanting passenger and signed every autograph, all the while plastering on an exhausting grin that hid the pain he truly felt. And the closer he got to home, the worse things got. He knew he was going to have to face his mother, and he felt so...ashamed. He'd broken her trust and then gotten insolent when she'd tried to correct him for it, as though he didn't deserve his entire punishment and more.

As Ethan entered the code into the security system of his Upper East Side apartment building, he took a moment to try to gather his emotions. Everything he'd been keeping bottled up for so long was bubbling over the surface of his control, and he knew he was about to lose it. He reached for the knob, but it turned before he could touch it. The door swung open, and before him was the face that cracked Ethan's control.

At the site of his mom, Ethan's guilt, and sadness, and remorse, and every other emotion that was swimming around in his system, made its way straight to his eyes. He shot a quick glance at his mother, waiting for her to yell at him some more, all the while unsuccessfully containing the moisture in his eyes.

But she didn't yell. She grabbed him and pulled him in, laying his head on her shoulder and running her fingers through his hair. He lost it. All of the anger he felt over the "what ifs" of his drunken excursion, all of the guilt he felt for lying to Alaina, all of the fear he held for Ben's future, and all of the sadness he felt over the loss of his first love came spilling out, all in one rush.

He tried to speak, to somehow find a way to explain why he was acting like such a sissy, when his mother had never seen him so much as shed a tear since the age of five, but only three words came out.

"I'm sorry, Mom."

The rest of the afternoon was a blur. Ethan had no one left to talk to. No one left to seek guidance from, so he told his mother everything. He admitted to all of the bad stuff that he'd been getting into before the accident. He told her all about how he'd acted toward Ted and Ben and Granny Mae when he first arrived in Fairhope. He told her about Alaina—every little detail down to the scent of her shampoo. He told her about Ben. And he told her about God and how He'd found him in the quiet town on the beach.

Finally, when Ethan had nothing left to tell, he gathered his things and headed for his bedroom. When he got there, he closed his door, feeling a wave of exhaustion wash over him. Despite his honesty session, he still felt something plaguing his mind. He felt better about admitting everything to his mom. She'd hugged him about a thousand times and told him how much she loved him and how she was sorry it took such drastic measures for him to realize how special he was. And it had all been great...but something was missing.

That's when he thought of Granny Mae. She said that when he needed answers, all he had to do was go to the book. It had all the answers he would ever need.

Feeling he had nothing left to lose, Ethan retrieved his grandfather's old Bible from his duffel bag and opened it to the page bookmarked about three-quarters of the way through.

The top right corner of the page read Colossians 1. And about midways down the page, highlighted in bright yellow was one tiny passage. Verse 21. Ethan read.

"Once you were alienated from God, enemies in your mind because of your evil behavior. But now he has reconciled you by Christ's physical body through death to present you holy in his sight, free from blemish, and without accusation."

It was at that moment that Ethan first felt it. He finally got it. God loved him.

He'd felt it for the last couple of weeks and had ignored it, not wanting to admit to himself that it could be possible after everything he'd done. But it was possible. He, Ethan Carter, could be holy, without blemish, and without accusation despite all the things he'd messed up and done wrong. Despite all of the bad decisions. Despite all of the times he'd denied Him. Because of Jesus's sacrifice, God still loved him.

All of the emotions Ethan felt he'd already finished releasing resurfaced, but this time in a different way entirely. This time they were emotions of gratitude and astonishment. And Ethan did the only thing that felt right—and it would be the first time of many to come.

He hit his knees and prayed.

Part Two

To Forget Would Be To Die

I will ransom them from the power of the grave; I will redeem them from death. Where, O death are your plagues? Where, O grave is your destruction?

Hosea 13:14

Chapter 25

Ethan

Eight months and sixty-nine concerts down—only one to go.

It had been a long and life-changing journey, but Ethan had done it. And now, it all came down to this night. The last show on his tour, taking place in New York City. Home at last.

Sound checks were over, the stage was built. The voice coach had just left the dressing room. All there was for Ethan to do now was to sit back and relish the fact that he was finally finished with singing the same songs and performing the same dance routines three nights a week, week in and week out. Not that he didn't love it. He did. And he loved the fans, but eventually, even he got tired of hearing his own voice.

Ethan was back to living life as a rock star—he had even gone back to his signature hairstyle—but, on the inside, he was a completely different person. These past few months had changed him in ways he'd never expected. After his moment of surrender upon arriving home from Fairhope, Ethan had never looked back. He'd talked to his mom about his decision, and she supported him whole heartedly. In fact, after time, she eventually gave up on the ghosts and pains of her past and jumped onboard with Ethan. Their relationship was better than ever. They spent daily time together in God's word, learning and growing stronger together, and Ethan couldn't be happier with his new life. He felt as if he finally had things figured out.

But there was still a gaping hole that Ethan couldn't quite figure out how to fill. He missed Alaina. He'd tried to forget her—to focus on his music and his new relationship with God and just forget about ever having met her in the first place. But that was a completely useless attempt from the very beginning. He couldn't forget her. She was a part of him, and he hadn't even so much as gotten a text from her since he'd left Fairhope. It was as if he loved this thought of a person he'd never truly met. As if his entire time spent with her was just some sick dream that continued to haunt his sleep.

Ethan had thought about calling her—probably more times than he could physically count. If nothing more, just to find out how Ben was doing. But something always stopped him. Things with him and Ali had ended badly, and he wanted to be one-hundred percent certain that if he ever had the opportunity to see her again, he would be everything he knew she deserved. He just hoped that if ever given the opportunity, it wouldn't be too late.

Ethan glanced up at the clock that hung above the mirrored vanity table in his white-walled dressing room. Fifteen minutes to show time. Normally, everyone would've been running around, frantically trying to make sure everything was ready to go for the show, but they'd done this so many times by now that the routines ran like clockwork. All Ethan had to do was meet up with the tour crew in the narrow hallway beneath the stage, say a quick prayer (a tradition he'd started upon his return from Fairhope), and then hit the stage. He was rising from the black leather couch when Bruce came bustling through the door, decked out in Armani from head to toe, glasses firmly in place over his eyes, and grasping his iPad.

"There's my rock star!" he said. "I just needed to go over a couple of things with you before the show because it's probably going to get pretty crazy when it's over."

"What kind of things?" Ethan asked.

"Well, first of all, I've scheduled you a press conference directly after the show. The entertainment magazines all want to get quotes from you in person on your opinion of the tour's success. A conference is the easiest way to get it over with all at one time."

Ethan nodded. "Good idea."

"Also," Bruce went on, never once looking up from the digital datebook screen, "we hit the studio day after tomorrow to start recording rehearsal sessions on your new album. We're looking at possibly upping the release date by a couple of months. We don't want too much time to pass between the tour and the album." He smirked. "Can't let you become old news can we, kid."

Ethan had actually been putting a lot of thought into his new album recently and figured there was no better time than the present to tell Bruce exactly what was on his mind.

"Actually, Bruce, I've been meaning to talk to you about the new album."

Bruce's eyes stilled never veered. "Oh yeah, you got ideas?"

"Uh yeah," Ethan paused. "I don't think I want to do it."

Bruce's finger froze in place on the iPad screen. His eyes bolted up from the rim of his dark sunglasses. "Excuse me?"

Ethan quickly tried to explain. "It's not that I don't want to do the album, it's just that I don't think I want to do those songs. They're not really...for me...I don't think."

"Hmm." Bruce didn't look cooperative. "And what exactly is...for you?"

Ethan turned and grabbed the little black notebook off of the table beside the couch. "Well, I know we've talked about this before, but I've written some new songs and I'd like to maybe replace a few of the songs on the album with some of these. If you'll just look at them, they're pretty good, I think."

Bruce's left brow raised. "I'm sure they are," he muttered. Ethan eyed him with hopeful eyes and finally he broke. "Okay, fine, show me what you got."

Ethan handed over the notebook, and Bruce flipped through the pages so quickly there's no way he could have possibly read more than a few words on each page. After about thirty seconds, he passed the book back to Ethan.

"No can do, kid."

"Why not?" Ethan stood firm. He'd had his own songs rejected before, but he knew he had talent and his songs deserved to be played. The problem was that his lyrics didn't match up with the perfect-haired girl-heartthrob pop star they'd turned him into. He awaited an explanation.

"We can't record these. They'll never sell."

"Again...why not?"

Bruce gave an impatient sigh and removed his glasses, looking Ethan directly in the eye. "Look kid, I know you've been on this new religious kick ever since your near-death experience, but it's just not you, okay. I can handle the prayers before the shows, but I'm afraid that's as far as it's going to go. There's no way I can take America's hottest boy toy and let him sing songs with the words 'God' and 'Jesus' in them. Who are you trying to fool, superstar? It'll be the end of your career."

"But Bruce," Ethan stammered, "I know I can make these songs work for me. I know that's not the platform I started with, but I think we can incorporate it in. My fans will respond positively." Ethan didn't want to say that he knew that if he followed his heart and was obedient to God in his music, then his career would be blessed. He knew Bruce would never understand that one.

"Listen, kid." Bruce wrapped his arm around Ethan's shoulders like a big brother, opened the door to the dressing room, and led him into the long, deserted hall. "Your buddy Bruce here has your best interests at heart. I've told you that before." Bruce's voice was like butter, but Ethan had long ago learned how convincing Bruce could be when he truly wanted. "I wouldn't tell you no if I didn't care about you. You're like the little brother I never had. Now take my advice and give up on this whole Jesus-freak bit and go back to how you used to be. I promise, things will be so much easier on you."

Ethan sighed, giving up on convincing Bruce of anything. "Yeah, okay."

Bruce ruffled the back of Ethan's hair playfully. "That's my superstar. You just stick with ol' Bruce, and I'll rock your world. Mark my words, Ethan Carter. You think you're big now, you just wait and see what I can turn you into."

"That's what I'm afraid of," Ethan muttered under his breath as Bruce led him around the corner. In the midst of the hall stood a group of Ethan's tour crew, with Ted eyeing the halls up and down like a good bodyguard, and his mom wiping tears from beside him.

Bruce returned the glasses to his head, adjusted the collar on his shirt, and murmured in Ethan's ear as they approached the group. "Okay, do your thing, Bible boy. We've got a show to put on."

~~**~~

The concert was a complete success. Ethan, the band, the dancers, the stage crew, and the wardrobe crew flowed like a smooth-running machine from one song to another, until finally, after all of the lights were down and the stadium roared with deafening screams from the satisfied fans, Ethan walked back out and delivered his encore performance.

Now, he stood backstage in the midst of a whooping victory celebration with his entire crew. Trays with elaborate fruit sculptures were being passed around the room. Some drank frosted bottles of Figi water while others clinked together sparkling flutes of champagne. They'd done it. Seventy venues in eight months. The moment was bittersweet for everyone.

Ethan brushed aside a strand of sweaty hair, still fully decked out in his stage clothes, and took a deep breath. He glanced forward to find his mother pushing her way through the crowd. She approached him with a triumphant grin and embraced him in a tight hug.

"Congratulations, baby," she said. "I'm so proud of you."

Ethan smiled. "Thanks, Mom. I love you."

She put a hand to his cheek and held back tears. "I love you, too."

"Superstar!" Their moment was interrupted as Bruce slid past two of the dancers who were jumping up and down and doing some sort of made-up handshake thing. "That was phenomenal, kid! Your best performance ever!"

Ethan plastered on a fake smile. "Thanks, Bruce."

Bruce turned to his mother. "Sorry, Mom, but I'm going to have to steal your kiddo for a minute. We've got a big time press conference to get to."

Ethan gave his mom an apologetic shrug and turned to follow Bruce down one of the long underground corridors of the arena. Ted, as always, followed silently behind. After a couple of right turns and one to the left, Bruce pulled Ethan through a doorway into a moderately sized banquet hall. A brightly lit stage, matching the color scheme of his tour, with a lectern in the middle, was placed at one end of the room. In front of it were multiple rows of chairs that were completely occupied by one person after another either holding a pen and pad of paper or balancing a camera on a shoulder. As Bruce entered the room, cameras flashed like wild, lighting the room up like a strobe light. Ethan held back in the doorway with Ted, awaiting his introduction.

When Bruce reached the lectern, he flashed a salesman-like smile and went into an obviously rehearsed spiel about how fulfilling it'd been to work with Ethan, how close they'd become over the past few months, and how much fun this tour had been. Blah blah blah. Now that Ethan's rock star blindfold had been removed, he saw Bruce for what he really was. Just a young guy living the city life, trying to make as much money as he could off of anything and everything involving Ethan's label. Bruce didn't have Ethan's best interests at heart. The only best thing Bruce wanted for Ethan was the thing that would be best for Bruce's wallet. Ethan couldn't believe it'd taken him so long to realize it. And as Bruce went on and on about the big plans that were being put into motion for Ethan's upcoming year—the album, talk show appearances, clothing lines, and colognes—Ethan began to realize that his life would be one giant chess game in which he was just a pawn being shuffled around the board. He had no control of his life or his career. He would never be able to perform his own songs. He would never be able to call his own shots. He would never be able to make the decisions that he knew were right because those decisions would not be the ones that would yield the most money for the people who were controlling his success. This was it for him. This or nothing.

"So, ladies and gentlemen, we thank you for your time and now I am very proud to present to you...Ethan Carter!"

Bruce's introduction snapped Ethan's attention back to reality, and Ethan stepped hesitantly onto the stage. Bruce gave him a brotherly slap on the back, flashed one last grin to the cameras, and murmured near Ethan's ear. "Drive it home, kid."

Ethan approached the lectern and gave a slight wave. The cameras went wild. Ethan didn't even realize it was possible for one camera to snap that many photos in a single second—and the room was full of them. After the buzz of photos finally settled and he raised a single hand to hush the onslaught of questions, the crowd slowly quieted and he chose his first reporter for inquiry.

From there, he answered one question right after another. He told the media sharks where the ideas for his stage setup came from. He let them in on some behind-the-scenes stories that he thought were humorous. He talked about the hours his band and crew had spent in dance rehearsals and sound checks. He thanked his choreographers and dancers and wardrobe team, not to mention the lighting guys and stage crew. All in all, the conference went quite smoothly. But as he was wrapping up his time on stage, one final question was asked that silenced Ethan for the first time all night.

"Mr. Carter!" The young female reporter in the back had been jumping up and down throughout the entire interview trying desperately to get his attention. "Mr. Carter, back here please!"

Ethan pointed to her and the room fell silent...sort of. "Uh, yeah, you in the back," he said.

"Yes, Mr. Carter, I just have one question. Word has it you were forced to postpone several shows in the midst of your tour. Can you give us a few more details on the cause for those postponements?"

Ethan's stomach tightened, and he opened his mouth to reply, but nothing came out.

"I...I'm not quite sure I understand the question," he said.

Truth be known, Ethan understood the question perfectly. Problem be known, Bruce had already told them a story and now they were checking to see if his would match up. Reporters never took a story that's only skin deep. He should have known they'd press for more details about his sudden absence. And the second Ethan stalled the question the reporters knew they had him. The room went silent, and all eyes focused on the audacious journalist in the back.

"I'm sorry, Mr. Carter. Maybe I should have explained myself more clearly. Reports were made that you suffered from a rather serious case of laryngitis. Can you give us some details of what that experience was like for you? Maybe even the name of the doctor you saw for treatment?"

"Right...laryngitis..."

Ethan's mind reeled. He was stuck. He could go along with Bruce's lie, or he could fess up and let the world know that he'd messed up. Ethan stared blankly as the hungry eyes zoned in on him from every angle. He turned to where Bruce and Ted stood in the doorway. Bruce, eyes practically bugging out of his head, was pointing over and over again to his throat, signaling for Ethan to hurry up and elaborate some fake details for the laryngitis story. Ethan ignored him and focused on Ted. Ted was a rock, but when he was sure Bruce wouldn't notice, he offered a slight smile and a wink.

Ethan's mind flashed instantly to the night on the deck of the ocean-view cabin. The night Ted led them in such an awesome prayer. What was it he'd said regarding Ethan?

"Lord we pray you will be the central focus as we're trying to figure out what kind of people we will choose to become."

Ethan had never forgotten his words.

This was Ethan's moment. This was his time to choose what he was to become. Was he going to be some little puppet on a string controlled by Hollywood idealism, or would he choose to be his own person? Make his own decisions? Do only what he knew in his heart was the right thing to do?

His mind flashed to Alaina. Beautiful, strong-willed, stubborn, adorable Ali. Would he choose to trust God enough to not rely on lies to win his battles for him?

He knew what he had to do.

Ethan stood up a little taller, turned his focus back toward the gawking reporters, and took a deep breath.

"The truth is...," he began again. "The truth is that I never had laryngitis." Ethan heard Bruce's gasp over the sound of the fanatically clicking camera flashes. "The truth is that I got a little carried away with fame and made some bad decisions. I had to take a few weeks off to regain my focus and learn a few lessons."

The buzz of questioning came all at once. Ethan went to quiet the reporters one last time in order to explain everything, but as they calmed, Bruce ran up on stage and practically pushed Ethan away from the microphone.

"I'm sorry everyone!" he called to the chaotic crowd, having difficulty pulling off the fake smile he'd previously flashed. "My boy here has had a long day, and I'm afraid we're going to have to call it a night!"

In that moment, Ethan realized that it was all or nothing. He wasn't going to be able to keep one leg in Bruce's world and one leg in his own. It was time to make a choice. A passage from Luke that he and his mom had read that morning flashed into his memory. Jesus said that anyone who doesn't give up everything he has for Him cannot be His disciple. Ethan had questioned himself while reading that passage. He'd wondered if he would ever be presented with that situation—if he would ever have to choose between living his dream or serving God. It seemed God wasn't giving him much time to prepare an answer.

Ethan braced a foot and gave Bruce a little shove, taking back his position at the microphone. "Actually, before we wrap this up, I've got an announcement to make." Ethan placed a hand over the microphone, muting his next words as he turned to Bruce, their faces only inches apart. "Bruce, I know who has my best interests at heart, and buddy, it's not you." With that he removed his hand and faced the reporters once more.

"I would like to announce that as of this moment, I am officially no longer a client of the Bruce McCloud Agency or any of its affiliates."

A reporter in front screamed loudest. "Ethan Carter, what are you saying?!"

Ethan smiled the first real smile he'd felt since those long nights in Fairhope, and for possibly the first time in his entire life, he felt peace. He was being obedient. He wasn't being a coward. He was being the person that he wanted to be, not the person that was chosen for him. "I'm saying...I quit."

Once again, the chaotic room erupted in flashes and screamed questioning. Ethan didn't bother to stick around. He turned toward Bruce, gave him a swift pat on the back, and said, "They're all yours now. Drive it home, kid."

Bruce's mouth gaped open, and Ethan exited the stage to rants of "You don't know what you've done! I'll ruin you!" and "You'll regret this, you pompous little teenage...!"

Ethan dismissed Bruce's temper tantrum and bolted for the door before the reporters could get it completely blocked, but he didn't quite make it fast enough. The cameras and microphones closed in on all sides. Ethan jerked his head side to side, trying to find a way out, about to resort to dropping to his knees and crawling through legs to the door, when he felt a hand enclose around his arm. Before he could tell who it was, he was being drug toward the door. Once there, he was flung into the hallway, the door slamming shut behind him. The hand on his arm never released as Ethan was tugged down the hallway.

Finally having a moment to breathe, Ethan peered to his arm, noticing the ebony color of the hand of his rescuer.

"Ted!"

Ted released Ethan's arm, and Ethan continued to run after him down the hall. Reporters were exiting the banquet room now and running after them in pursuit of a fuller story. Ethan had to admit, he'd definitely given them a lot to write about.

"Ted, what are you doing? You heard what I just did in there. You could lose your job for helping me!"

Ted smiled, his white teeth shining brightly as they continued to run. "I heard what you said. And that is precisely why I am helping, Mr. Carter. Anyone who shows as much guts as you just did deserves to be helped."

Sounded good to Ethan. Anything to get him away from those cameras. "So where are we going?"

"I've got a secret car parked not far from here." Ted grinned at Ethan's glance of curiosity. "It never hurts to have a backup plan, Mr. Carter."

Ethan caught his breath and let out a laugh. "Wow, you're good."

A loud bang resounded in the hall behind them as a few of the more persistent reporters found the latest door in which Ted and Ethan had bolted through.

"Uh...Ted..."

"Don't worry! We're here!" Ted raced Ethan down one last hall. There was a heavy metal door at the very end. When they reached it, Ted pushed the handle and busted them through to the outside. They were in an underground garage of sorts where only a few cars were parked. Ethan slammed the door completely shut behind him and ran after Ted toward a black Lincoln parked next to the lot exit.

"Where are we?" Ethan called out.

"Private parking deck," Ted answered. "Security staff only."

"Ted, you're a genius!" They were about halfway to the car when Ethan had a terrible thought. "What about my mom?! She doesn't have any security with her. If the reporters find her, they'll mob her with questions, and she doesn't even know what I did back there!"

"Don't worry, I told your mom I'd bring you home after the press conference. She has already left for your apartment. She's waiting for you there." Ted clicked a button on the remote key chain and the car roared to life. When they reached it, Ted pointed to the back seat. "Get in and duck down."

Ethan did as he was told, and Ted jumped into the driver's seat, yanking the shifter into drive. Ethan did risk one last peek out the window to see the reporters bust into the garage just as the car peeled out of the parking deck and pulled out into the busy New York City side street.

As Ted maneuvered the Lincoln down one street after another, somehow finding a way to make better time than the taxis, Ethan couldn't help but feel a bout of guilt for all of the risks and sacrifices Ted had made for him.

"I can't believe you're doing this, man," Ethan voiced from his hiding spot in the back floor board. "You just gave up your job for me."

Ted snickered. "Don't worry about me, Mr. Carter. I've got other connections in the music industry besides Bruce McCloud. There's always another job where that one came from. In fact, if it's okay, I was thinking about sticking with you for a while."

"Sticking with me?" Ethan laughed. "After tonight, I'm pretty sure my music career is over. Bruce will make certain of that."

"I wouldn't be so sure about that." Ted held an amused tone.

"Ted, do you know something I don't know?" Ethan asked.

"It's not what I know, Mr. Carter. It's who I know," Ted said. "My brother. He's a producer for one of the biggest inspirational production companies in the country. And don't get mad, but I took your little black book of songs the other day during your rehearsals and made copies to send to him. He loves your lyrics and wants to meet with you."

Ethan couldn't believe his ears or his excitement. "What are you getting at, Ted?"

Ted laughed. "Well, to put it simply, Mr. Carter, have you ever considered a career in Christian music?"

Chapter 26

Alaina

The intense summer sun beat down through the driver's side glass, and Alaina raised her forearm to wipe her brow. It would be on the hottest day of summer that the air-conditioner in her parents' worn out car would decide to quit producing cold air and make a strange grinding, clicking noise instead. But that was just typical, Alaina thought to herself. Chaos and misdirection was the story of her life these past few months.

Not only had the ambitious attempt to attend her senior year of high school been a complete bust from day one, but now, even as a high school dropout working double shifts at the restaurant and spending next to no time with Ben, she still wasn't making any headway on the medical bills. Granny Mae had offered to help, but Alaina knew that Granny was living on retirement alone. Granny Mae had already opened up her home to Alaina, and there was no way Alaina was going to allow Granny Mae to worry about any finances other than her own.

But it seemed the longer Ben held on and fought his fatal disease, the more complicated and more expensive things became. Not that Alaina cared, of course. She just wanted her brother. But it was becoming harder and harder to bear watching his bitter struggle for life. This fight was such a double-edged sword. In one respect, Alaina wanted nothing but more time with her brother. But in another, she wanted nothing but for him to find some kind of relief from the pain, even if that meant the unthinkable.

Ben's oncologist, Dr. Rouse, had said at the last appointment that the cancer was attached to most of Ben's major organs now and it was basically a waiting game at this point. Alaina had spent a lot of time under the staircase that day.

Alaina looked out across the sandy beach that ran parallel to the Fairhope main road and heaved a sigh. Work had been extremely slow that day, hardly even making it worth her time to show up, and the beautiful pink ocean horizon that stretched out before her was nothing but a taunt to her haywire emotions. She wondered what it would be like to just lay out on that beach; to watch her brother play in the water, smiling and full of life; to see her parents walking hand in hand in the tide; to simply be...happy. Alaina had been faithful in her relationship with God. She still read her Bible daily. She still prayed constantly. And God provided her with the peace of understanding. Alaina understood that her parents were gone. She didn't like it, but she accepted it. Alaina understood that Ben was in the midst of a battle that he simply was not going to win. She didn't like it, but she accepted it.

But that didn't make it any easier.

Alaina wondered what it would feel like to be happy again. She remembered having laughed before, but it was only a distant memory, and not an action that she'd managed in quite some time. She wiped at a drop of sweat escaping from her hairline and thought back to the last time she'd truly felt happy—a time that she rarely allowed to surface in her memory.

It was hard to believe that an entire year had passed since those late nights in the garden, talking and laughing. Those enchanted kisses underneath the Mobile Bay skyline. She remembered his perfectly placed brunette locks and wondered if he'd allowed them to go back to their original blonde by now. Alaina knew she easily could have looked him up on the internet—there would be a billion pictures there—but she'd never allowed herself. Somehow, she knew seeing his face would make her regret her decision.

The night of their separation still stung in her mind with a residual persistence. The sight of his kissing Vanessa had been more than she could handle. It'd been at that moment that Alaina realized she'd become too attached. Her relationship with Ethan was supposed to have been a mere distraction from her current crisis, but had quickly turned into much more than that. Ethan had not only stolen all of her time, but he'd also stolen her heart, and as much as she hated to admit it, he'd taken it with him when he left.

Not that she blamed him for leaving. She'd told him to go, after all, and wasn't surprised when he'd chosen to listen to her. And as much as it still hurt, she knew it was for the best. Ethan didn't belong in her world. He'd said he loved her. *Loved her*. The words still played over and over in an occasional dream. Even if that were true, Alaina couldn't have allowed Ethan to love her because, truth be known, she loved him right back. As much as she didn't want to admit it. As much as she hated herself for even allowing her heart to be put on the line in the first place, she knew there was no fighting it. She loved Ethan Carter with everything in her being, and that was exactly why she had to let him go.

Ethan looked to Alaina as an escape from his busy lifestyle. She was his vacation. But all vacations have to come to an end. Eventually, everyone has to return to reality and continue on with their lives as normal. Ethan had a life and it wasn't in Fairhope. He had a career and it wasn't being her crutch. She couldn't allow him to feel obligated to become a part of her mess and feel somehow responsible for fixing it because he wanted her to be happy. He was much better off thinking she never wanted to see him again and going on with his future. He had way too much going for him to be slowed down by some girl who was just around at a time of vulnerability.

Now that Alaina knew Ethan's true reason for visiting Fairhope, she realized why he'd wanted so badly to remake himself into a new person while he was there with her. It went so much deeper than just his hair. After all of their conversations, the things that Ethan had opened up to her about, she knew now that he'd been searching for something. Meaning and answers. She remembered a time when she'd done the same thing, and wherever Ethan was now, she hoped that he'd found his answers. And if not—if he'd decided to return to the life of drunken forgetfulness—she just prayed that God would protect him until he woke up and remembered.

Lost in thought, Alaina almost missed her turn for home. She swerved around the corner of the deserted intersection, completely ignoring the large red octagon—but somehow managing to find the curb with the back passenger side tire.

The car grinded along the protruding concrete, and Alaina let out a slight squeal, jerking the wheel to the side in attempts to free the car. The car bumped back down to the pavement, and Alaina let out a slow sigh, relieved that she hadn't managed to sideswipe a mailbox, or worse, a person. She took a moment to catch her breath, and then pressed back down on the gas to resume her drive home.

That's when she heard the noise—a loud pop followed by a low hiss as though someone was deflating a balloon in her right ear. It only took a matter of seconds for Alaina to realize what had happened when she began to hear the sound of rubber flapping against the pavement and felt the up and down motion of the no-longer-balanced vehicle.

The tire was blown.

Alaina hit the brake, threw the gear shift into park, and fell back against the seat. Her hands went to her head, and she ran one through her sweaty hair with more aggression than truly necessary. *What else?* she thought with a huff.

She wrenched the door open, popped the trunk latch, and stomped to the back of the car. Wiping another bead of sweat, she pulled on her long dark hair and rewrapped it back up into a messy ponytail. Upon viewing the contents of the trunk—the spare tire, the jack, a portable air tank, and a bag of tools—an inconvenient truth reared its ugly head.

She didn't have the faintest idea how to change a tire.

Oh well, no better way to learn than when under pressure, she decided. She was reaching in to pull the spare out when a loud engine came to a roaring halt behind her. She knew that truck. Had spent many a regrettable night riding in it with a regrettable ex-boyfriend. And as he jumped down from the driver's side, dressed in nothing but a pair of Hawaiian-print swim trunks, a pair of Billabong flip flops, and a narcissistic grin, Alaina wondered how much damage she'd cause by just forgetting about the tire and driving the car home right then on the rim.

"Flat tire, I see."

Cam's voice sent shivers up her spine. She flashed back to the night she'd spent on the beach with Ethan. The night Cam had revealed her secrets through a very drunken display of masculinity.

Alaina smirked. "Wow, you're observant."

"Ouch. What's with the hostility?"

"The fact that you even have to ask that question should be answer enough."

Cam was at the trunk now. "Move over, Ali. Let me get that spare for you."

She didn't budge. "My name is Alaina." She took a step in front of Cam, blocking his way to the spare, and reached in. "I got this, Cam. I don't need your help."

He gave a slight snicker. "Oh really?" He reached in and grabbed a long metal rod with an S bend in the middle and hexagonal indentions on both ends. "Well then, why don't you tell me what this is called?"

Alaina's mouth formed into a thin line. She opened it, but nothing came out.

Cam's brow turned up, a play of amusement gleamed in his eye. "Uh-huh. Can you at least tell me what it's used for?"

Once again, Alaina was at a loss. The best she could come up with was, "It turns those big screw things on the tires."

"They're called nuts," Cam said. "And sometimes they're really hard to turn, so just move over, drop the I-can-do-everything-myself bit for five minutes, and let me help you."

Alaina didn't budge, eyes locked with Cam's. She'd forgotten how blue they could be and how long his lashes were. Finally, deciding it wasn't worth the fight, and that dealing with Cam for ten minutes was worth getting home before dark, she took a begrudged step out of his way.

"There ya go," he coaxed. He reached into the trunk and pulled the spare tire out in one swift heave. He bent over and rolled it to the side of the car, propping it against the passenger side door. He returned promptly for the rod thing—a tire iron he later called it—an air pump, and a jack.

Pushing the jack underneath the back end of the car, he attached a pole thing to the end of it and began to crank it as though it was some sort of windup toy. Alaina watched with curious focus, wondering how he knew where to place the jack without it ripping a hole in the base of the car.

Is that even possible? Maybe Cam's help was more needed than Alaina cared to admit.

"Consider this your first lesson in the fine art of tire changing," Cam said. He then took the tire iron, fit it up against one of the nuts, grasped the cross sections, and gave a hard tug. The nut gave a slight whine as it loosened its grip and began to turn. Alaina couldn't help but notice that every single muscle in Cam's back flexed as he loosened each of the nuts, one right after another. It reminded her of the morning she'd run into Ethan in the hallway in nothing but a towel. Cam wasn't quite as built as Ethan, but he definitely gave him some competition.

Giving a slight glance her way, he grinned and winked. "Like what you see, church girl?"

Alaina gasped and turned her head. "Oh shut up, Cam. Just fix the tire so I can get out of here."

"Wow, you don't show much appreciation for a guy who comes to your rescue," he said. "Is this the kind of attitude you used with beach boy last year? No wonder he took off so fast."

His comment punched through her as if he'd actually used his fist and not his mouth. "That is absolutely none of your business." Alaina stepped out of the way as Cam yanked the blown tire from a circle of what appeared to be big screws. "Although you never have been good at minding your own business unless it's convenient for you," she muttered more loudly than intended.

Cam smirked and grabbed the spare tire. "Man, you're feisty. What's going on? Bad day?"

Alaina laughed. "Try bad year. Not that you would care. I haven't heard more than a 'I need more Pepsi' from you since that night at the beach when you tried to fight Eth...I mean Brandon."

Cam paused for a moment, eyes averted to his feet as if considering his next words. "Yeah, I actually wanted to talk to you about that night."

He bent back down, fitted the spare tire onto the screws, and began hand screwing the nuts back on.

Alaina scoffed. "Really? And what could you possibly have to say for yourself after that?"

He shrugged, refusing to look up at her. Something in his normal egotistical expression changed a little. Grabbing hold of the tire iron, he began tightening the nuts, as if grateful for the distraction. His words came out as more of a mumble. "Just that I was totally out of line that night. I'd had a bad day, drank a little too much at the pier, and sort of took it out on you. It was a mistake."

Alaina remained unmoving. "That's an understatement."

Cam fastened the remaining nuts and rose back up. "Look, Alaina, I'm sorry I blew your whole normal-teen-girl cover with that guy. I just didn't realize your situation was some big secret, that's all."

"It wasn't...it's not a...secret," Alaina said. "I just hadn't exactly gotten around to...telling him yet."

"Because you didn't want to scare him off."

Alaina opened her mouth to object, but knew it'd only be a lie. Instead she decided to do the typical girl thing and turn it around on him. "Well, it's not like I hadn't had a history of that already. I'm sure you remember the time you ran like your pants were on fire when you found out what a relationship with me was going to entail. A teenager who lives a forty-year-old's life isn't exactly the most desirable quality to attract guys."

Cam tugged at a smile. "Trust me, Alaina, you've never had trouble attracting guys."

Is that a compliment? Alaina shook it off. "Yeah, well...." She wasn't sure what else to say.

Cam leaned against the side of the car, arms crossed at his chest, and the sun casting a slight glow on his bare, tanned shoulders. "So what ever happened to beach boy?"

Alaina felt a slight twinge in the pit of her stomach. "Let's just say things didn't work out."

"Well he's an idiot. He doesn't know what he gave up."

"It wasn't him who gave it up," she replied. "The split was my idea."

Cam's brow raised, and Alaina thought she almost saw a hint of guilt cross his features. "You know you don't have to push guys away just because your life is complicated, right? I was stupid for taking off the way I did when we were together, but that was almost two years ago. We were younger then, you know? I was too busy trying to party it up. I just didn't realize what I walking away from."

"Yes, you did," Alaina said. She sighed. "And now that I look back, I know it was for the best. I didn't have a right to ask you to stay and be a part of that. Not that I wanted you out partying and acting like a total moron either..."

Cam laughed. "Don't hold back. Please tell me how you really feel."

"I'm serious, Cam," Alaina continued. "What are you doing hanging around those jerks, drinking at the pier every night, failing your classes? It's such a waste."

Cam's mouth turned up in a small grin. "You know, I've always liked that about you, Alaina. You know exactly what to say to make a guy rethink every decision he's ever made." He laughed. "No seriously, I'm just kind of relieved to know you still care about me enough to be disappointed. I guess disappointment is better than nothing. But if you must know, I slacked up on the partying quite a bit this past year. My mom found a bottle in my truck and cracked down hard core."

"Really?" Alaina said.

"Yeah, really." He smirked. "Practically threatened me with my life. Made me go to tutoring every day after school. I made A/B honor role for the first time in my life last semester of senior year."

"Wow," Alaina said. "Congratulations. Sounds like you've got things together."

Cam grinned. Alaina was a little taken aback. Now that she really paid attention, he actually did look better. Happier. "I wouldn't say I'm totally out of the woods yet, but yeah, I'm on the road to improvement. I got to graduate, at least," he smiled, "cap and gown and everything."

Alaina offered a faint smile. "I bet that was fun."

Cam immediately picked up on the tightness to her tone. "Hey, look Alaina; everyone understood why you weren't there. It really wasn't that big of a deal, you know. Just a bunch of sitting and standing and lots of camera flashes." Cam laughed. "Well, that and Skeeter Johnson went nude underneath his gown and mooned Principal Newman as he walked off of the stage."

Alaina felt a laugh spring to her throat for the first time since she could remember. It felt great. "Wow," she said, "maybe I don't regret missing it after all."

Cam laughed with her. The tension between them seemed to relax a little, and Cam shifted his stance against her car. "So what are you going to do about school? Do you have plans to come back, you know..."

Well, so much for the lightheartedness. His pause meant that he wondered if she had plans to go back to school after Ben died and was no longer racking up medical bills. She couldn't bring herself to think about the answer to that question.

She just shrugged. "I...I don't know what I'm going to do yet. I'm just taking it a day at a time."

"How is he?" Cam's voice was more serious than she'd ever heard it, and for the first time, contained a bit of compassion.

She sucked in a deep breath. "Not good." She refused to break down and cry while stranded on the side of the road talking to the ex-boyfriend whom she'd sworn to loathe for all eternity. But he must have noticed her sudden shift because he stepped forward, said a hushed, "Come here," wrapped his fingers in her hair and pulled her to his chest.

Surprisingly, Alaina didn't push him away. Shirt or no shirt, his embrace was comforting, and she missed the feeling of being held. Sensing her approval, he wrapped his other arm around the small of her back and pulled her in tighter. Her head fit comfortably in his shoulder, and she allowed her eyes to shut, losing herself in the comfort of his strong arms.

But what was she doing? This was Cam for crying out loud! She was about to pull away when her phone went off in her apron pocket. She felt Cam sigh in her ear, and he reluctantly let her go.

She pulled out her phone. It was Granny Mae. Never a good sign.

"Alaina, dear, it's Mae." Alaina could tell by her tone what her next sentence was going to be. "Now, I don't want you to rush and have a wreck, but you should know that we're on our way to the emergency room. Ben's having a bad day."

Alaina felt her gaze drop. This was the third trip in the past two months. Each time Alaina wondered if this was it. Would her little brother manage to come home with her again this time? The thought re-shattered the same piece of her heart over and over. "Okay, tell Ben to hold tight. I'm on my way."

Alaina clicked her phone shut and turned for the driver's side of the car, almost completely forgetting that Cam was still standing there, giving her a concerned gaze.

"I'm sorry," she said brusquely. I've got to go. It's Ben...." She glanced up and offered a civil smile. "Thanks for the help."

He nodded. "Anytime."

Alaina plopped down in the driver's seat, thrust the key into the ignition, and turned it...but nothing happened.

She tried again, but heard nothing but a sputtering engine that refused to turn over. She slammed her fist against the wheel and felt a sudden loss of control. A frustrated cry escaped her mouth. It seemed that everything on her parents' worn out car had decided to tear up recently. And she hadn't had the money to fix any of it. "Not now!" What was she going to do?

The roaring engine pulled up in the street next to her, and Cam's voice called out, answering her question. "Come on, get in."

She looked up to find the open window of the passenger side door to Cam's single cab truck. He was leaning across the bench seat and pulling the latch.

Alaina rose from her car but didn't move toward the truck. "What?" she asked, not sure if she'd heard him correctly.

"I said 'c'mon.' By the sound of that engine, you're not going anywhere in that lemon for a while. So get in. I'm giving you a ride."

Alaina took one last look at her parents' old car and decided that Cam was right. Now was not the time for pride. She had to get to Ben, even if it meant taking a ride from *him* to get there. She reached into the car, grabbed her purse, and locked the doors. After making the jump into the jacked up truck, Alaina noticed that Cam had miraculously found a shirt since their awkward embrace.

She looked up to him, and he met her eyes offering a slight smile. "Why are you being so nice to me?" she asked.

He reached over, gave her shoulder a light squeeze, and then pulled the gear shifter to drive.

"Let's just say I'm doing what I should have done a long time ago."

Chapter 27

Alaina

Alaina's door was already slightly open as Cam slung the growling truck into a tight parking space in the lot of the Thomas Hospital emergency parking. Without saying a word, Alaina jumped from the bench seat to the ground and took off for the electronic sliding doors at the entrance, with Cam trailing her heels.

When they got inside, Alaina bolted straight for the check-in desk. She kindly—attempting to keep the urgency out of her tone— told the receptionist who she was there for. While the woman clicked away on the mouse controlling the computer screen in front of her, Alaina turned to Cam.

"You didn't have to come in. You could have just dropped me off."

He gave her a slight shrug. "I know."

"Right this way, ma'am," the receptionist said. "He's already in a room in the back." The woman reached underneath her desk, and a light buzzer sounded, signaling that the door to the back was unlocked. Alaina reached for the handle and opened it slightly, but then re-shut it just enough to look closed but not latch.

She took a deep breath. "Look, Cam, I really appreciate all you've done for me today, but before you go back there, you need to understand something. Ben doesn't look the same as he used to. If you come back there...it's just not a pleasant sight, okay?"

Cam bent down, eyes level with hers. "I can handle it, Alaina. Let's just get back there so you can be with your brother."

A little shocked by his willingness to get involved, she nodded and opened the door to the emergency clinic. Along the opposite and adjacent walls were small rooms sealed off by navy blue sliding curtains. Alaina knew the room well. Had spent several nights there, in fact. Nearing the nurse's station, Alaina caught the eye of a familiar x-ray tech who directed her toward the room in the far back corner.

Alaina could hear Granny Mae's soft voice from behind the curtain as she hummed gospel hymns to Ben from the chair beside his bed. Alaina reached out and took hold of the curtain, sliding it open slowly in case Ben was already sleeping, which he was.

It was always like this. He'd get sick, get rushed to the ER, and be out on pain killers by the time Alaina got there to be with him. She just wished that for once she could be there with him when he felt this way. To hold his hand and hug him when he was scared. But she never was. She always waited with baited breath, praying with all her might that he would wake up again so that she could see him one last time. And so far, her prayers had been answered every time. But she knew that eventually it would be the last time.

Alaina shot Cam a weary glance, and he nodded, understanding that she needed to be alone with Granny Mae and Ben for a moment. "I'll wait out here," he said.

Alaina offered an appreciative nod and closed the curtain behind her. She knew that Cam could hear every word through the curtain, but she still admired the fact that he'd shown respect for her privacy. Maybe Cam was changing after all. He certainly seemed different today.

Granny Mae rose upon Alaina's entry. "Hey, hon," she said, her voiced tired.

Alaina made her way to Ben's bedside. What little hair had grown back after the discontinuance of his chemo treatments clung in a cold sweat to his forehead and dark circles shaded below his eyes. He'd been fighting for so long now. He looked so pale. So weak. "How is he?" she asked, already knowing the answer.

Granny reached out and took hold of Alaina's hand. "About the same as last time, I'm afraid. He's malnourished. The cancer cells are depleting his system. They've got him on some IV fluids to help keep him hydrated and try to get some nourishment to his blood stream. They think he can be stabilized in the next couple of days, but he will have to be admitted." She paused for a moment. "Sweetie, they want to air evac him to the cancer center in Birmingham this time."

"Oh." That was different. Normally they just admitted Ben into the local hospital, treated him for a couple of days, and then sent him home. "It's getting worse, isn't it?"

Granny nodded, trying to remain strong for Alaina. "I think so."

Alaina took a deep breath and leaned down to give her brother a long kiss on the cheek. "Granny..." she stopped there as her voiced cracked. She was about to lose it.

Granny Mae squeezed tighter on Alaina's hand and placed her other hand on Ben's arm. "I think we should pray," she said.

Alaina could only nod her agreement. She bowed her head and shut her eyes as Granny Mae led a whispered prayer for Ben's comfort and strength. Never once did she pray for his recovery or for some miracle cure. Granny Mae knew as well as Alaina that there was no miracle cure. Sure, Alaina didn't understand how someone as small and as innocent as Ben could be put through something so incredibly scary and grown up, but that didn't make any difference. Alaina understood that sometimes bad things just happened to good people. There was no explanation. There's just the fact that it happens, and through it all, the only thing that can truly provide a sense of comfort is trusting that God has his hand on the situation and everything will turn out good for those who believe in Him. Alaina believed in Him. And she believed that she would get her chance to tell her amazingly courageous little brother how much she loved him and how proud of him she was. But past that, she knew that she had to let him go.

When Granny Mae finished her prayer, she pulled Alaina in for a quick hug. "I'm going to go speak with the nurse and get the admission information for Birmingham."

"Okay," Alaina replied. "Oh, and will you tell Cam that he can come in if he wants?"

Granny cocked her head to the side curiously. "Cam?"

Alaina shrugged, giving her a look that indicated she didn't quite understand it either. Granny Mae returned an understanding nod and ducked behind the thick curtain. Seconds later, Cam entered looking about as white as she'd ever seen him.

"He's getting worse," Alaina said as he approached the side of Ben's bed.

Cam gazed down at Ben with his IV tubing running from a catheter in his bruised arm and his oxygen tubing taped to his nose. "Wow, he looks so...small."

Alaina couldn't respond. She could only change the subject. "They're evacuating him to the cancer center in Birmingham tonight."

"Yeah, I overheard your grandmother."

Alaina almost smiled. Nobody had ever said that to her about Granny Mae. It was nice to hear Granny Mae referred to as her grandmother.

Cam looked up from Ben's side, and his expression was one Alaina didn't recognize. Was it guilt again? "Alaina," he started, "I...uh..." He took a deep breath and finally spit out the words he was holding in. "I want to go to Birmingham with you. I want to help."

Alaina's eyes widened in surprise, a look he couldn't help but notice.

He shrugged and offered an explanation. "It's just that you guys are going to have to drive up there and if...if something were to...happen...while you're there, I think you should have someone to drive you back home."

Alaina couldn't help but ask. "Okay, Cam, seriously, what gives? A year ago you were making fun of me and giving me a hard time about the fact that I was working sixty hours a week, thirty of which were totally illegal by the way, just so that I could support my brother. And now you want to help out and accompany me to the hospital? It just doesn't add up."

Cam let out a frustrated sigh but his voice was as gentle as she'd heard it the first night they'd ever hung out together all those years ago. "I told you, Alaina, I acted like a jerk before and I'm trying to do better. There is no catch. No ulterior motive. I should have been there to help you the first time and I wasn't, so I'm here now."

Alaina paused and found her gaze shifting to Ben. Cam had a point. Ben looked as bad as she'd ever seen him. What if something happened? It would be nice to have someone around to help with things. In fact, it'd just be nice to have someone around who was close to her own age. Someone who could provide a means of company in the daily hospital waiting grind.

She looked back up to Cam, considering a silent ultimatum in her mind. Finally, she voiced it aloud. "So you really want to help?"

"I really want to help."

"And you promise you're not going to get up there and flake out and leave us stranded?"

He gave her an *are you serious?* look. "No, Alaina, I'm not going to leave you and your elderly grandmother stranded in Birmingham."

"And you're not going to be bringing any kind of mind-altering substances with you on our trip?"

Cam scoffed. "Really?" She shrugged. "No, I will not be bringing alcohol or anything else to the hospital with me." He let a light grin slip. "Are there any more questions?"

She considered and couldn't believe she was about to say what she was thinking.

"Uh, yeah, just one. If things really do get bad...and I start to kind of...lose it...can you maybe not say anything and just hug me like you did earlier?"

Cam's brow rose a bit, and he reached out an open hand. "So are you saying we're friends again?"

Alaina spoke softly. "Yeah, we're friends." She reached out her hand in return and gave his a slight shake. "And I think I might like it if you come with us to Birmingham."

~~**~~

It took less than an hour for the chopper to land on the rooftop pad at Thomas Hospital. An air evacuation team transported Ben from the ER to the chopper within only a matter of minutes. Alaina and Granny Mae caught a ride home with Cam who dropped them off in the driveway. Their stay in Birmingham was expected to be a couple of days, but somehow Alaina knew it was going to turn into more. She could feel it. It was different this time. Ben was different. She and Granny Mae were going to pack their bags and wait for Cam to return with his belongings. He would be driving them in Granny Mae's car so that they could get a little sleep before the long, constantly interrupted hospital nights.

The act of abandoning Ben to that chopper was almost more than Alaina could bear, but his medical team insisted it was for the best. They warned that she would need her things and some rest. The drive up to Birmingham would give the staff at the treatment center enough time to get Ben stabilized and tucked comfortably into a room. It had taken quite a bit of convincing on their part, but eventually Alaina had agreed to stay behind, admitting that what they were saying did make sense.

And as for her parents' broken-down car, well, turns out Cam was going to get the opportunity to help out with more than just the tire that day. Since graduation, he'd been working at old Mr. Martin's mechanic shop. All it took was one phone call, and the car was towed to the garage and put on the list to be repaired.

Now all that was left to do was drive and wait, and drive and wait some more. And as Alaina sat in the backseat, staring listlessly out the rain-soaked glass, she tried to will her mind to slow down and pass into sleep mode. But she simply wasn't tired. She tried reading her Bible with the aid of a clip-on book light. She tried listening to the radio. Nothing worked, and she was still awake when Cam finally found a parking spot on the fifth floor of the treatment center parking garage around three o'clock that morning.

Granny Mae called on the way down and reserved them a room in the Annex portion of the hospital—a hotel-type area attached to the South wing. Alaina didn't even bother stopping by the room to drop off luggage. Instead, she and Cam went straight for Ben's room and let Granny Mae take the comfortable bed for the night. Alaina checked in at the nurse's station on Ben's floor just long enough to get the details of his status. His vitals were improving gradually, but he was still in need of IV fluids for hydration. It was definitely going to be a while before he would be discharged.

When Alaina finished with the nurses, she and Cam made the trek down the cold, white-walled hallway to Ben's room. Beside his bed was a hard leather chair that appeared to have the capacity to recline. Against the opposite wall was a cot with a single pillow resting on top of a couple of meticulously folded blankets. Ben lay peacefully tucked underneath three layers of starched white sheets. His IV tubing was still in place, and the oxygen tube remained firmly attached to his nostrils. His eyes fluttered slightly as he dreamt. Alaina imagined that, between the morphine for pain and the sheer exhaustion his disease caused his body, Ben hadn't stirred since he'd been admitted earlier that evening.

Sometimes, Alaina couldn't help but look at Ben and the scene around her and wonder how it had all come to this.

"You want the bed or the chair?" Cam asked, breaking through Alaina's thoughts.

She took another look at Ben. "I'll take the chair." She sat down, but not before grabbing one of the blankets off of the cot. Cam tried to hand her the pillow, but she refused it. Instead, she pushed the recliner as close to Ben's bed as it would possibly go, curled up in a little ball under her blanket, and laid her head on the mattress next to Ben's shoulder.

His breathing was so faint. Steady enough, but Alaina knew her brother well enough to recognize the struggle in it. He was getting worse, enough to observe noticeable differences by the day. Alaina wrapped her fingers around her brother's tiny hand and gave it a light squeeze. What she wouldn't do to take the sickness away from him. Ben was nothing less than extraordinary. He was smart and talented and had the type of personality that couldn't help but grow on even the coldest of hearts.

Alaina loved him more than she loved herself, but she also knew that Ben didn't belong to her. Ben was God's child, and if it was time for him to go home, then she would have to accept that. God loved children. Jesus spoke of that love with his disciples on several occasions. Those passages were some of Alaina's favorites because they provided comfort. She knew that she didn't have to worry about Ben after he was gone. God loved him and would take care of him until they could be together again.

There were a lot of things in the world that provided distractions and temptations. Alaina wasn't above all of that. She felt those urges just like everyone else around her. And there were times when she wanted to ponder every misfortune of her past and get angry. It would be so easy to scream and curse and blame God for all of her struggles. For the unfairness of being forced to grow up long before she was supposed to. For the agony of losing her parents without a moment's notice, and then briefly after watching her little brother die before her very eyes. But Ben wouldn't want that. Ben was an iridescent light in a world that shown black as coal. His faith in God's power and love far surpassed anyone's that Alaina had ever met. Ben was ready to go home to his Father—ready to no longer feel the pain and just be in a place where he could run, cancer free, in heaven's garden. That thought, if nothing else in her entire life, would be enough to keep Alaina in God's will. She knew Ben's destiny, and there was no way she was going to mess up getting the chance to see him again after his life was over. She knew God had big plans for them, even if those plans were not to unfold during their short time on Earth.

Alaina understood that sometimes life threw curveballs. Well, she'd been thrown a bowling ball. But she would be okay because every step of the way, no matter what types of *unexpecteds* she encountered, Alaina felt God's hand on her life—guiding her path and providing her with everything she needed at just the right times.

With that thought, her gaze involuntarily shifted to Cam. He lay on the cot, curled up underneath the thin knit blanket with his blonde hair spiking out around the pillow, his back turned toward her as he faced the wall. He remained fully dressed, sneakers and all. It was strange to see him in that setting—in the hospital with her when they hadn't spent time together in almost two years. But oddly, it didn't feel wrong. Alaina didn't feel uncomfortable allowing Cam to see her vulnerability in the hospital setting because he'd seen it all before. They'd been dating only a few short months when Ben was diagnosed. A couple of doctor's visits in and Cam hit the door running. After that, Alaina had tried so hard to hate Cam, to remain angry and keep her heart closed to him as punishment for his rejection, but it didn't work. No one can love God, deliberately try to follow his will, and still despise another person. The two emotions won't fit within a person at the same time...or at least not without a battle, which was exactly what Alaina had felt ever since Cam left—a battle in her mind over her dislike for Cam and her obligation to forgive him.

She wanted to hate him for leaving her—for not sticking around and providing her with the strength and support and comfort that she'd needed—but he'd only been sixteen at the time. What had she really expected him to do? It only made sense for him to run, and now that she looked back on things, she was kind of glad he did. Cam deserved to have a childhood, and following Alaina around and playing grown-up with her wasn't in his job description. Through much prayer since their split, God had revealed to Alaina that Cam made the right decision in leaving, and she'd finally accepted that.

It was that realization that made her understand why it was impossible for Ethan to stay. Alaina had replayed that night over and over in her mind. Walking in to find Ethan's lips pressed against another girl's. The truth of his past being thrown at her through sardonic annotations. The desperate look on his face as he'd begged her to let him stay. She'd wanted to let him stay. Oh, how she'd wanted to let him stay. But it was Cam who taught her it was best for Ethan to go. Ethan deserved a childhood, too. He deserved to go out and live his dreams without Alaina's situation holding him back. And it was that thought alone that ran through her mind repeatedly that night at the pier as she'd insisted on his leaving. Without that realization, she would've had no choice but to tell Ethan that very second that he was forgiven and beg him to leave everything for her and stay. Just stay and be with her and help see her through this storm.

But like he *needed* to, Ethan had left. And it was for the best.

But Alaina couldn't shake him. Even now, sitting in the dark, chilled hospital room with the smell of antibacterial foaming soap in the air, Ethan was in her thoughts. He stayed in her thoughts, and every little thing reminded her of him. She remembered every detail of his face. Every expression and every type of smile. She could still smell his cologne as if he were standing right next to her. The memories were nothing but gut-wrenching depictions of what she could never have. And her prayer lately was more of a desperate plea. She needed relief. As much as her heart hurt for her brother, it hurt almost as much for the loss of her first love. He'd been the one thing that had brightened her dark nights. The umbrella in her thunderstorm. And now he was gone.

"Please God," she'd pray. "I can't do this alone. I don't want to burden anyone, but I need somebody. When Ben's gone, I'll be alone. I don't have anybody left."

And then there was Cam. Of all people. God had an interesting sense of humor. Alaina wasn't sure what had changed Cam's mind, and she still hadn't forgotten his drunken tirade at the beach, but things were different this time.

Cam had come to her. He'd *asked* to help. His involvement was his own idea, and Alaina didn't feel like she'd forced anything on him or asked him of something he wasn't ready for. Cam was there of his own accord, and his company alone was all Alaina needed to have the strength to make it through whatever would happen in the days to come.

Sometimes God answered her prayers in unexpected ways, and Alaina understood when God was speaking to her. Her prayer wasn't for a romance or a replacement to fill the hole in her heart with Ethan's name on it. Her prayer was for a friend.

Her answer was Cam.

Chapter 28

Ethan

Ethan felt as if his life was soaring by in a nauseating blur. Ted wasn't lying when he said he had connections. Within a week of leaving Bruce McCloud hanging out to dry, Ethan was hooked up with Ted's brother, Percy, at GIG Music Group, which was also located in New York City.

Once there, Ethan worked with a few musicians, put some notes to his lyrics, and clocked some hours in the recording studio. During his stay in Fairhope, he'd written his first Christian song based on the display of strength and faith he'd witnessed through little Ben and his sister. He'd shelled out several more songs while finishing up his tour, each a story depicting the walk of a new believer. Some were about the joys of surrender. Some were about the struggles of surrender. Some were just about how exceedingly lucky Ethan felt to have been plucked from the pit he'd been dipping into in his previous life. But despite the context, each song was a raw depiction of Ethan's heart and soul, and each was one-hundred percent the work of his own hands.

He was finally singing his own music.

One of the downfalls to Ethan's recent toggle of genres was the media attention he'd drawn to himself. Skeptical reporters sat around like vultures, mocking his decision for spirituality and seeming to simply wait for him to mess up one time so that they could snap that one incriminating picture that would ruin his entire testimony of change. In fact, Ethan had taken to holing up in a small writer's room at his record label's establishment just to find some peace. He spent most of his days there finishing up what little homeschooling work he had left to do to graduate, reading his grandfather's old tattered Bible for inspiration, and scheming up lyrics to a song that he only hoped would reach out to kids struggling with the same temptations he'd once succumbed to.

Percy had voiced to Ethan upon signing him that he thought that since Ethan was coming off of this big headline tour, it would be a good idea to get him out performing his new music as soon as possible as to spread the word of his new sound. The only problem was that Ethan only had a handful of songs in which to perform thus far, so the solution was to book him as an opener in Toby Mac's Winterslam Tour. If the fans were accepting of him, and his new music went over as well as everyone hoped, then he would be looking into possibly releasing a full album at the end of the tour and traveling solo for a while with those songs.

Percy had high hopes for Ethan. The news of Ethan's revolt against his bad influencing agent had spread like wildfire, and to Ethan's relief, his fans seemed to be siding with him. His social networking sites were blowing up with supportive comments. The song he wrote in Fairhope had been released on iTunes only a couple of weeks prior and was already in the top ten of the Billboard Charts for Christian music. Percy had even voiced recently that he hoped to begin plans on Ethan's own headline tour a few months after his album release.

All in all, life couldn't be going any better for Ethan.

Well, except for one thing. Ethan had been having a nagging sensation in the pit of his stomach lately, and it was around midnight when he finally discovered the cause. He knew something had been tugging at his subconscious, making it impossible for his mind to slow enough to sleep, but couldn't figure out what it was. It was in the midst of a restless prayer when the thought simply popped into his mind. And he knew he was right. As much as it pained him, he knew he was right.

At least once every day, Ethan checked his Facebook page. And not because he was addicted to social networking or because his new agent expected him to maintain a certain online status. He checked it because ever since he'd left Fairhope, Ben had written him messages almost every night. At first, they'd started out as angry little rants about Ethan just taking off and leaving him for no reason. Then they'd turned to pleas for him to come back. Then they'd morphed into letters of the type of forgiveness that only a child could muster. And finally, they were just updates on life. Ben told him about Granny Mae and church and how things were going around the house. He'd talk about Alaina and how she was still working all the time. He updated Ethan on how he was feeling. Some days Ben's messages had a happy undertone, and others were more of a quest for answers. And throughout it all, the days upon months of continuous messaging from his little friend, Ethan had never replied to even one of them.

Ethan had come a long way in his walk with God. He'd let go of many of the ghosts of his past. Found ways to forgive others and found ways to forgive himself. But the thing he'd never been able to get past was Ben. Ethan loved Alaina and missed her with all his heart, but he deserved what he got with her. He'd brought it on himself when he'd chosen to not be honest with her from the beginning. He understood that. But Ben...Ben was so little and didn't understand the complications a relationship could bring. Ethan had abandoned him. He'd walked in, treated the little guy like garbage, then befriended him, and then left him. Ethan understood why Ben was confused and wondered what Alaina had told him about why he'd left. He knew he owed Ben an apology and an explanation, but there was just something about the thought of that little face scrunching up in a stubborn look of disappointment that Ethan couldn't bear to see. So instead of doing what he knew was right and facing Ben like a man and apologizing...Ethan kept quiet and resorted to reading Ben's letters every day as if they were the most important piece of literature other than his Bible.

But there were days when Ben's letters didn't come. Ethan always wondered why they'd stop, only to figure out later that those were the days that Ben was sickest. Ethan assumed a hospital visit. He wasn't sure because Ben never spoke of his hardships in his letters. He only spoke of the strength God was giving him with wisdom that far surpassed the expectations of a little kid.

As Ethan lay in his cushy bed, in the apartment he shared with his mom in downtown Manhattan, he realized that he hadn't received a letter from Ben in several days. And it was a gut-wrenching intuition that told Ethan there was a reason. Ben wasn't home around his computer, which meant he was in a hospital somewhere. It'd happened before, but never lasted this long.

Something was wrong.

It was a call to Granny Mae that confirmed it. Ethan knew it was late, around eleven at night her time, but he needed to find out how Ben was. There would be no sleeping until Ethan knew Ben was okay.

"Sweetie, what's wrong?" Granny's tone was groggy. He'd woke her up. "You never call this late? Is everything okay?"

Ethan paused, almost afraid to ask the essential question. "How's Ben?"

It was Granny's sigh that told him all he needed to know.

"Where are you guys?" Ethan asked; his tone one of persistence.

Granny replied slowly, keeping her voice steady. "We're at the treatment center in Birmingham. Ben is not doing well this time."

"I'll be there tomorrow."

"Oh, baby, I know you love Ben...."

"Granny, I need to tell him good-bye...the right way."

"I understand," Granny said. "But Lil E, there's something you should know...."

But it was too late. Ethan had already hung up and lurched for his duffle bag. Ben was in bad shape. He could tell by his grandmother's tone.

And he didn't know how much time he had. Ethan had never responded to Ben; never explained to him why he'd left or how he'd changed since then and how it was partially Ben's influence that led Ethan to the best decision he'd ever made for himself. He'd never told little Ben any of that.

Because Ben deserved better than a half-hearted letter typed over some social network. Ethan needed to tell him everything face to face and take whatever Ben had to throw at him. Whether it be disappointment or forgiveness, Ethan would take it.

He just hoped he wasn't too late.

~~**~~

The airliner touched down at the Shuttlesworth International Airport in Birmingham at mid-afternoon the next day. The sun beat down on the blackened runway causing heat to radiate in seemingly visible waves as Ethan gazed out of the tiny oval window. This time he'd opted for first class. And not because he preferred the amenities it offered, but because he needed his privacy. His stomach was twisted in knots of anticipation for the reality that would face him the second he set foot in that hospital.

What would Ben be like? Would he see Alaina? How would she react to his presence there? The last thing he wanted was a scene in the middle of the waiting room, but he knew better than that from Alaina. She wouldn't make a scene. All it'd take was a look and he'd know he wasn't welcome. He just needed to see Ben before she knew he was there. That's why he'd called that morning and asked Granny Mae to keep quiet about his arrival. He had some stuff to settle with Ben, and it'd be a lot easier to accomplish without having to explain himself to Alaina—or having to deal with the pain of seeing her and not being welcome to touch her hair or hold her hand the way he had before messing everything up.

Ethan chose a blue Yankees cap and a pair of dark sunglasses as his disguise for the day, and he just hoped it'd be enough to get him as far as Ben's room unnoticed. Ironically, his departure from the secular music scene had not put an abrupt end to his career as he'd anticipated. Sure, he'd lost some of his fan base, but he'd gained a whole new wave. Turns out, people liked to see the real side of celebrities and his new fans felt that he had a backbone, that he'd made a stand for Christ and for his beliefs with his decision to switch to Christian music—which was great, but once again didn't aid to private ventures out of the house.

And then there was Ted. A constant companion and spiritual guide, he and Ethan had become what could only be described as friends. Ted was there for Ethan every time it really mattered, and it'd taken a while for Ethan to realize why, but now he understood that Ted was a man of God, and through His guidance, knew exactly what Ethan needed to hear at just the right moments. Ted offered advice and helped Ethan maintain his focus on what really mattered.

Ted was at Ethan's side as they rode in the yellow taxi from the airport to the hospital, and Ethan knew he could count on Ted to stay there indefinitely, even if not physically. Ted's wisdom would always remain etched in Ethan's memory and would pop to mind whenever he needed it. And now was one of those times. The monstrous brick conglomeration of buildings loomed in the street ahead. Ethan was there.

"I believe we've arrived, Mr. Carter," Ted said in his usual cool tone.

Ethan felt himself gulp. "Yep."

Ted didn't say anything else for a long moment, but then it came. The few words that Ethan needed to hear. "Before his downfall a man's heart is proud, but humility comes before honor."

A smile played at Ethan's lips. "Psalms?"

Ted nodded. "I'm impressed."

Ethan shrugged. "I read a lot of Psalms." He paused for a moment, feeling a little vulnerable by his next statement. "But what if he hates me?"

Ted placed his thick hand on Ethan's shoulder and gave it a supportive squeeze. "Just be honest, Mr. Carter. Be humble. Ben will understand."

The cab came to a stop at the main entrance of the treatment center, and Ethan readjusted his hat and glasses before opening the door. He took one last deep breath. "Humble. Got it."

Granny Mae had instructed them to go to the fifth floor, and the long trek there felt to Ethan as if he was trying to walk on eggshells without cracking them. Every girl with long dark hair, regardless of

height or size, made Ethan's skin jump. He just knew he was going to
turn a corner and meet Alaina face to face. He wasn't sure what he'd
say if that happened and really preferred to not have to find out.

But after about ten minutes and two elevator rides, Ethan and
Ted approached Ben's hallway and there had been no sign of Alaina.
Tenth door down on the right, Granny Mae poked her head out, and
met Ethan's gaze with a wide loving smile. When he reached her, she
embraced him.

"Oh, Lil E, I hate the circumstances, but it is so good to see your
face."

Ethan returned her hug. "How is he, Granny? Am I too late?"

He could see the sadness in his grandmother's eyes. "He's
hanging in there. Putting up a Ben kind of fight."

"Where is uh..."

Granny smiled a little. "I sent her for an early dinner. Ben
started stirring a few minutes ago. If you want to visit with him, you
better get to it because those pain meds will have him out again soon.
I know he'll be excited to see you."

Ethan's stomach tightened, and he offered Granny an
appreciative nod. "I hope so," he murmured. He looked up to Ted.
"You think you can give me a minute, man?"

Ted nodded and turned to Granny Mae. "Mae, I think I saw a
Starbucks on the way up here. How does a cup of coffee sound?"

Mae smiled and allowed Ted to take her by the arm back toward
the elevator.

They'd made it all the way to the opposite end of the long
hallway, and Ethan still remained frozen in the doorway to Ben's
room. He couldn't believe he was so nervous. He'd imagined this
moment going so many ways in his mind. The most preferable: Ben
would be ecstatic to see him and not even ask why he'd left in the
first place. The least desirable: Ben would completely go nuts and
yell at him and give him the same look and speech his sister had the
night she'd told him that he was a liar and needed to leave.

Ethan placed his hand on the doorknob and sent up a silent
prayer. *Lord, just give me the words to say. He's so young. Please
help him understand. Help him to see that I'm different.*

Ethan turned the knob and slowly pushed the wide door open.
The room was small, but fairly comfortable. The walls were white,
but a couple of pictures hung from each one, casting a little color to
the room. A small flat-screen television hung from a mount in front
of the bed. Linens draped messily from the recliner beside Ben's bed

and from a cot that sat up against the opposite wall. Ethan wondered why they both looked slept in. He knew Granny Mae was staying in a room in the annex. He figured Alaina was sleeping in the bed at night and using the chair to nap in during the day.

It took several moments for Ethan to allow his eyes to shift to the small figure occupying the bed in the center of the room. But when he did, he felt his emotions beginning to get the best of him. *Pull it together Ethan!* He hadn't even said anything yet. Now was not the time to go soft.

Ethan made his way a little closer to the bed, and the sight of Ben only became more painful. It'd been a whole year since he'd seen little Ben. He would be eleven now, and he looked it in size, but his face appeared much older. His sickness had drained his skin of its color. Dark circles hung below his eyes, and he was so thin, his skin clinging to his cheekbones.

"Oh, Ben." The words escaped Ethan's mouth as more of a sigh than anything else, and he almost jumped when Ben's eyes flung open.

The two boys stared at one another for a moment as if assessing if the other one was really there. Finally, Ben spoke in a voice much weaker than the one Ethan had heard from him last. The excited vibrancy was gone from Ben's tone.

"Ethan? Is that you?"

Ethan forced a timid smile. "Uh, yeah. It's me."

Ben's head cocked to the side, and he gave a confused puppy dog expression. "What are you doing here? Did Alaina call you?"

Ethan took the fact that Ben hadn't screamed at him or rolled over refusing to look at him as a good sign and moved toward the recliner. "No, Alaina didn't call me."

"Granny Mae?"

"Nope."

"Then what are you doing here?"

Ben's tone was sweet, almost as if absolutely no time had passed since the last time they'd seen one another. "You quit sending me messages. I got worried about you...so here I am," Ethan answered.

"I thought you had people who checked your messages for you?"

Ethan managed a real smile this time. "You're right. I did. But then this cool kid told me how my fans might appreciate me more if I took the time to actually read what they have to say. And I get worried when my biggest fan suddenly stops writing me with no explanation." Ben didn't respond. "Are you still my biggest fan, Ben?"

Ben scrunched his nose up in that cute little line that Ethan had never forgotten. "That depends," Ben said. "If you were getting my messages all this time, then why'd you never write me back? Fans also like it when you write back, you know."

"I know." Ethan said. "I'm sorry I never wrote you. I just...I just felt really bad about how I left you and I didn't want you to...hate me."

"Why would I hate you?"

"Because..." Ethan walked to the open area of the room. The words seemed to flow better while pacing. "Because I messed up, Benny Boy. I lied about why I was in Fairhope. I was mean to you when I first got there. Your sister hates me. And then I wasn't even man enough to stick around long enough to give you the truth about why I had to leave."

Ben didn't smile or frown. He remained expressionless. "Why didn't you tell me?"

"I...I don't know, kiddo. It's just that you've always looked up to me like I was some kind of hero or something, and at the time, I was so messed up inside. I was so ashamed of how I'd been acting that I was afraid that if I told you why I was really there you'd never look at me the same again."

Ben pressed his hand down to his sides and attempted to rise a little. The ghost of a grimace that crossed his features made Ethan's heart hurt. Ben was in pain.

"Can I do anything to make it stop hurting?" Ethan asked.

A faint smile tugged at Ben's lips. "I like Popsicles."

Ethan laughed. "Then Popsicles it is." He reached for the control hanging from Ben's bed and flicked the big red button to call the nurse's station. After placing their orders for Popsicles, Ethan looked back to Ben once more and spoke slowly. "I'm sorry, Ben. For everything. For not being the person you thought I was. For not being nice to you. For lying to you. For leaving you. I'm sorry for it all."

A nurse appeared then and delivered the Popsicles, which Ben eagerly ripped into. He swallowed his first bite, then spoke.

"Did you know there's a video of you getting baptized on YouTube?"

"Really?" Ethan said.

"Yeah. Didn't anyone ever tell you not to wear jeans when you're getting baptized? It soaks up the whole bathtub."

Ethan couldn't help but laugh. "But I got baptized in a lake."

"Yeah, but normal people get baptized in bathtubs."

"Ben, I don't really think it's called a bathtub...."

"Oh yeah?" Ben's stubborn tone was back, and for a moment Ethan felt a little life spring into the kid. "And what does it look like to you?" he asked.

Ethan smirked. "It looks a little like a bathtub."

"That's all I'm sayin'." Ben grinned. "So that note you left me; was that a song on the back of it?"

Ethan nodded. "Yep. My first single in my new genre."

"That's why I wasn't mad at you," Ben said, but Ethan didn't quite understand. "I used to pray for you all the time when I'd lay down at night. You were my favorite singer, but none of your songs were about God, so I prayed every night that someday you'd sing songs about God. Then when you stayed with me, you never talked about God. So I prayed that one day you'd talk about God all the time."

Ethan's eyes grew wider with each one of Ben's words. Ben continued. "Then you left me that note. And I was mad at first. And a little lonely. But then I saw all the news online about how you quit your agent and went to sing Christian music, and I remembered all of those prayers. I knew then that you were just going to do what I'd been praying about. You were going to sing for God."

Ethan pushed back the moisture in his eyes, refusing to let go of his emotions in front of the little tower of strength and courage that lay in front of him. There was no doubt in Ethan's mind that Ben's faith in him had been the turning point in his life. Ethan thought back to all those times in Fairhope when he'd feel this tug, like something inwardly pulling him to learn more about God and His word. He knew now that it was all because of Ben. God was answering Ben's prayers, and it had changed Ethan's life forever.

"Thanks, big guy," Ethan said. "I think you just might be my hero now."

Ben grinned big, but exhaustion was creeping back into his eyes. Ethan could tell that the medicine was starting to kick in.

"So how long are you staying?" Ben asked, trying to stifle a yawn.

"Actually, I go back tonight," Ethan replied. "My plane leaves at seven."

"But you could stay and hang out with me?" Ben said.

Ethan wanted so badly to take Ben up on that offer and to hang out with him every chance he could get until it was too late, but Ben wasn't his brother and it wasn't his place to monopolize all of Ben's time.

"I can't stay, Ben."

The understanding in Ben's eyes far surpassed his age. "Because of my sister?"

"It's just...complicated," Ethan replied.

"She really liked you, you know. She always acts sad when someone says your name." Ben sighed a little.

It was all Ethan could do to not ask little Ben a million questions about his sister, but this time was not about her. This time was for him and Ben. A time of reconciliation. A time of redemption. But there was one question he had to ask.

"Does she know?" Ethan asked. "About my getting baptized? About my switching to Christian music?"

Ben gave a slight shrug. "I don't think so. The radio in Mom and Dad's car broke down a while back, and she didn't have the money to fix it. And every time I try to show her videos of you online, she gets all quiet and goes to her room. She won't even let me show her pictures."

That was all Ethan needed to hear. Obviously, Alaina was still upset with him. He couldn't believe how bad he'd messed things up. The girl he loved wouldn't even look at his picture.

"I wish you and my sister were still together," Ben said, his eyes becoming heavier and heavier with each breath. "She was so happy. She's never happy anymore."

Ethan sat back in the recliner and stared at the ceiling. How could a simple conversation with a little kid stir up so many emotions? Ethan turned his head slowly and met Ben's bright blue eyes. "What do you want Ben? What would make you happy?"

Ben looked thoughtful for a moment, but then answered with words that Ethan would never forget—the most selfless thing that could have ever come from a child's mouth. Ethan only hoped that he would one day become the kind of man that Ben had already turned out to be.

"I want Alaina to be happy," Ben said. "I don't want her to have to work all the time because I never get to see her. She's always tired. She cries at night. She thinks I don't hear her, but I do."

"That's really nice, Ben."

A calm silence fell between them, and eventually Ben rolled a little to his side and reached for something that was stuffed beneath his pillow. When he pulled it out, a lump formed in the back of Ethan's throat.

"Ben is that..."

"Your song," Ben answered. "I saved it. I read it all the time." He smiled. "I heard it on the radio the other day. It's way cooler now that you've got music with the words."

Ben let in another deep yawn. "Can you sing it for me?" he asked.

Ethan sucked in a little breath. "Like...now?" he said. "But I don't have my guitar."

Ben shrugged, his eyelids sliding closed. "That's okay. I sing it all the time without your guitar."

Ethan knew he didn't have much time left with his buddy. Once Ben was asleep, Ethan would have to leave to catch his flight home. That would be it, and Ethan knew it. He could tell by Ben's current condition that his time left in this world was slim. So Ethan took hold of the paper from Ben's hand and ran his fingers over the words. This was the original copy. He still remembered how each individual word had felt entirely inspired.

Ethan opened his mouth and allowed the song to flow. He was never nervous during a performance, truly an experienced professional, but this performance had butterflies swarming in the pit of his stomach. This performance was different. It was special. This was the only thing he could give Ben. And for the first time, he truly understood what Alaina had meant all those months back. The words he was singing meant something. They had the power to make a difference. And right now, all Ethan cared about was finding a way to distract Ben from the pain searing through his tiny little body, and lulling him into a sleep of peace.

So Ethan sang with everything he had in him. And when he was finished, he looked down to find Ben's eyes completely shut, the grimace wiped clean from his face. Ethan sighed and leaned back in the recliner. He sat for a while, gripping Ben's little hand in his, and doing the only thing he knew to do.

Pray.

He prayed for God to take care of Ben. To lighten his pain. To give him strength. He prayed that Ben's heavenly mansion would be stocked with all the Popsicles he could ever eat. And when Ethan was finally finished, he wiped his tear-stained cheeks and rose from the recliner.

After peeking down both sides of the hall, he found no sign of Ted or Granny Mae. Deciding to go see if they were still hanging out in the Starbucks, he headed toward the end of the hallway where the elevators were. Ethan was lost in thought, reflecting on his time with Ben, as he neared the end of the hall, but when the elevator dinged open, the sound of a familiar voice blasted his mind back to reality. Could it really be?

He did all he knew to do. Three hallways jutted off of the elevator corridor, and Ethan darted into the nearest one, crouching down behind a medicine cart. He realized it was pathetic, but if just the sound of her voice made his heart race the way it was now, he couldn't imagine what would happen if he had to speak to her. And he also knew by Ben's words that Alaina wanted absolutely nothing to do with him.

What was she saying? Something about how good the food had been at wherever she'd just eaten. But who was she talking to? Granny Mae hadn't mention anyone going to eat with her.

That's when Ethan heard another familiar voice. One that was burned into his memory, and just the sound of it sent adrenaline pumping through his veins. The voices were past him now, making their way down the other hall back in the direction of Ben's room. Ethan crept out from behind the medicine cart and walked back to the elevator. He stood there for a moment, his finger frozen on the arrow button. He watched Cam and Alaina stroll down the hall, and just as they reached Ben's door, Cam's arm went around Alaina's shoulders and he pulled her in for a hug. Her head rested gently in his neck.

The same place it had one rested on Ethan.

Ethan thought he might throw up. How could she be with Cam now? Alaina hated Cam! How could she have given into that loser? And better yet, how could she have gotten mad at Ethan for drinking and then forgiven Cam for the way he'd acted that night on the beach!

Because he never lied to her.

Ethan shook the words from his mind and pulled his finger away from the elevator button. He felt his foot pull out in front of him, about to take a step down the hall toward Alaina. So many things raced through his mind at once. How could she have picked

Cam over him? What did Cam possibly have to offer Alaina? Ethan could give her everything. Could be her everything. He was *Ethan Carter* for crying out loud!

Suddenly, Ted's words floated into his mind...popping back into his memory at just the right moment like they always did.

"Before his downfall a man's heart is proud, but humility comes before honor."

If Ethan were to stomp down that hall and throw a little tantrum, shoving his popularity and his money in Cam's face, it would most definitely be to his downfall. The downfall of any hope of a future with Alaina and the downfall of his testimony. Ethan was not the same guy he once was. He was a new creation in Christ, and he would not take the path of his old ways. He would take the new path. The right path.

He would be humble. And it was at that moment that Ethan figured out what he could do to truly shine without being seen. What he could do to not only help Alaina because he loved her, but also give Ben what he really wanted.

But he would not do it for show. He would do it for Jesus. He knew it sounded crazy, but he knew that Jesus had sacrificed his own life in payment for Ethan's mistakes. It was the least Ethan could do to sacrifice something in return. He didn't know how much would be left when he was finished, but he didn't care if it took the last penny he had. It would be worth it.

Feeling God's approval of his spontaneous decision washing all through him, Ethan glanced back down the hall once more, making certain that he wouldn't be seen. Then he headed for the nearest nurse's station. A tall Hispanic nurse with a bright smile greeted him at the counter.

"Can I help you, sir?" she asked.

Ethan grinned, knowing with all his heart that he was finally making a real difference.

"Yes, ma'am," he said. "Can you please tell me where to find the billing department?" Ethan grabbed a sticky note from the counter and jotted down her instructions. When he was finished, he looked back up to the friendly nurse with sparkling eyes.

"And can you tell me if they will take an anonymous payment?

Chapter 29

Ben

Ben blinked, his lashes fluttering like little butterfly wings. The room slowly came into focus, and he realized that he was still there. Still in the same hospital room and the same unfamiliar bed that he'd occupied for the past few weeks. It'd only taken Ben a few days there to realize that he wasn't going home this time. He felt sick all the time now. He was always tired.

He was tired of fighting.

Ben moved his little hand and found his sister's, which lay limply next to his. Her dark hair cascaded down the edge of the stark white blanket underneath it. She sat in the recliner adjacent to his bed, with her head lying on the edge of the bed. Her hands had been clasped together in front of her face, but had fallen apart as her muscles relaxed. Ben knew that position. She'd fallen asleep praying again.

Ben looked around the room. He and Alaina were alone.

Everything looked different than it used to. The lights were dimmer. The white paint on the wall seemed a dingy shade of gray. It all looked so earthy.

Nothing like Ben's dreams. Recently, Ben's dreams were filled with the most beautiful colors he'd ever seen in all his eleven years. He saw himself running in streets of gold, body revived and cancer free. He had no cares, no worries, and no pain. He wasn't weighed down with the haze of pain killers. His mind was clean and pure. There were no cares and no worries. There was just being.

When Ben had first found out about his illness, he refused to believe it was true. He'd fallen into the rants of a small child who wasn't getting their way. How could it be possible that he had to stay inside and be bored and feel like junk all the time when his friends got to go outside and play and have a good time? It just wasn't fair.

So he'd agreed to the chemo even though it scared him worse than any idea of monsters in his closet. And he just knew it was going to work. And when it didn't the first time, he tried it again. And then again. By the time Ben figured out that the chemo was not going to make him feel better, he'd already come to terms with his future.

Ben had watched his sister's faith in God grow more and more as they journeyed together through his sickness. And, like always, he mimicked her every move. When she read her Bible, so did he. When she prayed, so did he. And what was so crazy...God talked back to him.

Not out loud, obviously, but in his dreams. When Ben was awake he was cooped up inside due to his diminished immune system. He was bored. He was in pain. He was restless.

But in his dreams...Ben was free. He ran the golden streets with smiling angels at his side. He felt the sun warm his skin and the wind whisk around his face. He was happy and content—totally and completely alive in every way.

He was no longer in his world where people hurt, like all of his friends at the cancer treatment center, or where people cried, like all of their families. Where Ben went in his dreams, no one cried because there was absolutely nothing to cry about. He had everything he ever needed.

Even his parents.

The first time he'd seen them, and ran into their arms, he thought he was really gone. When he woke up, he'd cried for their loss all over again. But the next time he slipped into a dream state, there they were again. With their smiles and their hugs and their protection. That's what God had given to him: a bright life of happiness in his times of darkness.

Ben no longer fought against the force of the pain killers, prying his own eyes open in attempts to stay awake a little longer. He no longer feared falling asleep and not waking back up. God had given him a new world to enter in his sleep. God's world.

And it was amazing.

In fact, Ben had taken to looking forward to those moments of slumber just so that he could return to his land of freedom. He felt at home there. He no longer looked at his world in the same light. He saw it for what it was. And he no longer feared for what he was leaving behind because it would never ever compare to what he was going to be a part of on the other side. All it'd take was going to sleep one last time and he'd be home.

Ben's only regret was his unbelievable sister who lay asleep next to him. He loved her more than she'd ever know. They'd grown up just like all other siblings—squabbling and quarreling about every little thing, driving their parents crazy. He'd done things to make her mad on purpose, and she'd tattled on him for things to get him back. They'd had screaming matches, and door slamming, and days when they both said that their lives would've been better if the other had never been born. But when it really mattered, Alaina had been there for him. She'd sacrificed everything for him—her friends, her school, her life—all for the little brother who annoyed her on purpose. There was no one who compared to Alaina, and Ben just wanted her to be happy.

And he knew that would only happen when she could finally let him go.

As Ben's eyes shifted around the hospital room once more, his gaze fixed on the neatly wrapped package that lay on the tray next to his bed. It was a gift for Alaina. Something to cheer her up after he was gone. It'd been all Ben's idea, and Granny had helped him with it, agreeing to not say anything to Alaina about it. And Ben was proud of his idea.

The only thing Ben regretted about the past few weeks was that he never told Alaina about Ethan's visit. It seemed that every time he brought up Ethan's name, Alaina would either get mad or her eyes would get all watery and she'd have to leave the room. Ben thought she was kind of being a sissy about it all, but who was he to say who she could be mad at and who she couldn't.

But Ben couldn't help but remember those lazy Fairhope nights when Alaina would get home from work and Ethan would play and sing for all of them as they ate dinner and talked about their days. Ben's days had consisted of Ethan—a distraction from his reality that showed up at just the right time. He'd had so much fun learning to play guitar and watching cartoons, going to the beach and playing board games. And Ethan had made Alaina happy, too. Ben was sure of it. He hadn't seen his sister that happy since they'd lost their parents. But it was gone away so quickly. Ben understood that Ethan had made some mistakes, but he'd forgiven him. Why couldn't Alaina?

Ben couldn't help but think that there was more to it than just her being mad at Ethan for lying. Ben had watched his sister give up everything for him, and he suspected that she was just following suit with her relationship with Ethan. Ben knew that until Alaina no longer had to worry about supporting him she would never allow herself to be with anyone who made her happy. Ben could see the guilt that washed through her expression every time she allowed herself to be happy. Alaina felt as though being happy was like rubbing it in Ben's face that he was the sick one and not her. So instead, she remained in her little bubble of work, and caring for her brother, and shut everything and everyone else out.

Ben felt his eyes falling closed once more. It wouldn't be long now. He thought of the bright world of life that awaited him, and all he wanted to do was to allow his eyelids to shut that one last time and run back into the arms of his parents and the angels. But he couldn't yet. There was one last thing to do.

Ben's little fingers found his sister's hand once more and gave it the firmest squeeze his fatigued muscles could manage.

"Sissy?"

Alaina stirred, and her head rose from the bed slowly. She sucked in an exhausted breath and swiped across her eyes. "Hey bub, how are you? Do you need me to get you anything?"

Ben shook his head. "Nah, I'm good."

She offered him a smile. "Well, what do you want to do? Wanna watch some TV? Or I can get the cards out if you're up for game of Go Fish?"

Ben remained silent for a moment, trying to figure out how to get out all the things he needed to say in the short time he had left. He already felt the darkness creeping in, but he would hold on for his sister. As much as he longed to return to the world on the other side of the darkness, he would hold on long enough to tell his sissy good-bye.

"I'm glad you got to quit your job and spend more time with me." He gave her as big a smile as he could manage.

Her expression faltered for only a split second, noticing that he hadn't taken her up on her offer for TV or cards. "Me too," she said. "I don't know how our church raised the money to pay off your bill, but however they did it, I will never be able to thank them enough."

"How do you know the church made that donation?" Ben asked trying to sound innocent. "It was made annononon...um...anoimus...uh..."

"Anonymously," Alaina said with a laugh. "Yeah it was, but who else could it be, Ben? I mean, that was a big bill. No one person would have that kind of money. Nobody we know anyway."

Ben couldn't help but smile this time. He let out a faint giggle. Alaina gave him a suspicious glance.

"Ben, what are you not telling me?"

Ben knew that his sister would get mad if she found out that Ethan had been there to visit and he'd not told her. He also knew that she'd be mad if he told her that it had to be Ethan who paid for his bill because it'd allowed for Alaina to spend these last few weeks with him. Ethan had given Ben his wish just like he'd hoped. He truly was Ethan's biggest fan.

Ben shrugged a little. "Nothing. You're right. It was probably the church."

Alaina didn't look completely convinced, but seemed to let it go. A comfortable silence passed between them. They'd grown accustomed to those lately. Totally comfortable around one another. They knew one another better than they ever had before. And Alaina could tell that Ben was restless.

"Wow, I bet you're sick of being cooped up in this little room," she said. "You want to get up and take a walk down the hall? Or I can go get a chair from the nurse's station and roll you outside for a walk."

Ben didn't reply. Instead, he reached forward and handed her the little package from his nightstand. "I want you to have this, sissy."

Alaina's breath caught in her throat, and a look of understanding washed through her eyes. "Ben, you don't have to do this now. There's still..." Tears welled in her eyes, and she fought to hold them back. "...there's still time. We can do all of this later, okay?" Her tone was pleading.

Ben shook his head. "No we can't. But don't open it now." He pointed to the little card taped to the top of the package. Alaina lifted the tab and read his scribbled script aloud.

To the best sister in the world, I love you and this is for you from me.
But you can't open it now. Thanks for everything,
Your best bubby, Ben

Alaina sniffed and, to her own surprise, stayed strong. Her wet eyes met his, and her voice shook as she spoke. "Is it really time?" she asked.

Ben gave a little nod. "I want to go back."

"To your dream world," Alaina said. She understood. A day never went by that Ben didn't give her every single detail about the place that Alaina knew without a doubt he'd be returning to the second his time was over on this earth.

"I'm tired of hurting," Ben said. His voice was so small. Desperate.

Alaina leaned forward and pulled him into a hug that she never wanted to release him from. How could this be happening? She'd known it was inevitable in the end, but the reality was nothing like anything she'd imagined. It was as if a piece of her soul was literally being ripped away from her. This was her little brother. He was funny and loving and so smart for his age. He never missed anything, and he could read her every move like an old worn book. He was a part of her. How could she really let him go?

God, please help! She inwardly pleaded. *I can't do this! Please help!*

Peacefulness eased into the room and seemed to wrap Alaina and Ben up in its arms. Ben took a deep sigh, a look of contentment in his eyes. It was as though the pain was completely gone. Alaina backed away, her hands grasping his. She could see his leaving her.

"I love you, Ben," she said in a whimper.

"I love you too, Alaina."

"Tell Mom and Dad I said I love them."

Ben smiled. "I do all the time."

Alaina placed her hand behind her brother's tiny neck and lowered him slowly down to the pillow so that he rested comfortably. With a deep breath and a strength that was not her own, Alaina said the words that contradicted every single emotion raging through her fleshly body.

"Go home, Ben."

Ben took one last look at the most important person in his world and knew with all his heart that his sister was going to be okay. And with the unexpected excitement of a child, he closed his eyes one last time.

The transition was easy. And when Ben reopened his eyes, the colors around him warmed his senses and a smile erupted on his little face. The angels were around like always, but this time a figure stood in the center of them. A man clothed in a robe of white and a grin that stretched from ear to ear.

Ben waved at his smiling parents who stood in the crowd of angels, expressions as proud as he'd ever seen them. And without a second thought, he took off in a sprint toward the figure in white, who wrapped Ben up in his arms when he reached him.

Ben giggled and hugged the man he'd seen so many times in his dreams but had never been able to touch.

"Well done, little Ben," Jesus said. "Welcome home."

Part Three

Sometimes He Opens a Window

For He has not despised or disdained the suffering of the afflicted one; He has not hidden His face from him, but has listened to his cry for help.

Psalm 22:24

Chapter 30

Alaina

Alaina dropped her gaze down to the ivory piece of parchment that rested in her hands with a mixture of emotions. It'd been one of the hardest tasks she'd ever accomplished, but she was glad Granny Mae made her go through with it. Alaina had to admit; if Granny Mae hadn't made her, she'd probably still be spending her every waking moment cooped up in the house moping around and going through all of Ben's clothes and toys that she adamantly refused to get rid of.

It'd been different with her parents. Everything had happened so fast with them. Once they were gone, and the bills started piling up, there was no other choice but to get rid of everything just to claim the small amount of money it might bring in. But it was different with Ben. He'd left behind no debt. His bills had been taken care of by an anonymous donor in the community. She'd found out that it wasn't her church, after all, which only left someone in the community who knew of her situation. She only wished she knew who so that she could properly thank them. If it hadn't been for that generous person, there's no way she'd be where she was now—standing on the sidewalk outside of the cinderblock walled institution, holding her very own high school diploma.

Granted, it'd been difficult—going back to school only a couple of weeks after attending the funeral for her little brother—but it was worth it, if for nothing more than to just get her mind off of things. Alaina was able to direct her sole focus into her work during those summer days, locked up in the school with no one around but herself and the vice principal, Mrs. Hall. When Granny Mae realized how badly Alaina was taking Ben's death, she'd called Mrs. Hall and asked if there was any way for Alaina to catch up on some of the hours she'd missed from dropping the previous year. Turns out, Alaina had only been a couple of credits away from graduating when she began her senior year. So Mrs. Hall set Alaina up a desk in her office and put together an independent study for her. It took all of July and August, including days of work in Mrs. Hall's office and nights of work at the house, but she'd done it. She'd finished. Credits complete. Diploma signed.

Now, Alaina stood on that sidewalk and looked out at the scene ahead of her. In reality, it was only the front lawn of the school and the asphalt circular drive around it, but Alaina saw none of that. She only saw a blank slate. No future and no plan. It was as though her life was at a standstill. She'd made it through the storm. She'd cried and felt beaten; battle scars were etched on her emotions. But she'd made it through.

Only one question remained. What now? With the financial freedom provided by the anonymous donation, Alaina's work hours had been reduced to only a couple of days a week—a schedule more conducive to the work week of someone her age. And Alaina knew she had absolutely no desire to wait tables at the restaurant on the pier for the rest of her life. So what was next for her? The future was imminent. Time would pass as time always does, and no matter how bad Alaina fought it, her life would continue on with or without her. But Alaina didn't want it to continue on. What did she have left that was worth moving forward to?

Her parents were gone. Her little brother was gone. Her friends were gone. Her home was gone. Ethan...was gone.

Alaina tried to keep her faith and to know that God's hand was on her life, holding it firmly in place with the strength that only He could provide, but she couldn't help but feel as though God had completely abandoned her to an existence of nothing but pain and loss. She could have faith all day long, but at the end of the day, one fact rang true—she was alone.

There was no sugar-coated solution to change that or bring her past back and fix everything that had gone wrong along the way. All that remained was reality. Hard, cold, unrelenting reality.

Maybe that was the reason for Alaina's sudden need to exclude herself from the rest of the world around her. She'd been secluded before in her busy schedule with work and Ben, but after Ben died, and there was no longer that situation to fill her time, Alaina had found no meaning and no purpose to her life. So she fell into a new routine. She went to school and then came home and did homework. Occasionally, she went to work where she punched her time card in and out at the exact scheduled times. She didn't watch television. She didn't listen to the radio. She just sat. Granny Mae worried about her, of course. And even Alaina couldn't explain the reason for her sudden change in attitude, but she just couldn't shake it. Alaina had felt a mixture of sadness and relief as she'd held her little brother and watched God take him from her—sadness for his loss, but relief for the end of his pain. But after that day, the feelings disappeared. All of them.

She felt nothing. She was numb.

When Alaina had first learned of Ben's illness, she'd prayed and drawn closer to God than she ever was before. She read His word and lived out what it said. She did everything it told her to do, but what happened? She still lost everything. She'd prayed for Ethan's salvation, but what happened? He lied to her and then left her. She'd prayed for Ben's healing, but what happened? He died.

God had not answered her prayers. How could He really be in this situation like she thought when there was no proof of His presence anywhere around her?

But the thing that bugged Alaina more than anything was the fact that she wasn't mad at God. She was mad at herself. She knew that she should be stronger in this situation. She shouldn't doubt her faith just because of her circumstances, but no matter how hard she tried, she couldn't bring herself back to the place with God that she'd been before Ben's death. Her heart wasn't in it like it was before. She felt as though God had left her, and she couldn't bring herself to go chasing after Him.

Ever since Ben's untimely death, Alaina had not been able to do anything but push through each day, trying to remain as wrapped up in her studies as possible, to distract her ever-racing mind from all of the thoughts and memories that kept it flooded. But she'd reached the end of that distraction. She was done studying. She had the diploma. Nothing remained but a vast array of indecisiveness and possibility. Which brought Alaina right back to her initial question.

What now?

The sun reflected in blinding beams off the mirror-tinted window as the roaring truck sped up the circular drive and came to a screeching halt in front of her. Alaina made her way to the passenger-side door and flung it open. She lifted a leg high in the air, grabbed the emergency handle, and pulled herself up into the truck. The driver glanced over with curious eyes, and Alaina tossed the roll of parchment into his lap.

A grin stretched across Cam's face. "Congratulations, graduate!"

Alaina rolled her eyes. "Thanks, but it's not that big of a deal."

"The heck it's not," Cam stated. "You just completed your entire senior year in two months. You can be stubborn all you want, Alaina, but I don't care what you say. That is a big deal."

A smile played at Alaina's lips. Cam was good at that. He had a way of not putting up with her down-in-the-dumps attitude and somehow making her feel better. Actually, Alaina couldn't believe the comfort that Cam had provided her in the past few months. Their relationship was purely friendship based and held no romantic undertones. They picked on each other. They played. They fought, but only in fun. With Cam, things were simple.

Granted, he wasn't perfect, but he'd kept his word. He'd stayed by her side all those weeks in the hospital as Ben lived out his last days. He'd accompanied her to the funeral home to make arrangements. He'd held her as she cried and cried until she thought she'd never be capable of producing another tear.

Cam had made up for lost time, and what they'd found in those experiences together was a deep friendship based on trust and respect. They didn't try to go back to what they once had. That was gone and in the past. But there was a future for them even if neither knew what it would contain.

Cam pulled the truck out of the school grounds and turned in a direction opposite that of home. Alaina wondered where he was going, but seeing as she had no plans for the rest of the night, didn't care enough to ask. "So aren't you glad you went through with it?" he asked after a bit. "You know, got the grade, did the time, walked the walk. All that good stuff. You graduated! You're officially a normal teenager again with a diploma and an undetermined future."

Alaina smirked. "I don't know about all that, but knowing that you'd made it further academically than me...well, let's just say that wasn't going to happen."

"Oh! I get it," Cam laughed. You think you're smarter than me, don't you?"

Alaina grinned. "I know I'm smarter than you."

"We'll see about that."

Alaina raised a brow at his comment, but he chose to not explain its meaning.

Cam reached his arm across the back of the bench seat, his fingers resting lazily a few inches from her shoulder. "So, Mae told me you've got the next few days off from work?"

Alaina felt a twinge in the pit of her stomach. She'd already thought of that and was anxious about the days of nothingness that lay ahead of her. Now that she no longer had her homework to keep her distracted, she dreaded finding the dark places her mind would wonder when left unoccupied.

"Uh, yeah," she said. "Almost a whole week, actually. I tried to schedule in extra days since I'm done with school now, but Tina refused. She insisted I go enjoy my last week of summer vacation." Alaina couldn't help but hear the sarcasm in her tone.

"Tina makes a valid point," Cam said. He continued down the highway parallel to the water, destination unknown.

Alaina snorted. "Yeah, except it's not technically summer vacation when you have nothing to bring it to an end. That's the whole idea behind summer vacation. You wait all year long for it to come and then you spend every day of it wishing it wouldn't end. I, however, have nothing to bring my summer to an end." She was trying to sound lighthearted but felt a sigh escape.

Cam sat for a moment and said nothing. Finally, he spoke with a tone that was not sarcastic or mocking. He was serious. "What if you could have something to end it?"

Alaina turned to face him. "What are you talking about?"

He gave a slight shrug. "Let's just say that in light of your new-found accomplishment..." He lifted her diploma in the air between them. "...you decided to continue on the path of teenage normalcy and dread the end of your summer like all the rest of us?"

"What are you getting at, Cam?"

He snuck a careful glance her way. "I'm saying, don't go back to Mae's house and mope around hating your life like you've done for the past two months. I'm saying, get out there and live it like the rest of us. Have a future, Alaina."

Alaina fixed her gaze on the flashing yellow lines that sped by under the truck's hood as Cam continued on his path. She felt her lips pressing together and tried to keep a grip on her anger, which seemed to be seeping from her emotions. She couldn't help but feel like a water balloon that had developed a slow leak due to increased pressure, but before long would finally blow and release every built up molecule inside of it.

When she spoke she focused to keep her voice calm and controlled. "And how do you suggest I do that, Cam? Just forget it all? Everything that's happened? Just put it in the back of my mind and leave it locked up and pretend like it never happened? Because I...I can't, Cam. I can't do that. I've tried and it never goes away. It's always there...haunting me."

Cam reached over and took Alaina's hand in his. The feel of his strong hand was a familiar one, and it instantly calmed her.

"Alaina, I'm not asking you to forget about your family. Or to pretend like they were never around. I'm just asking you to try to imagine the possibility of a life past the next few minutes. You do have a future, and it can be whatever you want it to be. But you're going to have to get out there and live it."

Alaina sighed again and fought back the tears she knew were trying to break the surface. "What if...what if I don't know how to do that anymore?" She glanced up at Cam and knew there was pleading in her eyes. Truth be known, she wanted to get out of this pit. She hated feeling the way she always felt. She wanted to be optimistic and cheerful and live in happy anticipation of a bright and shiny future. But she'd long forgotten how to feel all of those emotions. All she felt now was numbness and a suffocating inability to look past everything that had happened. "I don't even know where to start."

Cam gave her hand a slight squeeze, and his playful tone returned. "That's why you are so very privileged to have a friend like me. And you can start by not getting mad at me for taking you with me." Cam cast a guilty grin her way, and Alaina peeked in the rearview mirror curiously. They had now reached the outskirts of the Fairhope city limits, and Cam veered the truck onto the Highway 42 exit ramp.

"Which is where, exactly?" she asked. "Tell me where we're going, and then I'll decide whether to be mad or not."

"Nope, sorry, not an option," Cam chided.

"Why not?"

"Well, because you're going whether you want to or not," he said. "So it's not going to do you any good to go all Alaina on me and get mad. Technically, you can get mad if you want to, but you're still going."

Alaina huffed. "Where! Where am I going?"

Cam paused and finally answered under his breath. "The*cough*air*cough*port."

"The airport!" Alaina turned around to view the road behind them and realized that there were pieces of luggage in the back of the truck.

"Cam, why are we going to the airport and why is my suitcase in the back of your truck and why didn't you tell me sooner that you were kidnapping me for a trip I knew nothing about?"

An amused grin crossed his features. "Which one of those questions would you like answered first because there's an interesting story behind each of them?"

Alaina jerked her hand from his. "Just pick one, Cam!"

He raised his hand to calm her, but it didn't work. "Okay, okay calm down. I'll answer you." He paused. "Can you remind me what the question was again?"

"Cam!"

"Oh, right. I suddenly remember." He grinned and Alaina clenched her fists. "We are going to the airport because yours truly is set up to tour a college campus in—get this—New York City! And seeing as you are my new closest friend, I decided to bring you along. Your suitcase is in the back of my truck because I didn't figure you'd appreciate waking up tomorrow with no shower supplies and no clean clothes. And I didn't tell you because I knew you'd never agree to go if I'd simply asked you."

"So you figured sneaking around and forcing me to go against my will was a better option?"

"Well, I know it's a huge inconvenience to pull you away from your busy schedule and everything, but I figured you could do me this one favor in light of everything I've done...."

Alaina gasped. "Are you really going to play the favor card? You volunteered to do all those things...."

Cam halted her. "No, I'm not pulling the favor card. I was just hoping that maybe you'd come simply because you enjoy spending time with me and because I don't want to go alone. And I guess if you want me to turn around and take you home so you can sit around and sulk for the next week until your six-hour waitressing distraction, then I can." When Alaina didn't reply, Cam glanced up at her with puppy dog eyes. "Or you can relax a little and go with me. Decision is up to you. What'll it be, Alaina?"

Alaina opened her mouth a couple of times to reply with some acerbic retort, but found nothing coming out. Truthfully, she had absolutely nothing to go home to. And the fact that Cam would be gone for the next couple of days and unavailable to hang out with her made the idea even less appealing. But New York City? She'd always wanted to tour the city, but somehow she thought that when she did it'd be with...

Would he be there? That is where he lived, after all. But how many people lived in New York? Like over a million or something? It's not like she'd walk around the corner and run into him or anything...

Cam reached over and playfully poked her in the ribs, attempting to yank her thoughts back to his question, but two words were the only thing floating around in her mind, and they were echoing like a scream in a cavern. Ethan Carter.

"You better think fast, or we'll be in the air before you decide," Cam said.

Alaina sighed and took one last glance at the road to her past stretching out behind her. Finally she spoke.

"Fine. Just drive."

~~**~~

It was late afternoon by the time the massive airliner touched down at LaGuardia Airport. Alaina wasn't sure she'd ever seen so many people at one time in her entire life. Everyone was so busy and so focused on whatever they were doing or wherever they were going. No one even noticed her and Cam as they fought their way to the exit with their bags in tow.

Thirty minutes later, they finally found a cabbie who felt sorry enough for them to offer them a ride to Manhattan.

"Okay, you got me here," Alaina said to Cam who sat next to her in the backseat as the cab traveled at a pace she would have thought impossible for the amount of traffic around. "How exactly do you expect to pay for this little adventure, anyway? This cab ride alone is going to cost a fortune."

Cam flashed a deviant grin and pulled a little plastic card from his pocket, flipping it confidently between his fingers. "Mom sent the credit card. She was so excited to hear that I was interested in college, she was up for just about anything."

Alaina glanced out her window and tried to catch her breath. They were traveling across the Brooklyn Bridge—the same one she'd seen a hundred times in the movies—and the view was nothing like anything she'd ever witnessed. "Even if it meant your moving a thousand miles away?"

"Well, that part was my idea," Cam retorted. "But it's cool. You're going to love this campus. I checked it out online, and it's located right on the edge of Manhattan. Just a few blocks from the Hudson River, but still only a bus or cab ride away from Central Park. Just imagine, Alaina, living here in the city. No one around to tell us what to do or when to do it. We would run our own lives and still receive an education to be proud of. What could be cooler than that?"

Alaina knew what it was like to not have anyone to answer to.

She'd been living that life for a couple of years now, and frankly, "cool" would not be the first descriptive word to come to her mind. "Well, don't get ahead of yourself, big guy. This is your little adventure remember? I'm just along for moral support and to fulfill my favor debts."

Cam laughed. "I already told you I wasn't pulling the favor card. And don't reject the idea so soon, Alaina. This could be your adventure, too. You might love this campus, you know. If not the city itself, the campus might be the one thing New York offers for you to love."

Alaina kept her focus on the concrete jungle that stretched out before her. She would never tell Cam, but New York City had already provided her with something to love, and if the way that had turned out was any indication of how things would go at this college, the hopes of her wanting to stick around were slim to none.

It was evening by the time the cab came to rest on the chaotic street in front of a beautiful set of mahogany double doors with elegant artwork etched into the ivory columns and door facing. Morningside Inn was on a sign mounted to the side of the towering building. Alaina lifted her gaze as Cam unloaded their bags and paid the cabbie for the ride. She counted about six or so stories judging by the windows. The sounds of the city were just as she imagined them to be. Cars honking their horns, sirens sounding in the distance, music echoing from a place she wasn't sure of. People consumed the sidewalks all around her. Some strolled leisurely, taking their time to enjoy the beautiful night and magnificent city weather. Others raced past at a pace near jogging, chattering away on their cell phones, some as if their worlds were falling down around them. Alaina saw people of every nationality, every race, every color, every age, and every gender. New York City truly was the melting pot, but she couldn't help but find it all serenely beautiful in its own messy little way.

A bellhop kindly met them at the door, offering to rid them of their bags, in which Cam eagerly handed over. He offered Alaina an excited grin and walked her to the front desk. A young, probably college-age, brunette girl awaited them with her hands clasped in front of the keyboard on the desk.

"Welcome to Morningside Inn," she smiled. "How can we help you this evening?"

"We need a room, please," Cam said.

"One night, sir?"

Alaina's ears perked up instantly. She hadn't even thought to ask Cam how long they were staying.

"Yep," Cam replied.

"Okay," the girl said, clicking away at the computer mouse. "I assume you want a single room...."

Alaina interrupted with an amused sort of snort. "Uh, you assume wrong. I would like my own room, please."

Cam turned to her. "Alaina, just because I have the credit card doesn't mean I have an unlimited budget. These rooms are like two-hundred bucks each after tax."

Alaina paused for a moment, contemplating what he was saying. In other words, she was going to have to share a bedroom with Cam or fork over two-hundred dollars of her own nonexistent money. That wasn't even a possibility. Well, there was at least one thing she could do. Alaina turned to the desk girl and flashed a kind, but firm, smile. "I'm sorry for the misunderstanding. I meant single room...two beds."

The girl held back an amused giggle. "Yes, ma'am, no problem." She clicked away a few more times at the mouse, swiped Cam's borrowed credit card, and finally handed Cam an envelope with a couple of key cards in it. "Room 622, sir. If you need anything, please push the concierge button on your room phone, and he'll take care of everything. Thank you for choosing Morningside, and I wish you a pleasant stay."

Cam and Alaina thanked her and headed through the expansive lobby toward the elevator on the far wall.

"I'm beginning to think you don't trust me," Cam said as he pushed the elevator button. He glanced down at Alaina with an accusatory grin.

"It's not necessarily that I don't trust you," she answered thoughtfully, "it's more like your entire kind in general."

Cam laughed. "My kind?"

Alaina shrugged. "You're a boy. What can I say?"

The elevator reached the sixth floor with a ding, and Alaina followed Cam into a long, maroon-carpeted hallway. Taupe-textured wallpaper covered each wall above a line of mahogany chair rail. What seemed like a quarter-mile walk after they made all the twists and turns, Alaina came to a halt behind Cam as he stuck the key card into the lock. The green light clicked to life, and the door opened easily.

Alaina entered the room to feel a cool breeze wafting from the air-conditioner vent in the doorway. Two perfectly made beds with huge fluffy pillows rested in the room as promised, and a large double-paned window stretched out along the far wall. The bell boy from earlier stood in the corner of the room with their bags and an expectant smile. Cam thanked him and offered the customary gratuity while Alaina bolted straight for the window.

She reached up and found the little plastic sticks in the middle and pulled them in opposite directions. The tan insulated curtains separated noisily, and Alaina caught her breath at the view behind them. In every direction, buildings towered to the very edge of heaven itself. Some were glass. Some metal. Some seemed to be made of stone. Cars that resembled little ants raced in perfectly gridded patterns and dots of people meandered down the sidewalks.

"Incredible, isn't it?"

Cam had come up behind her and placed his hand on the small of her back. Normally, this would have irritated Alaina, but this was Cam. She'd turned to him so many times in the past few weeks; his touch was nothing but a familiar comfort now. She looked up at him and offered the smile she knew he expected.

But on the inside she wondered where, in the massive concrete jungle outside of her window, was Ethan Carter...and could it be possible that he was thinking about her, too?

Chapter 31

Alaina

It was around eight o'clock the next morning when Alaina and Cam reached the outskirts of City University. Alaina was wide awake and ready to go, having grown quite accustomed to early mornings. In fact, compared to the work schedule she'd held for so long, eight o'clock constituted sleeping in. Cam, on the other hand, had insisted on a stop-off at the Starbucks two blocks down from the hotel.

As they walked up the winding sidewalk that curled through the elaborate campus, Alaina couldn't figure out which direction to focus her gaze. Everything was so beautiful. The buildings that housed the classrooms looked absolutely nothing like a public school, which was basically a cinder block rectangle. No matter where she looked on this school campus, there wasn't a cinder block in sight. The buildings were massive structures constructed of rock and designed to resemble tiny castles. There was not a bare space of land at the bases of the buildings that was not perfectly mowed or landscaped. The campus was like a little grassy refuge hidden inside the concrete maze that surrounded it. The mixture of architecture and landscaping was as much classic as it was futuristic, blending together in a perfect balance of visual appeal.

Alaina glanced down at the outer screen of her phone. The digital clock read 8:02. "Uh, Cam, aren't you supposed to be there at eight?"

"Yep."

"It's past eight."

He seemed unconcerned, but Alaina noticed his pace quicken a tad. Her phone read 8:10 when they finally—panting and starting to perspire—reached the flag pole in front of Shepard Hall. A small group of about ten were gathered in front of a concrete structure made to hold an American flag. A boy who didn't appear to be much older than Cam climbed up on top of the concrete structure and held his hands up to get everyone's attention.

"If I could have your attention please!" The boy was tall and muscular with spiked dirty blonde hair and a killer tan. He wore a faded pair of jeans with a pair of Sanuks. His T-shirt was a deep red with three Greek letters over the left breastbone that Alaina recognized from her brief time in calculus before she was forced to drop out. The sigma and beta she knew, but the letter in the middle she couldn't quite decipher.

"We are about to begin our tour," the boy continued. "My name is Josh, and on behalf of the Sigma Lambda Beta fraternity (*Oh, it's lambda.*) welcome to City College, and thank you for taking the time to consider our university for your higher education."

Alaina could tell that the boy's intro was entirely rehearsed and wondered how many of these tours he'd given before he'd become so expertly skilled at reciting it. He seemed smooth...too smooth to be real. And then, the boy did something Alaina would never have expected.

Remaining on his concrete perch, Josh called out, "Before we get started, I need to know if Camaron Crawford is here."

Alaina glanced up at Cam with surprise.

Cam grabbed hold of Alaina's hand and led her toward the front of the group of campus tourists. "It's just Cam, actually," he said, holding his free hand out for the boy to shake. "Sorry, I was running a little behind."

Josh smiled a full mouth of teeth. "Cam, we've been expecting you! Nice accent, man. On behalf of Sigma Lambda Beta, I would like to offer you a special welcome and a VIP position in the front of the line."

Alaina nudged Cam in the ribs. "What's going on?" she muttered.

Cam thanked the frat boy as they departed. Following closely behind Josh, Cam leaned down near Alaina's ear. "I told you I was invited to tour the campus."

"You were invited by a fraternity? Is that normal policy? I thought those were kind of closed off groups, like you had to get voted in or something?"

Cam gave a wink. "Not when you're a legacy."

"Legacy, as in...already a member?" Alaina said. "How is that possible?"

"My dad. He went to school here. Grew up in New York, in fact. He met my mom at some kind of Greek-life National Conference, or something like that. His job eventually took them to Fairhope a few years before I was born."

"I'm starting to think there's a lot about you I don't know," Alaina said thoughtfully.

Cam grinned, wrapped his arm around her shoulder, and gave her a tight squeeze as they continued to follow behind Josh.

"Yeah, it's kind of sexy in a mysterious sort of way, don't you think?" His grin turned mischievous, and he fluttered his eyebrows.

Alaina snorted. "Whatever you say, wannabe frat boy. I was thinking it's more alarming in an I'm-alone-in-New York City-with-a-boy-I-hardly-know sort of way."

Cam laughed and turned his attention back toward Josh's riveting tour guide speech. Josh was waving with excitement from one direction to another, giving random historical facts about each building. Up ahead, a building dedicated strictly to the study of engineering. Another geared to nursing and physical therapy. One for science and another for mathematics. Others for the study of the arts and history.

Alaina tried to stay focused, but there was something gnawing at her concentration. Cam had been acting a little different ever since they'd arrived in New York. First, with the failed attempt to get a single room with a single bed for them to sleep in. Now, with the blatant flirtation and the constantly touching her. Alaina wondered if Cam was starting to get the wrong idea about their relationship. She'd allowed herself to get pretty close to Cam over the past few months when she needed his support. They hugged and he held her and occasionally gave her the supportive kiss on the forehead. But that's always where things ended, and she thought he was okay with that. They were just friends after all. Weren't they?

The traditional campus tour lasted two hours. Cam and Alaina followed Josh like leashed puppy dogs as he walked every square inch of campus and ducked inside some of the most frequented buildings, making certain to "Oooh" and "Ahhh" at all of the appropriate times. But then, after all of the other tour guests had left, Josh—who had seemed to be talking directly to Cam the entire morning—took Cam by the arm and led him around to parts of the campus not included in the previous tour. Alaina followed behind as Josh talked up every single little attribute of CUNY as if there was no better campus on earth, and she laughed to herself as Cam ate up every single word. It was around lunch time when Josh finally came to a halt at their original starting point in front of the flagpole.

"Hey, man, let's go check out the frat house," Josh said with a eager smile, slapping Cam on the shoulder as if they were old friends by now. "You can see where you'll be staying if you choose to go to school here. I'll introduce you to some of the guys. It's not normal practice, but you can even bring your girlfriend along. We usually don't let just anyone see the headquarters, but she seems pretty cool."

"Cam and I are just friends, actually." Alaina was quick to jump in. She wanted to add to Josh that she didn't appreciate the way he'd ran his eyes up and down her body when he'd said the words 'pretty cool,' but chose to just keep her mouth shut out of respect for Cam. "Besides, Cam and I have a plane to catch this afternoon so..."

"Alaina," Cam interrupted hastily, "our plane doesn't leave for several hours. We have plenty of time."

"Yeah, but..." Alaina went to interject, but Cam already had his wallet out and was pilfering through a stack of bills in the leather pocket. He pulled out a twenty and shoved it toward her.

"Here, go get some lunch and I'll meet back up with you in an hour or so. Check out the campus." He came closer to her, blocking Josh from their conversation. "Remember, this is your adventure, too. Go check out the stuff you're interested in. See if this could be something you'd consider for your future."

Alaina gave a frustrated sigh but didn't protest. "Okay, fine, but seriously, Cam. I don't want to miss that plane."

"You worry too much!" Cam grinned and took off after Josh, leaving Alaina alone by the flagpole.

Alaina turned in circles trying to remember which direction they'd gone earlier to get to the Student Center. After about half an hour and three wrong buildings, she finally figured it out. She entered the cafeteria, purchased a sub sandwich and a Coke, and found an unoccupied booth in the back corner. Little flat-screen televisions were mounted in every corner of the vast dining hall, and played some kind of university music station. None of the music was any that Alaina had ever heard. She only listened to Christian music, but after giving it a little thought, she realized that she hadn't really even listened to that lately.

Truthfully, since Ben's death, Alaina hadn't done much of anything, period. She never watched TV. Never listened to the radio. She just lived in her own depressed little bubble. Tears welled in her eyes as she realized how much Ben would hate that. Suddenly, she felt as if she'd let him down a little. She looked back up to the television. On the screen was some blonde girl dressed in a strange pink-and-black polka-dotted outfit that could just as easily have been designed for a baby doll. Her eyes were lined in dark shadow and thick liner that curled up her temples in a spiral. She sang a pop song with a dark undertone, and at some point Alaina realized that she wasn't even sure what the girl was singing about. Her mind wondered back to one of the first conversations she'd ever held with

Ethan. She'd told him that he was so talented and it was a waste to use his talent to sing songs that had no real meaning. He could make a difference with his voice. She wondered if Ethan was ever on this channel, dressed up in strange costumes, singing songs that didn't mean anything. She wondered where he was now. Surely his tour was over by now. She hadn't bothered to check online. Somehow, it would just make his leaving a permanent finality.

Alaina gave up on finishing her sandwich and rose from the table. Cam might have just been trying to get her out of his hair so that he could go hang out with the boys when he'd told her to check out the campus, but she had to admit that he was right about one thing. She had to start living her life, and there was no better time to start than now. So with that thought, Alaina left the Student Center and took a walk across campus—this time vowing to look at it with fresh eyes of optimism and possibility. Her life was moving on without her, and it was time she caught up to it.

Alaina made it a point to revisit all of the main buildings on campus, vowing to keep her mind open to the possibilities of one day pursuing a college education of her own. Her main concern, of course, would be the financial aspect of the endeavor, but after a short visit to the financial aid office, and a brief discussion with one of the financial advisors there, Alaina learned that with her present situation she qualified for more grants than she needed to fully cover all of her tuition, fees, and books. The college option was officially on the table for her. All she had to do was decide whether or not to go after it.

After one last walk through the library, Alaina decided that she had been to all the buildings she cared to visit, so she found a place to sit down on a bench under a nearby tree. A breeze blew on her face, and she leaned her head back to observe a passing cloud. The sun was no longer positioned directly above, and she wondered what the time was. She pulled out her cell phone. It was 4:30. Her heart skipped a beat, and she looked at her phone once more, praying she had read it wrong. Nope. Now it read 4:31. Their plane would depart in half an hour!

Alaina jumped up and found herself turning in a circle, trying to figure out what to do. There was no way to get from CUNY to LaGuardia in less than half an hour, not even going the pace the cab had brought them in the previous day. Not to mention, their luggage was still in the holding room at their hotel. What were they going to do? Alaina flipped open her phone and went straight to Cam's number on speed dial. He answered in a tone that was much more relaxed than her own.

"What's up, Alaina? Having fun?"

"Cam, we're about to miss our flight! I just looked at the time. The plane leaves in thirty minutes!"

His reply was just as calm as his greeting. "I know. Don't worry about it. I already called and canceled it."

"You did what?"

He continued as though she'd said nothing. "And I called the hotel. They're going to hold onto our luggage for a while longer. I'm over at the frat house. Josh invited us to stay for a grill-out. Come on over and meet me. Do you know how to get here?"

Alaina gave a frustrated sigh. The last thing she cared about right now was grilling hot dogs at a fraternity house. "Cam, how could you have called and canceled our flight without telling me?"

"Alaina, chill out, okay." She could tell Cam was moving away from the group of chattering voices in the background. "Like I said before, you worry too much. Planes fly out all the time. We'll just catch another one. It's not like you have anything severely pressing to get home to, anyway. Now come on over here and have some fun with us. These guys are great! You'll love them!"

Somehow, Alaina highly doubted that, but seeing as she had no other option, and technically, this was partially her own fault for forgetting to check the time, she sighed and gave up. Flicking her phone shut, she stomped off in the direction of fraternity row. Now if she could only remember the Greek letters on Josh's shirt, she might be able to figure out which house to go to.

Once Alaina reached fraternity row, she was surprised to find that all of the houses looked exactly the same. In the end, unable to identify Josh's house, she had to call Cam and have him walk her there over the phone. At first sight of fraternity row, Alaina wondered if it was always customary practice for five hundred twenty-somethings to be congregated in the middle of the street on a Tuesday afternoon.

Coincidentally, Josh's fraternity, Sigma something Beta, was not the only one who'd had the idea to grill. It seemed that every fraternity on the block was outside serving up everything from hot dogs to T-bones. Ten minutes into the chaotic crowd, Alaina finally found Cam leaned back lazily in a lawn chair surrounded by fifteen or so other boys who were doing the exact same thing. Girls roamed all over the place. Alaina guessed they belonged to the corresponding sororities on campus. Upon viewing their attire, she instantly felt underdressed. These girls wore skirts or dressy shorts that rode mere centimeters from the very top of their thighs. In fact, Alaina was fairly certain that she owned underwear longer than some of those shorts. Their makeup appeared to have been painted on with a spray gun. And their hair—whether it be bleach blonde, brunette, jet black, or streaked multi-colored—stood in perfect formation on top of each of their heads. Alaina glanced down quickly at her own customary jeans, tank top, and Converse attire. Her hair hung low below her shoulders and flowed there freely, absent of any product whatsoever. And she was pretty certain that the dab of eye shadow and mascara she'd applied earlier that morning had completely worn off at that point.

But to the boys around Cam, her appearance didn't seem to matter a whole lot. They all looked at her, running their eyes up and down her body the same way Josh had earlier, and frankly, it gave her the creeps. And to top matters off, Cam grabbed hold of her hand as she approached and swung her onto his lap so that she'd have a place to sit.

"Guys, this is my...friend...Alaina," Cam said with a grin.

"Your friend, huh, man?" A guy a few chairs down snickered and took a drink of something from a red Solo cup. "I wish I had friends like that."

Alaina had no idea what the guy was talking about, but she rose from Cam's leg as abruptly as she'd fallen to it. "Have you called the airport back yet? When's the next available flight?"

Cam seemed a bit annoyed, but smiled to cover it up. "Alaina, when are you going to stop worrying?"

"Cam, get up for a second. We need to talk."

"Whoa-ho-ho!" The boy with the cup called out. "You better go man, she looks serious!"

Alaina flashed the guy a dirty look and then directed it toward Cam. He arose slowly, and it was then that she noticed he also had a red cup in the holder of his chair. She really hoped that it contained soda or they were going to have bigger problems than merely missing their flight.

"What's going on with you?" she asked, once they were the most alone as was possible in the crowd of people. "We've done the tour thing, Cam. You've hung out. Why can't we go?"

Cam sighed and put on his best puppy dog face. "Look. If I do decide to go to school here, these are the people I'll be living with. I want to stay a while and get to know them. Hang out a little so that I won't feel so isolated when I start the school year. Can you just please support me on this? I've been there for you for months now. I just want one night, okay?"

Alaina opened her mouth to object, but realized he was right. And even though she didn't feel completely comfortable in the fraternity scene, Cam had been there for her, and he deserved for her to return the sentiment. "Fine," she sighed, "we'll stay for a while. But please don't go doing anything stupid like drinking with these guys. You're better than that, Cam."

An expression of guilt mixed with anger washed across Cam's face for a split second, but was abruptly gone. "I knew you'd understand!" He returned his arm to her shoulder and guided her back to the group of lawn chairs. When they arrived, a tall blonde, Barbie doll looking girl who was standing beside Josh bounced toward them with a blindingly white smile.

"Hi, Alaina! I'm Josh's girlfriend, Kim. Josh told me you were visiting and that I should show you around fraternity row and introduce you to some people."

The girl's smile was like a bright ray of sunshine, and she bounced when she talked like every word was of the utmost importance. Alaina was not the perky cheerleader type, but she'd deal with it if she had to. But first, she flashed Cam a look that said, "Oh I'm definitely returning the favor now," and allowed Kim to pull her off into the crowd.

Kim walked Alaina up and down the entirety of fraternity row, which ended up burning more time than Alaina would have ever thought possible. As Kim led her deeper and deeper into the extravaganza that was the world of frat, seconds turned into minutes, and minutes turned into hours. By nightfall, things were really starting to heat up on the street front.

Huge speakers had been loaded onto trailers and boomed music into the air that Alaina was sure could be heard for at least a mile. Huge jugs of liquid were cased in large metal trash cans and had a pump spout on the top that people continually walked up to fill their glasses from—their glasses being red Solo cups. Alaina's stomach churned, and she realized that it was time to find Cam. The "keg," as she heard it referred to by a redheaded girl in a dress that resembled a shirt, definitely did not contain soda. And Alaina knew Cam's history with alcohol. She'd thought he'd changed, hence the reason she'd hung out with him for so long.

Alaina thought about the cup in Cam's chair earlier. Had he already been drinking even then? Why hadn't he told her? Been honest with her? But then again, he hadn't told her about rescheduling their flight or calling the hotel about their luggage. Alaina turned in circles, having lost Kim at least an hour ago, and suddenly, rage burned behind her eyes. How could Cam possibly think that she would be enjoying this? This was not an innocent social gathering where he could meet new people and hang out with the guys he would be living with. This was a party! An all-out music-blaring, keg-drinking, dirty-dancing party. Alaina looked around, and as she took in the scene, she realized that she'd never felt more incredibly alone in her entire life.

There was not a single person within sight who wasn't holding a Solo cup, and she had walked through so many clouds of smoke, she was certain the smell would never completely wash out of her clothes. The girls wore clothes that advertised way more than the designer labels printed on them, and each guy she passed seemed to study her as though she was strictly there for their viewing pleasure. Couples danced in the street, rubbing on one another to the point Alaina was embarrassed to watch.

She peered farther down the street. At the frat house to her left, a swimming pool had been constructed in the front yard, and one by one, girls were stripping down to nothing but their underwear and diving in to meet the boys in the water. At a house to her right, a couple was lying on the lawn, sprawled on top of each other in the grass as if no one else was around.

Alaina had seen more than she cared to and bolted back toward Josh's frat house. She tried to dial Cam's number, but it went straight to his voicemail. She looked at nothing but the road and tried to keep her focus away from everything going on around her. She felt alone...isolated...dirty. Just being in the midst of the chaos of that street made her spirit feel tainted. She wanted to cry out to God to save her from this mess, but she'd held so much anger and so much bitterness for her brother's death in the past couple of months that she rarely felt God's presence with her anymore. Even in her morning studies, she could tell her heart wasn't in it as it'd once been.

But that's when the words floated into her mind. Not like a blasting intercom, but a faint whisper.

I urge you as aliens and strangers in this world to abstain from sinful desires which war against your soul.

The words came from 1 Peter. She'd read them only a few days ago, but at the time, she didn't fully understand their meaning. Now, the words rang out with perfect clarity. Alaina was an alien in the world of fraternity row. She didn't belong there. God didn't want her there, and she didn't want to be there. She couldn't believe it, but God had found her, even there in the midst of evil. She sent up a silent prayer of thanks and trudged forward even faster, looking everywhere for a sign of Cam. The longer she had to look, and the more she witnessed in that street, the angrier she became at him. How could he possibly think she would want to be there? Did he not know her any better than that by now? After all of the time they'd spent together and all of the talks they'd had? And why did he want to be there?

She knew he'd been the partier back home for a while, but he'd changed, hadn't he? She wondered now how true that was.

Alaina was dripping with sweat and approaching blind fury when she finally caught sight of Cam's bright orange Hollister T-shirt he'd thrown on that morning—except the shirt was upside down, as was Cam's entire body. Not only was Cam drinking, but he was being hoisted up by a couple of beefy frat boys, with the keg tube shoved deep inside his mouth. His eyes were closed as if every bit of his concentration was focused toward how much of the beer he could consume in the matter of a few seconds.

Alaina's heart dropped to her feet. Not only was she madder at Cam than she'd ever been at anybody in her entire life, but at the same time, her heart shattered in a million pieces for the loss of the friend she'd made over the past couple of months. The Cam who had left her stranded two years ago was the Cam who was back now. Full-fledged idiocy prevalent all over his features.

Alaina caught her breath and felt the words escape her mouth. "CAM! I need to talk to you!"

Cam's focus was yanked from the keg tube, and he looked up, his eyes meeting hers instantly. At first, his eyes portrayed guilt, but it was swiftly replaced with rage.

"Aww, close dude," said the boy who'd been holding Cam's right foot, "but I'm afraid I still hold the record for the night."

Cam gave the boy a playful punch in the arm and wobbled forward. "Alaina!" he said with a huge grin, all rage washed from him eyes. When he reached her, he grabbed her by the waist and pulled her off her feet into his arms and spun her around. "I've missed you, baby! Where have you been all night?"

"Baby?" Alaina grabbed Cams arm and drug him to a more private spot beside the side of the house, under a big tree. "Cam what the heck are you doing! You said you weren't going to drink, and I find you mid keg stand? I'm ready to go. I want you to take me home. Now."

Cam put his fingers under her chin and pulled his face close to hers. "Aww, you're so cute when you're mad."

The smell of beer on his breath was sickening, and Alaina knew instantly that he was completely wasted. Chances were Cam probably wouldn't even remember their conversation the next day.

"I'm not playing around, Cam. I want to leave now!"

The goofy grin on Cam's face fell. "Well, that is just...just too bad." His words slurred, and he struggled to speak right. "I am having...a fun time with my new friends. I...am...not ready to leave."

Alaina slapped her hand to her forehead and turned around. "I can't believe I got myself in this situation," she thought aloud. "I am so stupid! What was I thinking?"

"You...you were thinking...that you really like to spend time with me," Cam slurred. He moved closer toward her, but she backed away. "And you were thinking that you owed me for putting up with you and your problems for so long." Cam's voice was a bit high pitched and didn't convey even near the accusation that came from his words. "You were...were thinking that I deserve a night to have fun because I've had to...babysit you for so long just to get here."

Alaina felt her heart quicken with his words. She knew he was totally drunk and felt that there was no better time to get the truth from the real Cam Crawford before she fell for anymore of his lies. "What do you mean just to get here?"

Cam laughed and swayed from his right foot, shooting his hand toward the brick wall of the frat house to steady his balance. "C'mon Ala...Alaina. Do you really think my mom...my mommy...would have ever let me come to visit the lovely...beautimous campus of UC . . N...something...if I hadn't built a little...you know...trust with her first?"

Lightbulbs started flashing like strobe lights in Alaina's mind. She tried to remain calm and speak to Cam as though they were having a normal conversation so that he'd keep talking. As long as she played the game, he was too inebriated to notice something was off.

"Oh, I get it," she said, playing her part perfectly. "You mean that you hung out with me and helped me so that your mom would think you had changed and let you come to New York."

Cam's face lit up. "You are so...smart, Alaina! See this is why...why you should go to college with me. See...I...I helped you get through your...you know...stuff...." When he said 'stuff' he cupped his hand around his mouth and whispered as if it was some secret. "...and you helped me get my campus tour. We...we make the perfect team!"

Cam reached his hand out to high five her, but Alaina couldn't bring herself to play the game that well. Anger boiled in her veins. All she wanted to do was scream, "YOU USED ME YOU JERK!" But she held it in. There was no point in making a scene. But she couldn't stand to look at Cam any longer. His face had morphed back into the one that she remembered from the first time he'd betrayed her. Nothing had changed except for the improvement in his acting skills. She couldn't believe she'd been naïve enough to fall for his tricks this time.

"I...I'm going to go...go have some more fun, okay?" With that, Cam turned and stumbled back into the party.

Alaina felt her breath escape in a swift whoosh, and all strength left her knees as she slid down the brick wall to the grass under the leafy tree. *Can this night really get any worse?* she wondered.

Her answer came in that instant as a hand reached out under her gaze. She looked up. It was Josh.

"Hey, it's okay. Every couple gets in fights." His voice was smooth. Too smooth.

Alaina didn't take his hand. She rose on her own. "We're not a couple." She heard the shake in her tone that she knew Josh would mistake as hurt from Cam, when it was really just blinding rage that she was internally battling to keep inside.

Josh moved a little closer to her. "Yeah, Cam told me about you guys' arrangement." He held up quotation marks with his fingers and smiled playfully. "I thought it was pretty cool." He reached his hand farther up and pushed her hair gently behind her ear, closing the space between them so that she was backed against the house. His tone grew deeper and seductive, and he placed his lips up to her ear. "I wouldn't mind having a friend like you, Alaina."

Is this really happening?! Alaina shook all over. Cam had reached an all-time low. Not only had he lied to her, but he'd told all his new buddies that they had some type of friends-with-benefits arrangement worked out between them. Alaina had never felt more violated in her entire life. The most she'd ever done with a boy was the innocent kisses she'd shared with Ethan outside his grandmother's garden.

Josh's lips touched her ear and began to move down her neck, and panic raced through Alaina's bloodstream. She prayed loud, pleading prayers of rescue in her mind. The night couldn't end like this. She couldn't find out that her supposed best friend was a totally fake liar and have her innocence forcefully yanked away at the same time.

The words *Please God! Please help!* played over and over again in her mind.

Suddenly, when all hope seemed lost, her mouth opened next to Josh's hot breaths and the words that came out didn't even seem to be her own—as if she was having an out-of-body experience. Her tone was surprisingly steady, her strength returned, and as Josh was moving his hands to the skin of her torso underneath her shirt, she spoke the words that brought him to an abrupt halt.

"I think you need to go find Kim before I do."

Josh backed away and glared into her eyes. Alaina wondered for a moment if he was going to hit her or just go back to taking advantage of her. But then, to her relief, he backed away.

"You know, Cam was right," he said. "You are a..."

Alaina cringed at his last word, but all she cared about was the fact that he was gone. When Josh was completely out of sight, she did the only other thing she knew to do.

She ran.

Alaina ran as fast as she could. She dodged the dancing couples and jumped over the passed-out bodies in the street. She ran and ran and ran until a good distance separated her and fraternity row. It wasn't until she'd almost reached the edge of campus that she finally slowed her pace to a swift walk. Tears streamed from her eyes; she was no longer able to contain them. Alaina looked to the sky above her as she reached the edge of campus and turned onto St. Nicholas Avenue. The time was nearing midnight, and the sky should have been black, but the lights of the city made it glow an iridescent greenish yellow.

Alaina paused at the campus entrance and tried to regain her focus. What was she going to do now? She was stranded in the middle of New York City with no money and no place to go. She didn't know anyone. Didn't have anyone to call....

Or did she?

No, she couldn't possibly call him after all this time. Would he even care enough anymore to come?

Alaina took one more glance up and down both sides of the dangerously dark city street. The protective crowds of people from earlier that morning were no longer there. Alaina was alone...she hoped. Yep, she had to call. Alaina yanked her phone out and found his number with ease. She'd almost dialed it probably a thousand times over the past year or so but had always turned back. But not this time. This time she had no choice. She just hoped that the biggest pop sensation of her decade hadn't forgotten about her completely.

Five solid rings sounded, and Alaina was about to give up on his answering when a drowsy voice came on the line.

"He...hello?"

"Ethan it's me, Alaina."

The voice awoke instantly. "Alaina, oh my gosh! How are you...wait what's wrong?"

His excitement to hear from her mixed with his concern where he'd immediately picked up on the fact that something was wrong, made her heart break all over again. He did remember her, and he still knew her well enough to know when to be concerned. Tears broke loose from her eyes again as she explained to Ethan where she was and what had happened. The words came out in a rush, and it was all she could do to get them out. She wasn't sure when Ethan interrupted her, but she heard the worry in his tone.

"Alaina, listen to me and do exactly what I say, okay? Go back inside the campus. Get off the street. Go to the Student Center and find a table that's well lit. I'm coming to get you, but it's going to take me a bit to get through town. If you feel uncomfortable there, go wait for me at the campus police station, okay?"

Alaina nodded.

"Alaina?"

"Yeah, I'm nodding," she said. "I'll be there. Thanks, Ethan. I owe you one."

Ethan didn't reply. He'd already hung up. Alaina turned and headed back into campus, quickening her pace toward the brightly lit Student Center. She understood Ethan's concern. An eighteen-year-old girl out alone in the middle of the night in an inner city college campus didn't exactly scream safe.

But if she could only hold on for a little longer, everything would be okay. Because, unlike Cam, Alaina trusted Ethan. He'd lied to her about his visit to Granny Mae's, but she'd realized long ago that he'd only done it to keep from hurting her. All Ethan had ever done was things to make her feel better and to laugh. He'd made her feel safe. He'd made her happy. And the excitement of the chance to finally see him again, face to face, shrouded Alaina's fear as she found a booth in a well-lit corner of the Student Center. And it was there that she waited for him.

Chapter 32

Ethan

Ethan's heart pounded as he jumped from his bed in the Upper East Side apartment he shared with his mother. He didn't even bother to wake Ted, who'd moved in only a month prior. Luckily, he no longer needed Ted's driving assistance in the city—their companionship now was one based on friendship and trust. Ethan had recently purchased a black Expedition with the money he'd pulled in from the release of the single he'd written during his stay in Fairhope. He raced down the apartment building stairs and launched into an all-out sprint toward the parking garage.

The sound of Alaina's voice was all it took to flood Ethan's mind with memories of their time together. Ethan had done everything in his power to forget Alaina, but it wasn't happening. She was permanently etched in his soul, and he hadn't felt whole since he'd left her. And now, she was there. She was in New York City, and she was calling him. But Ethan knew Alaina's tones by heart, and he could tell when she was happy, or mad, or sad. Her tone tonight held the latter two of these qualities, but it also contained something else that he'd never heard from her.

Alaina was scared.

All he'd translated from her blubbering story was that she was in New York at the City College with Cam. Something about a tour and a party. Some guy named Josh. Something about a plane and luggage. And then all he'd heard were the words that echoed over and over in his mind as he pulled out of the private parking garage onto Lexington Avenue.

Ethan, I need you.

He'd longed to hear nothing else since she'd yelled at him to leave her alone on the pier that dreadful night this time last year. He knew that she was only asking for his help now as a favor to a friend, but Ethan couldn't care less. Anything just to see her again. Luckily, he wasn't too far from the university, and being that it was in the middle of the night, traffic would be slightly lighter than normal.

Ethan drove as fast as he could without getting pulled over, sending up verbal prayers for Alaina's safety until he could get to her. Ethan wasn't certain of the details, but somehow he knew this mess had something to do with Cam. Ethan could hardly believe it when he'd seen Alaina and Cam together at the hospital outside Ben's room, but he had seen it. He'd wondered then what Alaina was thinking hanging out with that loser, but he'd hoped that somehow

Cam had changed like he had. Alaina was an amazing girl, and Ethan held faith that she could change anybody if they only hung around her long enough. But something had happened tonight. Cam had not pulled through for Alaina. Somehow, she was alone on a deserted street with no one there to protect her and absolutely no experience in how to deal with the dark nights in a city like New York.

The possibilities of what could happen to her if she didn't make it to the Student Center raced through his mind and caused his stomach to do flip flops. His foot pressed a little harder on the gas pedal as he turned from East 116th Street onto St. Nicholas Avenue. The campus loomed ahead under the dull sky. Ethan pulled into the campus and swerved into the first visitor's parking space he could find. He'd performed at this college several times when he was first building his career and knew its layout fairly well, at least enough to find the Student Center.

This time Ethan didn't even bother donning his baseball cap and sunglasses. He didn't care about the fans or the paparazzi or the cameras. All he cared about was the girl who sat alone in the building ahead and needed him.

Ethan bounded up the concrete staircase two stairs at a time until he finally reached the large double glass doors to the Student Center. He entered the dining area and darted his eyes in every direction trying to find Alaina.

And there she was.

Sitting all alone and looking just as tiny and beautiful as ever, was the girl Ethan had sworn to never stop loving. He moved toward her at a pace near a jog but stopped in his tracks when her eyes darted up to meet his. Their gazes held for what felt like an eternity, and Ethan stood frozen, unsure of what to do next. All he wanted was to run to her and pull her into his arms, but so much time had passed between them. And he'd caused her so much pain. Did she even know he'd changed? Did she even know that it was because of her that his life was on the right track? Did she know she'd saved his life? He looked deeper into her eyes, but he couldn't see anything behind the tears. And just as he couldn't hold back going to her any longer...he didn't have to.

Alaina jumped up from the deserted booth and raced toward him. He thought his heart would pound right out of his chest as she reached him and buried her head in his neck.

"Thank you, Ethan." It came out as a whimper.

Ethan couldn't reply. All he could do was relish in the feel of her head in its rightful place on his shoulder. The familiar scent of her perfume and shampoo. Involuntarily, Ethan's arms wrapped around her and his fingers ran through her hair just as they had always done before everything crumbled. She broke out into sobs, and all Ethan could do was try to comfort her. He didn't understand what she'd been through tonight, but he understood how she felt right now. If he hadn't worried that she'd think him a big sissy, he would have cried right along with her. This moment, Alaina in his arms, was all he'd wanted for the past year.

"It's okay," he said gently. "It's okay. I'm here."

Ethan held Alaina for a solid fifteen minutes as she cried out all of her tears and got a grip on her emotions, but to him it only felt like seconds. Eventually, she pulled away a few inches and buried her head in her hands, shaking it with a groan of frustration.

"Ugh! Why is it that every time I see you, I cry about something?"

Ethan let out a slight laugh. "Don't worry. I have that effect on girls." He swiped the hair out of her face and reached his thumb under her chin, lifting her head so that her eyes met his. "What happened tonight, Alaina? What are you doing in New York? Why are you crying?"

Alaina sniffed and took a deep breath. She linked her arm in his, the fingers of her other hand grasped around his inner elbow. "C'mon," she said. "Let's get out of here. I'll explain on the way."

Alaina did explain. She explained everything, starting with how she and Cam had come to hanging out again in the first place. She told Ethan about Ben's stay in the hospital. She told him about the generous donation from the anonymous giver that allowed her to quit her job and spend time with her brother before he died. Ethan remained quiet during that part, but couldn't help but smile. She told him about how Ben passed on to be with Jesus and her parents. She told him about finishing school over the summer and receiving her diploma. Then she went into how she'd wound up in New York and how it'd led to her calling for his rescue services in the middle of the night.

When Ethan learned of Cam's drunken confession and the things he'd said about Alaina that had provoked Josh to corner her in a way that made his skin crawl, it was all he could do to not forget everything God had taught him in the past year, and march into that frat party and show Cam just how far he was willing to go to protect

Alaina. But it wouldn't have done any good. Cam was just...Cam. That's all there was to it. Alaina should have seen it coming from day one. Ethan knew it and she knew it, too, whether or not she would ever admit it. Instead, Ethan tried to stay focused on keeping his breaths steady and dwelling on the fact that Alaina was safe now. In the end, that was really all that mattered. Cam would get what was coming to him whether it be in this life or the next. God would see to that, and Ethan would leave it up to Him. Right now, his sole focus was directed toward the girl with the cascading dark hair and illuminating eyes who occupied the passenger seat of his vehicle.

He'd pulled out of the college and was headed toward some place called the Morningside Inn. Alaina said that her luggage was there. When they arrived, he pushed the gear shift into park and started to turn the motor off, but Alaina held her hand up to stop him.

"Don't worry about it," she said with a smile. "I'm just going to run in and get my bag. I'll be right back."

"Okay, I'll be here."

A few minutes later, Alaina returned with a dark purple rolling suitcase in tow. This time Ethan did grab the hat and glasses, seeing as there were a lot more people around the entrance to this hotel than there had been on the deserted campus. He jumped out of the Expedition and jogged to the passenger side to help Alaina load her suitcase into the back seat.

"Still a gentleman, I see." She smiled as Ethan pushed the bag a little farther in and opened her door for her.

Ethan just shrugged, closed her door as she reclaimed her seat next to him, and went back to the driver's side.

"So what happens tomorrow when Cam doesn't know where you are and comes here to find your luggage is gone?" Ethan asked as he drove back onto the quickly populating street.

"I left him a note," Alaina replied nonchalantly. "It said, 'You're a jerk. I went home. Don't call me.'" A light giggle escaped her mouth. "Too much?"

Ethan grinned. "Nah, sounds pretty good to me."

Alaina tilted her head to the side, her eyes shifting up and down Ethan, studying him to see if she'd remembered everything accurately—his eyes, body shape, hair, lips. Everything. Turns out, she hadn't forgotten a single thing.

"I want to thank you again for coming to my rescue tonight," she said. I don't know what I would've done if you hadn't been home or hadn't answered your phone or hadn't been...willing to come."

Her focus went back to the front window, her eyes averting his.

"That would never happen, Alaina." Ethan couldn't hide the sincerity in his tone. "I would never ignore your call. I would never refuse to come if you needed me."

Alaina had a wistful look, but her focus remained fixed on the window. "I think I knew that deep down, or I wouldn't have called."

Ethan took a chance and reached his hand over to give her shoulder a light squeeze. "You can always call."

A silence fell between them, and Ethan turned back onto Lexington. Finally, Alaina broke the silence.

"So, what have you been up to? Is your tour over?"

Ethan tried to hold back laughter. Was his tour over? That was an amusing understatement. In the respect Alaina was referring to—the pop singing, Bruce worshiping, teenage girl heartbreaking singer he'd once been—his career was over. Was it really possible that she hadn't stayed caught up on his life at all since they'd parted? He wasn't sure whether to feel slighted or to be proud of her for once again being different than every other girl he'd ever met. He contemplated telling her about everything that had happened since they'd last spoken—the press conference where he'd come clean about the drunken driving, the leaving his record label, the leaving behind his old life and dedicating his new life to the service of God instead of himself. He contemplated telling her about how he'd switched to singing Christian music and how God had finally provided him with a way to write and sing his own songs. He wanted to tell her that he was singing with a purpose now and that he owed it all to her.

But somehow, the time didn't feel right. He didn't want to have to convince Alaina that he'd changed. He wanted her to notice based on his fruit. And if she was anywhere near as perceptive of his actions as she'd once been, he was sure she'd figure it out soon enough.

The sun was just beginning to peek out between the edges of skyscrapers when Ethan pulled back into the private garage of his apartment. Losing the hat and glasses, he made his way to Alaina's side of the vehicle, removed her suitcase from the back seat, and opened her door for her.

"Where are we?" she asked, stepping out onto the gray concrete.

"My place. Well, mine, my mom's, and Ted's place."

"Oh, what are we doing here?"

"I thought you might appreciate a hot shower," he laughed. "I never thought I'd hear myself say this, but you, Alaina, smell like cigarette smoke and beer."

Her cheeks flushed just like he remembered, and her head once again went to her hands. "Yuck! You're right, I know. Shower it is. Just point the way."

Ethan walked Alaina into his building and led her toward the apartment. Once inside, they tried to keep quiet to avoid waking his mom and Ted. He led her to the doorway at the end of the hall. His bedroom.

"I've got a bathroom that adjoins my bedroom," he said. As they entered he flipped his light switch on. He wondered if Alaina noticed any of the posters on his walls of various Christian artists that he'd befriended recently, or the Bible that sat on the nightstand next to his bed. He didn't think so. It seemed after his comment on her current stench, Alaina focused on nothing but the beeline path to the shower. Ethan followed her into the bathroom, making sure she found everything she needed.

As he turned to exit, she spoke. "Thanks again, Ethan. I don't know what I would've done without you tonight."

Ethan allowed his eyes to find hers, and that's where they stayed, transfixed and unmoving. How was it possible that she was really there in his room? Spending time with him again? Her presence was an answered prayer. His first love had returned to him, and as he finally broke his gaze and left the bathroom, latching the door behind him, he wondered one thing.

How long could it possibly last?

~~**~~

Alaina

Alaina ran the thick chocolate-brown towel through her drenched hair as she sat on the floor of Ethan's bathroom, leaning against the base of the shower. Her suitcase lay open at her side, and she pilfered through it to see what all Granny Mae had packed for her. That morning, she'd only had time to grab what was on top and hadn't actually paid attention to anything else that was packed. Now, she saw that Mae had prepared her for at least a four- to five-day trip. There were several outfits, some casual, some dressy, and two pairs of shoes. Not to mention, her Bible, her journal, and something else in the bottom corner that Alaina couldn't quite make out. She reached a hand deep into the bag and clasped her fingers around the object in question.

Once she pulled it out, she knew at first glance exactly what it was. A little box wrapped delicately in paper with a small bow on top. Taped to the front, a piece of paper with messy crayoned writing.

It was the last thing Ben had ever given Alaina. The little present that she'd never quite found the strength to open. Why would Granny Mae have packed it? She knew that Alaina would never open anything that personal in front of Cam. Ethan on the other hand…well, that was probably a different story and Granny Mae knew it.

But Mae couldn't have known that Alaina would wind up seeing Ethan during her trip to New York City, could she? Surely not.

But Alaina had wound up seeing Ethan, and for the first time since Ben's death, she felt as though she had the strength to check out the contents of the little box.

Alaina finished towel drying her hair, threw on a pair of faded jeans and a red Skittles T-shirt she'd bought at the mall during the Steve and Barry's closeout a couple of years ago, and stretched her arms up high, stifling a yawn. It was then that she realized how long it'd been since she last slept. She was fairly certain that, at that moment, she could lie down on the bath mat and get some pretty great sleep, but she was there with Ethan. She couldn't sleep now. It would be a stretch to stay awake for him, but somehow, she'd find a way to do it.

Alaina checked her reflection in the mirror one last time—laughing to herself as she recalled how little she'd been doing that recently—grabbed Ben's gift, and opened the door to Ethan's bedroom.

She wanted to look around and check out what the room of the nation's most popular pop singer looked like, but when she found Ethan sprawled out on top of his covers with his muscular arms folded neatly behind his head, which was propped on a pillow, the light from a small lamp on his nightstand shadowing his features, she couldn't quite bring herself to look at anything else but him.

How was it that a year of absence had only served to intensify her attraction toward him?

"What do you have there?" he asked, pointing to the little box in her hand. Alaina made her way over to Ethan's bed and took a seat at the foot of it. He sat up and moved next to her. "Looks like a present."

"It is," she said. "Ben gave it to me the day he passed away." Alaina could already tell she was more comfortable talking about this with Ethan than she'd been with anyone else. With Ethan, she didn't have to push through an explanation of what had happened and how she was feeling. He could tell all of that about her without having to hear a word. With Ethan, she could just relax and talk about Ben with a happy fondness and recollection. "I never really got around to opening it, but I just found it in my suitcase. I think Granny Mae put it there."

Alaina looked up to Ethan, meeting his eyes once more with a smile. "Mind if I open it now?"

Ethan nodded. "I'd like that."

Alaina took a deep breath. "Okay, here goes." She placed gentle fingers on the bottom of the little box, pushing the tape loose from the paper. For some reason, ripping right into it just didn't seem appropriate. Once the paper came loose, an old cardboard jewelry box fell into her hand. She guessed it had once belonged to Granny Mae, whom she also assumed was the one who'd done the wrapping. Judging from Ben's help that past Christmas, present wrapping definitely wasn't his specialty. Alaina paused for a moment before opening the box, wondering what Ben could have possibly left behind that he thought would mean so much to her. What could mean that much and fit into such a tiny box?

The top of the box slid off with ease. Inside laid a folded piece of paper. It was wrinkled where Ben had obviously opened and closed it numerous times. Alaina's fingers trembled as she slowly unfolded the paper. Her eyes scanned over the words quickly, and she heard Ethan catch his breath next to her, but he remained silent. There were handwritten words on the paper, but not in Ben's handwriting. There wasn't a signature anywhere, but there was a title at the top of the page: "Redemption Song."

The words were lyrics. Ben had left her a song. At the bottom corner, in her brother's sloppy little boy handwriting, there was a web address. Something with the words "YouTube" and "famous baptism."

Alaina's head shot up, and her eyes connected with Ethan's. He held a knowing smile, and his eyes glistened as if he was excited in some way, but at the same time he seemed to be holding back tears of his own.

"I need to use your computer," Alaina said with hushed urgency.

Ethan nodded toward the laptop sitting on the computer desk beside his bed. Alaina, feeling as confused as she ever had, rose from the bed and sat in front of the laptop without a word. The computer booted up easily, and within seconds, she'd found the website.

Alaina found her focus transfixed to the screen in front of her. The video was taken in front of a lake. There was a tall man, his arms wrapped around a boy. They both held huge grins. Another woman stood off to the side, proud tears streaming from her eyes. The actions in the video were silent, but a song played as the events unfolded. It was a boy singing. He sang the words that were etched on the paper that Ben had left behind for her. Alaina would know that voice anywhere. She would never forget the face of the boy in the video.

It was Ethan.

His voice rang out through the laptop speakers, as clear and as confident as Alaina had ever heard from him. The words were those of an apology. A confession. A plea for forgiveness. As the title read, it was a song of redemption.

And as Ted folded Ethan's hands over his chest and spoke words that were not audible over the sound of the song, and then dunked Ethan into that lake water only to pull him back out a new creation, Alaina saw the expression on Ethan's face.

He was saved.

Ted slapped Ethan a high five, and his mother ran right into the water to hug him. The scene was beautiful. And with that, the picture faded to black and the last chord of the song sounded to silence, leaving the breathing of Alaina and Ethan as the only perceptible sounds in the room.

Alaina sat, frozen in place by unreserved shock. Ethan believed! After all of the time she'd spent with him, all of the hours of talking, sometimes even arguing …he finally believed. Just when Alaina thought that God had turned His back on her life—that He had given up on a chance of ever using her for anything other than taking care of her own life and her own problems—Ben had gone and shown her what a difference she could truly make in another person's life. Her little brother hadn't just given her the best present she'd ever received. He'd given her life back.

Alaina wasn't certain of the exact amount of time that had elapsed before she finally turned back around in that computer chair, but when she did, she finally saw Ethan's room for what it was. Christian posters hung on the wall. A Bible laid open on his nightstand. His guitar was lazily placed over the arm of the recliner in the corner of the room on the opposite side of the bed. Ethan was no longer America's hottest teen pop sensation.

Ethan was a Christian singer. He was using his talent for God's glory and not his own. And Alaina had never been more proud of anyone in her entire life.

"I knew you were different," she said thoughtfully, finally meeting his eyes. "You never said it out loud, but I could tell you were different."

Ethan remained seated on the end of the bed across from her. "I'm sorry I didn't tell you. I didn't want to have to convince you. I just wanted you to be able to see it for yourself." His eyes fell to his hands on the bed, a look of vulnerability flashed across his features before his eyes rose back up to meet hers. "You have to know that it was because of you. You saved me, Alaina."

Alaina felt the tears welling in her eyes. No longer tears of pain or tears of suffering. These were tears of joy. But she fought them off anyway. She was tired of crying. She was ready to live. "You know, the people I really care about call me Ali."

Ethan's lips stretched into the grin that Alaina had longed to see for the past year, and in one swift motion, he rolled to her side of the bed, grabbed her hands, and pulled her up out of her seat to standing position. His hand rested on her right ear as he pushed the hair away from her eyes. He was cautious, and when Alaina didn't object, his lips found hers.

The kiss was brief, but as Alaina's head buried into his neck, Ethan's arms wrapped around her in a hug that she never wanted to be released from, her heart pounding so loudly she suspected he could hear it.

His voice came out as a trembling whisper. "I missed you, Ali."

"I missed you, too."

It felt as if eternity had passed before Alaina finally found the strength to pull away from him.

"I can't believe we're finally getting to see each other again and now I have to leave," she said, not even trying to hide the whine in her tone.

Ethan took a sharp breath. "When does your plane leave?"

"I don't really know. I haven't rescheduled my flight yet."

"So don't go."

Alaina peered into his eyes trying to find meaning behind his words. "What are you saying?"

He gave an innocent shrug. "I'm saying, don't go. Stay here…stay with me."

Alaina felt her heart quicken. What was he asking of her?

"Like, move to New York? Leave everything behind?"

"Well, technically, you'd only be in New York for a little while." Ethan shrugged with hopeful innocence. "Toby Mac just signed me to his Winterslam Tour. Rehearsals start in a week. Then in a couple of months we'd hit the road. Think about it, Alaina. You could hang out with all of your favorite artists, tour the country, and see places you've never seen. And…we could be together."

"You…you want me to go on tour with you?"

Ethan gave a slight shrug. "Why not? It could be great."

Alaina opened her mouth to reply, but paused as she considered what he was offering her—which was basically the world. How could she turn down the opportunity to meet famous people and tour the world? And how could she turn down the opportunity to do it all at Ethan's side? The one boy on the entire planet who had managed to steal her heart away was offering her everything. How could she possibly turn that down?

But she knew she had to.

"Okay, I know that expression." Ethan gave her a knowing look and backed away to give her some room to think. "How about I lay off the life-changing talk for now and we start with today? We'll go find you a flight that leaves out tonight. Please, Ali? You don't have to make your decision right now, but can I just have a little time with you? Just spend the day with me, and you can think things through, okay?"

Alaina wasn't certain what her future held, but she knew that one day wouldn't be enough to tip the balance of the scales forever. So, she smiled—ignoring all feelings of exhaustion—nodded her head, and went to retrieve her suitcase from the bathroom. When she returned, Ethan stood by the doorway waiting for her with a look of anticipation.

"Okay," she said. "One day."

~*~**~*~

Ethan

One day.

It seemed so unfair that one day was all he could have. He'd already waited one year. It seemed that he should at least be allowed the same amount time to make up for all that he'd lost. But if one day was all he could have, then one day was what he would take. And he would make it the best one day of his life if it was the last thing he ever did.

They started out at the airport. Thirty minutes later, Alaina had a flight booked for eleven that night. They both knew it would put her getting back to Alabama in the early morning hours, but Ted had agreed to fly home with Alaina, rent a car at the airport, and drive her the rest of the way to Fairhope. Ethan would love to have tagged along and gotten the chance to visit with his grandmother again, but he had his own plane to catch the next day. He was scheduled to interview at the K-Love studios in Rocklin, California, on the morning show to discuss his first Christian album release and the opportunity he'd been given to tour with Toby Mac.

But none of that mattered right now. All Ethan was concerned about was the next twelve hours. He prayed with all he had that Alaina would consider his offer to go on tour with him. He couldn't imagine getting the opportunity to sing and perform—two of his absolute favorite things—and getting to spend time with Ali while he did it. The possibility seemed too good to be true. Yet, technically, she hadn't said no. He could see the reservation in her eyes, but she hadn't said no. Which meant he still had time.

But no matter how much Ethan wanted to spend the next few hours trying to convince Alaina that the advantages of going with him far outweighed the disadvantages, he had already decided that their day together would have nothing to do with that. His ultimate goal was to simply spend time with Alaina and hope that she understood just how much he'd missed her over the past year.

After the airport, he asked Alaina where she wanted to go. Of course, she didn't even know where to begin, so Ethan opted for the customary tourist attractions of the Big Apple. They did the Empire State Building thing and the Statue of Liberty thing. They walked through China Town and ate pizza in Brooklyn. And finally as the sun was beginning to burn over the edges of the skyscrapers that lined the Manhattan horizon, Ethan led Alaina by the hand into Central Park.

"Your city is beautiful," she said as they passed by the lake where a team of paddle boaters were out practicing. They came to a stop there, at the edge of the water, the full view of Manhattan in the distance over the tree tops.

"It's home, I guess."

"I've seen this place a thousand times on TV and in movies, but somehow it's just not the same as actually being here and experiencing it."

Ethan squeezed her hand and turned her body to face him. He'd held back all day, but he couldn't any longer. He bent to her level and found her lips with ease. He heard her sigh as she fell into his kiss in the cool city breeze. "I know exactly what you mean," he murmured as they slowly parted.

Her eyes danced as she gazed up at his with excited curiosity. He wondered if she'd made her decision, but he refused to ask. It wasn't time for that yet. He still had a couple of hours with her, and he intended to use every single second.

"Come on," Ethan said. "I want to give you something to take home to remember this day by."

Alaina grinned and fell into step beside him, her hand never leaving his the entire way. A few hundred yards down the winding concrete path, Ethan slowed his step next to an older redheaded gentleman with a flaming goatee and sideburns to match. He wore a plaid beret and sat on a stool in front of an easel. A long narrow paintbrush lay with experience between his fingers while his other hand grasped a circular board colored like the rainbow with various oil paints.

Ethan reached his hand into his pocket and pulled out a couple of bills. He held them out toward the man. "You have a few minutes for us, man?"

The man's eyes widened at the money Ethan offered, and a wide smile spread across his cheeks. "Oh, yes sir! Right this way, sir." The man had a thick Brooklyn accent and seemed quite pleasant. He led Ethan and Alaina to a little pallet he'd set up in the grass on the edge of the sidewalk. "Just have a seat here with your girl, and I'll paint you up something real pretty."

Alaina giggled and knelt down next to Ethan on the blanket. When the man raised his paintbrush to the canvas, Ethan held up his hand and said, "Oh, yeah, hold up a second." He pulled the cap off his head and removed his glasses. "Okay, sorry about that, now you can start."

The man lifted his gaze to study the objects he was to paint, and his eyebrows rose. He paused for a brief moment, but said nothing and went to painting. The brush connected with the canvas, and his hand whirled around as if their images were simply coming to life on the paper through his fingers. Ethan and Alaina remained as still as possible: Ethan's arm wrapped tightly around Alaina's waist and their cheeks pressed together as they struggled to hold smiles longer than naturally possible. When the man claimed to be finished, Ethan and Alaina rose from the blanket, opening and closing their mouths to stretch their jaws back out.

The man tore the paper from the huge pad on the tripod and handed it to them. "I hope I did you justice," he said kindly.

Ethan held out the painting for him and Alaina to view together.

"Wow, that's amazing," she said. "You're very talented, sir."

He smiled thankfully and held out Ethan's hat. Ethan took it from him and peered inside to find his sunglasses and the bills he'd handed the man earlier.

"You might want to put that back on, Mr. Carter," the man said. "I'd hate for a bunch of people to go ruining your day with your girl here."

Ethan gazed back at the man in surprise. "But I don't understand," he said. "You know who I am, but you won't let me pay you? Please, sir, your work is beautiful. Take the money."

The man let out a hearty laugh. "Trust me, Mr. Carter. You have already given me so much more than money." When Ethan and Alaina exchanged confused expressions, the man went on. "You see, I'm actually a pastor at this little street church in Brooklyn. This painting thing is just something I do to minister to people I come into contact with in the park. But I have a daughter about your age who loves you, kid. But for the longest time, I couldn't get her to listen to a word I said about God. She just didn't want to hear it. But when you stood up for what you believed in and gave up everything to sing for your Savior, well, she finally started to listen. She got baptized just this past Sunday. You're making a difference in the lives of your fans, Mr. Carter. So please understand that this painting is the least I can do to repay you for your service."

Ethan couldn't even speak. He knew he'd made changes in his own life, and he knew that his amazing fans had transitioned pretty well to his new genre of music, but he'd never thought about how many of them would be led to Christ because of him. He'd never felt more useful in his entire life. He prayed for it all the time, and it was happening. God was using him.

When Ethan continued to not say anything, Alaina spoke for him. "Thank you very much for the painting, sir. And we're really happy to hear about your daughter."

Ethan finally found his voice and agreed with Alaina. He also asked the man for permission to use his canvas, insisting on leaving an autographed message for his daughter, congratulating her on her decision to give her life to Christ and thanking her for staying faithful to his music.

The rest of the night spun by in a blur. Ethan treated Alaina to a lakeside dinner at one of the restaurants inside the park. Then they finished the night off with a carriage ride back to the edge of the park where he'd left his vehicle earlier that afternoon. He'd lived in New York his entire life, but decided then that he'd never truly felt its magic until that night. Alaina was right. It was beautiful. And so was she.

The sun had long since set over the horizon by the time Ethan pulled into the parking lot at LaGuardia Airport. They'd remained silent the entire ride there, each unsure of how to proceed from that point. It was a bittersweet ending to an utterly perfect day.

They continued to walk in silence, with their hands clasped firmly together as if prepared for a battle meant solely to yank them apart. They walked for what felt like miles to the Central Terminal until they finally reached the very end of Concourse C. Idling outside the window of Gate C14 was the plane what would fly Alaina back to Alabama and, once again, out of Ethan's arms and life. Ted was seated comfortably in a padded chair next to the attendant desk. When they approached, Ted stood to greet Alaina with a welcoming smile and a ticket.

"It's so nice to see you again, Alaina," Ted said. "I'm so glad you are allowing me to accompany you home. I'm looking forward to getting to visit with Mae."

Alaina smiled, but it was obvious she was battling something inside. "Thanks, Ted. She'll be real excited to see you, too."

Ted, being ever perceptive, knew precisely when to take a hint. He gave a slight nod. "I think I'm going to grab one last cup of coffee before we take off." He left them alone by the window.

Ethan took a deep breath, not fully believing that this moment had arrived so soon. Wasn't it only moments ago that Alaina was in his room agreeing to spend the day with him? How could his time with her possibly be over so soon?

She looked up at him and gave a pained smile.

That's all it took. "Come here, you." He reached out and pulled her to his chest. He grasped her hair, his lips just above her ear. "I can't believe you're leaving already." She didn't answer, but he felt her head bob in agreement. His face fell to the nape of her neck and rested there with the smell of her shampoo filling his senses. "I'm guessing by your silence that you've decided to opt out of the tour idea?"

She pulled her head away slowly and peered up at him with confused eyes. "Ethan, I..." But then she fell silent again.

"Can I just ask why?"

She pulled back farther but left her hands clasped in his, holding on to them tightly. It was as though she was struggling with an inward battle, just trying to hang on long enough to make it through. Ethan didn't understand the problem. Just stay…that's all there was. That was the only option. Just stay with him and be with him and love him. That's all he wanted.

But it was then that he realized he hadn't yet considered what she wanted.

"Is it me?" he asked quietly. "Do you not want to be with me?"

Alaina reared her head back and let out a frustrated half laugh half sigh. "Do you really think that's it?" she said. "You think I don't want to be with you?"

Ethan shrugged. He didn't see any other alternative.

Alaina removed her hands from his and put them up to his face, grasping both of his cheeks between her hands so that he was forced to look her square in the eye. And then, she said the words that would eternally turn his world upside down.

"Ethan, I love you."

Ethan struggled to catch his breath. Three short weeks with Alaina had been all it took for her to steal his heart. Just three short weeks. But when he'd messed things up, he never thought he'd be able to salvage their relationship. He never expected her to forgive him. He'd prayed and prayed until he couldn't even find the right words to pray anymore, but he never truly expected God to answer that prayer. But there she was, the girl who captivated his very soul, telling him that she loved him.

He reached up, took her hands in his again, and a frustrated sigh escaped. "Ali, you cannot tell me that and then get on that plane." He paused, trying to get every word to come out perfectly. "You know I love you, too. I mean you must know that, right? I have missed you every second of every day since that night on the beach. How can you really be leaving?"

Ethan looked around not even sure what he was looking for. He wanted something...anything that would change her mind. "Why won't you go on tour with me? We can be together, Ali. You know what we have. We could be so great together."

She sighed, obviously trying to fight back tears again. "I know," she said quietly, "but I just can't."

Ethan wasn't giving up that easily. "Look, Ali, you have done nothing but work your brains off for the past two years playing the adult of your family. You've been released from that, now. It's time for you to live a little."

"I know." She sighed again and looked up to meet his eyes. "I know it is...and that's why I can't go with you, Ethan. If visiting that campus yesterday taught me anything, it's that I want to go to college." She elaborated when Ethan eyebrows scrunched with confusion. "I missed out on a good majority of high school, including all of senior year. I have no idea what I would have been capable of achieving. I want to go to college and work my butt off to make good grades. I want to pull all-nighters and stress about project deadlines. I know it sounds crazy when you're offering me so much by going with you, but the tour is just..."

"Not your dream," Ethan finished for her. "It's my dream. Not yours."

She nodded. "Yeah."

"Flight C14; it is now time to board! I repeat Flight C14 to Birmingham, Alabama; it is now time to board the aircraft!"

The flight attendant's voice sounded over the loud speaker above their heads and put a solid end to Ethan and Alaina's last moments together. Ted returned at that moment, realizing he was barging in on a farewell moment. He smiled at both of them and said, "I'll see you on the plane, Alaina."

Alaina turned back around to Ethan and tears welled in her eyes. "I promised myself I wasn't going to cry this time." She gave her head a solid shake and pulled herself back together.

"So this is it," Ethan said. "This is good-bye?"

Alaina shrugged. "Does it really have to be? I mean, I won't be in school forever. There will be holidays and breaks. And your tour only lasts during the winter, right? Technically, there are possibilities here…"

Alaina's tone had turned lighthearted as she tried with all her might to shed light on the situation, but all Ethan heard was one message that rang loud and clear in her words.

She was not closing her heart off to him.

Just because she wasn't going with him didn't mean that she was giving up on the possibility of their being together one day. And if that's the best Ethan could have from her, then that's what he would take.

Before she could finish her sentence, the flight attendants voice rang out a last notice to board the plane before it took off. Running out of time, Ethan didn't let her finish. He pulled her to him once more and gave her a kiss that he was sure she wouldn't forget anytime soon.

When he finally pulled away, her eyes remained closed as if she was still relishing the feel of his lips on hers. Ethan felt his cheeks tint red with satisfaction.

They had to part now.

The flight attendant was giving them an annoyed look from the terminal door. But they would not part with good-bye, because there was no good-bye in store for them. Just like Ethan had learned when he'd given his life to Christ; the world was open to all sorts of possibilities if he just had enough faith in God to provide him a way. And this was also true of his relationship with Alaina. God had put them together, of that he had no doubt. And with enough faith, He would provide a way for them to find each other again.

So Ethan's eyes met Alaina's once more, and she nodded, understanding that their time was up. But there was something else to accompany that, and it made both of them smile because they both understood that, this time, they weren't parting to a future of ill feelings and depressing uncertainty. Their future, however unclear, seemed bright and welcoming with an array of endless possibilities. And as Alaina turned, rolling her dark purple suitcase toward the door of the terminal, only one parting phrase seemed appropriate.

"See you later, Ali."

Alaina paused at the edge of the doorway, the air blowing her dark hair as she turned and flashed a smile that would remain etched in Ethan's mind until he was able to see her again.

"See ya later, superstar."

Book Club Questions

1. In the beginning of the book, Ethan was a very different character than he was at the end of the book. Discuss how his attitude changed as the story progressed. What events do you feel contributed most to these changes?

2. Ethan's mother had to make a tough decision when choosing how to punish him for his mistakes. If you are a teen, have you ever received a harsh punishment that you knew you deserved? How did you handle it, and if you could go back and do things over, what would you do differently? If you are a parent, have you ever had to punish your children in a difficult way? Do you feel you handled it correctly? Why or why not?

3. Alaina went through some very difficult situations, but she found strength through daily devotionals. Have you ever received comfort in hard times by reading scriptures? What were the scriptures, and how did they speak to you? Do you think there is value in performing daily devotionals?

4. We might not have realized it in the beginning, but by the end of the book, it was obvious that Ethan and Alaina had fallen in love. Do you feel that they were too young to have developed such strong feelings for one another? Could their circumstances and lifestyles have contributed to such a mature relationship? How did their relationship differ from most adolescent relationships?

5. Alaina agreed to go to New York with Cam, unaware of his dishonest intentions. Do you feel that she was acting naïve by placing so much trust in him, or was she simply being a good friend? Do you think Granny Mae made the right decision by allowing her to go? Could she have had ulterior motives for Alaina?

6. Ethan eventually gave up his rebellious ways and gave his life over to the Lord. How did he show that he was truly changed on the inside? What kinds of sacrifices did he make? What changes and sacrifices have you made in order to live by Christ's standards? Have they been worth it?

7.   The title of this book is *Redemption Song*. Do you think the title simply came from the song that Ethan wrote, or could it relate to other aspects of the story, as well?

Acknowledgements

I would first like to thank God for the abilities He has given me to do the things I love and desire to do. I am so blessed to be given the opportunity to use these gifts to share His word with the rest of the world. My prayer is that this novel has, in some way, encouraged you or lifted you up to a stronger relationship with your Savior.

To my husband. Thank you for all of those times you helped me with the kids and took care of the house so that I could write. Also, for those countless conversations where I ramble on and on about the business of writing and publishing and you pretend to be insanely fascinated, even though I know it's not your thing. Thank you for your love and support as I pursue my dreams. I hope this novel makes you proud.

To my mom. Thank you for your encouragement and your eagle-eye editing skills. I can't imagine completing a novel without your help. Thank you for reading and rereading this novel over and over without ever losing your original enthusiasm.

To my sister. Thanks for your awesome musical guidance in creating the trailer to accompany this book. Love you.

To the women at my church. You guys are my lights on dark days. Your smiles and encouraging words spur me to be a better person in Christ. I thank you for all of your words of support and for test driving this novel for me.

To my editor, April Michelle Davis, with Editorial Inspirations (www.editorialinspirations.com). Thank you so much for your amazing work. You truly made this novel the best it could be, and I look forward to working with you on future projects.

To my formatter, Larry Kaye (larrykaye@shaw.ca). Thank you for your timely work. You make the act of digital publishing look easy.

Finally, to my students. To all of those unnamed faces who inspired the characters in this story. You are so special whether you believe it or not. Know that God has a plan for you. I pray you grab hold of Him and never let go. I promise; it will be a wild ride.

About the Author

Melodie Murray is a high school mathematics teacher and a writer. She lives with her husband, two boys, and a dog in Pocahontas, Arkansas. When she is not doing math or writing, she is at church singing with the Praise Team or at home cuddled in a Snuggie reading books.

~~**~~

Connect with Melodie Murray online at:

Website: www.melodiemurray.com
Twitter: www.twitter.com/@murraymelodie
Facebook: www.facebook.com/murraybooks
Blog: www.murraybooks.blogspot.com
Email: murraymelodie@yahoo.com